RED
1-2-3

JOHN KATZENBACH is a bestselling
author of psychological thrillers.
His work has been published in more
than 25 languages. Four of his books
have been turned into films. He won
the Grand Prix de Littérature Policière
for his novel *The Analyst*. He lives in
Western Massachusetts.

RED
1-2-3

JOHN KATZENBACH

A Mysterious Press Book
for Head of Zeus

First published in 2014 by Mysterious Press,
an imprint of Grove/Atlantic, New York.
This paperback edition published in the UK in 2014 by Head of Zeus Ltd.

975312468

A CIP catalogue record for this book is available from the British Library.

Paperback ISBN: 9781781859469
eBook ISBN: 9781781859452

Printed and bound by CPI Group (UK) Ltd.,
Croydon CR0 4YY.

Head of Zeus Ltd
Clerkenwell House,
45-47 Clerkenwell Green
London EC1R 0HT

www.headofzeus.com

RED
1-2-3

ALSO BY
JOHN KATZENBACH

FOR THE ENGLISH DEPARTMENT FACULTY,
BARD COLLEGE, 1968–72

Prologue:
The Unwanted Mail

Red One was standing by helplessly watching a man die when her letter was delivered to her isolated house in a rural part of the county.

Red Two was dizzy with drugs, alcohol, and despair when her letter was dropped through the mail slot in the front door to her split-level suburban home.

Red Three was staring at a failure, thinking that more and far worse failures were awaiting her, when her letter arrived in a mail depository just down the stairs from her dormitory room.

The three women ranged in age: Seventeen. Thirty-three. Fifty-one. They did not know one another, but they lived within a few miles of each other. One was an internist. One was a public middle school teacher. One was a prep school student. They had little in common, save for one obvious detail: They were all redheads. The doctor's straight auburn hair was beginning to show gray around the edges, and she wore it pulled back sharply in a severe style. She never let it flow freely when she was at her medical practice. The teacher was luxuriously curly-haired, and her bright red locks fell in wild electric currents from her head to her shoulders, disheveled by the unlucky hand that fate had delivered her. The prep school student's hair was slightly lighter, a seductive strawberry color that would have been worth singing about, but it framed a face that seemed to pale a little bit more each day, and blanched skin that seemed lined with care.

What linked them together much more than their striking red hair, however, was the fact that each, in her own way, was *vulnerable*.

The white envelopes, postmarked *New York City*, were common security-tinted envelopes available with self-sealing flaps that could be purchased in any office supply store, grocery store, or pharmacy. The message within was printed on plain white 20-lb. weight common note-paper by the same computer. None of the three had any of the forensic skills necessary to tell there were no fingerprints on the letters, nor was there any telltale DNA substance—saliva, a stray hair, skin follicles—that might give a sophisticated detective with access to a truly modern labora-tory some idea who mailed the letters had the letter writer been in some national criminal database. The letter writer was not. In a world of instant messaging, e-mail, texting, and cell phones, each letter was as old-fash-ioned as smoke signals, a carrier pigeon, or Morse code.

The opening lines were delivered without salutation or introduction:

"One bright, fine day Little Red Riding Hood decided to take a basket of deli-cious goodies to her beloved grandmother, who lived on the far side of the deep, dark woods . . ."

You undoubtedly first heard the story years ago when you were small chil-dren. But you were probably told the sanitized version: The grandmother hides in her closet and Little Red Riding Hood is saved from becoming the Big Bad Wolf's next meal by the brave woodsman with his sharp axe. In that retelling, everything ends happily ever after. In the original, there is a far different and

2

much darker outcome. It would be wise for you to keep that in mind over the next few weeks.

You do not know me, but I know you.

There are three of you. I have decided to call you:

Red One.

Red Two.

Red Three.

I know each of you is lost in the woods.

And just like the little girl in the fairy tale, you have been selected to die.

1

At the top of page one he wrote:

Chapter One: Selection

He paused, waved his fingers above his computer keyboard like a magician conjuring up a spell, and then bent forward, continuing.

The first—and in many ways foremost—problem is selecting your victim. This is where the thoughtless, the impatient, and the rank amateurs make most of their stupid mistakes.

He hated being forgotten.

It had been nearly fifteen years since he'd published a word or killed anyone, and this self-enforced retirement had become extremely painful to him.

He was a year shy of his sixty-fifth birthday and he did not expect to see many more. The realist within reminded him that despite his excellent overall fitness, true longevity was not in his family gene pool. Virulent cancers had claimed both his parents in their early sixties, and heart disease his maternal grandmother similarly early, so he thought his own time was probably close to up. And although he had not been to a doctor in many years, he could feel mysterious steady aches, small, sudden, sharp, and inexplicable pains, and odd weaknesses throughout his body that heralded the advent of old age and perhaps something far worse growing within him. Many months earlier he had read everything Anthony Burgess frantically wrote in the year of productivity the famous novelist had when he was misdiagnosed—told he had an inoperable and fatal brain tumor, when none really existed. He believed—without any real medical confirmation—that his situation just very well might be the same.

And so he had become determined that in whatever time he had left—whether it was twenty days, twenty weeks, or twenty months—he should do something absolutely significant. He knew he needed to create something deliciously memorable, and something that would resonate long after he'd passed from this earth and gone directly to hell. He fully and somewhat proudly expected to assume a position of honor amongst the damned.

So, on the evening that he put what he considered to be his last and greatest work into motion, he felt a long-absent extraordinary child-on-Christmas-morning excitement and an overwhelming sense of deep heart's release, knowing that not only was he returning to the games that he'd petulantly abandoned, but that what he'd designed for his masterpiece would be talked about for years.

Perfect crimes rarely existed, but there were some. These were usually created less by the genius of the criminals and far more by the consistent incompetence of the authorities, and they were usually defined by the pedestrian question of whether the perpetrator got away with it or not. *Accidents of ideal homicide*, he believed they should be called, because getting away with murder wasn't really much of a challenge. But crimes *of perfection* were a different standard, and he truly felt he was launching into one. His invention was designed to satisfy on many different levels.

Pull this off, he told himself, *and they will study you in schools. They will argue about you on television. They will make movies about you. A hundred years from now, your name will be as well known as Billy the Kid or Jack the*

6

Ripper. Someone might even sing a song about you. Not some soft and melodic folk song. Rock and roll.

More than anything, he despised feeling ordinary.

Lasting fame was something he craved. The smaller tastes he'd had of notoriety over the course of his life had been a fleeting narcotic, momentary highs replaced by crushing returns to routine. After many years of drudgery at the late night copy desk at various mid-level newspapers, correcting careless reporters' grammar mistakes in a never-ending assembly line of news stories, he felt an electric thrill when his first novel was accepted by a reputable publishing house. It had come out adorned with a flurry of modestly good reviews. "A gifted natural," one critic had opined.

After he'd quit his job, his subsequent books had been highlighted with the occasional interview in a literary magazine or the arts sections of local papers. A local television news program had once done a small feature on him when one of his four mystery-thrillers had been optioned for the movies—although nothing had ever come of the screenplay some forgettable West Coast writer had produced.

But sooner than he'd expected, sales waned and even these modest accomplishments had faded when he'd stopped writing. If no one was going to pay attention to what he wrote, why write it? He could no longer find a copy of one of his novels on a bookstore shelf, not even on the tables devoted to publishers' overstocks and remainders. And they'd stopped calling him *sophisticated*, *gifted*, or *a natural* as he'd inexorably grown older.

Even death had lost its luster for him.

Murder had lost its cachet in the news business, he believed. The most ordinary of crimes were hyped by reality television shows, trying to create mystery out of the mundane. Well-known spasms of gunshot violence by psychotic head-case killers trapped in wild-eyed delusions still garnered breathless headlines in the few newspapers that continued to struggle out daily editions. Mass killings in drug wars still bought out the television cameras. Gunning down a passel of coworkers in an office rampage would electrify the radio airwaves and drive commentators on the left and right into wild suppositions and nonsensical conclusions.

But the relentless lone killer was no longer a celebrity. Instant sensationalism had replaced steady, cautious design—which left him feeling utterly useless. *More than useless*, he thought—*impotent*.

For years, he had kept a leather-bound scrapbook, filled with clippings from his four murders next to collections of his reviews. Four books. Four killings. But where once he'd reveled in the details of each paragraph, now he could barely stand to examine them. Whatever sense of accomplishment and satisfaction these deaths or the books he'd written had once given him now tasted acid. And so he had bitterly turned away from who he was, because what good was it? If no one took note, what did it mean? Personal satisfaction was nice—but without the accompanying attention of headlines, killing and writing had lost their gleam. He *knew* he should have been an important writer and a notorious killer.

To keep himself sane and exert some control over his growing bitterness, he had turned his back on the world, because the world had turned its back on him.

That fame had not been delivered to him in larger doses continually gnawed at his insides, twisting his waking hours into frustrating knots, turning his sleep into sweat-stained dreams. He thought he was every bit as good at what he did as any Stephen King or Ted Bundy—but no one seemed to know that. He thought the only real passions left to him were anger, envy, and hatred, which were more or less like having a kind of near-fatal illness—only one that couldn't be treated with a pill or a shot or even surgery. Over the course of the last year, as he'd painstakingly prepared his ultimate scheme, he'd come to realize that it was the only route forward for him. If, in his remaining years, he wanted to belly-laugh at a joke, or to enjoy the taste of a fine wine and a good meal, feel some excitement over watching a sports team win a championship or even vote for a politician with a sense of optimism—then creating a truly memorable murder was of paramount importance. It would give life and meaning to his remaining days. *Special*, he told himself. It would make him *rich*—in all the senses of that word.

After fifteen years of self-imposed denial, he had decided to return to doing what he did best—in a way that could not possibly be ignored.

Create. Execute. Escape.

He smiled, and he thought this was the Holy Trinity for all killers. It surprised him a little that it had taken him so many years to realize that he had to add a fourth and unexpected term to that equation: *Write about it.*

He tapped hard on the computer keys. He imagined that he was the same as a drummer in a rock band, devoted to maintaining rhythm and creating the backbone of the music:

While there is much to be said for and much to admire in the sudden, random murder—where you suddenly happen upon an appropriate victim and instantly indulge—these sorts of killings ultimately lack true satisfaction. They become merely a stepping-stone, leading to more of the same. Desires dictate necessity, and those same desires eventually overcome you, clouding your ability to plan, and may actually lead to detection. They are clumsy, and clumsiness translates into a policeman knocking on your door, gun drawn. The best, most rewarding killing is one that combines intense study with steady dedication and, lastly, desire. Control becomes the drug of choice. Out-think, outmaneuver, out-invent—and the killing inevitably will become outstanding. It will satisfy every dark need.

Anyone can kill someone.

And maybe get lucky and get away with it. Probably not. But there's always a chance of blundering into success.

Anyone maybe can go on, taking what they've learned, and kill another and another and another. And maybe get away with all of these, because they are all truly the same killings, just repeated. Ad infinitum.

But kill three strangers on the same day, within hours, each in their own special way?

And walk away, leaving death and confused policemen behind?

Now that is truly unique.

And the killer who can pull that off will be remembered.
And that was precisely what I had in mind with my three Reds.

The evening he mailed the letters, he stopped at a small kiosk on the 42nd Street causeway leading into Grand Central Terminal and paid cash for a half-stale croissant stuffed with unrecognizable cheese and a plastic cup of bitter, scalding black coffee. He had a dark leather briefcase-satchel hung over his shoulder, and he wore a slate-gray woolen topcoat over his dark navy suit. He'd colored his salt-and-pepper hair a sandy blond, and matched that with dark-rimmed eyeglasses and a fake beard and mustache purchased from a store that specialized in providing disguises to the film and theater industries. A tweed driver's cap was pulled down on his head, further obscuring his appearance. He had done enough, he believed, to fool any facial recognition software—not that he expected any enterprising detective to use any.

The coffee filled his nostrils with warmth and he headed into the cavernous station. Soft yellow light reflected off the green-blue ceiling with its curiously reversed constellations and a steady hum of noise greeted him. The drone of train arrivals and departures was like canned background music. His shoes clicked against the polished surface of the floor, which reminded him of a tap dancer or maybe a marching band moving through precise steps.

It was at the height of the daily rush hour. He walked with practiced speed, chewing on the croissant and idly bumping up against thousands of other commuters—most of whom looked very much like he did. He passed by a pair of bored New York City cops as he angled toward a mail drop just outside the platform entryway for a Metro-North commuter train. For an instant he wanted to spin in their direction and shout out *"I'm a killer!"* just to see their reactions, but he easily fought off this urge. *If they only knew how close they were . . .* This made him grin, because that irony was part of the whole theater. He made a mental note to reflect on his observations and feelings in prose later that night.

He wore surgeon's latex gloves—it amused him that neither of the cops seemed to have noticed this telltale detail. *They probably thought I was just some paranoiac overly worried about germs.* He paused at a trash container to dump what remained of the croissant and the coffee. In a movement he'd practiced in his house, he unslung the satchel from his shoulder and seized three envelopes. Clutching these, he let the crush of hurrying-home-from-work people carry him toward the mail drop. Keeping his head down—he suspected there were security cameras hidden in spots he couldn't identify on the lookout for potential terrorists—he swiftly dropped the three envelopes into the narrow slot above a sign that warned people about the dangers of mailing hazardous materials.

This, too, made him want to laugh out loud. The United States Postal Service meant illicit drugs, poisons, or bomb-making liquids. He knew that carefully chosen words were far more threatening.

Sometimes, he told himself, the best jokes are those you alone can hear. The three letters were now in the hands of one of the busiest postal processing systems in the United States—and one of the most reliable. He wanted to howl out loud with anticipation, bay at some distant moon hidden by Grand Central's cavernous roof. His pulse raced with excitement. The din of the trains and people around him slipped away, and he was abruptly enveloped in a warm, delicious silence of his own creation. It was like descending into azure-clear Caribbean waters and floating, watching shafts of light slice through the enveloping blue world.

Like the diver he imagined himself to be, he exhaled slowly, feeling himself rise inexorably toward the surface.

He thought:

And so it begins.

Then he let himself be swept forward with the rest of the anonymous masses onto a jam-packed commuter train. He did not care where it was going, because wherever it stopped wasn't his real destination.

2
The Three Reds

The day that she became Red One had already been a difficult one for Doctor Karen Jayson.

First thing in the morning she'd had to tell a middle-aged woman that her test results showed she had ovarian cancer; midday she'd received a call from a local emergency room that one of her longtime patients had been severely injured in an auto accident; at the same time she was forced to hospitalize another patient with a crippling kidney stone that couldn't be managed with routine pain medication. Then she had to spend nearly an hour on the phone with an insurance company executive justifying her decision. Patients in her waiting room had backed up, everything from routine physicals to strep throat and flu, which each sufferer had blissfully spread to everyone else waiting in various states of frustration and illness.

And then, late in the afternoon of what she thought was already a relentlessly bad day, she was called to the hospice wing at Shady Grove Retirement Home—a nearby place that was neither in a grove nor particularly shady—to attend the final moments of a man she barely knew. The man was in his early nineties, with not much more than a sunken-chest-and-gaunt-eyes wisp of him left, but he had clung to life with pit-bull tenacity. Karen had seen many people die over the course of her professional life; as an internist with a subspecialty in geriatrics, this was inevitable. But even so, she could never get accustomed to it. Standing at the man's bedside doing nothing other than adjusting the IV Demerol drip, it roiled her emotions. She wished the hospice nurses hadn't called her, had managed the death on their own.

But they had, and she'd responded, and there she was.

The room seemed stark and cold, though the heat was blasting through old-fashioned radiators. It was shadowy and dark, as if death could enter more easily into a dimly lit room. A few machines, a shuttered window, an old metal bedside lamp, some tangled, dingy white sheets, and a faint odor of waste were all that surrounded the old man. There was not even a cheap but colorful painting on any of the flat white walls to fracture the atmosphere in the bleak room. It was not a good place to die.

She thought: *Poets be damned, there's nothing even slightly romantic or elegiac about dying, especially in a nursing home that has seen better days.*

"He's gone," the attending nurse said.

Karen had heard the same things in the final few seconds: a slow release of breath, like the last bit of air leaking from a balloon, followed by the high-pitched alarm from the heart monitor familiar to anyone who'd ever watched a doctor drama on television. She reached over and turned the machine off after watching the flat, lime-green electronic line for a moment, thinking that the routine of death had none of the cinematic tension people imagined it to have. It was often just a fading away, like banks of lights in a huge auditorium being shut down after a crowd has dispersed, until only darkness is left behind. She sighed, told herself that even this image was too poetic, and let habit overtake her. She placed her fingers against the old man's throat, searching for a pulse in his carotid artery. His skin seemed paper-thin beneath her hand, and she had the odd thought that even the softest, gentlest touch would leave telltale scars on his neck.

"Time of death, four forty-four," she said.

There was something mathematically satisfying in that series of numbers, like squares placed inside each other, fitting together perfectly. She examined the old man's DNR form and then looked over at the nurse, who had begun to unhook wire leads from the man's chest. "When you finish Mister"—she glanced at the DNR form again—". . . Wilson's paperwork, will you bring it around for me to sign?"

Karen was a little ashamed that she stumbled over the old man's name. *Death should not be so anonymous*, she thought. The old man's face looked—as she expected—peaceful. *Death and clichés*, she thought, *simply go together*. She wondered, for a moment, precisely who Mister Wilson was. Lots of hopes, dreams, memories, experiences disappearing at four forty-four. What had he seen of life? Family? School? War? Love? Sadness? Joy? There was nothing in the room in his last moments that said anything about who he was. For a moment, Karen felt a surge of anger over death's arriving alongside anonymity. The hospice nurse must have sensed it, because she interrupted the creeping silence.

"It's sad," the nurse said. "Mister Wilson was a lovely old man. Do you know he liked bagpipe music, of all things? But he wasn't a Scot. I think he came from the Midwest somewhere. Like Iowa or Idaho. Go figure."

Karen imagined there had to be a story behind that love, but now it was lost. "Any family I should be calling?" she asked.

The nurse shook her head, but answered, "I'll have to double-check his admission forms. I know we didn't call anyone when he came in to hospice."

The nurse had already passed from one routine—helping someone who had reached his nineties pass from this life to the next—to her subsequent responsibility, which was properly processing death bureaucratically.

"I think I'll go outside for a moment while you get the paperwork together."

The nurse nodded her head slightly. She was familiar with Doctor Jayson's postmortem order of business: sneaking a cigarette in the far corner of the nursing home's parking lot where the doctor believed no one could see her, which wasn't actually the case. After this solitary break, the doctor would head back inside to the main office, where she kept a desk solely for filling out Medicare and Medicaid forms and signing off on the inevitable conclusion to stays in the home, the state-mandated death certificate. The home was several blocks away from the square redbrick medical building where Karen practiced internal medicine alongside a dozen other doctors competent in everything from psychiatry to cardiology.

The nurse knew that Karen would smoke precisely one-half of a cigarette before coming back inside to complete Mister Wilson's paperwork. In the pack of Marlboros that Karen thought she had hidden in her top desk drawer, and which all the staff at the hospice wing were aware of, the doctor had carefully and painstakingly measured each smoke and marked the midway point with a red pen. The nurse also knew that regardless of the weather, Karen would not bother with a coat, even if it was pouring rain or freezing cold in western Massachusetts. The nurse imagined that this lack of concession to the vagaries of the weather was the penance the doctor paid for continuing to be addicted to a disgusting habit she fully knew would kill her before too long and one that was held in total contempt by virtually everyone in the health care business the doctor was a part of.

It was night and well past the dinner hour when Karen pulled onto the long dirt and gravel driveway that led to her house, stopping at the beaten old mailbox by the side of the road. She lived in a rural part of the county, adjacent to conservation land and walking paths through dark woods, where modestly expensive homes were pushed back away from any roadway and many sported views of distant hills. In the fall this landscape was spectacular as the leaves changed, but that time had swept past, and now it was trapped in cold, muddy, and barren winter.

The lights were ablaze inside her home, but this wasn't because there was someone to meet her; she'd had a timing system installed because she lived alone, and she didn't like coming home to a dark house on sad nights like this one. It wasn't the same as being greeted by a family, but it made the return home slightly more welcoming. She had a pair of cats—Martin and

Lewis—who would be waiting for her with feline enthusiasm, which, she was sad to admit, wasn't really very much. She was torn about her pets. She would have preferred a dog, some bounding, tail-wagging golden retriever who made up for lack of brains with unabashed eagerness, but because she worked such long hours away from her house, she hadn't felt it fair to a dog, especially a breed that suffered without human companionship. The cats, with their lofty self-determination and haughty approach to life, were better suited for the isolation of Karen's daily grind.

That she lived alone, away from city lights and energy, was something she had simply fallen into over the years. She had been married once. It hadn't worked. She had a lover once. It hadn't worked. She'd engaged in a relationship with another woman once. It hadn't worked. She had given up on one-night-meet-you-in-the-bar stands and Internet service dating sites that promised real compatibility once you filled out the question-naire and suggested that love was waiting right around the corner. None of these had worked, either. She had discovered that solitude didn't bother her in the least. It gave her confidence.

What she had was her job and a hobby that she kept hidden from her physician coworkers: She was a dedicated if completely amateur stand-up comic. Once a month she would drive to any of the dozen or so comedy clubs throughout the state that had "open-mike" nights and would try out various routines. What she loved about performing comedy was its unpre-dictability. It was impossible to gauge whether any given audience would be howling with laughs, guffawing with hilarity, or sitting stony-faced, lips curling up, before the inevitable catcalls started to ring out and she would be forced to make a rapid retreat from the unrelenting spotlight. Karen loved making people laugh, and she even oddly appreciated the embar-rassment of being hooted off the stage. Both reminded her of the frailties and eccentricity of life.

She kept a small Apple laptop with only a few applications on it to write her comedy routines and try out new jokes. Her regular computer was jammed with patient records, medical data, and the ordinary elec-tronic life of a busy professional. The smaller one she kept locked away in the same way that she concealed her hobby from coworkers and her few friends and distant relatives. Comedy, like smoking, she told herself, was an addiction best kept secret.

Her mailbox door had been left slightly ajar—a habit the delivery person had that often resulted in her mail being soaked by the elements. She got out of her car, jogged around to the mailbox, and grabbed everything inside without looking at any of it. It had started to spit freezing rain, and a few drops hit her neck and chilled her. Then she hustled back behind the wheel and launched herself up the driveway, tires spinning against loose gravel and some ice that had already formed.

She found herself fixating on the old man who had died that day. This wasn't uncommon for her, when she signed off on a death. It was as if some sort of vacuum had been created within her, and she felt a need to fill it with *some* bits of information. *Bagpipes. Iowa.* She had no idea how that connection was made. She began to speculate, trying to invent a story that would satisfy her curiosity. *He first heard the pipes when he was a small child, after a new neighbor arrived from Glasgow or Edinburgh into the weather-beaten house next door. The neighbor would often drink a little too much, and he'd become melancholy and long for his native land. When this loneliness came over him, the neighbor would bring down his instrument from a shelf in the closet and decide to pipe in the evening dark, just as the sun would set over the flat Iowa horizon, all because he missed the rolling green hills of his home. Mister Wilson—only he wasn't yet Mister Wilson—would be in his bedroom, and the rich, unusual music would float through his open window: "Scotland the Brave" or "Blue Bonnet." That was where the fascination came from.* Karen thought that as good a story possibility as any.

She wondered: *Is there a routine in this?* Her mind churned up *So, I watched an old man who loved the bagpipes die . . .* and could she make it seem like it was the unusual notes from the instrument that killed him and not old age?

The car crunched to a halt by the front door. She grabbed her briefcase, coat, and the pile of mail, and arms filled, she hustled through the gloomy darkness and damp chill toward her home.

The two cats sort of stirred to greet her as she came through the front door, but it seemed more an idle curiosity combined with dinner expectations that had forced them from slumber. She headed into the kitchen, intending to pour them a new bowl of dry food, fix herself a glass of white wine, and consider what leftover in the refrigerator wasn't too close to homicidal spoilage to reheat for dinner. Food did not interest her much, which helped keep her build wiry even as she crept in age into her fifties. She dropped the coat on a bench and shoved her briefcase beside it. Then she went straight for the trash bin to sort through the mail. The letter without any identifying characteristics other than the New York City postmark was stuck between a telephone bill from Verizon, another from the local electric company, two promotional letters for credit cards she didn't need or want, and several solicitation letters from the Democratic National Committee, Doctors Without Borders, and Greenpeace.

Karen set the bills on a counter, tossed all the others into a bin for paper recycling, and tore open the anonymous letter.

The message made her hands twitch, and she gasped out loud.

When she became Red Two, Sarah Locksley was naked.

She had stripped off first her pants and then her sweater, dropping them to the floor beside her. She was slightly drunk and slightly stoned from her usual afternoon combination of vodka and barbiturates when the postman pushed her daily mail delivery through the slot in her front door. She heard the sound of envelopes slapping against the hardwood floor of the vestibule. She knew most would be marked *Overdue* or *Final Notice*. These were the daily deluge of bills and demands that she had no intention of paying the slightest attention to. She stood up and caught a glimpse of herself in the reflection of the television screen and thought it made no sense to go halfway, so she tugged off her bra and stepped out of her underwear and tossed it all onto a nearby couch with a flourish. She pirouetted right and left in front of the screen, thinking how little of her seemed to be left. She felt scrawny, emaciated, too thin by a half, and not from obsessive exercise or marathon race training. She knew that she had been sexy once, but now her slenderness was caused solely by despair.

Sarah picked up the remote control and switched on the TV. Her own reflected image on the screen was immediately replaced by the familiar characters of an afternoon soap opera. She found the *mute* switch on the remote and killed off the dialogue. Sarah preferred to make up her own story, substituting what she believed they should be saying for whatever the writing staff had come up with. She wanted her dialogue to be more trite. More clichéd. More stilted and more stupid. She did not want to allow even the slightest touch of emotional accuracy or acceptable reality into her versions of the soap operas. She wanted it to be sloppy and overwrought and she did not trust the soap opera's writers to be as over the top as she could be. She did not expect to be able to do this for much longer—the Big Box store where she'd purchased the television on credit was likely to come asking for it back any week. The same was true for her furniture, her car, and probably her house as well.

Her voice seemed to echo around her, her words slurred slightly, as if they were photographs taken out of focus.

"Oh Denise, I love you so much . . . especially your unbelievable Barbie-doll figure."

"Yes, Doctor Smith, I love you too. Take me in your arms and spirit me and my medically augmented breasts away from here . . ."

On the television screen, a dark-haired, strapping man who looked significantly more like a male model than a heart surgeon was embracing a statuesque blond woman whose most serious disease ever might have been a cracked nail or the sniffles. The only time she'd ever had to see a doctor was when she'd had her teeth capped. Their mouths moved with words, but Sarah continued to supply the dialogue.

"Yes, darling, I will . . . except your test results have come back from the laboratory, and, I don't know how to say this, but you haven't much time . . ."

"Our love is stronger than any disease . . ."

Hah! Sarah thought. *I bet it isn't.*

Then she told herself: *I guess I'll be writing the lovely Botoxed Denise and the handsome Doctor Smith out of my life.*

Sarah walked over to the front window as the show's credits scrawled across the screen. She stood motionless for a few moments, arms lifted above her head, totally exposed, half-hoping one of her nosy neighbors would see her, or that the afternoon yellow school bus from the junior high school would roll past jammed with students and she could give all the preteens a real show. Some of the kids on the bus would remember her from her days in the classroom. Fifth grade. Mrs. Locksley.

She shut her eyes. *Look at me*, she thought. *Come on, goddammit, look at me!*

She could feel tears starting to well up uncontrollably in the corners of her eyes, running hot down her cheeks. This was normal for her.

Sarah had been a popular teacher right up to the moment she resigned. If any of her former students saw her this day framed in her living room window stark naked, they would probably like her even more.

She had quit a little less than a year earlier, on one of the last days of the semester before summer vacation started. She quit on a Monday, two days after the bright, warm morning her husband had taken their three-year-old daughter on the most innocent of Saturday errands—a trip to the grocery store for milk and cereal—and never returned.

Sarah turned from the window and stared through the living room to the front door where the pile of mail was bunched up on the floor. *Never answer the door*, she said to herself. *Never answer a ringing doorbell, or a hard knock. Don't pick up a telephone when someone unknown calls. Just stay where you are, because it just might be a young state trooper with his Smokey the Bear hat in his hands, looking embarrassed and stammering, "There's been an accident, and I hate to have to tell you this, Mrs. Locksley . . ."*

She sometimes wondered why her life had been ruined on such a fine day. It should have been a raining, sleeting, miserable, gloomy wintry mix, like this day was. But instead, it had been bright, warm, an endless blue sky, so when she fell to the floor that morning, her eyes had scoured the heavens above her, trying to find some shape that they could fix on, as if they could tether her to even a passing cloud, so desperate was she to hold on to something.

Sarah shrugged at the injustice of it all.

She looked outside the window. No one passing by. No naked sideshow this day. She ran her hands through her mane of red hair, wondering when it was that she'd showered, or taken a comb to the tangled thatch. A couple of days, at the least. She shrugged. *I was beautiful once. I was happy once. I had the life I wanted once.*

No more.

She turned and looked at the pile of envelopes by her front door. *Reality intrudes*, she told herself. She wished she were drunker or more stoned, but she felt totally sober.

So, she walked over to the pile of dunning letters. *Take it all*, she said. *I don't want to have anything left.*

The nondescript letter with the New York postmark was resting on top. She didn't know why it grabbed her attention, but she reached down and picked it up from the pile. At first, she imagined this was a really clever way some creditor had devised to get her to respond. Putting *Second Notice* in large red letters on the outside was really designed to have her ignore whatever the notice was demanding pretty rapidly. But *not putting anything*—well, she thought, that was smart. Her curiosity was pricked. *Reverse psychology.*

Okay, she told herself, as she idly tore open the envelope, *I'll give you this one. You won this round. I'll read your threatening letter requiring me to pay money I don't have for something I no longer want or need.*

She started reading, and swiftly realized that whatever she had had to drink earlier and whatever pills she had taken that morning, it might not have been enough.

By the time she'd finished the message, for the first time she actually felt naked.

It was just after her last morning class when Jordan Ellis became Red Three, and she was utterly miserable. She did not know about her new

21

role immediately because she was preoccupied with her latest in a year-long series of failures: American history. She was staring at her most recent essay in the required course, which was emblazoned with a cryptic note from the professor *See Me* and a desultory grade: D-plus. She crumpled the sheets of typing in her fist, then sighed deeply and smoothed them out again. The grade had little to do with her ability; this she knew. Words, language, ideas, details—all of it came naturally to her. She had been an A student in the recent past, but she was no longer sure that she would ever be again.

Jordan felt a surge of anger. She knew that everything was tied together, all knots pulled tight. She was failing math, barely passing history, on the cusp of flunking Spanish and science, and just creeping along in English literature—and college applications hung over her head like a sword. She could no longer concentrate, no longer focus. No longer do the work that had once been so pleasant and had come to her so easily. The school psychologist had sat across from her a week earlier and glibly talked about *acting out* and *behaving self-destructively in order to gain attention* and wrapped up every failing grade with the easiest of emotional equations: "You were delivered a blow, Jordan, when your parents announced their divorce. You need to rise above it."

It hadn't been anywhere near that simple.

She hated trite psychology. The school therapist had made it seem like life was little more than hanging on to a rope and swinging back and forth above some abyss and that Jordan had allowed her grip to slip loose.

She felt like she had no home any longer, that everything in her life was a lie, that the two people closest to her were nothing more than illusion and deception. She had decided that she would never love anyone. Not anymore. And as angry as she was, she could not shake loose from the sensation that she was somehow to blame for something terrible, something that had ripped her life apart as casually as one might tear a shred of worn cloth into a rag.

When she surveyed the landscape of her senior year of school, she could see nothing but rocks and crevasses strewn across dirt and mud.

Boys she'd once happily experimented with sexually now mocked her. Girls she'd once thought were her friends now spent all their time trashing her behind her back. Her life had become so entwined, so knotted, that she didn't know where to turn. *Jordan's typical day*, she imagined: *A miserable grade on a test in the morning; fumble the ball during basketball practice in the afternoon so often that the coach yells at you and then removes you from the starting lineup; eat alone in the dining hall at dinner because no one will sit with you.*

She wished she could hide somewhere, but even this was impossible. Her damn red hair—she hated it—made her stand out in every crowd, when all she wanted was to fade away into anonymity. She even tucked it up beneath a knit ski cap, but this hardly helped.

She was walking along a pathway between the art studio and the science labs, head down, her parka scrunched up, her backpack jammed with books tugging at her shoulders. Cold rain dripped from the ivy that covered the dormitory buildings at her exclusive private school. *At least*, she thought, *the weather fits my mood.* Jordan plowed along, a little glad that the weather was driving everyone along the black macadam trails that crisscrossed the campus with the same rapid pace. It was early in the afternoon, although the dark gray skies made it seem like night was about to tumble down. She had basically skipped lunch, only ducking into the cafeteria for an orange, a hunk of French bread, and a small milk carton, which she stuffed into her parka pocket to eat in the solitude of her room.

As a senior, she had managed to get a single—no roommate—in one of the smaller, converted houses that rimmed the campus. A regular New England white clapboard home built a century earlier, it had a wide front porch and a stately mahogany center stairwell. It had once been home to the school's chaplains, and had a ghostly smell of religious devotion inside. Now it housed six upper-class girls and the women's lacrosse coach and Spanish instructor, a Miss Gonzalez, who was supposed to act as a dorm parent and confidante, but who spent most of her free time meeting with the assistant football coach, young and married with two little children. Their sounds of their unbridled—and the girls thought *sporting*—passion

23

penetrated the walls and gave the girls in the dormitory something to laugh about and secretly envy.

Thinking about the squeals, moans, and sighs of cheating that came from Miss Gonzalez's suite actually brought a grin to Jordan's lips. *Letting go like that must really be wonderful,* she imagined. It didn't seem at all like her fumbling, self-conscious experiments with boys.

She shook her head and slowly all her troubles crept back onto her shoulders and into her heart, as if the jammed backpack that weighed down on her neck was filled with far more than books. For the first time since the day she'd finished packing for school and her parents had interrupted her with a *Jordan, we need to speak with you . . ."* summons, she truly wondered whether continuing was at all worthwhile. She knew nothing was truly her fault, and yet it felt as if everything was her fault.

Filled with confusion about seemingly everything in her life, Jordan stepped inside the vestibule of her dormitory. She shook some of the dampness from her head and scooted some from her parka. She tugged off her ski cap, letting her hair fall loose because no one was around. Everyone was still at lunch and there was a little time left before the afternoon sports activities took over the private school routine. The quiet calmed her, and she padded over to the table where the dormitory's mail was sorted into six different trays. She saw there were three letters in hers.

The first two were in familiar hands: her father's tight, barely readable scribble and her mother's more flowery, expansive script. That these two letters arrived simultaneously made perfect sense to Jordan. There was some new excessively dramatic dispute, some new and overblown bone of contention between the two of them. Since their announcement hardly a week had gone by without some new bickering back and forth. This had allowed their lawyers to posture and threaten like the blowhards they probably were. Her parents both considered Jordan to be the ultimate emotional battlefield, the Waterloo over which they could compete like Bonaparte and Wellington. She knew what was inside each letter: an explanation of each one's latest nonnegotiable position, and why Jordan should side with the letter writer's interpretation of events. *"Wouldn't you really rather live with me, darling, and not your father?"* Or: *"You know how your mother can't think of anyone except herself, honey."*

Her parents had only recently taken to communicating with her through the formality of the U.S. mail. Both had realized that she simply ignored e-mail and allowed her cell phone to go straight to voice mail when they called. But the tactile presence of the written word on her mother's pink-hued, expensive stationery, or her father's business-weight bond, seemed harder for her to shunt aside. But, she thought, *I'm learning.*

She shoved the two letters into her backpack. Ignoring whatever falsely urgent dispute between her parents that needed her immediate attention gave her a small sense of satisfaction.

The third letter surprised her. Other than her name and a New York postmark, she could not tell what it was about. Her first thought was that it was from one of the many attorneys handling the divorce, but then she realized that wasn't the case, because those folks all had very fancy stationery emblazoned with their names and addresses so there was no doubt of the importance of whatever was contained within. This letter was slender, and as she walked to her room, pushed open the door, and stepped inside, she turned the envelope over two or three times, inspecting it. She was reluctant to open any mail. It was never good news.

She dropped her coat to the floor and dumped her backpack on her bed. She took out the orange for her lunch and started to peel it, but stopped midway through and, shrugging, tore open the letter.

She read the message slowly, then read it again.

After she finished, Jordan looked up, as if someone had entered the room beside her. Her lip quivered.

This has to be a joke, she thought. *Someone is playing a trick. It can't be real.*

It was the only explanation that made sense, except she could feel a lurking darkness deep within her telling her that making sense wasn't really what was important to whoever had written this letter.

Earlier that morning, she had not thought that she could possibly feel more alone, but suddenly, right at that moment, she did.

3

Panic One.

Panic Two.

Panic Three.

After reading their letter, each Red panicked in her own unique way. Each Red mistakenly thought she was maintaining control over emotions that seemed suddenly explosive. Each Red imagined she was reacting to the threatening words appropriately. Each Red believed she was taking the right steps. Each Red felt that she—and she alone—could keep herself safe, if safe was what she actually wanted to be. Each Red assessed the stated threat to her life and reached a dizzyingly different conclusion. Each Red was unsure whether she was truly in danger or just ought to be annoyed, although neither alternative made complete sense. Each Red struggled to grasp the truth of her situation, only to be stymied. Each Red slid into confusion without knowing that was what she was doing.

None of them were completely right about anything.

Karen Jayson's first instinct, after absorbing the shock delivered by the words on the page, was to call the local police.

Sarah Locksley's initial impulse was to find the handgun that her dead husband had kept locked away in a steel box, hidden on a top shelf in the small room that had doubled as his home office.

Jordan Ellis did nothing except flop down and curl up on her bed, doubled over as if cramped and sick.

Karen's conversation with the detective was brutally unpleasant. She had read the letter thoroughly twice, and then slapped it down on the kitchen table and angrily seized her telephone from a hook on the wall. Her imagination reeled with barely contained fury. She was not accustomed to being threatened and she hated the coy fairy-tale underpinnings of the letter, so the officious, determined, well-educated *I'm not scared of anything or anyone* side of her rapidly took over. *So, who are you, some big bad fucking wolf?* she thought. *We'll see about that.* Without really considering what she would say, she dialed 911.

She expected the dispatcher who answered to be helpful. She was wrong.

"Police. Fire. Emergency," he said.

She thought the voice sounded very young, even with the curt words.

"This is Doctor Karen Jayson over on Marigold Road. I believe I need to speak with a detective."

"What is the nature of your emergency, ma'am?"

"Doctor," Karen corrected him. She instantly wished that she hadn't.

"Okay," the dispatcher responded instantly, "what is the nature of your emergency, *Doctor*?" She could hear a tired end-of-shift contempt in the way he forced out the word.

"A threatening letter," she answered.

"From who?"

"I don't know. It wasn't signed."

"An anonymous threat?"

"Yes. Precisely."

"Well, you better speak with someone in the detective bureau," the dispatcher said.

That's what I said, Karen thought but did not say.

She was put on hold, presumably while the phone line was switched. The local police force was small and occupied a stolid brick building in the center of the closest town, just off the main common, adjacent to the town's only ambulance and fire station and across from the modest town hall. She lived in the countryside at least five miles away and the only time she passed the police headquarters was when she took her weekly Saturday morning trip to the Whole Foods Market nearby. She guessed that most of the police work was dedicated to keeping the highways safe from bored and speeding teenagers, stepping between husbands and wives who had come to blows, and working with the nearby bigger city forces on drug investigations, because many dealers had come to understand that being out in the rural sections allowed them considerable peace and quiet while they cooked up crystal meth or chopped up rock cocaine for distribution on much harder urban streets and nearby colleges. Karen wondered whether there were more than ten actual police officers on duty at any time in her town and if any had even the smallest amount of sophisticated training.

"This is Detective Clark," a sturdy, no-nonsense voice came over the line. She was relieved to note that this policeman at least sounded older.

She identified herself and told the detective that she'd received a threatening letter. She was surprised that he did not ask her to read it to him, but instead launched into a series of questions, with the most obvious first.

"Do you know who might have sent it to you?" he asked.

"No."

"Does it have any identifying marks that might indicate—?"

"No," she interrupted. "A New York City postmark, that's all."

"You have no idea who the writer is?"

"None."

"Well, have you been through any personal issues—"

"No. Not in years."

"Have you made any enemies at work?"

"No."

"Have you recently had to fire an employee?"

"No."

"Have you had any run-ins with neighbors? Like maybe a nasty dispute over a property line, or your dog got out and chased their cat, or something like that?"

"No. I don't have a dog."

"Has there been anything out of the ordinary in the last few days or weeks that you noticed, like telephone hang-ups, or vehicles following you on your way to or from work?"

"No."

"Have you had any recent thefts, or a break-in either at your home or office?"

"No."

"Have you lost your wallet or a credit card or some other type of personal identification?"

"No."

"How about Internet? An identity theft, or—"

"No."

"Can you think of anyone, anywhere, for any reason who might want to harm you?"

"No."

The detective sighed, which Karen thought was unprofessional. Again, she did not say this out loud.

"Come on, Doctor. Surely there's somebody out there you might have crossed, maybe even inadvertently. Did you ever misdiagnose some patient? Fail to provide some medical service that caused someone to get ill, or even to die? Ever been sued by some unsatisfied customer?"

"No."

"So you can't think of anyone . . . ?"

"No. That's what I told you. No."

The detective paused before continuing. "How about someone who might want to play a practical joke?"

Karen doubted this. Some of the other performers she met at comedy clubs had what she considered pretty far-out senses of humor—and there was a style of *punking* other comedians with pranks that verged on the sadistic and cruel—but a letter like the one on the kitchen table in front of her seemed way beyond any comedian's idea of good fun, no matter how twisted he or she was. "No. And I don't think it's very funny."

She could imagine the detective shrugging on the other end of the line. "Well, I'm not sure there's much we can do right now. I can have regular patrol cars frequent your street a bit more often. I'll have an announcement made at our daily staff session. But until there's some sort of overt act . . ." The detective's voice trailed off.

"The letter isn't an overt act?"

"It is and it isn't."

"What do you mean by that?"

"Well," Detective Clark said in a voice that was probably designed for giving a lecture to a high school class about the law, "a written threat is a second-degree felony. But you say you have no enemies—at least, none that you are currently aware of—and you haven't done anything to warrant a threat and no one has actually *done* anything, other than write this harassing letter. . . ."

"I think, Detective Clark, that someone saying '*You have been selected to die*' might register as more than merely harassment." Karen knew she sounded overly stuffy and stiff. She hoped that this would energize the policeman in some way, but it had the opposite effect.

"Doctor, I think I'd just chalk it up to some bizarre moment, or someone with a lousy sense of humor, or someone who wants to mess you up a little bit for whatever reason and forget about it until something actually happens. Unless, of course, you see someone following you, or someone raids your bank account or something like that. Or else they demand money. Then maybe . . ."

He hesitated before continuing, "The cases we see where there is a threat—well, usually we're talking about a stalker. Someone obsessed with a teacher or a coworker or a former boyfriend or girlfriend. But it's always someone they had a relationship with. The threat is part of some larger picture of compulsion. But that's not what you're saying, is it? Do you think you're being stalked?"

"No. Or I don't know."

"Well, look at your life. Anything else unusual?"

"No."

"Well, there you have it."

"You mean there's nothing at all I can do?"

"No. I mean there's nothing *we* can do. You should certainly take some precautions. Do you have an alarm system in your house? Better get one, if you don't. Maybe get a big dog. Take a much closer look at the people you've come into contact with over the past few months. Start to put together a list of anyone you *might* have crossed, or anyone you *might* have wronged. Maybe take a closer look at all your patients, and consider their families. Maybe someone you've been treating with less-than-great results has a psychotic brother-in-law or a cousin that just got out of prison. Think about that. Usually in threats like these people can't see the person doing the threatening even though they're standing right next to 'em, because they just don't expect it."

The detective continued to drone on. "You know, you could consider a private detective service, see if they can't trace the letter—but that's damn difficult. An e-mail? Well, that they could manage. But an old-fashioned letter? Even the FBI has trouble with that sort of thing. Remember those anthrax letters? Or the Unabomber? Big-time hassle even with all their modern, up-to-date resources. And here in our small town we don't have anywhere near their capabilities or manpower. Hell, even the state police don't. But, if I were you, the most important thing is coming up with that list of who there is out there you've managed to offend, because there might be someone you're just totally unaware of. Most likely that's it. You come up with a name, even ten names, well, I'll be more than happy to go have a real direct and not-too-pleasant conversation with them. Put the fear of God and the mighty resources of the great Commonwealth of Massachusetts into them. Until then . . ."

"You mean threatening to kill someone isn't a crime you want to investigate?"

"Well, I'll file a report so your complaint becomes a part of the legal record. But to be frank, Doctor, people make idle threats all the time."

"This doesn't seem idle."

"No. But you just don't know, do you? It's probably nothing."

"Yeah," Karen said. "Probably."

She hung up. *Except if it isn't*, she said to herself.

Sarah Locksley was quivering when she slowly walked through the door to her dead husband's small office. It was a narrow room, with only a single window in the back with the blinds shut and a scarred old oaken desk with an out-of-date computer on it. It was where he'd done their taxes and paid their bills and off and on worked on a memoir of the dangerous months that he'd spent driving supply trucks and heavy machinery up and down the Baghdad Airport Road in the early part of the Iraq war. The idea all along was that when she got pregnant again, it would be turned into the nursery for the new baby.

There were framed pictures on the walls of the two of them on their wedding day, then the three of them, and of Sarah and their daughter. There was a Red Sox pennant signed by several of the players after the 2004 championship and a picture of her husband with his National Guard unit during their deployment. There were some other memorabilia, photographs, the sorts of knickknacks and silly stuff one collects that have small meanings—a seashell painted in pink and orange with a big heart in the middle that she'd bought him as a joke on a Valentine's Day; a gimmick fake trophy fish, a fad a few years back, that sang a tinny version of "Take Me to the River"; a scale model of a black turbo Porsche that occupied a corner of the desk. This had been a birthday gift. One exhausted, colicky night shortly after their daughter was born her husband had made a series of jokes about why he needed something utterly irresponsible in his life instead of all this dedicated-parent stuff—and he was going to buy a sports car, preferably the most expensive and fastest he could find. He'd laughed wildly months later when he'd opened up the brightly wrapped toy car.

In all the time following the accident that killed her family, she had entered the room only two or three times, and each time she had not lingered, but had grabbed whatever it was she'd gone in for and then quickly shut the door tight behind her. The same was true for her daughter's room, just next door. Each had been left as it was on the day the pair of them had died. Sarah knew that it wasn't unusual for people who were grieving, but entering either of the rooms scared her, because when she did, she thought she could hear her daughter's or her husband's voice echoing in the shadows and she could feel their touch on her skin. It was like they were crying for her, and the eerie sensation of their touch and the hallucination of their voices always caused her to break down sobbing.

He had promised her many times he would get rid of the gun. He hadn't had time.

Of course, she thought, as she stood in the doorway afraid to even turn on the light, *there hadn't been time for anything that they had planned*. The trip to the Grand Canyon. The trip to Europe. The bigger house in a nicer suburb. A new car. They hadn't known this, of course, because if they had, things would have been different. At least this was what she imagined, but there was no way to be certain.

She glanced across at a bookshelf that was jammed with his favorite mystery novels and thrillers, alongside a number of World War II and Vietnam memoirs that her husband had been studying as he'd worked on his own. On the very top shelf concealed behind well-read, dog-eared copies of Val McDermid and James W. Hall and John Grisham, there was an old military surplus olive-drab metal ammunition case, with a combination lock keeping it shut. That was what she'd come in to get.

She knew the combination. It was their daughter's birthday.

"I'm sorry," she said out loud, as if apologizing in advance to the pair of ghosts who were watching her. "I've got to get the gun."

Her husband had been a lieutenant in the local fire department. She taught children. He put out fires. She corrected spelling tests. He rode in a red fire truck, sirens blaring. It was never going to be a life with exotic vacation homes and large black Mercedes-Benzes. There was little ostentatiously first-class about them. But it was always going to be a good, solid, American life. They were always going to be middle-class, liberal, and respectable. They bought their clothes at the local mall and watched television together at night after dinner. They rooted for all the New England professional sports teams and considered a trip to Fenway Park or Gillette Stadium for a game to be the ultimate indulgence. They would be union members and proud of it. They would complain about their taxes, and occasionally work overtime without pay because they loved their jobs. And there was never a night that they fell tired into bed in each other's arms that the two of them hadn't looked forward to the sun rising.

Sarah thought that was even true on the last day of her life, the day Ted had swept little Brittany up and held her above his head, tickling his daughter so that she was red-faced with laughter before he carefully strapped her into the car seat in the rear of their six-year-old Volvo. She had seen him fasten his own belt before giving a jaunty wave, grinning, and taking off.

Nine blocks. Grocery store. Death.

It was not an equation anyone would ever have imagined. There was no actuarial table, no sophisticated algorithm that could project the heating oil fuel delivery truck that ran the red light and slammed into them. She had always hated that detail madly. It was nearly summertime. The weather was mild and warm. No one in New England was still using an oil burner. There was *no need* for the truck to be on the road.

They were properly belted. The air bags instantly deployed. The Volvo's steel frame, designed to crumple protectively upon impact, had performed exactly as its engineers had designed.

Except none of it worked, because they were both dead.

Still hesitating in the doorway, Sarah said, "Look, Teddy, someone says they're going to kill me. I promise I won't get it and use it on myself. Even if I really want to, I promise, I won't do that. Not yet, at least."

It was almost as if she needed his permission to find the ammunition box and get the gun. Both of them had been raised in devoutly Catholic households and there was that profound prohibition against committing suicide. *A sin*, she thought. The most reasonable and logical sin she could imagine, but a sin, nevertheless.

She thought she was a complete coward in so many different ways that she could hardly count them. If she were brave, she could have decided to kill herself. Or, if she were brave, she would have decided to go on with her life and not let it disintegrate around her. If she were brave, she would have dedicated herself to something meaningful, like teaching special education in the inner city or going on missions to help AIDS babies in the Sudan, as a way of honoring her dead husband and dead child.

"But I'm not brave," she said. It was sometimes hard for her to tell if she had been talking out loud or not. And sometimes she had entire conversations in her imagination that ended up with some sentence blurted out that made sense only to her. "Definitely not brave."

But, she thought, *I still need the gun*.

It was, she guessed, some leftover frontier gene that lurked within her. Someone makes a threat, and like a cowboy in a Western, she would reach for her weapon.

She paused in the doorway for another moment. Her eyes scanned the room—and then she launched herself inside, moving rapidly. It was as if by looking around she would be inviting the memory attached to each item to punish her further. She went directly to the bookcase, pushed aside the novels that hid the dust-covered ammunition box, seized it, and then retreated as fast as she could, slamming the office door shut behind her.

"I'm sorry, Teddy, darling, but I just can't stay in there." She knew this was a half-thought, half-whisper.

Holding the olive-drab ammo box under her right arm, she lifted her left hand to the side of her face, blocking the sight of her dead daughter's room. She did not think she could handle another conversation with a ghost that day, and she hurried down the hallway back to her kitchen.

She was still naked. But there was something about getting the weapon and the reverberating noise from the threatening letter that made her suddenly feel modest. She plucked her clothes from where she'd discarded them, and tugged them back on.

Then she took the letter and put it next to the ammo box on a coffee table in her living room. She dialed the combination and reached inside.

A cold black Colt Python .357 Magnum rested on the bottom, next to a box of hollow-point bullets. She removed the weapon, fiddled with it for an instant, and finally cracked open the chamber. Seeing it was unloaded, she carefully steered six live rounds into the cylinder.

The gun seemed incredibly heavy in her hand, and she wondered how anyone had the strength to lift it, aim, and fire. She used both hands, and adopted a shooter's stance as she had seen in television melodramas. Using two hands helped, but it was still difficult. *A guy's gun*, she thought. *Teddy would always want a real guy's gun. Not some flimsy little girly shooter.*

This thought made her smile.

She looked down at the words on the letter.

"You have been selected to die."

Sarah put the gun down on top of the typed page

That might be true, she silently told whoever it was that was out there planning to kill her, *but I'm more than half-dead already, and this is one Little Red Riding Hood that isn't going down without a fight. So come on. Give it your best shot, and let's see what happens.*

Sarah was astonished at her response. It was the exact opposite of what she'd expected herself to think. Logic suggested that because she wanted to die, she should do nothing and just open her door to the Big Bad Wolf and let him kill her and put her out of her misery.

But instead, she spun the cylinder of the gun, which made a clicking sound before coming to a halt. *Okay, let's see what you've got. I may be alone, but I'm not, really.* She had absolutely no desire to call her aging parents, who lived in the eastern portion of the state, or any of the people she once thought of as friends but whom she now ignored. She did not want to call the police or an attorney or a neighbor or anyone else. Whoever it was that had *selected* her, well, she was going to face him all by herself. *This just might be crazy*, she told herself, *but it's my choice. Whatever happens, it's okay with me.*

And oddly, she felt a sense of warmth, because for a fleeting instant, she thought her dead husband and her dead daughter just might possibly be proud of her.

* * *

Jordan seemed frozen on her bed, hunched into a fetal position. She wondered whether she should ever move again. Then, as seconds blended into minutes, and she heard some of the other girls in the dormitory returning—voices raised, doors slamming, a sudden burst of laughter, and a fake wail mocking whatever phony trouble someone had—Jordan began to stir. After a few more moments, she sat up and swung her feet to the floor. Then she picked up the letter and reread it.

For an instant, she wanted to laugh.

You think you're the only Big Bad Wolf in my life?

It was almost like *get in line*. Everyone else—from her estranged and constantly arguing parents, to the faculty at her school, to her ex-friends who'd abandoned her—was in the process of killing her off. Now, added to that was some anonymous joker.

She suddenly felt rebellious, confrontational. She still figured that whoever wrote the letter was just taunting her. Prep school students could be incredibly inventive and incredibly cruel. Someone wanted her to react in some manner that would amuse him. Or her. She reminded herself to not rule out girls just because the letter writer promised violence. Some of her female classmates were capable of administering astonishing physical beatings.

Screw you, she thought. *Whoever you are.*

Jordan picked up the letter and began to go over it carefully, the way she once would do when she was absorbing a detailed question on a difficult test.

The words on the page seemed to leap at her. The letter didn't seem juvenile. It had a more sophisticated tone than that of her classmates. But Jordan knew she needed to be careful before she reached any conclusion. Just because it didn't *read* like it came from another teenager didn't mean that one hadn't written it. Like Jordan, many of her classmates had actually absorbed the language lessons taught by Hemingway and Faulkner, Proust and Tolstoy. Some were capable of very sophisticated prose.

She stepped across the room to her small work space. Desk. Laptop. A jar of pens and pencils and a stack of unused notebooks. In a top drawer, she found a tan folder that she usually used for collecting stray class notes in one location. She put the letter into the folder.

Okay, what's the next step?

Jordan felt cold inside. She realized there was little right then that she could do, or should do, but one thing did jump out at her. *"It would be wise for you to keep that in mind . . ."*

She nodded. *All right. You want me to learn about the real story of Little Red Riding Hood. Well, that I can damn well do.*

It was time for basketball practice. After working up a sweat on the court and showering, she would have plenty of time to go to the school library and find the Brothers Grimm. She was pretty much flunking everything, so spending her time analyzing a centuries-old fairy tale because she was either being stalked by a crazy killer or was the butt of some elaborate joke by a mean classmate made perfect sense to her.

4

The Big Bad Wolf regretted not being able to see the reactions of each of his Reds when they read his message on the page in front of them. He was forced to indulge in fantasy—racing through delicious mental images of each, and anticipating the emotional contortions each was stumbling wildly into.

Red One will be angry.

Red Two will be confused.

Red Three will be scared.

He took a moment to look at slightly blurry pictures of each woman, taken with a long-lens camera. On the wall above his computer he had tacked more than a dozen pictures of each Red, along with note cards filled with information about each woman. Months of observation—from a distance yet intensely personal—were delineated on the wall. Little bits of their history, small aspects of their lives—all gleaned from cautious study—became words on a note card or glossy full-color pictures. Red One was caught smoking. *A dangerously bad habit*, he thought. Red Three was sitting alone beneath a campus tree. *Always lonely*, he reminded himself. Red Two was pictured emerging from a liquor store, arms filled with packages. *You are so weak*, he whispered. He had placed that photograph above a newspaper clipping that was frayed around the edges. The headline was *Fireman and Daughter, 3, Killed in Crash*.

It was not unlike the sort of display that police detective bureaus collected so that the cops could have a visual representation of the way a case was progressing. It was a staple cinematographer's shot in a hundred movies—with justification, because it was so commonplace. There was one large difference, however: The police tacked up crime scene photos of murdered bodies because they needed answers to questions. His array was of the living, destined to die, most questions already answered.

He knew each Red would respond differently to the letter. He had spent considerable time examining literary and scientific works that assessed human behavior in the turmoil that direct threats create. While there were common reactions associated with fear—see a shark's fin and the heart skips a beat—the Big Bad Wolf instinctively believed fear was processed individually. When an airplane hits unexpected turbulence and seems to stagger in the sky, the passenger in seat 10A screams and grips the armrests white-knuckled, while in seat 10B the traveler shrugs and goes back to reading. This fascinated him. He liked to think that in both his careers, novelist and killer, he had explored these things deeply. And he was not one to underestimate the correlation between fear and creativity.

He expected several concrete things to happen after they'd read his letter. He also tried to anticipate some of the emotions that were within them. *They will stumble and fall*, he thought. *They will twitch and shake*. He had recently watched a television show on the History Channel that interviewed famous military snipers. Using high-tech camerawork, it had reconstructed some of the remarkable assassinations they had performed, in Korea, in Vietnam, and in the Iraq war. But what struck him was not merely the extraordinary competence of these snipers who stole lives, but the emotional detachment they displayed, what the French call *sangfroid*. The military killers called their victims *targets*, as if they had no more personality than a black-and-white bull's-eye, and boasted that they had not the slightest hint of a subsequent nightmare. He did not know that he believed this. In his murderous experience, the stealing of a life was only as significant as the mental reverberations afterward. Indeed, reliving moments was where the real satisfaction rested. He embraced nightmares. He guessed that the snipers did as well. They just weren't about to say that in public with a documentary camera rolling.

That, too, made him special. He was documenting *everything*. That was what he found delicious: actions and thoughts, the stew of death. He typed furiously, words racing at him.

One of them—at least one, but not all—will call the police. That's to be expected. But the police will be as confused as they are. Preventing something from happening is precisely not what the police are skilled at. Maybe the police are capable of finding out who performed a murder, after it happens—but they are relatively incompetent at preventing one from taking place. The Secret Service protects the president, and they devote thousands of man-hours, computer time, psychological analysis, and academic study to keeping one man safe. And yet—they fail. Regularly.

No one is protecting the Reds.

One—maybe all three of them at some point—will try to hide from me. Think of the children's game of hide-and-seek. The advantages are always with the person doing the seeking: He knows his quarry. He knows what drives them into concealment. He probably knows the places they will try to hide, and he knows the uncertainty that fuels their fear.

One—I'm sure at least one—will refuse to believe the truth: that they are going to die at my hands. Fear corners some people underground. But sometimes fear insists that people ignore danger. It is much easier to believe nothing will happen to you than it is to think each breath you take may be one of the last you'll ever enjoy.

One—maybe all three—will think they need to seek out assistance, only to have no idea what sort of assistance they need. So they will be stifled by uncertainty. And even were they to seek out another person's counsel—well, that person is likely to downplay the threat, not underscore it. This is because we do not want to ever believe in the capriciousness of life. We do not want to believe in thunderbolts and accidents. We do not want to believe that we are being hunted, when in truth, we are every day of our lives. And so, whoever they consult will want to reassure my Red that everything is going to be all right, when the exact opposite is the case.

What is the challenge facing me?

My Reds will try to protect themselves in any number of ways. My task, obviously, is to make certain that they cannot. To achieve that, I have to get close to each of them, so that I can anticipate each pathetic step they will try. But at the same time, I have to maintain my anonymity. Close, yet hidden—that's the approach.

He paused. It was nearing the dinner hour. His fingers flew across the keyboard. He wanted to finish up with some of his initial thoughts before breaking for the evening meal.

No one has ever done what I intend to do.

Three wildly different victims.

Three distinct locations.

Three different deaths.

All on the same day. Within hours of each other. Maybe within minutes. Deaths that tumble together like dominoes. Each one falling against the next. Click. Click. Click.

He stopped. He *liked* that image.

Maybe one of those military snipers had achieved multiple kills all on the same day, or in the same hour, or even in the same minute, he thought. But they had a single enemy to focus on that walked stupidly and thoughtlessly directly into their line of fire. And there were killers he had studied who had achieved multiple murders in short order. But again, these were genuinely random acts—shoot this person, walk across town, shoot another person. The D.C. Sniper. Son of Sam. The Zodiac.

There were others. But none had done anything as special as what he planned. What he was attempting was truly something that no one had ever tried. *Guinness World Records*-worthy. He could barely contain his excitement. *Proximity*, he told himself. *Get closer.* That was what the Big Bad Wolf did in the children's story. That was what he was busy planning.

5

At the top of the key, Jordan heard the play called, the point guard's voice just overcoming the crowd noise filling the gymnasium. She hesitated, unsure why the coach would signal for a play that had never once worked in practice. Then she spun to her right and set a pick for the weak-side forward. The play was designed for an easy layup right down the lane. Jordan loved the architecture of the game, how every small detail became an element in an equation that resulted in success. But every time they'd run this play in training, it had broken down, because the girl who was supposed to drive her defender into Jordan slowed, allowing the opposing player to slide into the small space that indecision created and not be picked off, but to maintain steady defensive pressure. There were variations that they'd attempted, but these, too, would fall apart if the other girl didn't commit to initially forcing her defender into Jordan's chest. Things happen quickly on a basketball court. Motion is defined not only by speed, but also by placement. Angles are critical. Body position is crucial. Everything depends on that first thrust and motion.

Jordan hated all these plays, because the failure to pick off the defender was always seen as *her* fault. She was the only one on the floor aware of the poor angle her teammate invariably took. It was like her teammate was afraid to cause anyone to get hurt—but the result was that the other girls all thought it was Jordan who was being weak and timid, when in reality she liked nothing more than the sensation of bodies clashing.

Small moments of danger and threat of injury—that was what Jordan lived for.

She lowered her arms close to her body so that she was like a pillar on the court. She knew that the point guard was dribbling behind her, perhaps ten feet away. There was a steady cacophony of noise that seemed to hover just above the court, so that the squeak and squeal of basketball shoes against the polished wooden floor rose up and mingled with cheers and exhortations from the people jammed into the bleachers.

Jordan saw her teammate faking along the baseline, and then turning and digging hard for the elbow—the spot where the foul line ends, and where Jordan waited. She could see the defender moving fast to keep pace, and instantly Jordan saw that, as she expected, her teammate hadn't taken the right angle. She was *close* but not close *enough*.

Jordan despised the lack of passion she felt from some of her teammates, when she felt every minute on the court as one of total devotion and release. The game would start and she could forget everything. Or so she thought. She imagined if she were religious, the ecstasy of prayer would be exactly the same as the feeling that overcame her in the game she played.

She imagined: *I am a nun on the court.*

She bent forward at the waist and tensed her muscles.

But not so innocent.

She knew that was she was about to do was illegal, but she also knew that a great journalist had once written that basketball is a game of subtle felonies, and so, in a split second, she decided this was a good moment to risk one.

Jordan saw that the defender was moving fast into the gap between her teammate and herself—a space that shouldn't have been there. And so, just as the three of them closed, she slightly dipped her shoulder and moved forward an inch or two at the moment they came together. The girl on the other team took the force of Jordan's shoulder in her chest. Jordan could hear wind knocked from her body, and a grunt and a small gasp as the two of them locked together. Her own teammate slipped past the instant tangle of players, emerged free on the far side, and took the pass. *An easy two*, Jordan thought, as she rolled toward the basket, not expecting a rebound, but moving into position as she had both been coached and had learned by instinct.

She fully expected to hear the referee's whistle. *Foul! Number 23!*

She could hear the crowd cheering. She could hear the opposing coach from his sideline bench, frantically screaming, "Illegal pick! Illegal pick!"

You're damn right, coach, she thought.

To her side, the opposing player, having regained her wind, whispered, "Bitch!"

Damn right again, she told herself. She didn't say this out loud. Instead, she loped back down the floor to take up her defensive position, knowing she should watch out for a stray elbow aimed at her cheek, or a fist shoved into her back where the ref couldn't see it. Basketball is also a game of hidden paybacks, and she knew she was due at least one.

The noise from the crowd rose in anticipation, filling the gym—there wasn't much time left and the game was close and Jordan knew that every action on the court in the seconds remaining would define who won and who lost. The dying moments of a basketball game require the greatest focus and most intense concentration. But something quite different popped into her head. *The Big Bad Wolf outthinks Little Red Riding Hood. He outmaneuvers her at every point. No one comes to her rescue. No one saves her. She is completely alone in the forest and she can do nothing to stop the inevitable. She dies. No, worse: She is eaten alive.*

Jordan tried to shake loose the prior evening's research. She had spent two hours in the library, reading the Grimms' fairy tales, then another ninety minutes on the computer examining psychological interpretations of the story of *Little Red Riding Hood*. Everything she'd learned had terrified her and fascinated her. This was an awful combination of feelings.

She heard one of her teammates yell, "D-Up! D-Up!" And when her opposite number came into position, Jordan set her shoulder against the girl's back in an *I'm right here* movement. She could hear voices shouting warnings. "Back pick! Watch the screen!" *Organized chaos,* Jordan thought. It was the part of the game she most loved.

A girl on the opposing team took an ill-advised, hurried three-pointer. The combination of cheering, the clock winding down, the closeness of the score, and the girl's overconfidence all conspired to push the ball away from the rim. Jordan jumped, reaching for the rebound, snatching it from the air, swinging her elbows wildly to clear away anyone who might try to steal it from her. For a second she felt as if she were alone, soaring angel-like above the court. Then she thudded back to the hardwood floor. She could feel the rough surface of the synthetic leather beneath her sweaty palms. She wanted to hit someone, just foul her savagely, but she did not. Instead she flipped the ball to a guard and thought, *Now we'll win,* but understanding that the point of the fairy tale was that death of innocence was unavoidable and that the Big Bad Wolf and everything he symbolized about the inexorable force of evil would ultimately win out. *No wonder they changed the story around,* she thought. *The original version was a nightmare.*

The whistle blew. One of her teammates had been fouled. The other team was resorting to hacking its way back into the game. *Just pathetic hope,* Jordan imagined. *They believe we'll miss our free throws. Not goddamn very likely.*

But she did not believe that she had won anything that evening. The game perhaps. But nothing else.

In the stands, in the seconds following the final whistle, especially in a close contest, there is a surge of relief crashing against waves of disappointment. Elation and disappointment are like conflicted currents in a tight channel as the tide begins to change. The Big Bad Wolf basked in the palpable ebb and flow surrounding him. Winners and losers.

He was incredibly proud of Red Three. He loved the way she fought on every single play and the way she had taken advantage of every mistake her opposing number had made. He thought he could taste the sweat that matted her hair and glistened on her forehead. *She's a real competitor,* he thought. Affection and admiration only made his desire to kill her increase. He felt drawn to her, as if she exuded some magnetic force that only he could feel.

He let out a loud, "Yeah! Way to go!" like any parent or spectator rooting in the stands.

He closed up his notebook and stuffed his mechanical pencil into a jacket pocket. Later, in the privacy of his writing room, he would go over his scribbled observations. Like a journalist's, the Big Bad Wolf's rapid notations tended toward the cryptic: Single words, like *lithe, nasty, tough,* and *fierce* mixed with larger descriptions, such as *seems possessed by the game* and *never appears to talk to anyone else on the court, either on her team or the other. No trash-talking and no encouragement. No high-fives for teammates. No "In your face" or shouts of "And One!" directed at the opposition. No self-satisfied, chest-pounding, preening for the people watching. Just singular intensity that every minute exceeds that of the other nine players on the floor.*

And one other delicious observation: *Red Three's hair makes her seem on fire.*

The Big Bad Wolf could hardly rip his eyes away from watching Red Three, but he knew that he should think of himself as on stage, so he forced himself to avert his gaze and watch some of the other players. This was almost painful for him. Although he knew no one was watching him, he liked to imagine that *everyone* was watching him, every second. There were marks that had to be hit, and lines that had to be uttered at just the precise moment, so that he seemed no different from anyone else crammed into the wooden bleacher rows.

Around him, people were standing, stretching, gathering coats as they readied to leave, or, if they were students, looking for book bags or backpacks. He stole one look back over his shoulder as he pulled on his jacket, and watched the team—with Red Three bringing up the rear—as they jogged off the court. The boys' varsity game was scheduled to start in twenty minutes, and there was a press of people moving out of seats and newcomers working their way in. He tugged on his baseball hat, emblazoned with the school's name. He believed deeply that he looked like any parent, friend, school official, or townie who just enjoyed high school basketball. And he doubted that anyone noticed his note taking; there were too many college scouts and local sports reporters who watched the games with notebooks in hand to draw any real attention to his interest.

This was something the Big Bad Wolf loved: looking ordinary when he was far from it. He could feel his pulse accelerate. He looked at the people pressing around him. *Can any of you imagine who I truly am?* he wondered. He took a final glance toward the door to the locker room and caught a glimpse of Red Three's hair, disappearing. *Do you know how close I was today?* He wanted to whisper this in her ear.

He thought, *She does not know it, but we are more intimate than lovers.*

The Big Bad Wolf began to make his way out of the gym, caught up in the throng of moving people. He had much to do, both planning and writing, and he was eager to get back to his office. He wondered if he'd acquired enough knowledge in what he'd seen to start a new chapter of his book, and his mind suddenly went to beginnings. He wrote in his head: *Red Three wore a look of utter determination and total devotion when she snatched the rebound from the air. I don't think she could even hear the cheers that rained down on her. Even knowing she was scheduled to die did not distract her.*

Yes. He liked that.

He suddenly heard a quiet, cheery voice coming from right beside him. "Are you absolutely sure we shouldn't stay for the boys' game?"

He hesitated as he turned to Mrs. Big Bad Wolf. She, too, had pulled on a well-worn baseball cap with the school's name on it.

"No, dear," he replied, smiling. He reached out like a teenager in love for the first time and took his wife's hand. "I think I've seen more than enough for one day."

Walk out the door. Just turn the handle and walk out the door. You know you can do it.

Sarah Locksley twitched with tension as she stood in the small vestibule of her house. She was dressed in brown leather boots, tight jeans, and a long tan winter overcoat. She had showered and brushed her hair and even applied a small amount of makeup to her cheeks and eyes. She had her large multicolored pocketbook slung over her shoulder and she could feel the bricklike weight of the loaded .357 Magnum pulling it down.

She knew she appeared completely presentable and totally put together and that any stranger walking by would think that she was just another woman in her early thirties on her way out for groceries or on some other errand. Maybe a trip to the mall or to meet with some girlfriends for a ladies' night out of shared appetizers and calorie-conscious salads followed by some inane romantic comedy at the multiplex.

That Sarah was crippled by despair was effectively hidden. All she had to do was open the door to her house, step outside into the wan afternoon light, make her way to her car, start the engine, put it into gear, and off she would go, just like any normal person with something to do on a weekend evening.

But she knew that she was not a normal person. She shivered as if she were cold. *Not normal in the slightest way whatsoever. Not anymore.*

Strange, conflicted thoughts crashed into Sarah's mind: *He's right outside. He will kill me before I have a chance to pull out Ted's gun. But at least I look nice. If I die in the next minute, at least the EMTs who arrive at my murder and the medical examiner who inspects my dead body will think I'm clean and organized and not like I really am. Why does that make a difference?*

She wasn't sure, but it did.

He's not out there. Not yet. The Big Bad Wolf didn't act swiftly. He stalked Little Red Riding Hood.

There was a part of her that wanted to wall herself into her home, build barricades and protect herself, waiting for the Big Bad Wolf to show up and try to blow her house down. *Except,* Sarah shook her head as she reminded herself, *that's the wrong damn fairy tale. I'm not one of the three little pigs. My house may be made of straw, but that's the wrong story completely.*

Again she hesitated, reaching her hand around the door handle. It was not as if she was scared—a significant part of her welcomed death. It was more the uncertainty of everything. She felt caught up in a vortex, like there was a maelstrom spinning her around, threatening to pull her under dark waves. She could hear her breathing coming in raspy, fast gasps—but she could not *feel* the shortness of breath. It was almost as if the sounds were coming from someone else.

She shut her eyes. *Okay. If this is it, at least it will be fast. Just like Ted and Brittany. They never saw the truck. Just one minute they were alive and laughing and having a fine time, and then they were dead. Maybe it will be like that for me, too. So okay, Big Bad Wolf. Just shoot me right now!*

She pulled the door open savagely and stood framed in the space. *Take your damn shot!*

She closed her eyes. Waited.

Nothing.

She could feel the evening's chill descending. It cooled her, and she realized that she was sweating, hot, as if she'd been exercising.

She blinked. Her street was as it always was. Quiet. Empty. She took a deep breath and stepped out. *Maybe there's a bomb attached to my car and when I start it up, it will explode just like in some Hollywood gangster movie.*

She slid behind the wheel and, without hesitating, turned the key over. The engine fired up and hummed like a cat being stroked.

Well, maybe the Big Bad Wolf will slam some truck into me, and I can die like Ted and Brittany did.

She steered the car into the street and stopped. Again she closed her eyes. *Broadside. Forty, maybe fifty miles an hour. Just like the oil truck. Come on. I'm waiting. I'm ready.*

Sarah's eyes again were squeezed tight. *Any second now,* she thought.

The car horn seemed to blast inches away from her left ear. The sound sliced the air like an explosion. She gasped and involuntarily held up her arm, as if to shield herself from impact. Her eyes flew open and she cried out some half-scream, half-sob.

The horn beeped again. Only this time, it seemed childlike, like a toy noise.

She half-turned in her seat, and saw that she was obstructing a couple in a small Japanese compact car. The man behind the wheel, who looked to be in his early sixties, and his wife, who was still dark-haired and appeared a little younger, were waving at her, but not in an impatient, unfriendly fashion. It was more like they were concerned and confused. Sarah stared at the couple, and then haphazardly pieced things together in her head. *I'm blocking the road. They want to get past me.*

The woman in the passenger seat rolled down her window. From perhaps ten feet away, she called out in a questioning tone, "Is everything okay?"

Yes. No. Yes. No. Sarah didn't respond other than to wave her hand as if to say *Sorry* without an explanation. She fumbled to get the car into forward gear. Then she quickly thrust her foot down on the accelerator and without looking back drove rapidly down the street. She did not know exactly where she was going, but wherever it was, she went in a hurry, breathing hard, almost hyperventilating, like a swimmer preparing for a dive into uncertain waters or waiting for the starter's gun to sound the start of a race.

"Odd," said Mrs. Big Bad Wolf.

"Maybe the young lady got a cell phone call, or remembered that she'd forgotten something. But you shouldn't just stop in the middle of the road," the Big Bad Wolf replied. "That's really dangerous."

"It's a good thing you were paying attention," his wife said. "People just certainly are strange."

"Indeed they are," he answered as he drove slowly forward. "Don't want to be late." He smiled. "Shall we listen to the radio?" he asked, pleasantly enough, fiddling with the dial until he found the classical music station. He *hated* classical music, although he had always told his wife he loved it. Little dishonesties, he thought, were good practice for the necessary larger ones.

Karen Jayson sat at her desk, an electronic medical notebook on the flat wooden surface in front of her, her head in her hands. The day was crawling toward an end. It had been long, but not crazily so, and she should not have felt as exhausted as she did.

She was a woman accustomed to being if not exactly certain about matters, at least confident, and the letter from the Big Bad Wolf had scoured her emotions. After speaking with Detective Clark, she had set the letter aside and told herself, *Forget it.* Then she had picked it up again and told herself, *You need to act.* But precisely how eluded her. She had the sensation that she needed to be actively doing *something* but had very little idea what that *something* was. She had done everything Detective Clark had told her. She had called a security company—they were scheduled to install an alarm system in her house the next day. She had gone over patient files, looking for some error that might have led to a threat. She had racked her memory for any slight, real or imagined, that might translate into *"You have been selected to die."* She had even checked out the website of the local animal shelter to see if they had some big mean dog for adoption. She had looked up the numbers of some private detectives, checked with various consumer ratings programs to see who received the best reviews, and written down the telephone numbers of two different men. She had half-dialed one number only to stop and hang up her telephone.

Above all, Karen despised panic. Or even the appearance of panic.

In medical school, doing her internship rotations, she had seriously considered a career as an emergency room physician, because even with blood spurting, cries of agony, and the need to move quickly to save a life she had always found herself preternaturally calm. The more things were disintegrating around her, the more her own pulse would slow. She thought that her response to the threatening letter should have been precisely the same as when some accident victim arrived in front of her, ravaged and in imminent danger of dying.

She liked to think of herself as a completely rational person, even with her comedy half occasionally surfacing. But since she'd opened the letter, she had been unable to even consider a comedy routine. Not a single joke, no sarcasm, no play on words or clever political observation—nothing that was the usual stuff of her routines had leapt into her thoughts. Her nighttime dreams had been tortured, which made her tired and angry.

She leaned back and rocked in her desk chair. She was shaking her head back and forth, as if disagreeing with something she'd told herself, when the door to her office opened.

"I'm sorry, Doctor, I didn't want to disturb you . . ."

"No, no, it's okay. I was just a little lost in thought."

Karen looked over at her nurse. Only two other people worked in her small practice: a young nurse two years out of a college program who had only recently, and hesitantly, asked Karen how to have the tattoo of a sun rising on the back of her neck removed, and her longtime receptionist, an older woman who knew many of the patients and their ailments far better than Karen did.

"Last patient of the day," the nurse said. "She's been waiting in exam room 2 for a couple of minutes and . . ."

She let her voice trail off before any sort of rebuke passed her lips. Karen understood two things: The nurse wanted to get home to her EMT boyfriend and Karen shouldn't keep the last patient of the day waiting no matter how unsettled she felt. She took a deep breath and jumped out of her chair, launching herself into her *attentive doctor* mode.

"It's just a routine follow-up exam," the nurse said, "She's already been checked by her cardiologist. His report is in her file. She's doing fine. This is just a follow-up physical. Nothing too important."

She handed Karen a clipboard with a file folder attached. Karen didn't even look at it, feeling suddenly a bit guilty for making a patient wait unnecessarily. She adjusted her white lab coat and hurried down the hallway into the exam room.

The patient was seated on the exam table, wearing a johnny-gown and a smile. "Hello, Doctor," she said.

"Hello, Mrs . . ." Karen glanced quickly at the folder to grab the woman's name. She hurriedly said it, trying to cover up her failure to greet her as she did all her patients: with a familiarity that implied that she had spent the entire day studying whatever medical issues the patient had. Ordinarily she had no trouble remembering the names of her patients, and inwardly she berated herself for the lapse. She knew that stress sometimes caused blanks in the memory. That an anonymous threat could intrude on her day-to-day life seemed horribly wrong.

She had absolutely no idea that her greeting that day actually should have been: "*Hello, Mrs. Big Bad Wolf . . .*"

Nor had she any inkling that sitting patiently in her small waiting room, reading an out-of-date copy of the *New Yorker,* was the man who secretly longed to catch a glimpse of the doctor whom he'd dubbed Red One.

6

Death is the big game and one that everyone plays and everyone loses at the final whistle. But murder is slightly different, because it is far more like that moment within each game when the outcome is decided. We sit in the stands, never knowing when that precise second will arrive. Will it be this goal, or that free throw, or the base hit with the man on second, or the defensive back failing to make a tackle? Perhaps it's the moment when the referee blows his whistle and points to the penalty spot. Murder is more like sport than anyone knows. Murder has its own clock and its own rules. Like sport, it's about preparation and determination. It's about overcoming obstacles. Someone wants to live. Someone wants to kill. That is the playing field.

He looked at the words on the computer screen. *Good*, he thought, *People reading this will start to understand.*

Karen awakened exhausted from a night of restless dreams at 6 a.m., her customary time in the morning, a few moments before her alarm clock would have rung. She had always had an inner clock that would wake her up shortly before the hotel wake-up call or her alarm. Her habit was to roll over and punch the *off* button on the alarm, thrust herself up from beneath a handmade quilt she'd acquired at a local crafts show many years earlier, and make her way to a pink exercise pad set up in a corner of the bedroom, where she would indulge herself with exactly fifteen minutes of yoga stretches and exercises before heading to the shower. In the kitchen, the automatic coffeepot was already percolating. The clothes she had selected for that day's work were set out the night before, after she checked the weather report. Routine, she insisted, set her free, although there were mornings when it was hard to persuade herself this statement was true.

She sometimes thought her entire world was constructed upside down, or perhaps back to front. She devoted all her organizational energies to her medical work, and thought of her comedy as liberating. Two Karens, she told herself, who might not even recognize each other if they met on the street. Comic Karen was creative, spontaneous, and quick-witted. Internist Karen was dedicated to her work and patients, steady, organized, and always as precise as illness allowed. Her two sides seemed to share little, but had managed to accommodate each other over the years.

This morning, she wondered if perhaps she needed to create a third.

She glanced over toward the alarm system pad that had been installed on the bedroom wall two days after the letter from the Big Bad Wolf had arrived. It blinked red—letting her know that it was on and functioning. She felt an odd discomfort. She had to get up, turn it off so that the motion detectors mounted in corners throughout the house would not catch her instead of the fictional bad guys they were designed to raise alarm about. She needed to get the day started. But she lingered.

Predictability is my enemy, she thought.

Someone unknown sends me a threatening letter, and I do exactly what every book, manual, or website says to protect myself. That was what made sense. A checklist. Call the police. Inform the neighbors to be on the lookout for any strange activity. Her isolation made that difficult, but she had still dutifully called the families that lived closest to her.

Simple, straightforward calls: *"Hi, this is Karen Jayson down the block. I just wanted to tell you that I've received some anonymous threat. No . . . No . . . the police don't think it means anything much, but I just wanted to ask some of the neighbors to keep an eye out for anything unusual. Like strange cars parked on the road or something. Thanks . . ."*

The responses had been solicitous, concerned. *Of course* everyone would keep eyes peeled for any suspicious behavior. The families with small children had reacted strongly—wondering whether they should keep the kids indoors until this formless threat had dissipated, as if it were some oil slick on the surface of the ocean. The weather being what it was, which was lousy, Karen thought it unlikely the kids would be outside anyway.

Her next call had been to the alarm company, which had promptly sent out an overly enthusiastic workman to install the system, all the time happily and ominously opining about how *you can't be safe enough* and *people don't understand how much danger is lurking out there* before managing to sell Karen an enhanced security package with a monthly charge deducted from her credit card.

She had subsequently gone through the entirety of the policeman's recommendations: *Get a dog.* No, she hadn't done that, but she was considering it. *Get a gun.* No, she hadn't done that, not yet, but she would consider it. *Call a private detective.* No, she hadn't done that, but she was considering it. In fact, she realized, she was considering everything and nothing all at the same time.

How is any of this going to keep me alive? Wouldn't the Big Bad Wolf have visited all the same online advice pages, read all the same words, and figured out all the same things?

Wouldn't he know precisely what all the experts suggested she do? How smart is he?

Martin and Lewis had already set off the system twice in the two days it had been functioning. This meant that either she had to get rid of them or figure out some way to make it work in concert with cats. This seemed an insurmountable problem. It dogged her as for the first time in years she ignored the exercise pad and made her way into the shower.

Warm water and suds cascaded over her body.

She scrubbed herself vigorously, soaping every spot she could reach once, then twice, and finally a third time, as if soap could erase the lingering sense of exhaustion from her unsettled night. She held out a hand against the tile wall, steadying herself against the flow of water. She felt dizzy.

Her eyes were closed when she heard a sound.

It was not a recognizable noise, nothing clear-cut like a car door slamming, or a radio being switched on. It wasn't loud—not a *crash!* or a *clang!* It was more like the first second of a hissing kettle, or a stiff breeze rustling through nearby tree branches.

She froze in position. A sudden burst of adrenaline coursed through her body so that she felt like she was abruptly spinning a million miles per hour, though she was immobile. Steam surrounded her like a fog, clouding her comprehension. The noisy flow of water obscured recognition.

What was that? What did you hear?

She was abruptly aware of her nakedness. Dripping. Vulnerable. She sharpened her hearing, trying to determine what the sound was.

It was nothing. Nothing. You're alone and jumpy.

The house is empty. It always is. Just two cats. Maybe they made the sound. Maybe they knocked over a lamp, or a stack of books. They've done that before.

The steam curled around her, but she had the sensation the water was no longer warm, that it had turned icy. She took a deep breath, shut off the shower, and stood in the stall, listening. Then, instantly, she thought: *If someone is out there, switching off the shower will tell them I'm about to get out.* She jammed her finger twisting the shower dial back on, and she jumped as too-hot water spilled over her back.

Conflicting thoughts screamed inside her head.

It was just anxiety. Nothing was there.

Straighten up. Step out. Act your age. Stop behaving like a child.

She turned the shower off a second time. The air seemed cold to her, as if a window was open.

This is a cliché. Like a bad horror film. There should be a dark John Williams Jaws-like score playing relentlessly in the background.

Then a more complicated thought: *Did you shut down the alarm properly?*

She went over in her mind's eye every step of the procedure, pushing each button of the security code, seeing the LED lights go from red to green. *Did they?* She was stifled by uncertainty. She could hear her own voice echoing within her, shouting advice, insisting, *You're acting like a fool. Get out. Get dressed. Get the day going.*

But she remained locked in position.

She thought, *The noise came after I shut off the alarm. Was someone waiting for those indicator lights to change color?*

It took Karen an immense amount of willpower to step from the shower and grab a towel from the rack by the door. She wrapped herself up and then paused to listen again. She could still hear nothing.

Dry off. Go get your clothes. Dab on a little makeup. Come on, just like every day. You are hearing things. Hallucinating noises. You're on edge for no reason. Or yes, there is a reason, but it's not a real reason.

The water was pooling beneath her feet and with a terrific effort that made her gasp out loud, she rapidly dried herself off, then dragged a stiff brush through tangled hair so quickly that had she not been so unsettled, she would have shouted at the self-inflicted pain. She stopped. *This is crazy. Why am I brushing my hair if someone is waiting to kill me?* She gripped the brush handle like a knife and kept it in her hand as if it could be a weapon. Then she hurriedly approached the bathroom door that led into the bedroom. Closed, but not locked. A part of her wanted to simply lock the door and wait, but it was the flimsiest of locks, just a turn-button on the handle, and wouldn't prevent the weakest, most incompetent intruder from breaking in.

Karen imagined him on the other side of the door, listening for her, just as she was listening for him.

She could not picture a person. All she could imagine were shiny white bared teeth: an image from a children's story.

Then, just as swiftly, she told herself that she was being ridiculous. *There's no one there. You're just acting nuts.*

Still, it took another surge of will to open the door, then step into the bedroom.

It was empty—save for the two cats. They lounged on the bed, already bored.

She listened again. *Nothing.*

Moving as quickly and as quietly as she could, she grabbed at her clothes and pulled them on. Underwear. Bra. Slacks. Sweater. She slammed her feet into her shoes and stood up. Being clothed reassured her.

She went to her bedroom door. Again she paused to listen. *Silence.*

Small noises seemed to surround her: a ticking clock; the scratch of one of the cats shifting position on the bed; the distant sound of the heating system switching on.

Her own labored breathing.

She imagined that *no* noise would be way worse, and then she told herself that this made absolutely no sense. *No fucking sense*, she thought. *It's my goddamn house. I'll be damned if I'll let anyone . . .*

She stopped. She picked up her cell phone from her bureau, flipped it open, dialed 911, and then poised her thumb over the *call* button.

This made her feel armed, and she began to slowly walk through the house, holding the cell phone like it was a weapon. Kitchen *empty*. Front foyer *empty*. Living room *empty*. Television room *empty*. She went from room to room, each quiet space both reassuring her and making her more nervous. At first she couldn't bring herself to throw open a closet door; a part of her expected someone to jump out. The rational part of her warred with this sensation, and with another large effort she tugged open each closet, only to be greeted by clothes or coats or piles of stray papers.

She was hunting for a noise. Or evidence of a noise. Something that would make the fear that surged through her make some rational sense. She could find nothing.

When she was finally half-persuaded that she was alone, she went back to the kitchen and poured herself a cup of hot coffee. Her hand shook slightly. *What did you hear?*

Nothing. Everything. She let the coffee fill her, let the adrenaline rushing through her ears settle. She wondered, *Can a letter make a noise? Can an anonymous threat make a sound?*

In an erratic mix of tensions, Karen grabbed her coat and headed out to her car to go to work. In her confusion and anxiety, for the first time in years she neglected to put out the cat food.

7

Jordan walked across the campus in the early evening gloom, going back to the library, a distant redbrick building with bright light flowing from large plate glass windows that threw odd cones of illumination across the grassy lawn. The cold breeze seemed to predict a change in the weather—but it was impossible for her to tell whether it would worsen or improve.

Like most students out after the night started to tumble around them, she had been pacing quickly, slightly hunched over, bent to the task of getting from one brightly lit spot to the next, as if time spent on the dark pathways was unsettling or dangerous. She thought, *It probably is*, but found herself slowing nonetheless, like an engine running out of fuel, until she finally stopped dead in her tracks and pivoted around, surveying the world around her.

It was all familiar, all alien, at the same moment.

She had spent nearly four years on the prep school campus, yet it did not seem like home.

She could see inside dormitories—she could name each one. Behind the windows, she saw students bent over textbooks, or sitting around in conversation. She recognized faces. Shapes. An occasional loud voice that seemed to come from nowhere, but which she knew emanated from some dorm, pierced the night, and it seemed to her that she knew who was speaking but just couldn't quite connect a face to the elusive sounds. From adjacent walkways, she could hear footsteps, and she could make out the darkened forms of other students. Some of the shrubbery and the trees seemed to catch the light that came from the student center or the art building in their swaying branches and toss it haphazardly across the lawn, as if taunting her with shadows.

She thought, *In the real fairy tale, the Big Bad Wolf tracks Little Red Riding Hood through the forest. Nothing stops him. Nothing gets in his way. He's like relentless. He fucking knows everything she's going to do before she does it. It's like he's at home and she's just a stranger in the woods. She's got no damn chance at all. Not even when she thinks she's safe because she gets to Grandmother's house, because the wolf is already there and pretending to be the person she thinks can protect her.*

What does that tell you?

She imagined that the man who had designated her for death could be in any shadow. He could be hiding behind any tree. He could be watching from any dark space or from behind any closed window.

Jordan took a quick stride forward, angling a few steps toward the lights of the library, feeling an electric surge of fear coursing within her.

Then, abruptly, she stopped.

Again she slowly looked around. A part of her still wanted to believe that the letter and the threat it contained were all part of an elaborate practical joke. *If so many people hate you,* she thought, *it makes sense.* Students like to pick on the most vulnerable. Despite all the well-meaning bans on hazing and emphasis on friendliness at the school, there was always an undercurrent of tension. Jealousy, anger, sexual predation, illicit drug or alcohol use—all the things that caused frightened parents to send their children away to avoid what existed in the shadow school.

Why wouldn't murder?

Jordan remained frozen in place. Her eyes drifted to the dark edges that surrounded her. She tried to identify shapes, but the night made them seem like hundreds of pieces of several jigsaw puzzles all mixed together. Each belonged to a single answer, each could be joined with others to make a single clear picture, but all tossed together, they formed an impossible and incomprehensible mess.

For a second, the fear-wave within her made her unsteady. The breeze seemed to swirl around her, threatening to pick her up and shake her. She felt cold and sweaty all at once.

She lifted her head, like an animal seeking a strange scent.

Alone is good, she thought. It might have been a contradiction to all good sense, but she clung to it, speaking to herself, as if the Jordan walking through the darkness could have a conversation with the Jordan filled with doubt and worry.

If you told someone, if you shared the threat with anyone, all they would do is tell you what they imagine you should do. They won't have any damn idea whether it's right or wrong. That's what the Wolf will want. He wants you to listen to others—a friend, although you don't have any; a teacher, although there are none you trust; an administrator, who will be more worried about the school's image than your life; or your parents, who have no time for anything but themselves and who probably would find it better if the Wolf succeeded and you were no longer out there creating a problem for them to fight over.

Jordan actually managed a wry grin. She cast her eyes about, searching every odd shape and dark corner. *Alone in the woods*, she thought. *Well, you're goddamn right about that.*

She started to move forward slowly, only one thought ricocheting around within her:

Alone is the only way to win.

Not knowing for an instant whether to believe herself, Jordan hurried out of the darkness toward the lights of the library. She intended to read much more that evening. Not history or science or foreign languages, like all the other students at the school. Jordan had decided to study murder. She thought it was fortunate that she was such a quick learner. And she also told herself that this was one course she could not afford to flunk.

The Big Bad Wolf had awakened early in the morning in order to do some work in the final minutes of dark before dawn light filled his small office. This was always a productive time. Most people, he believed, awakened sluggish and irked at the thought of another day of soul-deadening routine, in a fog until they slammed down a cup or two of coffee.

Not him. The Wolf was filled with enthusiasm and excitement over the coming day, because he had planned something he thought would be truly inventive and unsettling. He imagined it was the way an athlete would feel awaiting the opening whistle of a big game. Murder, as he'd written, lent itself to sporting metaphors.

Words crowded the screen in front of him. His focus was intense. As always, he spent a few moments considering his position in the world of violent death.

As he typed furiously, in an almost a stream-of-consciousness style—though he detested that type of writing, because he thought it lazy and indulgent—he imagined himself some sort of existential hero. Grendel, he believed. Hannibal Lecter. Raskolnikov. Meursault.

I am not precisely an assassin, although we share many qualities. An assassin has some political fury behind his act. Whether this is John Wilkes Booth leaping from the balcony to the stage shouting "Sic semper tyrannis!" or an anarchist taking aim at the archduke riding in his car down the wrong street in Sarajevo or even a Borgia plot that imagines death as the easiest way to consolidate power. To an assassin, the end justifies the means. That same quality may be true for me and my three Reds and for many murderers—but the difference lies in the approach. The assassin settles in to the Book Depository's sixth floor and aims down the barrel of his Carcano 6.5 mm carbine at the president's head and remembers his Marine Corps training as he gently squeezes the trigger. "Red mist," they call it now in shooting circles. But for me, that moment is the easiest. It is the buildup that creates the real excitement of that inevitable gathering together. I do not imagine that an assassin gains the same pleasure as I do in planning the act. Perhaps it is the difference between foreplay and orgasm, between being an attentive lover and merely being eager to conclude. Maybe.

But the thing that distinguishes me from an assassin is the nature of our intimacy. While we each may have studied our victims with precision, the assassin hates what he intends to kill and wants to make some allegedly important point. Everything he does is designed for that moment. A death is scheduled to create a vacuum that the assassin believes will be filled by what he wants. In a way, this is limiting. My own approach with the three Reds is far more intense. I have no political restrictions on my design. The three Reds are part of a grand design. What I plan is far closer to art than politics. I may have important points to make, but these are like brushstrokes, not loud speeches. I won't be leaping from any balcony to a stage shouting "The South is avenged!" but someday soon I will be just as famous.

For me, it's not about hatred. Instead, I am in love with my three Reds.

But each love is different.

Just as each death has to be different.

A powerful smell of bacon began to penetrate the office. The Big Bad Wolf craned his head, and he could hear sizzling coming from the stove. The popping noise was likely to soon join with the more subtle sounds of eggs being scrambled and the toaster ejecting slices of toast. It would probably be sourdough, which Mrs. Big Bad Wolf made in her own electric bread maker, and which she knew was his favorite.

Mrs. Big Bad Wolf liked to prepare large breakfasts. *Most important meal of the day.* He remembered that phrase from the movie *Ordinary People. When did it come out? Twenty years ago? Thirty?* Donald Sutherland was seated across from Timothy Hutton in their Lake Forest mansion and was trapped by his son's grief and confusion and trying desperately to inject some sort of understandable normalcy into their day-to-day turmoil. Except he was thwarted when Hutton hesitated and Mary Tyler Moore, who played the cold and damaged mother, swept the breakfast away from her son and dashed it into the sink and the disposal.

The Wolf pictured the scene. *It was pancakes*, he thought. The actress had made pancakes. *Or maybe French toast. I'm sure of it.* Then he doubted himself. *It might have been waffles.*

He didn't like pancakes as much; they made him feel overfull and sluggish, unless there was really fancy Vermont maple syrup purchased from a gourmet market available. He hated the fake syrup the big grocery chains carried. It tasted like oil to him.

Again the wolf smiled. *I am a gourmand of breakfasts*, he thought, *and a gourmand of killing.*

He heard his wife calling his name. He closed up the computer and encrypted the latest files, using a predictable password: *Grimm.* He was suddenly famished. *Even the greatest killers need to eat*, he told himself as he pushed back from his desk. *It's just that they feed on more than eggs and bacon and freshly baked sourdough bread.*

He thought he needed to make that point in his manuscript, but it could wait until later. He was also stretching his imagination. There were a few necessary upcoming excuses he needed to make to his wife. Places he needed to be and things he needed to do that he didn't want to be questioned about. This was something that really intrigued him: the need to appear normal when great things were in motion around him. He thought: *The backdrop music of my life needs to be a simple, solitary violin. No huge symphonic chords that attract attention.* He smiled. *And no heavy metal screeching guitars, either.*

From down the hallway, he heard a cheery, "On the table. Eggs and bacon."

"Coming, dear," he shouted to Mrs. Big Bad Wolf, not unpleasantly, eager to get the day started.

8

Mrs. Big Bad Wolf collected the breakfast dishes and dutifully scraped the remains into the trash compactor before loading knives, forks, plates, and cups into the electric dishwasher. As usual, her husband had carefully sliced the crust edges away from his toast, using only the crisp center portion to sop up the runny eggs. She had seen these orphans on his morning plates for fifteen years, and although she thought it wasteful, and a part of her believed the crust was the best part of the toast, she never said anything to him about this eccentricity. Nor had she ever—even though she knew he would invariably do this when she put the plate in front of him—sliced the edges off for him before they sat at the table.

This morning she was late for the work that she more often than not disliked, and she knew she had a desk piled up with mundane duties that would drag on throughout the day. She imagined that after putting in her eight hours the list of to-do items clogging her calendar would be only modestly diminished. She envied her husband. Her workaday life seemed devoted to ever-increasing amounts of the deadly same, over and over. He, on the other hand, was the creative force in their relationship.

He was the writer; he was special. He was unique, like no man she'd ever known, and that was why she married him. He provided vibrant color in her dull dirt-brown world and nothing made her feel better than introducing him to coworkers, saying, "*This is my husband. He's a novelist.*" She sometimes berated herself by thinking that all she brought to their relationship was comprehensive health insurance and a regular paycheck and the occasional hurried bout in bed, and then she would dismiss this awful idea and persuade herself that even if it seemed like a cliché, every great writer needed a muse, and she surely was his. This idea made her proud.

She sometimes imagined herself to be willowy, slender, gossamer-dressed, which was the image she suspected an illustrator drawing a writer's *inspiration* would create. That she was short and stocky, a little overweight, with mousy brown hair and a smile that seemed lopsided no matter how much pleasure she meant to express, was irrelevant. Inside, she was beautiful. She knew this. Why else would he have fallen in love with and married her?

And, after so many fallow years, so many literary fits and starts and frustration, to see him once again eager to lock himself away in the spare bedroom that he'd taken over as his writing studio, colored her day and made heading off to work less painful. She envisioned bundles of words, filling pages, relentlessly stacking up by the printer.

Mrs. Big Bad Wolf often wished she had his imagination.

It would be nice, she thought, *to be able to live in made-up worlds where you control the outcome of all the characters. You can make whomever you want fall in love. You can kill off whomever you want. You deliver success or failure, sadness or happiness. What a wonderful luxury.*

It was not unusual for her to steal a glance at the closed door to the office, wondering what special world was taking form inside. Like Odysseus strapped to the mast of his ship, she longed to hear the siren's songs.

She paused, standing at the sink. Water was running over her hands and she knew she should reach for the dishwashing soap and start the machine before leaving for her office, but in that second of envy, she felt a twinge on her left side, just below her breast. The sensation—it wasn't even significant enough to call *a pain*—sent a shaft of fright directly through her, and she gripped the counter edges to steady herself as a rapid dizziness swept over her. For an instant she felt hot, as if an oven door within her had been opened, and she caught her breath sharply.

The only words she could think of were *not again*.

She slowed her intake, tried to force her pulse to return to a normal pace. She closed her eyes and cautiously did an inventory of her body. She felt a little like a mechanic working over a car engine with some mysterious failure.

She reminded herself that she had just the other day been in to see her doctor and received a completely clean bill of health. She'd gone through the routine of poking and prodding and answering questions, opening her mouth wide, feeling the electrocardiograph leads placed on her body and waiting while the machine chewed out an assessment. And when her doctor had smiled, and begun to reassure her, it had been musical, even if she hadn't quite believed it.

No signs.

She almost said this out loud.

This was the trouble with having a faulty heart. It made her imagine that every twinge and every misplaced beat signaled the end. She thought to herself that she didn't have an interesting enough life to be this paranoid.

Mrs. Big Bad Wolf reached over to a countertop drainage rack, where she had placed a few of the bigger pans that wouldn't fit into the dishwasher. She lifted out a large skillet made of stainless steel and held it up in front of her eyes. She could see her reflection in the clean, polished metal. But unlike with a mirror, the portrait that stared back at her was slightly distorted, as if it was out of focus.

She told herself: *You were beautiful once*, even if this wasn't true.

Then she searched for pain: None in the eyes. None in the corners of her mouth. None in that extra flesh that sagged around her jaw.

She pushed further. None in her feet. None in her legs. None in her stomach.

She held up her left hand and wiggled the fingers.

Nothing. No sudden shock of hurt plunging through her wrist.

As if entering a dangerous minefield, she began to mentally examine her chest, an explorer searching some unknown territory. She breathed in and out slowly, all the time watching the face in the steel reflection, as if it were someone else's and would display some telltale sign that she could spot. There were experts who had studied facial expressions, and detectives who believed that by merely examining a face they could tell when someone was lying or cheating or even covering up some illness. She had seen these people on television.

But her breathing seemed regular. Her heartbeat seemed solid and steady. She touched her rib cage with her fingers, prodding it. Nothing.

And her face remained flat, without affect. *Like a poker player,* she thought. Then she slowly lowered the pan back to the drying rack. *No. Okay. It was nothing. A little bit of indigestion. Your heart isn't going to stop today.*

She reminded herself to go to work—and to hurry, maybe even speed, to make up for the minutes lost to dying fears. "I'm leaving now," she shouted. There was a small silence, then a muffled reply from inside the locked office.

"I might be out a bit doing some research, dear. Maybe late for dinner."

She smiled. The word *research* encouraged her. She believed he was really making progress, and she knew enough to make sure that nothing she did would upset that fragile state.

"Okay, honey. Whatever you say. I'll leave a plate for you in the microwave if you need to get home late."

Mrs. Big Bad Wolf didn't wait for a response, but she was happy. This sounded like the most mundane conversation any couple could have. It was so ordinary, it reassured her. The writer was *working;* and like the worker bee she considered herself, she was heading out to her job. Nothing as *different* as a heart attack could ever enter into a world so determinedly normal.

She drove through the faculty-and-staff parking lot twice before she found a spot near the back, which added fifty yards of rain and chill to her exposed travel. There was nothing she could do about this, so Mrs. Big Bad Wolf slid her car into the space, gathered her satchel, and maneuvered out of her door, trying to get a small umbrella raised before she got soaked.

She immediately stepped into a puddle, and cursed. Then she hurried across the lot, head down, making for the school administration building.

She hung her damp coat on a hook by the door and slid behind her desk, hoping that the dean wouldn't notice she was a little late.

He emerged from his office—her desk guarded the entry—and shook his head, but not at her tardiness or at the lousy weather that was turning the school into a dark and dreary place. He had a file in his hand and he seemed dismayed.

"Can you send a message to Miss Jordan Ellis?" he said. "Have her come in this afternoon to see me during a free period, or maybe after her basketball practice?"

"Of course," Mrs. Big Bad Wolf replied. "Is it urgent?"

"More of the same," the dean said ruefully. "She's doing poorly in every subject and now Mr. and Mrs. Ellis want *me* to referee their custody battle, which will only make matters significantly worse." He managed a wan smile. "Wouldn't it be wonderful if some of these parents just left their children alone and let us deal with them?"

This was a familiar complaint and a prayer that never had any realistic chance of being answered.

"I'll see that she's here to see you today," Mrs. Big Bad Wolf replied.

"Thank you," he said, nodding. He glanced down at the sheaf of papers in his hand and shrugged. "Don't you just hate it when seniors throw their futures away?" he asked. This was a rhetorical question, and one that Mrs. Big Bad Wolf understood didn't need answering. *Of course everyone hated it when seniors did poorly. They struggled in school and then got into lower-tier colleges, and that skewed the school's Ivy League statistics.* She watched as he retreated back into his office, still clutching the file, although eventually it, and all the confidential information it contained, would arrive on her desk for sorting away in a large black steel file cabinet in the corner of the room. It had a combination lock. *8-17-96.* Her wedding day.

9

Sarah Locksley shifted about uncomfortably in her seat. She was dizzy, twitching, and felt both exhausted and energized, as if the two opposing sensations could happily coexist within her. Every second that passed was boring and exciting. She felt on the verge of something, whether it was passing out unconscious for twenty-four hours or taking aim and shooting the next person—who would be the first person in weeks—to knock on her door.

Over-the-counter NoDoz, Stolichnaya vodka and fresh orange juice, a large supply of candy bars, packaged donuts, and sweet rolls, and an occasional peanut-butter-covered banana had fueled her over the past few days. Fattening, calorie-filled, but she felt like she hadn't gained a pound.

She wanted to laugh out loud. She imagined a cynical advertising copywriter: *The dead woman's diet. Just have an anonymous someone threaten to kill you and watch the pounds melt away!*

She had placed a stiff chair in a spot where she could cover both the front of the house and much of the kitchen entranceway in the rear, and she had arranged a few pillows and an old sleeping bag nearby, so that when she'd had to sleep, snatching a few hours from night, she'd been able to tumble half-drugged and half-drunk into the makeshift bed. She was avoiding her bedroom. There was something frightening about concealing herself inside the place she'd shared with her husband. The room seemed suddenly prisonlike and she was determined that she would not allow herself to be murdered in the place where she had once known so much pleasure.

She knew this seemed totally crazy, but crazy was a state that she was willing to embrace.

She had constructed a homemade alarm system by the rear door— hanging a string across the doorway and tying empty cans and pots and pans to it, so anyone bumping into it would rattle and clang with noise. Just beneath the windowsills she had shattered empty liquor bottles into glass shards and spread them around, so a person—*no*, she thought: *a Big Bad Wolf*—breaking in that way would likely slice hands or feet clambering into the house. On the stairway leading to the basement she had strung strands of wire an inch or two above each riser to trip the Wolf if he tried to use the steps. She had also spread some ball bearings and old marbles around on the basement floor and unscrewed the light, so that the room was pitched into darkness and likely to cause her stalker to trip.

She had her dead husband's gun close by and she periodically checked it to make sure that it was loaded and ready, even though she knew she had already checked it a hundred times. The area around her was a mess of plastic wrappers, empty Styrofoam cups, and discarded bottles. Sarah kicked away some of the trash accumulating next to her bare feet and sighed deeply. *Well, this isn't working, goddammit.*

Her defense systems seemed straight out of the *Home Alone* movie, better preparation for a slapstick comedy than preventing a killer from sneaking unseen and unheard into her house and slaughtering her in her sleep. She knew she was likely to pass out at any moment and that when she did succumb to inevitable exhaustion, no clattering of pots and pans would wake her. She was all too experienced in the fog that accompanied booze and narcotics.

And mostly, Sarah doubted that the Big Bad Wolf was anything less than completely skilled at murder and professional at killing. She had no evidence to support this feeling, but she believed it to be the truth. Instinct. Sixth sense. Premonition. She didn't know what it was, but she knew he would wait until the right moment, which would be the moment he knew she was at her most vulnerable.

Vulnerable. What a god-awful, pathetic, barely adequate word, she thought. *More likely it described her every second of every day and every night, regardless of whether she was asleep or sitting waiting by the front door, gun in hand.*

She looked around. Her back was stiff. Her head ached. Everything she'd done to protect herself seemed precisely what a middle school teacher *would* do. Scissors, sticky glue, and brightly colored construction paper—it was very much like a class project. All that was lacking were some excited fifth graders and happily raised voices.

She could see herself, clapping her hands together sharply to get their attention. *All right, class! Mrs. Locksley has to protect herself from a psychopathic killer. Everyone bring their favorite materials to the middle, and let's build a wall so she will be safe!*

Ludicrous. This she knew. But she did not know what else to do.

She took a long look down at her right hand gripping the pistol. *Maybe I should break my promise to my dead husband*, she thought, *and turn the gun on myself just before the Big Bad Wolf arrives at the door.*

Sarah laughed bitterly. A sudden burst, as if from an unexpected moment of humor. *Now, that would be a hilarious sight to see, when the Big Bad Wolf sneaks inside to kill me and discovers that I've beaten him to the punch. What the hell could he do? A killer without a target. Joke's on him.*

Except I couldn't see it because I would already be dead.

Words to a song penetrated her memory: "'*No reason to get excited,*' the thief he kindly spoke. '*There are many here among us who feel that life is but a joke.*'"

She could hear the guitar riff as if it were being played in the distance. She could hear the gravelly voice. It made sense to her. No reason to get excited.

She sighed deeply, but that release nearly turned to scream when she heard a sudden sound at the front door. She first lurched away, as if she could hide, then she stumbled forward, gun outstretched, ready to shoot.

She thought she was shouting aloud incomprehensibly, but then realized that all those noises existed only in her head.

There is nothing worse, Karen Jayson thought, *than the racket caused by silence*.

This held true, she insisted to herself, whether she was on stage, in her office surrounded by work, or alone in her home.

She was driving home after the day's work. She had quickly adopted a habit that cost her time: After pulling off the main highway onto the quieter rural roads leading to her isolated house, if she spotted someone behind her in the rearview mirror, she would pull to the side and patiently wait for the car or truck or whatever to sweep past her before resuming her drive. No one was going to tail her. This constant stop, go, find another pullover, stop, wait, then resume made the trip tediously slow, but gave her a sense of satisfaction. She was not in any rush to return home. It no longer seemed safe.

The trouble was, at the same time that she felt unsettled about returning, she kept insisting to herself that there was no reason to feel that way.

She approached the turnoff for her gravel driveway. She could just make out the outlines of her house, partially obscured by the foliage even with the leaves all down for winter. Dark pines and deep brown oak trees, lined up like sentinels, were barriers to her sight. She took a quick glance behind her, just to make sure no one was there, and pulled into the driveway. Just as she always did, she stopped at the mailbox.

But now she hesitated. *Crazy thinking*, she told herself. *Get the mail*.

She did not want to get out of the car. She did not want to open the mail container. It was almost like she expected a bomb to explode if she did.

There was no reason for her to believe that the Big Bad Wolf would use the mail to contact her a second time. And no reason to believe he wouldn't.

She tried to impose rationality on her heart. *Medical school discipline*, she recalled, summoning up memories of long shifts and soul-deadening exhaustion that she had managed to overcome. *Get out. Get the mail. Screw him. You can't let some anonymous joker disrupt your life.*

Then she wondered whether this made sense. Maybe what made sense *was* to let him disrupt her life.

Karen remained frozen behind the wheel. She watched shadows slice through the trees like sword strokes of darkness.

She felt trapped between the ordinary—the mundane task of getting the daily collection of bills, catalogues, and flyers—and the unreasonable. *Maybe a second letter.*

Karen took her car out of gear and waited. She insisted to herself that she was being silly. If someone were to see her hesitate before doing something as routine as collecting the mail she would be embarrassed.

This did not reassure her.

She very much wanted to talk to someone right at that moment. She suddenly hated being alone, when for so many years that was *all* she wanted to be.

With a final glance up and down the road, she got out of her car, mumbling to herself that she was being paranoid and stupid and there was nothing to be afraid of. But still, she cautiously opened the box as if she were afraid there was a poisonous snake coiled inside.

The first thing she saw was the white envelope resting on top of a bright J.Crew catalogue.

She pulled her hand back sharply, as if it was indeed a snake. Fangs bared and ready to strike.

"Jordan, I am so very concerned," the dean said with appropriate sonorous, serious tones. "Every one of your teachers is surprised by the precipitous drop-off in the quality of your work. We all understand the pressure that your home situation creates. But you need to recognize how important this year is for your future. College awaits, and we fear you will cripple your chances at the better universities unless you pull your academic record together rapidly."

The dean, Jordan believed, could not possibly sound more pompous. But then, a daily dose of pomposity was the natural state of existence for all deans at all prep schools, so he couldn't really be criticized for acting like he was supposed to.

If a mad dog bites you, is that dog being unreasonable? If a squirrel runs away when you come too close, is it being foolish? If a murderer wants to kill you, is that really a surprise?

Jordan imagined that she was becoming a philosopher. She only half-listened as the dean continued to mix encouragement with criticism, thinking somehow that just the right mix of pep talk and sympathy, colored with dire threats, would combine to make her shape up.

"We need to help you get back on track," he said, as if this was an important, earth-shattering point he was making.

Back on track was the sort of phrase she'd heard a lot in the past months and which didn't really mean anything to her anymore. It referred to the old Jordan, the one who was, if not popular, at least accepted, who got good grades, and who was looking forward to her next year. New Jordan wasn't even sure she was going to live much longer.

She looked around the office. There were books in an oaken case and a large brown desk that matched. There were some framed diplomas on the wall adjacent to framed children's drawings that splashed color into the room. There were also framed pictures of the smiling dean and his happy family on a rafting trip, another in which they were all arm-in-arm and posed in front of the Grand Canyon, and finally a montage of them all at the peak of some conquered mountain. An active, energetic, unified family. Not at all like hers. Hers was fracturing.

Something he said distracted her. "What can I do to help you, Jordan?" the dean asked.

Jordan realized that she was hunched over slightly in her seat, arms tight to her stomach as if she was in pain. She slowly rearranged herself so she wouldn't appear so crippled. "I'll work harder," she said.

The dean hesitated. "I don't know that it's about hard work, Jordan. It's about trying to regain your focus."

"I'll focus harder," she said.

He shook his head, but only slightly. "You have to try to put some of these distractions aside and concentrate on what is important to you."

"I'll try," she answered. She did not blurt out, *Don't you goddamn think that staying alive is what's important to me?*

"We all want to help you, Jordan, because getting through this difficult time is crucial for your future."

I might just not have a future.

She took a deep breath and composed herself. The dean, she thought, wasn't a bad guy. He really did mean well. She had a tinge of envy. She didn't think her parents had any pictures on any wall of anything she had ever done, or anything they had all done together in happier times, although she couldn't recall any *happier times* at all, or when they'd ever done something together.

She thought for a moment about her response. She understood that if there was a moment where she should bring up the Big Bad Wolf, this was it.

You think it's just my parents' ugly divorce that's fucking me up? Hell no. Screw them. It's really that there's some crazy guy out there who thinks I'm Little Red Riding Hood and he wants to eat me. Not really eat me. He's just going to kill me. It's the same thing.

But she didn't say this. It sounded too wild.

A part of her was shouting inside her head: *You all want to help me? Well, get a gun. Hire a bodyguard. Call the damn Marines. Maybe they can protect me!*

None of these angry thoughts tumbled out of her mouth. Instead, she quietly replied, "I'll do the best I can." She kept her voice low, almost as if speaking in a confessional, except she had never been to a confessional and wasn't about to start anytime soon.

It wasn't really the right thing to say. And she could see disappointment in the dean's eyes. She liked that. At least he wasn't being phony.

She started to open her mouth again, to let loose some great stew of pain over her parents, over her failures, over her isolation, and finally over her fear that she was being stalked and on a list to die and there was nothing she could do about it. She was halfway to letting it all tumble out, when she stopped.

She nearly gasped out loud.

If I tell him about the Wolf, maybe the Wolf will come for him, first.

She glanced around. Happy family pictures. She couldn't put them in danger.

She saw the dean lean forward. Most people would have seen the motion as concerned. She saw it as predatory.

Maybe he's *the Wolf,* she thought suddenly. She felt her stomach tighten. She clamped down, lip to lip, keeping her secrets to herself.

The dean hesitated, letting uncomfortable silence fill the room like pungent smoke. After what seemed like a very long time, he said, "Okay, Jordan. You know you can come talk to me anytime you want to. And you know I think you should return to seeing the school therapist. I can make the appointments, if you're willing and you think it will help . . ."

A therapist with a big goddamn gun, she told herself. *That might help. Or maybe a therapist who can double as the sturdy woodsman who saves Little Red Riding Hood with his stout axe. Except that's not the ending that the Big Bad Wolf intends in this retelling, is it?* She didn't answer her question.

Instead, Jordan pushed herself out of her chair and nodded, but the nod quickly turned into a shake of the head *no.* Then she left, moving rapidly past the dean's secretary, who half-smiled, half-scowled in her direction, and down a wide flight of stairs and through the doors leading to the school grounds.

The air was raw, but fresh, and she felt like she could bite off pieces of cold and chew them. What she wanted to do was head to the gym, get to practice early, and run harder than any of the other girls on the team. She wanted to sweat. She wanted to smash into other bodies. If she took an elbow to the lip and started to bleed, that would be okay with her. If she did that to a team-mate, well, that would be okay, too. She took a couple of strides toward her dormitory, planning on tossing her book bag onto her bed and exiting for the practice courts, when she was suddenly overcome with a single, discouraging thought: *The mail will be delivered by the time I get there.*

She did not know there would be another letter from the Wolf. But the electric panic that raced around unchecked within her insisted that would be the case. She hated the sensation of knowing something that couldn't possibly be true, but nevertheless *was*. It made her stop in her tracks, letting the cool air surround her. *There will be another letter,* she thought. *I don't know how I know it, but I know it.*

She was partially correct.

There was an envelope waiting for Red One, Red Two, and Red Three.

But this time there was no letter.

Each envelope contained a single line of type specific for each Red.

Karen Jayson received: *http://www.youtube.com/watch?v=wsxty1xl.Red1.*

Sarah Locksley received: *http://www.youtube.com/watch?v=wftgh1xl:Red2.*

And waiting for Jordan Ellis was: *http://www.youtube.com/watch?v=hgtsv1xl:Red3.*

Each was signed with the initials BBW.

10

The killer's largest dilemma, the Big Bad Wolf eagerly wrote, *is precisely assessing the right sort of proximity. You need to be close—but not too close. The danger lies in the old cliché: Like a moth to a flame, you are drawn toward your intended victim. Don't burn yourself. But interaction is an integral element to the whole death dance. The desire to hear, to touch, to smell is overwhelming. Screams of pain are like music. The sensation of closeness as murder is delivered is intoxicating. Think of all the elements of a gourmet meal, how each spice, each foodstuff, blends its flavor with the others in a single unique experience. Conjuring up a five-star dinner is no different from sculpting a proper killing.*

In the fairy tale, the Wolf doesn't merely stalk Little Red Riding Hood through the forest. That's far too simple an interpretation. He is at home there. His resources are double, maybe triple, hers. His eyesight is sharper. His sense of smell is immensely better. He can outrun her. He can outthink her. He is deep in his element, familiar with every tree and every moss-covered rock. She is only a frightened interloper, alone and way out of her depth. She is young and naïve. He is older, wiser, and far more sophisticated.

In reality, the Wolf could kill her at any point as she stumbles helplessly through the thick thorns, brambles, and dark shadows. But that would be far too easy. It would make the kill too routine. Mundane. He has to move closer. He has to communicate directly before death. It's those moments that make the killing experience come alive. Ears. Eyes. Nose. Teeth. He wants to hear the tremble of uncertainty in her voice and sense the rapid beat of her heart. He wants to see panic grow on her brow as she slowly comes to the realization of what is going to occur. He wants to smell her fear. And ultimately what he wants is to hold all the intimacies of murder in his paw . . . before he tastes what he has dreamed of and bares his teeth.

Just like an author, the Wolf needs to write her death.

He had been typing quickly, but as he wrote the word *death* he suddenly pushed back in his office chair, bending over slightly. He rubbed his open palms hard against his old corduroy jeans, feeling the fading ridges of the soft material, and creating heat in the same way that rubbing sticks together can create flame. He wished he could stand next to each Red, just to see the impact of his second letter. This was a desire so intense that it abruptly drove him to his feet, where he punched the empty air in front of him with a series of quick, short jabs, like a boxer who has just injured his opponent and closes in on him as he senses weakness and opportunity at the same instant, oblivious to the rising noise from the crowd and the imminent ring of the bell. The Wolf turned away from the computer and his desk and exited quickly. He locked his office and then hurried through the house. He remembered to grab an overcoat from the rack by the front door, although he thought he wouldn't need it. He was warm enough already.

He drove hard, maybe a little too fast, cutting corners and running through yellow lights, until he reached the school. He parked on an adjacent street, where he had a distant view of the main campus walkways through black iron fence bars.

"Where are you, Red Three?" he whispered. He took a quick glance at his watch. He inwardly counted down: *five, four, three . . .* knowing that a bell would peal and fourth-period classes would shift to fifth period. *American history to English comp*, he told himself.

He scrunched down in his seat. "Come on, ring, damn it," he said. Obligingly, the bell sounded, just as he knew it would.

There was a brief moment of hesitancy, as if the entire campus landscape had shrugged and then doors started to open and squads of teenagers filled the quadrangle, moving from one obligation to the next. It was a sea of blue jeans and parkas. He bent forward, wiping the moisture off the interior glass of his car window.

"Where are you, Red Three?" he repeated.

He caught a glimpse of strawberry red, stuffed beneath a woolen cap. He spotted a hesitant stride a few paces behind a clutch of students. He wanted to see her stumble, maybe even collapse in fear, lying in a heap on the black macadam path.

He smiled.

"I'm here," he spoke softly. "And you know it, don't you?"

The real answer to this question was *no*. But the better answer was *yes*.

The Wolf watched as the far-off image of Red Three disappeared into another classroom building. For an instant he glanced around. He was alone, in his car, on an empty street. He thought that he was camouflaged, just like any forest predator: an ordinary man, behind the wheel of an ordinary car, on an ordinary day, seemingly doing nothing out of the ordinary whatsoever.

He started the car up. *Two more stops*, he told himself. *Maybe just a lucky drive-by. And we shall see what we shall see.*

He inhaled sharply. He could smell uncertainty. Doubt. Subtle scents that shortly would be replaced by the stronger odor of terror.

None of the three Reds had immediately searched out the YouTube address that had arrived in the daily mail. Each stared first at the envelope, and then when indecision grew like a shriek within them and they tore open the gummed paper, they each stared at the letter-and-number hieroglyph centered on each page. One minute became two. Two became ten.

Each Red felt as if she was sliding recklessly out of control.

* * *

Karen Jayson dropped the sheet of paper into her lap. She had climbed back behind the wheel of her car, locked the doors, and then froze in place until she got up the courage to open it up and read the single line contained within. She then gripped the steering wheel so tightly that her knuckles whitened as she lost time to fear. It was a little like passing out, or going into a fugue state. She was staring through the windshield up the driveway to her home, but she no longer could see the trees, the twisting gravel trail, or the outline of her house just beyond. She had plummeted into some different place, where she teetered on panic. When she finally, painfully drew herself back into the world in front of her, she realized that in a short time whatever the Wolf wanted her to see would likely twist her further.

Lost in a type of daze, she felt a sudden shaft of fear when a car passed behind her on the country road that led to her driveway. She pivoted about, imagining that the car had slowed, inspecting her—but by the time she turned, the car was gone.

If there even was a car.

She was no longer sure.

She could not organize her thoughts or her feelings. For a woman who prided herself on knowledge and the steady application of facts to any situation, it was this that frightened her as much as anything. She realized she had a death-grip on her steering wheel and thought she would break it off in her hands. She slammed into gear and crushed the accelerator beneath her right foot, spitting stones and dirt from beneath the car, swerving madly as she fruitlessly tried to flee from her emotions.

Sarah Locksley hid in the bathroom.

She locked the door behind her, then pushed herself toward the sink, ran cold water into the basin, and dashed it on her face, where the droplets mixed freely with her tears.

Her breath came in short gasps ripped from her chest. Her hands felt clammy against the porcelain. She could feel her grip weakening and she felt dizzy. *It has to be all the booze and all the drugs*, she told herself, insisting on a falsehood when she knew that the truth was that it was fear.

She could feel her balance fleeing, as if whatever held her upright was draining out of her like blood from a wound. She glanced down at the sheet of paper. She wanted to crumple it up and toss it into the toilet and flush it away like so much waste. But as strong as this desire was, she knew she wouldn't do it.

Not, at least, before she had seen what it was the Wolf wanted her to see. She did not want to see it. She did not want to know what it was. But at the same time, she knew she had to.

She gripped the letter in her hand, and then, overcome suddenly by nausea, she pivoted to the toilet bowl and was violently ill.

Jordan Ellis first curled up on her bed as if stricken by an abrupt illness, the letter clutched in her hand. She remained locked in position for nearly fifteen minutes. She stared across her tiny dormitory room to the desk, and the laptop computer lying open there.

It took a great effort to push her legs off the mattress and onto the floor. It took a second effort, equal to the first, to rise up and take a step toward the computer. And finally, as she dropped herself into the stiff-backed desk chair, it took a third effort even greater than the first pair to draw her hands above the computer keyboard and type in the first letters of the web address that BBW had sent her.

Each letter or number or backslash she typed was like a needle probing her flesh. When the entire address was completed, she hesitated before hitting the return key, which would send her electronically into whatever world the Wolf wanted her to be in.

Jordan paused. She tried to imagine what hitting that final key was doing to her and for him. She asked herself if she was helping her cause or hurting it. She thought she was entering into some dangerous arena in which a deadly game was being played, but without being told the rules, and without being given the right equipment, so that she would be hamstrung from the beginning and winning was not only unlikely, but impossible.

I can play, she thought, trying to fill herself with some sort of phony confidence. *I can play any game. Better than he knows.* Still she hesitated.

She bit down on her lower lip until it was nearly painful and then she said *Fuck it* to herself and punched the return key with a heady determination that astonished her.

The familiar logo of a YouTube page came up on the screen. In the frozen video in front of her, all she could see was a close-up of a barren tree, branches denuded, against an overcast sky.

She had no idea what it was and a confusing *what the fuck* series of thoughts crowded into her head. She moved the cursor over to the *Play* arrow and clicked. In the box on the screen, images leapt to life. She hunched forward, watching carefully.

At first the camera—held unsteadily and amateurishly—wobbled as it lingered over the tree. Then it swung about rapidly, and Jordan understood that it was a forest. She could see leaves collected on the floor, dark-stained tree trunks melding together in a tangled mess, bushes, and fallen logs. But the camera seemed light, almost at ease, at it effortlessly traveled through the dark woods. Shafts of weak sunlight occasionally interrupted the scene. Jordan thought the footage was taken near the end of a gloomy day.

She watched, fascinated. The point of view suggested that whoever was behind the camera had no trouble following a designated path. But she recognized nothing. The footage could have been taken anywhere.

Suddenly, the camera stopped. A large flash of light washed out the view and Jordan rocked back as if she'd been slapped.

There was a moment of grainy, out-of-focus, hard-to-identify images, and then Jordan realized that she was watching a long-distance shot of someone walking through the late afternoon.

She saw the red hair.

She saw the school pathways.

She saw herself. Alone.

She thought she was about to scream. But her mouth opened wide and no sound came out.

The camera image lingered for an instant as she watched herself disappear into her dormitory. She saw the front door swing shut behind her.

Then the screen went black.

11

Karen tried to adopt a carefree, unaffected tone on the telephone. She had dialed the number for the Apple Store in a shopping mall some twenty-five miles away, and been connected to a young man at their "Genius Bar," who had given his name as Kyle.

"I have a computer question," Karen said, keeping her words as short as possible.

"Sure. Shoot," Kyle replied, without pointing out the obvious, that there was no other reason for calling the store. In the background she could hear other responses from blue-shirted Apple "geniuses" answering questions about bits and bytes and downloads and memory.

"Is it possible to post something on YouTube anonymously? We're trying to do something special for my husband's birthday, and the kids and I wanted to put up a video we made as a surprise for him—he's in the service overseas, you see—and part of the surprise is doing it so he can't trace it back, because we don't want to give away the second surprise we have planned for him when he comes home . . ."

She stopped her story there. It didn't really make any sense, she knew, and it was a complete lie, but she imagined it would be enough to get Kyle the Genius to tell her what she needed to know.

"Ah, sure. Posting anonymously? No problem. It's not really any big deal," he said.

"I mean untraceable completely?"

"Yep," he replied.

"So, like if I did want to trace something back to the poster, how would I do that?"

"Easy to post. Hard to trace," Kyle said simply.

"Can you fill me in a little?" Karen asked. She hoped that none of the tension she felt within her was leaking into her voice.

"Well, two different questions really," he answered. "First, posting anonymously. That's not too difficult. You need to take your laptop to just about any public server, like in a coffee shop or a library. Then you create a proxy account with a website like Tor, which will give you a program that guarantees anonymity. By the time you're posting on YouTube, you're using a server that can't be traced to you and a site that hides all the relevant computer info, so that even if one were to get to the location, they'd be up against a wall."

"Sounds like a lot of work."

"Not really. Just a short drive in the car, buy a cup of overpriced coffee, and make some discreet clicks. Use some alias that means nothing to nobody. Seems like a relatively small inconvenience for total secrecy." Kyle seemed a little bored by the question.

"But the cops—"

"Nah," he interrupted immediately, with significantly more enthusiasm, "no chance, no way. They just run into the same electronic walls. And, assuming the public server in the library or coffee shop doesn't have any security cameras, well, there you have it. Your post is up and running, you cancel out of Tor or wherever, and no one knows the difference and you've disappeared."

The Big Bad Wolf, Karen thought, would know about security cameras. He had to. He would know about computers. He would know about websites that create anonymity. She suddenly imagined that he would know about *everything*.

"And back tracing . . ."

"You mean if someone posted something anonymously that you wanted to track down? Like someone did to you what you want to do to your husband?"

Kyle's reply had a slightly mocking tone, as if he understood she wasn't really talking about a husband, but that he was willing to play along.

This was what she truly wanted to know. She felt her insides constrict, as if someone were hugging her. She could feel sweat beneath her arms and she reminded herself to keep her own voice airy, light, and unconcerned, even if this was nearly impossible.

From what she could hear, Kyle was young—probably in his early twenties, she thought—but in computer years he was significantly older than her. "Exactly," she said.

"Well, I think YouTube is required by law to keep as much of that information available as possible, in case the cops come calling, or some lawyer with a subpoena. They're really sensitive to Internet bullying and intimidation because of all the cases that have come up all over the place. They get a whole lot of bad publicity when some high school creep posts something to humiliate or intimidate some ex-boyfriend or -girlfriend. Facebook is no different. But they're just going to run into the same problems as they break it down. Now, I don't know about the military or like the CIA—you know, spooks. They've got some pretty cool top-secret stuff for tracing bad guys, like in Iraq. But for everyone working for the feds with real expertise, there are a dozen or a million computer pros working to get around them. And the guys that aren't collecting a government paycheck are really a whole lot more skilled."

Karen didn't know what to ask next, but Kyle obligingly continued, his voice picking up some excited momentum.

"It's like you see in the movies and television," Kyle said. "You know there's always a scene where either the good guys or the bad guys hack this or that and come up with some killer piece of information about some guy or some plot or something cool that's just floating about in cyberspace and it all seems to like make sense and you believe it?"

"Yes?" Karen asked. Nothing she had heard from Kyle reassured her. Instead, she felt queasy.

"Well, that's because it usually does make sense."

"Thanks, Kyle," Karen said. "I might have to call you again."

"Hey, anytime, Doctor," he said as he hung up.

It took her a moment to realize that she hadn't identified herself. And she hadn't told Kyle her profession. Caller ID on her phone, she thought. For a moment she stared at the black receiver she held in her hand. *What else did it tell him?* Home phone, landline, cell phone, office line. Where had her privacy disappeared? It frightened her.

Then she turned back to her computer screen. It frightened her more.

Sarah's tears had dried.

She felt like she had walked headlong into some dark room and she knew that somewhere in the floor was a trapdoor that would drop her into some sort of endless oblivion. It made no difference how carefully and cautiously she felt her way forward, because the door yawned open in front of her and there was no way to avoid it.

For a moment or two, she stared at her computer screen, watching the YouTube posting for the third or fourth time. Maybe it was the fifth time. She didn't keep track.

Suddenly, she reached out and seized her husband's gun from the table beside her. Before she fully understood what she was doing, she clicked off the safety, rose from her chair, and stomped across the house, finally reaching the front door. Without hesitation, she flung the door open and stepped outside on the front stoop, swinging her gun right and left, sighting down the barrel, her finger tight on the trigger, ready to fire instantly.

Come on! Goddammit! Come on! I'm ready for you!

She thought she was shouting, but then she understood that her teeth were clenched tight, so tight that her jaw began to ache.

She pivoted to the right a second time, then repeated the movement to the left, a little like a top spinning on a table.

Finally, she lowered the weapon and flipped the safety switch back on. Sarah breathed out slowly, tasting fresh air and wondering whether she had been holding her breath for seconds, or a minute, or the entire day.

The gun suddenly felt heavy, and it bounced against her hip.

Sarah wanted to laugh.

No one in sight. No one walking up or down the street in front of her house. No cars moving past slowly. No one within her view at all.

They were all lucky, she thought. All the neighbors who never called on her anymore. All the strangers who might have taken that moment to amble past her house.

They were all lucky to be alive.

She told herself that she would have leveled the pistol and pulled the trigger and killed anyone she saw. It would have made no difference if one of them was the Big Bad Wolf or not. She had begun to think that *everyone* was the Big Bad Wolf.

She sighed and stepped back inside. Sarah had the odd thought that she had been completely forgotten in her neighborhood. No one wanted to catch the virus of despair that she carried. So no one acknowledged her existence. Not anymore.

I can stand naked in my window. I could walk naked down the street with my gun in my hand. I could dance naked in the center of the road firing shots wherever I liked and no one would pay any attention, she told herself. *I have become invisible.*

She was tempted to try. But instead, she went back inside, locking the door behind her and rearranging her flimsy homemade alarm system of cans and bottles, and returned to her computer screen.

A second thought slithered into her head: *I'm invisible to everyone except one person.* She could hear her breathing coming in short, tortured bursts.

Sarah reached down and pressed the *Play* arrow with the barrel of her gun and began to watch what was posted another time.

But as she did so, she raised her weapon and aimed it at the images in front of her.

Red One's YouTube video began in the same manner as Red Three's—with the camera tracking rapidly through some anonymous stand of trees, like an animal moving quickly over familiar ground. When Red One saw this for the first time, she imagined that it was the woods behind her house. *Had to be*, she thought. A terrifying thought. Then the video dissolved into a long-distance shot of her in the back of the parking lot at the hospice, stealing one of her post-observed-death smokes, thinking naïvely that she was indulging in her dangerous vice alone and unobserved.

Red Two's YouTube entry mimicked the others with its fast-filmed forest beginning. But hers faded into a shot taken through a car window in the parking lot of a big discount liquor store. It was a local store that Red Two knew all too well. The camera held that position for what seemed an interminable moment, until Red Two emerged through the wide glass doors of the store, arms filled with paper parcels jammed with liquor bottles. It tracked her to the point when she got into her car and drove unsteadily away down a familiar street.

Each minimovie had been taken at some time over the past months. The footage didn't necessarily match the bleak early wintertime that trapped the three Reds. In the videos, trees were blanketed with leaves. The clothing spoke of a warmer season.

Two of the videos lingered on the final image. Red One's froze on the wisps of cigarette smoke rising above her head. Red Three's ended with her disappearing into her dormitory, as if swallowed up by evening shadows. But Red Two's video had a gratuitous cruelty added to the end.

After her car had exited the liquor store parking lot, the image had dissolved into another picture, one that when she saw it for the first time caused Red Two to keen out loud with an unrecognizable sound of pain:

A grave site. A headstone. Two names followed by the same date. Beloved husband. Beloved child. Dead.

12

It took great strength for Jordan to concentrate during the afternoon basketball practice. Every cut she made, every screen she set, every shot she took felt as if it was somehow misshapen or distorted. When she clanked an easy layup, rolling it off the front rim on a wide-open shot, there was the usual hooting from her teammates and a quick reprimand from an assistant admonishing her, "*Take your time, Jordan, and finish!*" But she imagined—even though the stands were completely empty—that someone else was watching her and that even the momentary lapse of a missed shot in the midst of a practice scrimmage meant something far bigger.

She believed that she should display no outward flaw. None whatsoever. Not even a momentary failure. Any weakness might be the route that the Big Bad Wolf used to catch her. Somehow, she had to be perfect in all things, even when she knew she was far from it, in order to keep the Big Bad Wolf away. This might make no sense whatsoever, but it pressed on her shoulders like a weight. She wondered whether the Big Bad Wolf was preventing her from jumping for a rebound. Maybe he could hold her down when he wasn't even nearby, just by making her think he was.

Close, but not too close. Near, but not too near.

Jordan clenched her fists.

An idea came to her. She was running down the court, doing obligatory "suicides" at the end of the session: baseline to foul line and back, baseline to mid-court and back, baseline to far foul line and back, baseline to baseline and finish strong. Everyone hated the conditioning runs and everyone knew the value they held. Jordan typically finished first and prided herself on being able to make that extra effort. Her mind should have been cleared of everything except the pain and short-breath of exertion, but as she bent down to touch the far foul line, she realized that she had to find a way to contact the other two Reds, even if that just might be exactly what the Big Bad Wolf wanted. And she thought she knew how to do it.

She did not know if there was truth to the cliché *Strength in numbers*. She doubted it.

Jordan waited until late that evening before she opened up the YouTube video showing her walking to her dormitory. She had ignored most of her homework, spending hours staring at the computer's background screen—a picture of the Earth taken from space—letting the minutes flow toward midnight. She told herself that even the Big Bad Wolf *had* to sleep sometime, and besides, what did he have to worry about? She and the other two Reds were the sleepless ones. The wolf probably slept soundly each night.

In one corner of the screen that displayed her video, there was the *views* counter. It seemed stuck on 5—which indicated the number of times she had watched it. She kept her eyes on that number. "*Five five five,*" she repeated to herself.

With a deep breath and the sensation that she was stepping into something unknown, Jordan reached for the keyboard and started typing rapidly.

First, she did a quick search using the keyword *Red* and ordering them by date. A menu arrived on her computer screen, a series of frozen images and a YouTube address. There was a punk leather-and-tattoo rock group and what she guessed was a family vacation and an avant-garde and probably pretentious artist in front of a vibrant red painting that was of something but she couldn't tell what. But in the stack of potential answers to her search were two videos that showed nothing except a forest—like the beginning of hers.

The first opened in the trees, and then blended into a woman wearing a physician's long white lab coat smoking in a corner of some anonymous parking lot at some distance. The woman looked to be about her mother's age. Jordan waited until the video ended. It was short, as short as hers was. Then she clicked on the second and saw the same rush through the woods blurring into a younger woman coming out of a liquor store. This woman seemed to be distracted. She watched the woman get into her car. Jordan's fingers were hovering over the keyboard, about to stop the video, when she saw a new image pop up in the box screen. It was slightly out of focus, but she saw two names on a headstone.

She grabbed a pencil and paper and wrote down everything she could before the picture faded away. Then she replayed the video a second and a third time, to make sure she had all the information from the grave.

Two names. One date.

Then she went back and watched the white-jacketed woman a second time, trying to make out a street sign or a business, anything that might tell her something. But a white-coated woman smoking in a parking lot could be anyone and anywhere. She did not have to read the web address to know she was looking at Red One and Red Two.

The red hair told her that.

Her first instinct was to whisper to the screen, *"I'm here! I'm right here!"* She hesitated.

For the first time, she really understood: *I am not alone.*

Before, it had seemed abstract. Two other women? Where? Who? But now she could see them. And they could see her, if they tried.

She tried to control her thoughts. For a moment she imagined that everything in her life was whirling about out of her grasp but that this one thing was the only important thing, and if she couldn't do anything about everything else, she knew she had to be disciplined and smart about what she did in this single arena. *There is only one school, one family, one world,* she told herself. *The Big Bad Wolf and you and you and me. He will know what we are all doing. He's watching. You can count on that.*

She minimized the YouTube window and opened up Gmail. It took her a few minutes to create a new account with a new electronic address: *Red3@gmail.com*.

Then she returned to YouTube and posted the same message beneath each video:

It's Red Three. We must talk.

She posted a link to her video and hoped that Red One and Red Two would see what she had done and mimic her. She tried to send mental waves of thought out to the two other women: *The Big Bad Wolf will see this. Don't imagine for an instant that he hasn't tapped into these videos and isn't monitoring them every minute, expecting you to do what you've done.*

She tried to encourage herself but wondered whether she was opening up some door that she did not want to see inside. *A world of shadows*, she thought.

She did not have to wait long for an answer. The counter on her video suddenly clicked to 6.

She held her breath counting the seconds it would take for someone to watch her video.

Then her computer *pinged* with her "new mail" sound.

Karen Jayson watched.

She gasped as the shaky camera left the forest and focused on a distant figure. She whispered out loud, "But she's just a child!" as if there was something inherently unfair in the age of Red Three.

She told herself to be cautious, that it could all be a trap. But even as she warned herself, her fingers were flying across the keyboard, tapping out a message on the computer she used for her comedy. It wasn't as if she really imagined that switching computers afforded her any new security, but she was happy enough with the illusion that this side of her might still be secret from the Big Bad Wolf.

She followed suit. She created a new e-mail address. _Red1@gmail.com._

Then she wrote:

Who are you?
And who is Red 2?

13

The Big Bad Wolf dressed carefully—an old tweed jacket, blue button-down shirt, slightly frayed at the collar and cuffs. Wrinkled striped tie. Khaki pants that had faded and scuffed brown shoes.

He placed a slender brand-new high-tech digital voice recorder and a small notebook into an old green canvas shoulder bag, along with a collection of cheap pens and a paperback copy of his last book. The novel sported a serrated-edged, bloody knife on the silver and black cover, even though there was no character that used such a knife on any of its pages.

He paused, turning to the mirror just at the moment he slid his tie snug to his throat, and remembered a nasty complaint he'd made to his former publisher trying to point out this discrepancy. *"The damn cover artist didn't bother to read one fucking word I've written! He couldn't even pass a true/false quiz about what's in the book!"* Outrage and insult, expressed in a frantic, no-compromise voice. He'd been summarily ignored. Apparently redesigning the book jacket was an expense they weren't willing to accept. The memory gave him a sour taste and made his face redden, as if the affront weren't fifteen years old, but had just happened that morning. His new book, he thought, wouldn't get such short shrift.

He checked his appearance in his wife's full-length mirror, spinning around like a teenage girl on prom night. Then he topped it off with horn-rimmed eyeglasses that he perched on the end of his nose and an old tan trench coat that seemed to flop shapelessly around his body and flapped with every step he took. Through the bedroom window he could see it was a damp, raw day, and he considered an umbrella, but then realized that a few raindrops and some breeze mussing what remained of his thinning hair would probably make him look slightly disheveled, which was precisely the image he was working to establish.

He was a man of utter precision, but he would appear to any observer to be more than just a little disorganized and totally head-in-the-clouds harmless.

He made a mental note to add a new chapter to his current book called *On Blending In*.

When you're special, when you're truly unique, he told himself, *you need to hide it carefully*.

He gathered himself, checked his wristwatch, and imagined where each Red was at that moment. He could hear their voices. *Trembling. Scared.* He considered the sensation of their skin beneath his fingers. *Goose bumps.* He took his time picturing them, as if he could fill himself with something stolen from them.

He spoke out loud, imitating voices appropriate to reading a children's book aloud. He looked at Red One, Red Two, and Red Three.

High-pitched, sniveling: "Oh, what big eyes you have, Grandmother . . ."

Firm, deep, growling, and in control: "Yes. All the better to watch you with, dear. And you, dear. And you too, dear."

Then he laughed as if he'd just told them the funniest, most outrageous knee-slapping, back-pounding joke, turned, and made his way out of his house. It seemed to the Wolf that he could hear laughter echoing behind him. He walked quickly toward his car and the sounds faded away. He did not want to be late for his appointment.

Outside the police station, it was spitting light rain. Not enough to soak anyone, just enough to give the chill a damp, nasty feel. He hunched up his collar and hurried across the parking lot.

The station was a modern building, in sharp contrast to the stately brick Victorian designs that had housed the town's other departments for decades. His town—just shy of a size to be considered a city, but larger than a quaint village—was like many in New England, a mishmash of old blending with the new. There were tree-lined streets of singular antique beauty next to developments that screamed of undistinguished postwar hurry-up-and get-it-built squares and rectangles.

A pair of tall oak trees guarded the walkway leading up to the police station. They had just shed their leaves and looked like twin skeletons. Just beyond these there was a concrete set of stairs that led to a wide set of glass doors. He headed in that direction.

There was a gray-haired, potbellied uniformed officer behind a bullet-proof glass partition, which seemed to the Big Bad Wolf to be unnecessarily excessive. It was unlikely any desperado was going to break through with guns blazing. The police department itself was typical for a town that size. It had a three-member detective branch and a patrol segment. It had specialists in domestic violence and rape and a traffic squad that turned a significant profit for the town annually with the number of tickets it wrote for speeders. It even had a modest fraud office, which spent its time handling calls from elderly residents wondering if the e-mail they received from a Nigerian prince asking for money was legitimate. Like any modern, organized department, each element had its own cubicle, and there were helpful signs on the walls directing him through the warren of police work.

It did not take the Big Bad Wolf long to find Detective Moyer, sitting behind a cluttered desk and a computer screen filled with FBI lookout notices. Moyer was a large man who sported a jolly look that made him seem more suited to department store Santa Claus than major crimes detective. He shook hands with an enthusiasm that matched his bulk.

"Glad to meet yah," the detective boomed. "Man, this is an unusual request. I mean, most of the time when some citizen has some questions it's because they want their brother-in-law followed because they think he's dealing drugs or cheating on his wife or something. But you're an author, right? That's what the chief's public relations assistant told me."

"That's right," the Big Bad Wolf answered. He dug about in his satchel and produced the bloody-knife paperback. "Here," he said, with a grin. "Dramatic proof. And a gift."

The detective took it and stared at the jacket.

"Cool," he said. "I don't read many mysteries. Mostly sports books— you know, like about championship basketball teams or famous coaches or breaking the four-minute mile. But my sister's husband, he's like addicted to these things. I'll give it to him . . ."

"I'll sign it for him," the Big Bad Wolf said, producing a pen.

"He'll get a kick out of that," the detective replied.

The Big Bad Wolf finished with a flourish. Then he produced the small digital recorder. "You don't mind?" he asked.

"Nope," Detective Moyer answered, smiling.

The Big Bad Wolf smiled in return. "I really like getting my research right," he said. "You really don't want to make mistakes on the pages. Readers are sensitive to every word. They'll call you on an error faster than . . ."

He let his voice trail off. Detective Moyer nodded.

"Hey, it's the same for us. Get second-guessed all the damn time. Except for us, well, it's real. Not made up."

"That's my luxury," the Big Bad Wolf joked. Both men smiled, as if sharing a small secret.

The Big Bad Wolf pulled out his notebook and pen. These items were more like props. They allowed him to avoid eye contact when he wanted to. The digital tape recorder would capture every answer accurately.

"And sometimes it's really helpful to have both notes and exact words," he said.

"Sort of redundant systems," the detective said. "Like on an airplane."

"Exactly," the Big Bad Wolf replied.

"So what is it you want to know?" the detective asked.

"Well," the Big Bad Wolf said slowly, hesitantly, before beginning to probe. "In my new book, I have a character stalking a person from afar. He wants to get closer, but he doesn't want to do anything that will attract the police, you see. Wants it to be just one-on-one, if you get what I'm driving at. Got to have it all play out before the cops get involved."

The detective nodded. "Sounds tense."

"That's the point," the Big Bad Wolf answered. "Got to keep readers on the edge of their seats." He smiled and clicked on the recorder and bent to his notebook, as the detective rocked back and forth in his desk chair before starting to describe in friendly, substantial detail just exactly what the police were—and were not—capable of doing.

As a general rule, Mrs. Big Bad Wolf always took an entire hour for lunch away from her desk in the dean's office. When the weather was nice, she would make a quick salad or sandwich in the school's dining hall, then go outside and sit beneath the trees, where she could be by herself and idly watch students pass by. When the weather was poor, as it was this day, she would head inside with her meal to any of the small spots around the campus where she knew she would be left alone: an alcove in the art gallery, a bench outside the English department's offices.

This day, she hunkered down in an empty lecture room. Someone had written on a blackboard: *What does Marquez mean at the end?* Honors Spanish, she told herself, but she was just guessing the assignment had been *One Hundred Years of Solitude*. She tore through her light meal and then sat back in her chair and opened up a copy of her husband's last book, which was the novel with the serrated-knife jacket. She had already read the book at least four times, to the point where she could actually quote some passages verbatim. She had not let him know she could do this—it was a part of her love that she liked to keep to herself.

He also did not know that shortly after she'd learned about his complaint to his publisher about the jacket cover, she had sent the editor at that house a furious letter, underscoring the same problem. They had been married barely a year, but loyalty, she thought, was an integral part of love. She had harangued the editor that the jacket was misleading and inappropriate and told him that she would never buy another novel from that publisher again. Uncharacteristically, she had filled her letter with violent threats and rampaging obscenities. Carried away, she at least had the good sense to not sign her name.

The lecture room was hot. She closed her eyes for a moment. When she allowed herself to daydream, she often imagined herself in some sort of public setting—a restaurant or a movie theater or even a bookstore —where she would have the opportunity to loudly verbally assault the editor—all the editors—who hadn't seen her husband's genius. In her imagination, she was able to gather them together, alongside all the film producers, newspaper critics, and occasional Internet bloggers who had failed him or been snide and less than complimentary.

When she painted this inward portrait, the men—they were always small, sallow, balding men—reeled under her volley of criticism and humbly admitted their mistakes.

It gave her great satisfaction.

Every author's wife would have imagined the same scenario, she believed. It was her job.

Mrs. Big Bad Wolf opened her eyes and let them drop onto the open pages and creep over the words gathered in front of her. She placed her finger in the midst of a paragraph describing the very beginning of a car chase. *The bad guy gets away*, she reminded herself. *It's very exciting*. When she was a little girl she hadn't been popular in school, and so she had descended into the safety of books. Horse books. Dog books. *Little Women* and *Jane Eyre*. Even after she grew up, titles and characters remained her truest friends.

Every so often she wished she had been blessed with the right sort of eye and the command of language that would have turned her into a writer. She longed for creativity. In college she had taken writing courses, art courses, photography courses, acting classes, and even poetry courses—and been decidedly mediocre in all. That invention had always eluded her, saddened her. But she gave herself credit for coming up with the next best thing: life at the side of someone who *could* create magical things.

She stopped reading. She could feel a quivering inside of her. What she held in her hands was beautiful—but it was familiar. She left the book open on her lap and leaned back and closed her eyes a second time, as if in her darkness she might picture her husband's new story unfolding right before her. There would be a relentless killer, she knew, and a clever detective hunting him down. There would be a woman at risk. Probably a quite beautiful woman, although she hoped that after the expected large bust and long legs, he'd modeled the character after her. The book's pace would be steady, filled with unexpected and surprising twists and turns that, no matter how outlandish, would build toward a dramatic confrontation. She knew all the requisite elements of a modern police-thriller.

She kept her eyes closed, but reached out with her hands as if she could touch the words she knew were being created almost in front of her.

Mrs. Big Bad Wolf stroked nothing but empty air.

After a moment, she felt a little cold, as if the heat in the room had suddenly slid away. She sighed deeply and packed up her paperback and her lunch utensils and took a quick look at her watch. Her lunch hour was almost finished; it was time to return to work. There was a faculty meeting that afternoon, which her boss, the dean, would surely be attending. Maybe she could steal a few moments to read familiar passages when he was out of the office.

14

After dark, cool air settling over the campus, Jordan slipped into torn jeans, old running shoes, and a black parka, and found a threadbare navy watch cap which she pulled down over her hair as tightly as possible. She waited in her room until she heard some of the other girls in her dormitory gathering to head out to an evening lecture—the school was forever bringing in writers, artists, filmmakers, businessmen, and scientists to speak informally to the upper-class students. Jordan knew the other kids would gather in the vestibule of the converted house and then launch themselves out in a giggling, tight-knit group. Teenagers tended to travel in packs, she knew. Wolves did as well, except she doubted that the wolf that concerned her joined any group.

Lone wolf, she thought. The phrase made her shudder.

Jordan exited her room and hesitated at the top of the stairs until she heard four other girls, voices raised, laughing and teasing each other, barrel loudly through the front door.

Moving swiftly, taking the stairs two at a time, she sprinted out just behind them, trying to make it seem as if she were a part of that group without getting so close that they would turn and draw attention to her. She wanted to make it seem to anyone watching that she was hurrying to catch up with her friends.

She trailed a few feet distant, but as they turned left, heading toward the lecture halls, she abruptly ducked into the first deep shadow she could find, pinning herself against the side of an old redbrick classroom building, scrunching up against twisted knots of ivy branches that poked her in the back like an unruly child vying for attention.

Jordan waited.

She listened to the sounds of her classmates disappearing into the evening and waited for her eyes to adjust to the night. Hidden in shadow, she counted seconds off in her head: *one, two, three*. She did not know if she was being followed, but she assumed she was, even though the rational side of her told her loudly that this was completely impossible. No wolf, no matter how clever, how dedicated, or how obsessed, could spend all his time outside her dorm room just waiting for her to emerge and then trail after her.

She repeated this to herself insistently, but she was unsure whether she was reassuring herself or lying to herself. They seemed equal possibilities. *Yes he is. No he isn't.*

She wondered if she should be scared, and then realized that the mere act of wondering made her muscles tense up and her breathing grow shallow. It was cold, but she felt warm. It was dark, but she felt like she was beneath a spotlight. She was young, but she felt old and unsteady.

Jordan squirmed closer to the side of the building. She could still feel the Wolf's presence, almost as if he was jammed into the ivy branches beside her, hot breath on her neck. She half-expected to hear his voice whispering "*I'm right here*" in her ear and she exhaled sharply, the *whooshing* noise seeming as loud as a train whistle. She clamped down on her lips.

When silence—or *enough silence*, because she could still hear distant voices echoing across the quadrangles from other students, and a Winter-pills song she really liked playing inside a dormitory—surrounded her she stepped out of her shadow, and hunching her shoulders up against the chill, keeping her head lowered and her pace fast, she wove her way rapidly across campus, zigzagging erratically, avoiding every light, turning up one dark path, then cutting across the grass to another, backtracking before racing inside a dormitory, and then using a different door at the far end of the building to exit back into the night.

Finally, persuaded that no wolf could successfully follow her drunken trail, she sprinted out through a set of tall black wrought iron gates that marked the school's entrance. She quickly turned onto an ink-shadowed side street. She slowed slightly to a jog as she headed toward the center of the small town that encapsulated the school. She felt a little like she was acting in some Hollywood spy movie. It was cool enough so she could see her breath.

Antonio's Pizza was lit up. Bright lights and multicolored neon signs. There were a half-dozen schoolmates of hers gathered around the stainless steel counter in front of the oven, waiting for a slice or two. She watched two men wearing white smocks and aprons serving up the orders. They did this with a flourish, using large wooden paddles to shoot the pizzas into the oven and then remove them moments later.

From where Jordan lingered on the street, she could imagine happy voices and the sound of the cash register. The pizza joint was like that—a difficult place to be depressed or distracted. There would be a happy buzz inside, laughter and raised voices mingling with the enticing smells of roasted meat and spices and the welcoming blasts of heat that rolled from the ovens each time they were opened.

She waited, half-hungry in that way that teenagers are; she could easily have stuffed herself with hot pizza. Except every time she thought about the Wolf, her hunger fled, replaced with a gnawing sensation in her stomach. Fear versus food. An unfair fight.

A cold breeze rattled an awning above the sidewalk in front of an antique store that was shut down for the night. Jordan was about to glance at her watch when the spire that rose above the small town's offices chimed seven times.

She looked up and saw a small station wagon pull up in front of the pizza place. She hunched back, once again seeking a shadow to conceal herself in, and waited. *Right on time*, she thought. She didn't know whether this was good or bad.

The car put on its flashers. Yellow lights painted the sidewalk. She could see the driver leaning across the front seat, staring into the restaurant, searching hard.

That was where Jordan had said she would be.

But instead, she was just down the street, in a vantage spot between two buildings where she could see without being seen.

She waited, holding her breath.

Jordan watched the figure in the station wagon sit upright and undo the seat belt. Then the figure opened the car door, stepped out and stood close to the car, continuing to stare at the group of teenagers inside the restaurant.

It was dark and the bright neon lights from the few stores open threw odd rainbow colors across the street, reflecting off glistening black macadam. Yellow sodium vapor streetlights tossed sickly shades down on the cement. It was a confusion of color; blacks and reds and greens and whites all mingled together, making lies of realities: A green car looked blue. A scarlet parka seemed brown.

She could not tell with certainty that the person's hair was red. She bit down on her lip and decided that she had no choice but to chance it.

Jordan stepped from the shadow and walked quickly forward to the car. She saw the woman turn in surprise toward her. She had a sudden look of shock, as if Jordan were holding a knife. "Red One?" Jordan asked. She wanted her voice to be firm and confident, but she could hear a crack, like ice fracturing under too much weight on a frigid day.

The woman nodded. Her face seemed to relax.

"Hi. I'm Red Three."

"Jump in," Karen replied, gesturing toward the passenger side. She was trying to sound as if this were the most natural meeting in the world.

When Jordan hesitated, Karen said, "I'm not him. I promise." She watched the younger woman seem to assess the validity of her statement,

111

then cautiously slide into the car. Karen only had a few seconds to measure Jordan, especially the few strands of her red hair that escaped from beneath the tight-knit hat. *She's so young*, the older woman thought as she got behind the wheel of her car.

"I'm Jordan," Jordan said quietly.

"And I'm Karen," the older woman replied. Jordan nodded. "Where shall we go?" Karen asked.

"Anywhere," Jordan replied as she shrunk down in her seat, as if by lowering her profile she could avoid being seen. "Anywhere you think it's safe."

She paused, then said in a low voice, "No. Anywhere you are absolutely fucking *certain* it's safe."

Karen unwittingly mimicked Jordan's evasive path as soon as she put her car in gear. She accelerated hard one instant, turned down a side street, squealing her tires with the sudden turn, then backed into an alleyway and made a U-turn. A mile outside the town there was a modest strip mall, where Karen turned in to a McDonald's and drove through the take-out window before exiting in yet a different direction. She steered the car onto the interstate highway, drove fast for a few miles, then pulled into a scenic rest area and waited, her eyes constantly scanning the rearview mirror to make sure no one was following them. Finally, when she had seen nothing but darkness for a few minutes, she once again drove fast, heading toward a spot she knew that fit Red Three's standard of being safe and *fucking certain*.

Jordan said nothing during the trip. Not even when she was thrown sideways and jerked forward as Karen pushed the car wildly around a corner. Karen imagined that the teenager was probably accustomed to wild, aimless rides.

"This is getting to be my regular driving style," Karen said briskly. She half-hoped that a little light talk might help them to connect. But her passenger remained quiet, as if lost in thought. Karen glanced from time to time at the younger woman. She thought Red Three preternaturally calm.

The hospital complex was lit up with security lights, especially near the emergency room access. There was a small white kiosk with a bored rent-a-cop guarding the doctors' parking lot. Karen pulled in there, giving the sullen security guard her name and a five number code, which he checked on his computer before waving her in wordlessly.

Karen found a spot near the back, hidden from view.

"Let's go inside," Karen said. "Follow me."

Again without speaking, Jordan complied.

The two women marched across the parking area. They passed from shadows into the cones of wan light dropped from above by high-intensity lamps. The light made their skin seem sallow, sickly. Each thought the same thing: that even if they had been followed at the start, their precautions had to have done enough to lose any wolf on their trail.

Neither of the two really believed this.

Shoulder to shoulder, they hurried out of the night into the hospital. There was a triage nurse at a desk in a brightly lit waiting room outside the emergency room. She looked up at the two of them with a world-weary look. There was a water fountain in a corner, and two state policemen in gray-blue outfits and three navy-blue jumpsuited EMTs were sharing a joke nearby. There was a burst of laughter from the three men and two women. Jordan glanced at the people waiting on uncomfortable molded plastic chairs. An old man buried under winter coats. A young Hispanic couple with a child in a pink parka seated between them, and a baby in the woman's arms. A pair of college-aged boys, one of whom looked both sick and drunk and was, somehow, sitting unsteadily.

No Wolf, she thought, *waiting for us.*

Karen dug around in her large, oversized leather purse, found an ID card, and waved it toward the triage nurse, who in turn hit a buzzer entrance. Karen gestured as the automatic doors swung open. Inside the emergency-room treatment suites, she waited for the doors to slam shut with an electronic locking *thud.*

With Jordan in tow, she passed the curtained exam rooms, pausing only to wave at a physician she seemed to know, before exiting through another set of doors and then traveling down a long sterile corridor that opened up into a cafeteria.

"Do you want something to eat?" She asked. "Or coffee?"

"Just coffee," Jordan replied. "Cream and sugar."

She sat at a corner table away from white-jacketed or green-surgical-gowned groups of interns and residents as Karen went to the counter and fashioned two steaming cups of coffee. Jordan nodded to herself and thought, *This is a good place. If the Wolf came in he'd stand out unless he was in scrubs.* She half-smiled when Karen returned to their table.

The young woman and the older woman sat across from each other, sipping the coffee, not saying anything for a few moments. It was Jordan who broke the silence.

'So," she said, "I gather you're a doctor."

"Internal medicine."

Jordan shook her head. "I was hoping you were a shrink."

"Why?" Karen asked.

"Because then maybe you'd know something about abnormal psychology, and that might help us," Jordan answered. "I'm just a student," she continued. "And not a real good one lately, either."

Karen nodded, and then said, "But we're both something else, now. Or, at least, it sure seems that way."

"Yeah," the teenager responded with a sudden burst of bitterness. "Now we're targets. It's like we've got bull's-eyes painted on our backs. Or maybe we're just soon-to-be-dead victims. Or some combination of the two."

Karen shook her head. "We don't know that. We can't . . ." Her voice trailed off. She looked up into the harsh ceiling lights of the cafeteria, trying to think of something reassuring to say. And then she gave up. She took a deep breath. "What do we know?" she asked.

Jordan paused before answering. "Not too fucking much."

The obscenity rolled freely off her tongue. Ordinarily she would never have used that sort of language with an older person. It gave her a sense of freedom to be so rude with Karen.

"No," Karen corrected her softly, "we know a few things. Like there are three of us. And one of him—"

"We don't know that," Jordan interrupted instantly. She had a queasy feeling in her stomach, because her next thought—the one she was about to speak out loud—had just struck her. *Lone wolf? How do we know?* "We only know that it feels like there's just the one guy out there hunting all three of us. That's because in the fairy tale there's just the one Big Bad Wolf. But we don't know for certain that there aren't two or three guys out there, like a little club. Maybe they're like the Knights of Columbus or some fantasy football team, except they're all about killing. And maybe they're lounging around some nice rec room in somebody's basement drinking beers and eating pretzels, giggling and guffawing and thinking this is just the damn funniest thing ever, before they get their acts together and come kill us."

Karen hadn't considered this. She felt cold, almost iced over inside. The two messages from the Wolf just automatically led her to certain assumptions. She looked up at Jordan. It took a child to make her understand that nothing was clear.

Karen gripped her coffee tightly to hold the cup steady. "You're right," she said slowly. "We can't assume anything."

The two women watched each other, letting a small silence fit into the table space between them. After a moment, Jordan shook her head and smiled weakly. "No," she replied. "I think we have to. I think we've got to make some decisions. Otherwise, we're just walking alone through the forest, just like he told us we were."

"Okay," Karen said, slowly elongating each syllable. "What do you think . . ."

"I think we need Red Two," Jordan said briskly. "That's the first thing. We have to find Red Two."

"That makes sense."

"Unless, of course, Red Two is the Wolf," Jordan said.

Karen's head spun. This thought seemed impossible, but at the same time eerily accurate. There was no way of telling.

She saw the teenager shrug. "We shouldn't guess. Find her and then the three of us can start to plan."

Karen nodded, although she was surprised. She had thought that it would be her leading the teenager, not the other way around, even though she had no real idea where to lead anyone, given their situation.

"Okay, how . . ."

"I can find her," Jordan said. "I'll do it."

Karen breathed out slowly. *Leave it to the teenager,* she thought. *If there's anything a teenager knows, it's computers.* She reached down and brought up her purse from the floor. "Here," she said. She opened it up and removed three disposable cell phones. "I bought these this morning: One for you, and one for Red Two when we find her, and one for me. This way, at least, we can communicate privately."

Jordan smiled. "That's smart." She took the phones and immediately started to program them with all three numbers.

"I'm not a *complete* idiot," Karen said, although she felt a little like one. "I'll try to figure out some safe places, like this"—she gestured around the cafeteria—"where we can all meet if we need to."

"Okay. That's a good idea, too."

"Yes," Karen said, "But that's pretty much the end of my good ideas."

"Well." Jordan shook her head. "I've been thinking. And I think it's pretty simple."

"Simple?"

"Yes. We have to find him before he finds us."

"And what do we do . . ." Karen said slowly. The teenager in front of her seemed both intimately familiar and a total stranger simultaneously.

"You know what we do then," Jordan said.

"No, I don't," Karen replied. But she did, even before Jordan filled in the silence.

"We kill him first," Jordan said matter-of-factly, just like she was slapping away a stray mosquito that had landed on her arm. The teenager leaned back in her seat. She was a little astonished at what she'd said. She did not know precisely where the idea had come from, but she thought it must have been hiding behind all her fears, just waiting for the brightly lit, oppressively clean place she was seated in to emerge. But just as quickly, she was pleased. For the first time in days, maybe even months, she thought, she *liked* the direction she was suddenly going in. Cold-blooded and determined. She could feel her pulse quicken. It was a little like jumping up toward the basket and releasing the ball and realizing that her fingertips had scraped the bottom of the rim. *Boys*, she thought, *dream of high-flying slam dunks, so they can pound their chest with look-what-I-did bravado. I'm more modest. I just want to be able to reach the goal and touch it.*

15

Red Two stared from the questionable safety of her house at the car parked across the street. She had first noticed it perhaps fifteen minutes earlier, as she had staggered aimlessly about her living room, pistol in one hand, some pills in the other, unsure which to use first. Ordinarily she would have paid no attention to a nondescript car pulled to the side of the road just beyond the reach of a streetlamp's glow. Someone in search of an address. Someone stopped to make a cell phone call. Someone momentarily lost, seeking their bearings. This last possibility made Sarah think, *Maybe someone like me.*

But Sarah Locksley suspected that nothing was ordinary in her life any longer, and despite the gray-black gloom of rapidly falling night, she could just make out the shape of a person seated in the car. Man? Woman? The shape was indistinct. For a moment or two she watched through her window, waiting for whoever this was to exit the car and walk up to one of her neighbors' front doors. A light would go on, a door would swing open, there would be voices raised in greeting and maybe a handshake or a hug.

That would have been my life not so long ago. No more.

She continued to wait, counting seconds as her mind blanked to everything except the steady accumulation of numbers.

The expected scenario didn't materialize. And when she reached 60 with the figure remaining obscured inside the vehicle, her pulse quickened. Like a picture slowly coming into focus, some sort of off-kilter algorithm coalesced in her mind: *I'm alone waiting for a killer. It's almost dark. There's a car parked across the street. Someone's inside, watching me. They're not just visiting the neighbors. They're here for me.* She slammed herself to the side as the formula took shape within her, dodging out of the sight of the person she suddenly absolutely 100 percent knew was staring back at her with murderous intent. Sarah hugged against the wall, breathing hard, then crept sideways to where she could just tug a small amount of worn chintz curtain away, and peered out at the vehicle.

Evening sliced away her ability to see clearly. Shadows slipped like razor blades across her sight line. She ducked backward, as if she could hide. She had an impossible thought: *He can see me, but I can't see him.*

Sarah twitched. She quivered. She thought *This is it* and thumbed back the hammer on her weapon. It *clicked* into position with an evil sound.

A hidden part of her—*the reasonable part*—understood that this couldn't be the way a killer would work. He would be cautious, prepared, and precise. The first moment she would be aware he was beside her would be her last. The Wolf wouldn't simply park out in front of her house and then after a suitable wait, giving her enough time to get fully ready, march up to her front door and announce, *Hi! I'm the Big Bad Wolf and I'm here to kill you.*

But logic seemed slippery and elusive, and it took tense muscles and a sweaty grip to grab any away from her imagination.

Wait, she abruptly insisted to herself, *that's exactly what he does in the fairy tale. He comes right up close to Little Red Riding Hood and she can only recognize that his eyes, his ears, his nose, and finally his teeth aren't quite right.*

She craned her head forward once again and stole another glance at the car.

It was empty.

She shrank back again, trying to imagine how she could make herself seem small, feeling the wall closing in on her almost like it was pushing her into the light. A panicky voice within her—she knew it was the drugs and the booze and the despair—screamed at her, *Run! Run now!* And she looked around wildly for an exit, although she knew there was none. For a single instant she had a vision:

Sarah flings open the back door.

Sarah dashes across the lawn in back, vaults the old wooden fence.

Sarah flees down the space between houses. Dogs bark. Neighbors hear her urgent footsteps and cry out in alarm. The police are summoned. They arrive, sirens blaring, just in the nick of time.

Sarah is saved!

She sucked in air and held her breath. The vision faded. She knew: *There is no escape. Not out the back. Not out the front. I can't fly away through the ceiling. I can't bury myself in the basement. I can't become invisible.* Her mouth was dry and she had trouble making her eyes focus, as if they both had suddenly decided to betray her. The hand with the pills dropped them all to the floor, where they rattled and bounced away from her. The hand holding the gun seemed to be dragging her down, as if the weight of her husband's pistol had suddenly increased tenfold. As fears and doubts sparked through her body like so many explosions, she was unsure whether she would be able to lift the weapon and whether she would be able to summon the strength to pull the trigger when the time arrived and she faced the Wolf.

And then, just as abruptly, she saw the weapon raised up in front of her, gripped in both hands, and she realized she had bent into a shooter's crouch.

For a moment Sarah wondered whether it was some other person steering the weapon. It was as if she was only peripherally connected to the gun. She wondered when she had last taken a breath. Her lungs demanded air and she gasped out like a swimmer breaking the surface.

Bizarre, contradictory thoughts like *I'm ready for anything* or *I'm dying now* raced through her.

She wanted to speak out loud, say something strong and brave, but when she tried the words "C'mon, damn it, I'm waiting," they croaked and shattered and were only barely comprehensible.

The doorbell rang.

It was a cheery chime, three notes that made absolutely no sense to her. *A killer rings the doorbell?*

She found herself half-hopping, moving almost crablike as she crossed the living room, gun still raised. She paused in front of her door.

The bell rang again.

Why wouldn't *he ring the bell? Or knock on the door? Or just call out her name to announce he was there? Hello-o-o, Sarah! It's the Big Bad Wolf. I'm here to kill you . . .*

She suddenly had no idea what a wolf would do. Nothing happening made any sense to her. It was all Alice in Wonderland: Up was down, front was back, high was low.

She could feel her finger tightening on the trigger. It occurred to her to simply fire. *The bullet will go straight through the wood and kill him where he stands.* It seemed like a good idea. A really good idea. Almost sensible.

A part of her stifled a laugh from bursting out. *What a joke*, she thought. *What a great slap-your-knees and wet-your-pants joke. I'll just shoot him right through the door.*

She aimed the pistol, leveling it right at the spot where she imagined the Wolf's chest would be. It was like doing measurements in her head: *Is he tall? Short? Don't want to miss.*

The gun quivered, yawing back and forth like a small ship being slammed by storm waves. She saw her left hand reach out and seize the doorknob, defeating what seemed like an eminently fine plan and replacing it with something completely foolish. She imagined that she was opening the door to death.

With a single, mighty lurch, she flung the door wide. In the same motion, she released the knob and reached back with her left hand and steadied the pistol. She was bent slightly, leaning forward and ready to fire.

Silence stopped her finger on the trigger.

Two women stared across the threshold at her. Their faces seemed shocked beneath the wan porch light. Someone inhaled sharply, but Sarah was unsure whether it was one of the two women or herself.

The two of them seemed frozen. Looking into the gaping barrel of a pistol with the hammer cocked has a way of discouraging most ordinary conversation.

They can't be the Wolf, Sarah thought. *Two Wolves?* But her finger caressed the trigger. Somewhere deep in her understanding, she knew that the slightest pressure would fire the weapon.

After a heartbeat in which Sarah fully expected to hear the thunderous roar of the gun as she killed whoever it was standing in front of her, she watched completely dumbstruck as one of the women slowly pulled a woolen knit navy watch cap from her head and carefully shook free great waving locks of strawberry-red hair, never taking her eyes off Sarah and her gun.

Then, as if following suit in a card game, the other woman—older, face lined with concerns—lifted her hands and unpinned her hair, which fell like a dull sheet of fading embers to her shoulders.

"Hello, Red Two," the older woman said. "Please don't kill us."

Sarah was ashamed of the way the house looked.

For the first time in days, she was aware of the trash and debris—the empty liquor bottles and prepared-food containers, candy bar wrappings, and potato chip bags that were littered around the space. She was also embarrassed by the *Home Alone* defense system spread beneath windows and across doorways. She wanted to apologize to the two women and explain that this really wasn't like her, except that it would have been a lie and she thought it would be unwise to start her dealings with Red One and Red Three with such an obvious falsehood. So she kept her mouth shut and watched the reactions of the two others as they surveyed the landscape of despair.

It was Red Three who spoke first.

"I'm Jordan," she said. "Do you have a picture of your husband and your daughter? The ones who died?"

Sarah was taken aback by the question. It seemed incredibly intimate, as if she were being asked to remove her clothes and stand naked.

She stammered her reply. "Of course, but . . ."

And then her words faded away. She went to a bookcase in the corner and brought out a framed picture of the three of them, taken shortly before the accident. Wordlessly, she handed it to Jordan, who looked at it carefully and then passed it over to Karen. She, too, examined the photo carefully.

There was a small silence. Sarah thought that usually someone examining a photograph like the one of herself, her child, and her husband taken on a summer day at the beach would say, *Isn't that cute* or *They're sure beautiful.* But she realized those responses were meant for the living. She was suddenly not exactly angry, but upset, or uncomfortable, and she reached out for the picture.

"What are you looking for?" Sarah asked.

"A reason," Karen replied.

It took Sarah a few seconds to understand that Red One wasn't searching for the reason why Red Two's husband and daughter had been killed. She didn't want to hear about a runaway fuel oil truck and the capriciousness of fate.

"Or maybe an explanation," Jordan said. She wasn't talking about the accident, either.

"How did you find me?" Sarah started.

Karen looked over at Jordan, who shrugged. "Your video on YouTube. It ended with a picture of a headstone. I fired up the computer and then worked backward from those names.

"It didn't take me that long," Jordan continued. "The local paper had a story about the memorial service at the fire station. They had a color picture. You were there. With this . . ."

Jordan pointed at Sarah's red hair. She remembered how bright Red Two's hair had looked spread across mourning black.

Sarah thought she should say something, but fell into silence. After an uncomfortable moment, Karen spoke up. "We shouldn't stay here," she said. "We need to go to a safe place to talk." Sarah seemed about to say something, so Karen spoke quickly, stopping her before she spoke. "Look, when Jordan and I first met yesterday, one thing we realized is that if and when the three of us are together, it increases our vulnerability. All of us being in the same spot, at the same time, makes us all into a much simpler target."

"It's kinda like us getting together is what he really wants and he throws a hand grenade at us," Jordan said. "*Boom!* Red One, Red Two, and Red Three all disappear at once." Cynicism mingled freely with anxiety in her voice. Karen didn't bother to expand on the hand grenade concept, although a part of her thought, *It makes as much sense as anything. Because none of it makes sense. Or all of it does.*

"But we've still got to talk, to figure out what we're going to do . . ."

"I know what we're going to do," Jordan muttered beneath her breath. Karen didn't turn toward the youngest of the trio. Instead she kept her eyes fixed on Sarah. "So, we need to go someplace where we know we can plan without being watched." Her eyes flicked over to the large living room window. "We don't know," she said, "we can't be sure he's not right out there . . ." Her voice trailed off.

Sarah felt dizzy. She thought there were a hundred things she needed to say, but all of them escaped her tongue. What she managed was, "Let me get my coat."

"Hey," Jordan said briskly. "Bring the gun."

16

There are three stages to a killing, the Wolf wrote when he finally got back to his office after his lengthy interview with the police detective and was able to lock the door and revel for a moment in quiet concentration.

Planning. Execution. Aftermath.

 Neglect any of these three phases, and failure is inevitable. The key is demanding more of oneself. It's crucial to recognize that at the conclusion of the second stage, as profoundly emotional and satisfying as that might be, and as much as one has built to that moment, there are still critical steps that need to be taken. Simply put, it's not over. It's just begun. I believe it's a little like the soldier coming home from the war trying to negotiate a fast-food restaurant after months spent in deprivation and fear, or perhaps the astronaut returning from a lengthy stay in space confronting the motor vehicles registry. There is decompression necessary before returning to ordinary life, a stepping-back time, where the killer needs to slide out from beneath the excitement and passion of the hunt and the murder and let it flow into sweetened memory. Creating the emotional context for enjoyment requires as much careful plotting as does the actual killing. It's where the clumsy amateurs and the unprepared wannabes fail. After they accomplish the death they've invented, they then don't know how to savor that moment. And it's important to be aware that not anticipating the needs of this final stage engenders frustration and dismay—and leads to mistakes in the first two stages. There is great danger in not fully preparing for post-death enjoyment.

When you've accomplished something special, it takes great nerve and focus and strength of character to allow yourself to become outwardly ordinary once again even when you know that the persona others see is a complete lie.

As always the words came in a rush to the Wolf. His fingers seemed to dance above the computer keyboard, his concentration entirely on the entry that was taking shape in front of him. He felt a kind of ease, as if he were an athlete settling into the routine of a workout, where the miles he stamped beneath his feet or the water that flowed underneath him with every overhand stroke were like so many familiar pushes from behind. He paused briefly to steal a thought about each Red and believed that he was fast approaching the time when he would have to begin the hands-on process of each specific death. *Red One is special because she has faced death so frequently with consummate professionalism, but now she must confront a death that has no diagnosis. Red Two is unique because she's so eager to die, and now is confronted by her very secret wishes coming true, just not how she expected them to. And Red Three is exceptional because she has done so much to toss her future away, and now must face someone else stealing from her what little remains of that future.* He shook his head and grunted out loud. Appetizer. Main course. Dessert. Each stage of murder had its own tastes.

He wrote down: *I want to let each phase run its course.* The Wolf was acutely aware that as in any relationship, a murder needed to be fulfilling at every level. Like machine-gun bullets, words leapt at him: *Threat. Fear. Process. The moment. The follow-up. Memory.* Any slippage at any point would detract from the overall experience.

He hesitated again, this time letting his eyes scan his latest entry on the computer screen. *What makes a book really work?* he wrote at last. *It must take risks. It must suck the reader inside the story. Every character has to be fascinating in his or her own special way. It must make it a paramount necessity for readers to turn each page. This is equally true for a novel of manners or a science fiction thriller. The same rules of murder apply to writing. What good is telling a story that doesn't resonate long after the final page has been read? Doesn't the killer face the same question? Both writer and killer are engaged in creating something that will last. The writer wants the reader to remember his words long after the final page. The killer wants the impact of the death to linger. And not just for him, but for all the others the death has touched.*

Murder isn't about a single killing. It's about a ripple through the lives of many.

He drummed his fingers against the wooden desktop, as if this rapid tapping would accelerate his thoughts into new words that he could write down. For a moment he envied artists who simply drew a line on a blank white canvas and let that small motion define everything that was to follow. *Painting, that's easy,* he thought. He understood that the similarity between a killer and an artist was that both already had firmly in their mind a finished portrait of what would emerge when they drew their first stroke. This notion made him grin.

Then he wrote at the top of a new page: *Why I Love Each Red.*

The Wolf sighed. He told himself, *It is not enough to tell readers how you expect to accomplish their deaths. You need to explain why. In the fairy tale, it's not just a fine meal that the wolf wants as he stalks Little Red Riding Hood through the woods. He could sate that hunger at any point. No, his real starvation is far different and it has to be addressed with intensity. The wolf wants to eat. But he also wants a relationship.*

Again, the Wolf hesitated. It was dark outside, the afternoon having given way to night, and he expected Mrs. Big Bad Wolf to arrive home shortly, the way she did every day, just a few minutes before 6 p.m., letting out a cheery "I'm home, dear . . ." as she passed through the front door. The Wolf never immediately responded. He allowed her a few moments to observe his overcoat hanging on its customary hook, his umbrella in the stand in the vestibule, and his shoes thoughtfully removed by the living room entrance, replaced by slide-on leather slippers. Her pair, which matched his, would be waiting for her. Then she would tiptoe past his closed office door—even if she had grocery bags in her arms and could use a little assistance. He knew she would immediately go to the kitchen to fix their dinner. Mrs. Big Bad Wolf felt that making certain he was overstuffed was a key element to fueling the writing process. He didn't disagree with this.

So, as soon as he heard pots and pans clatter in the kitchen as the meal began to get under way, he would call out an answer, as if he hadn't heard her entry. "Hiya, honey! I'll be out in a sec!"

He knew his wife enjoyed the bellow from behind the office door, so he shouted out his greeting regardless of his mood or the moment happening on the page in front of him. He could be writing about something as mundane as the weather or something as electric as how he intended to kill. It made no difference. He still raised his voice so she could hear him. They played the same lively tunes daily:

"*How was your day?*"

"*What's going on at school?*"

"*Were you able to work hard?*"

"*Did you get around to paying the electric bill?*"

"*There are some odd jobs around the yard we need to get to.*"

"*Would you like to have Chinese for dinner tomorrow?*"

"*Shall we watch a movie on the TV tonight, or are you too tired?*"

"*Maybe we should take a cruise this year. There are some great sales on Caribbean trips. We haven't had a real vacation in months. What do you think; shall we make a reservation and start saving our money?*"

The Wolf heard a distant rattle. It had to be the front door. He waited, and then he heard the expected greeting. This signaled him to start the electronic process of closing up everything he was working on and encrypting it. All this was actually unnecessary. The wall of photographs was incriminating enough—a factoid he knew from his discussion with the detective. "Killers—the type who like to plan, not the thug robbing a convenience store or doing in some competitor in the drug business with a whole lot of automatic weapons fire—like to keep souvenirs," the policeman had told him in a smug, self-satisfied tone of voice. *As if he really knew what he was talking about*, the Wolf said to himself. The cop had been very helpful, and had answered all his questions, although sometimes the policeman had sounded like a teacher trying to explain things to a distracted elementary school class.

But securing the files made the Wolf feel his privacy remained intact when he shut down his computer. It was a little like turning off a machine but switching on his imagination, because each Red would glow in his thoughts right through the remainder of the humdrum evening that awaited him.

If you are a plumber, make sure you wear your utility belt and carry your tools. If you are a salesman, make sure you maintain that glib, quick, handshaking demeanor at all times. And if you are a writer, make sure you ask questions like you're looking for information to put on a page.

"I'll be out in a sec!" he called, just as he did every night and precisely as he knew she expected him to. "Just finishing up in here!"

Meat loaf, he thought. *That would be great tonight. With gravy and mashed potatoes.*

And then, if his wife wasn't too tired, after they'd finished clearing the table and doing the dishes, a movie. They rarely went out to the cinema anymore, preferring to hunker down in front of their wide-screen television. The Wolf was very sensitive to the fact that Mrs. Big Bad Wolf worked hard at a job critically important for their lives—it paid the creditors and allowed him to be who he was—and with her past heart problems, even with the recent clean bill of health, he didn't like to create stress in the household. He rewarded her with loyalty, which helped provide a nice quiet, private life for the two of them.

It was the least he could do. If he thought she needed something special, he would surprise her with the occasional night out to a nice restaurant or front-row tickets to a local acting company's rendition of *Macbeth*. These outings helped cover up the inevitable disappointment he could see in her eyes when from time to time he announced he had to go out alone "on research."

This night he thought he'd check the on-demand television listings and attempt to find something funny and romantic that wasn't too modern. He didn't like the latest crop of films, which substituted gross-out for slapstick. He preferred classics. The Marx Brothers and Jack Lemmon and Walter Matthau, right up through Steve Martin and Elaine May. He knew about Judd Apatow, but couldn't really understand what the kids saw in his brand of cinematic comedy. He and his wife would agree on one of the old-time channels, and he would sit in his reclining chair, and she would plop down in the adjacent love seat. She would fix them each a bowl of vanilla ice cream with some chocolate sprinkles on top right before the movie started.

They would laugh together and then head up to bed.

To sleep.

He suspected that he actually did love his wife. He still enjoyed making love to her from time to time—although in recent months he'd pictured one of the three Reds beneath him as he covered his wife. He didn't think she had ever noticed this distraction. *Perhaps*, he thought, *it makes me more intense.* But he was also aware that since her illness, the moments of coupling had diminished. Frequency was down to maybe once or twice a month, if that.

His desire was still intact, however. And he took some pride in the fact that even as he was closing in on getting truly old, he didn't need the little blue pill to help him perform. But the idea that he might look for sex outside of his marriage had never occurred to the Wolf.

He strayed—but only in his imagination.

The Wolf looked at the computer screen and the page in front of him with his new chapter heading. He read it out loud, but quietly: "Why I Love Each Red."

Then, still speaking softly, he answered the question.

"Because of what they give me."

True passion, he thought. He needed to capture that intensity on the pages of his book.

He imagined that stalking them and planning their deaths was a little like having an affair. He didn't think of it as cheating, however.

Certainly, they were like lovers waiting patiently for him. But, each in her own way, they were also like faithful wives.

17

The three Reds drove in Karen's car to the largest local enclosed mall, where she dropped Jordan at the east entrance by Sears, then drove around and delivered Sarah to the west entrance near Best Buy. After waiting a few minutes, Karen steered her way to the top floor of the parking garage adjacent to the mall. She turned her car around so that she could see if any car had followed her up. She shut off the engine and switched off the headlights and waited exactly seventeen minutes. The advantage of this parking garage was that it had separate ramps for heading up and heading down. At the seventeenth minute, she fired up the engine and raced down the circular drive, tires squealing against the pavement. She accelerated across the expanses of vacant parking to the mall's north exit. "Follow that," she muttered to herself. *I don't care how damn clever you imagine yourself to be, Mister Wolf.*

As before, when she had first met with Red Three, she had a distinct sensation that it was important to not allow herself to be followed, although she was unsure precisely *why*. A part of her felt completely ridiculous. She had adopted evasive steps when she returned home in the evening and when she went to work in the morning. She had driven like a crazy person when she had picked up Red Three. Now she was repeating the same erratic formula—and she was pretty certain that the other two Reds were doing the same thing—and she could not answer the essential question: *Why are you doing this?*

She answered herself: *So he doesn't kill you in a parking garage.*

Then she hesitated, gasping out loud as if there were no air in the car, realizing, *Anything is possible. You don't know how he's going to kill you.*

The physician within her recognized paranoia. *Except there's nothing made up about this. No delusions. It's real.* She tried to think back to her brief rotation as a medical student in a psychiatric wing of a large state hospital, but whatever lessons she had learned in those weeks had dissipated through years of internal medicine. *All my—no, all our—behavior is being defined by fear.*

She closed her eyes tightly.

Put a name to it, she told herself. This was impossible. She tried to think: *Fear of heights. That was acrophobia. Fear of spiders? That was arachnophobia. Fear of dying?*

Thanatophobia.

What she felt seemed like a combination of those and every other fear she could draw from her heart.

Put a name to it, she repeated to herself.

Easier said than done.

Karen tried to clear her mind of various deadly images that began to intrude wildly on her imagination, and tried to concentrate on watching for the other Reds. *Guns. Knives. Poisons. Choking.* All she could see were dozens of murders, all spread out like a bloody buffet before her, and as if caught in a nightmare, she was being forced to choose one.

She wiped her hand across her face. She could feel sweat beneath her arms. Her breath was short and raspy. She looked around. There was no obvious reason to be on the verge of panic. There was no lurking figure in a shadow staring at her. There was no man racing toward her brandishing a weapon. There was no set of auto headlights burrowing into her from behind.

But all these things were there, even if they weren't there.

Her eyes swept around the empty spaces of the shopping mall. "Come on," she whispered out loud, speaking to the other two Reds. "I want to get the hell out of here."

Within seconds of her arrival, Red Two and Red Three emerged through the wide mall doors, walking swiftly toward her. They had each traveled haphazard routes through the shops, hurrying down aisles, ducking in and out of toilets, backtracking, riding escalators up and then down, crossing paths twice before joining up and exiting. Trailing them would have been difficult, even with the smaller-than-usual crowds of people inside the cavernous building.

"Think that will work?" Sarah asked breathlessly as she launched herself into the car.

"Sure," Jordan replied confidently from the backseat.

The others both nodded, although Red One and Red Two secretly thought, *I don't know about that.*

Karen saw that Jordan wore a small grin, and the doctor within her wondered whether the teenager was enjoying the situation. Then she saw Red Three turn in her seat and peer out the back window, as if checking once again to make certain they weren't being followed. *Nervous energy*, she thought. *No, it's fear. It's just a little different for each of us.*

It was Red Two who asked next: "Where are we going now?"

Karen smiled wryly, although she knew there was little to smile about. "Yesterday, Jordan told me to come up with *absolutely fucking safe* places where we can talk. I know a good one."

The Moan and Dove was an old-fashioned, college-town, dark-wood, shadowy bar that featured single malt whiskeys and more than seventy varieties of beer, served from a polished long wooden counter that ended abruptly before giving way to a space for a small stage with a tattered black curtain as a backdrop. There was room inside for two dozen small tables. On most nights it was crowded with university students, loud and overly boisterous. But Tuesdays it featured local folk singers—Joni Mitchell and Bob Dylan wannabes—and occasionally it scheduled Saturday night open-mike comedy shows. This was how Karen had come to know it.

But on Thursday evenings, which this was, it catered to the local gay women's groups by having a "Ladies Only" night. So, when the three Reds came through the front door, they were greeted by a loud and packed bar with not a single man in sight. Even the bartenders—usually weight lifters with the muscles to handle unruly college students—were women: thin, young, nose-pierced, purple-haired punk-rock-type women, all of whom seemed to be aping Lisbeth Salander from the books and movies. The crowd ranged from tough-looking types wearing tight black jeans and leather jackets and knocking back shots to flower-children types who favored sweet mixed drinks with the occasional decorative paper umbrella and spoke in high-pitched enthusiastic bursts.

Red Two and Red Three joined Karen in the doorway, taking it all in. Karen grinned a bit, and said, "I'd like to see the Wolf come walking into this crowd. I don't think he'd last long."

Sarah laughed out loud. It seemed crazily ironic, which seemed to capture the flavor of her existence. *That would be great*, she thought. *The Wolf walks into a gay women's bar and all I have to do is stand up and point him out saying "Here's a man who kills women!" and like modern-day maenads, these ladies will immediately rip him to shreds and we can happily go on with what little remains of our lives.*

Jordan seemed a little distracted. "I'm underage," she whispered to Karen. "If my school finds out I was here, I'll get kicked out."

"So, we'll make sure they don't find out," Karen replied. Jordan nodded, then looked around and grinned. "You know, the field hockey coach might be here . . ." and then she stopped, shrugged, and said, "Maybe we could just sit in the corner."

They found an empty table near the stage, which had the added advantage of being positioned so they could keep an eye on the front door, although none of the three Reds thought that *any* wolf would be brave or stupid enough to follow them inside. A tattooed waitress in a tight black T-shirt came to take their order, looked askance at Jordan, and seemed about to ask her for an ID when Karen said, "My daughter will have a soda." Jordan nodded and added, "Ginger ale." Karen ordered a beer and Sarah first ordered vodka straight on the rocks, but then was overcome by the idea that somehow this might be wrong, and she, too, asked for a ginger ale.

The Goth waitress rolled her eyes. "This is a bar," she said unpleasantly.

"Okay," Sarah replied. "Put a little twist of lemon in the glass, so it looks like a real drink."

This made the other two Reds smile and drove the waitress away sour-faced. It wasn't much of a joke, Sarah thought, but at least it was an attempt at humor, which was more than she had managed in months.

The three were quiet for a moment, waiting for the waitress to return with their drinks. The youngest spoke first. "Well, here we are. What do we do now?"

After a moment Karen asked the practical question: "Does anyone think that it's just someone fucking with us? You know, it's all a game, like we're the butt of some not-very-funny joke and that nothing will really happen?"

Both Sarah and Jordan knew that this question had been considered and dismissed by each separately, but neither wanted to blurt this out. It was Sarah who reached just beyond all the pain she felt within and said, "I don't think I'm that lucky."

Again, quiet afflicted them. None of them felt *that lucky*.

"So . . ." Karen started, then stopped. She felt herself choking, as if she had stage fright. When she continued, her words came out as cracked as dry leather. "We need to make some kind of sense of this."

Jordan responded, feeling like someone else was speaking. "What do you mean, *make sense*? Some crazy guy wants to kill us because we've got red hair and he's all obsessed with Little Red Riding Hood and we've got to figure out what we're going to do about it. I mean, what sense is there to make? And, while we're trying to make sense of it all, maybe he's stalking us and lining us up like targets on a firing range and getting ready to pull the trigger. *Bang bang bang, y'er all dead*."

Jordan's voice had picked up momentum with each word until it was racing, even as she dropped it to barely a whisper.

"Beat him to the punch, beat him to the punch, beat him to the punch," the teenager repeated three times, once for each of them.

Karen reeled back. She had ignored the teenager's homicidal suggestion the first time she'd offered it. But with the three of them gathered around the table, it wasn't so easily dismissed. She did not know why she didn't think this was a viable approach. She heard herself saying, "Look, Jordan, we're not killers. We wouldn't know what to do. And we can't stoop . . ."

She stopped, because she thought she sounded foolish and she could see the youngest of them shaking her head violently in disagreement. She shifted in her seat. *Be logical!* a voice within her fairly screamed. But obeying this command took a great effort on her part. She could feel her throat closing up and her mouth drying. She licked her lips and took a swig of beer. "Look, the first thing," she said. "Something locks us together." She spoke as slowly as possible. "We need to figure that out."

"Yeah, red hair," Jordan said.

"No. It has to be something more than that."

"What do you mean?" Sarah asked. She felt a little intimidated, as if the other two were more in control and had far greater resources than she did, although with the talk having shifted to killing, she remembered that she seemed to be the only one who actually owned a weapon.

"He had to find us," Karen said. "So, something links us. It can't just be random."

"Why not?" Jordan asked.

The three women looked at one another. Each imagined that the other two were as different from her as possible. Other than their hair, nothing rang out loudly. No alarms, bells, or sirens sounded that announced a similarity.

Again, the three women were silenced by their thoughts. And again, it was the youngest who broke the quiet. "Yeah, but even if we can figure it out, what then? Call the cops?"

"I already tried that," Karen said. "Of course, if we figure out who's stalking us and we can take that name to the police, maybe they'll be able to do something . . ." She hesitated. This most logical path seemed utterly unreasonable. *When you're tossed into insanity*, she thought, *what makes you think logic will help you?*

She slumped in her seat. All her training and all her adult life had been devoted to reason, to making a diagnosis: Run this test and that test, take into account this symptom and that symptom, put it all together into the mix of education and experience, and come up with an answer. A *reasonable* answer. Maybe it wouldn't be a *happy* answer, but it would be an answer nevertheless. She shook her head.

Jordan looked at the older woman. Karen Jayson was completely respectable—educated, responsible, and mature and Jordan had expected that she would know exactly what to do because she was the type of woman who always knew exactly what to do. She was the type of woman that teenagers like herself were urged to grow up and become. And so, when she saw the same confusion and doubt on Red One's face that she imagined was on her own, it frightened her. She half-turned, to see if she saw the same look in Sarah's eyes, but the third member of the trio was leaning back, staring at the ceiling, as if hoping for some thunderbolt of guidance from the heavens to penetrate the walls and strike her with a clear path forward. Jordan thought, *It's like being cast adrift at sea with two strangers.*

She did not say this. Instead, she blurted out, "There's only one way to protect ourselves."

"How is that?" Sarah asked, as if sliding slowly down a ladder to earth.

"The Wolf has all the advantages over Little Red Riding Hood," she said, "except one."

"What's that?"

"He's a prisoner," she said.

"What?" Karen grunted.

"Of what he wants."

"I don't follow," Sarah said.

"What trips him up? His own desires."

Sarah and Karen looked at Jordan.

"I've read the fairy tale," she said swiftly. "I went to the library the other night. I've read all the versions."

"Yes," Karen said, discouraged. "But that's a fairy tale . . ."

Jordan persisted, leaning forward and talking quickly, as if the speed of her words would overcome the noisy buzz of the bar. She ignored Karen's interruption. "And the only version where Little Red Riding Hood gets saved in the end is the phony, politically safe one that mothers tell their daughters. Sort of the sanitized Disney version. In the real story . . ."

She stopped. She saw doubt in front of her.

Jordan nodded her head. She imagined she sounded young, but she had youthful determination. "That's our only chance. Turn the old story into the new one. The story where we all get eaten alive needs to change into the safe one where we get rescued."

"Sounds nice," Sarah said, bitterness that she did not want or think was helpful creeping into her voice. "I'm sure there's a helpful strong woodsman just waiting to come running with his trusty axe . . ."

Jordan held up her hand. "We have to rescue ourselves," she said. "It's our only chance."

Karen jumped in. "Okay," she said, "but how do we do that?"

"I don't know exactly," Jordan said. "But it seems to me that we won't be doing any good for any of us if we all just sit around waiting for the Wolf to kill us. I mean, if he can stalk us, why can't we stalk him right back?"

"A nice idea, but how?" Sarah asked.

Jordan didn't know how to answer that question, but Karen did. "The way we started this. We find out what links us. And what I mean is, no one do anything that's out of the ordinary. Do whatever it is you do on schedule and at appropriate times. Don't let the Wolf know anything different."

"I don't get it," Sarah asked.

Karen shut her eyes for an instant. She couldn't believe what she was about to say. "At some point," she said slowly, "we're going to have to draw him in. Close enough so that we can see who he is."

She almost gasped. This thought was too terrifying. She placed her hands beneath the tabletop, because she was afraid the others might see them quivering.

Jordan, however, smiled. "*What big teeth you have, Grandmother,*" she said. "Makes sense."

The three Reds were quiet for a moment. "How much time do you think we have?" Sarah asked.

This question went straight to the pit of each Red's stomach. *A day. A week. A month. A year.* There was no way of telling.

The three women stared at one another. A physician with a secret life as a comic in a world where nothing was funny anymore, a widow lost in relentless grief, a teenager trapped by circumstances and failure.

"I don't want to die," Sarah said abruptly. The words surprised her, because up until that moment she had believed that this was *all* she really wanted to do.

18

In what the Wolf thought was a wonderfully serendipitous bit of good fortune, the following day he received a chain e-mail from the New England chapter of the Mystery Writers of America, announcing a special seminar with the Massachusetts State Police's top forensic analyst. Although he had joined the organization shortly after his first book was published, he had never attended any of its lectures, which were designed to help members with tricky issues that cropped up in their struggling narratives. He had felt above these "how-to" sessions and preferred researching on his own. The local police were always helpful, as were many criminal defense lawyers. He sometimes wondered whether they would be equally eager to speak to a real killer.

But this e-mail seemed to play into his current needs, and he reserved a space for the seminar, paying the $50 fee with a credit card and getting directions to a hotel convention room for the talk. It was going to be a two-hour drive to just outside Boston, but he felt it would be worth the trip. The Wolf liked to think that he was constantly on the lookout for small pieces of information. Little details of crime made his writing come alive, he believed. In that regard, he imagined himself like all the other writers of crime fiction.

This notion of joining a pack amused him. *Because I'm not like any of those others struggling to find a good agent and get a book contract and maybe a movie deal for their detective series.*

It was to be an evening session—which he didn't like. He no longer enjoyed driving at night. His eyesight was still good enough, but the creeping early winter darkness seemed to slow his reactions down, which made him tentative behind the wheel. This sensation of vulnerability or mortality—he hated it—reminded him he was steadily aging. This caused him, in turn, to feel more energized when he thought about the three Reds.

Killing, he wrote, *brings out the youth inside.*

Do you remember what it was like when you had your first kiss? The first time you touched a girl's breast? The first time you caressed a knife blade with your thumb and drew a little line of blood? Do you remember that taste? Or the first time you hefted a loaded pistol, and placed your index finger upon the trigger, knowing that all the power in the world would be released with just the gentlest tug?

Perfection.

Those are the passions that constantly need to be restored and renewed.

The Wolf reluctantly set aside his musings on murder and devoted some time to drearily writing down questions for the seminar speaker and trying to anticipate the scientist's answers. He thought of himself as a dedicated graduate student preparing for an oral exam. This would be the final step before being awarded a doctorate. This idea made him grin. *A higher degree in killing.* Still, he considered it necessary to be prepared for the seminar. He wanted to be able to display enough understanding that expert knowledge would flow back toward him. It was like knocking on the door to a sophisticated, exclusive club, demanding entrance.

He did make one more note in the chapter he was working on: *To be a truly successful killer, you must always be eager to learn. Too many death-row inmates stare out between iron bars waiting for that final bad word from the warden and wondering where exactly everything went so wrong. "I'm sorry. All your court appeals have failed. Would you like a priest? And chicken or steak for that last meal?" If you don't educate yourself about death, death will decide to educate you. And you don't want that lesson.*

This, he thought, was probably obvious to every reader but deserved being stated in clear, concise prose anyway. *Sometimes*, he told himself, *you have to be totally explicit. Pornographically clear. In words and in killing.*

Jordan counted quietly to herself. One step. Two. Twenty, twenty-five, and thirty. She angled across the open quadrangle, measuring carefully, ignoring the other students walking to late classes.

In her hand, she clutched a small video camera. She had borrowed it from one of her dorm mates, a slightly younger girl who seemed less intent than the others on either taunting her remorselessly or taking pains to avoid her. Jordan imagined that it was used mostly for out-of-bounds fun—maybe taking incriminating pictures of other girls making out with football team boys or breaking the school rules by drinking wildly at parties.

Moving across the campus, Jordan periodically lifted the camera and looked back through the lens. When the distance seemed right, she stopped and checked the viewfinder. Then she smiled and took a quick glance around.

"That's where you were standing," she whispered to herself. She half-lifted her hand to point, as if there were someone standing next to her.

Jordan had duplicated the first shot the Wolf had taken of her in her Red Three YouTube video. The distance was approximately the same. The angle was nearly identical. She had done her best to gauge the light to replicate the time of day.

She was stopped a few feet outside a small space between a science lab and a boys' dormitory. It was a dead-end alleyway—no longer than eight or ten feet deep—that was blocked by a gray concrete wall at the back that connected the two buildings for no apparent purpose. There were several trash bins located at that end and the wall was scrawled with obscenities and vaguely pornographic drawings, phone numbers, and protests of undying love or promises of oral sex. It was not unlike a typical bathroom stall wall in a bus station.

Both buildings were the ubiquitous redbrick so familiar to schools and colleges, covered with tangled ivy, although the cold weather had stripped all the branches of leaves. The space seemed almost cavelike. It was, Jordan thought, a bad place for trash containers, but a fine place to hide for a few moments while sneaking a video.

Had to be last spring term. Plenty of greenery, she thought. *And the evening shadows would have made this spot dark, while the last bit of sunlight hitting the quadrangle would have made it possible to see me clearly.*

She bit down on her lip. It was a smart place to choose for a secret videotaping. Jordan stepped back slightly, looking first right, then left. *No one could see what you were doing unless they accidentally walked right past and happened to look directly at you.*

In her imagination, it was like she was conversing with the Wolf—as if she wanted him to hear how much she had already figured out about him. She stared at the spot she believed he'd occupied. She wanted to whisper something defiant, but no words came to her. She pictured him—a lurking man's dark form that seemed part animal, almost cartoonlike—lowering the camera, wide wolf's grin on his face, teeth bared. Again, she let her eyes travel the adjacent areas. *Plenty of parking on the side street just twenty yards away. A few quick steps and you would be gone. No one would know what you'd been up to. So, you must have felt pretty damn safe.*

Jordan worked hard to reconstruct every element of the filming moment in her head.

You couldn't just wait here for hours, hoping eventually I would happen by and you could take your pictures. That would be far too suspicious. Someone might spot you and maybe call security. No one's allowed to just hang out around the school. So that's a chance you wouldn't take. Any smart wolf would know to be far more cautious, right?

Her throat felt sore, her mouth dry.

You had to know when I was going to pass by. Maybe not exactly, but damn close. You had to have a sense of timing. My timing. You know my school. The smart wolf knows exactly when he can spy on his prey in complete safety.

That observation told her something.

You must know the same things for Red One and Red Two.

She lifted the video camera up to her eye, but did not push the *record* button. She had already seen all she wanted.

Jordan could feel a rush of warmth, even though the air was chilly. *Here is the first fight,* she told herself. *Don't panic. He was standing right here, right where you are right now. What else does it tell you?*

One answer she already knew, and she reminded herself of it, speaking out loud to no one: "He's been watching all of us for months." The video was the culmination of many hours. It wasn't some spur-of-the-moment picture.

This seemed completely unfair to her. It was like a surprise test in a classroom on material that she'd neglected to study. Only failure here meant much more than a lousy mark.

She reached out and idly ran her fingers over the pitted brick of the science building, as if the old stone could tell her something else.

Jordan had the sensation there was some reply to her touch to be found, but it seemed to elude her in the late afternoon gloom. Torn—a part of her wanted to flee, a part of her told her to keep looking because there might be other answers just lying about near the trash—she pivoted. For a moment, she stared at the gray concrete wall behind the trash containers, her eyes flowing over all the faded and misspelled messages. She took a couple of steps closer, reading.

Kathy gives good head. Call her 555-1729.
Fcuk the class of 2009. There assholes.
I Luv S. Forever.

She was about to turn when her eyes spotted a small hand-drawn heart shape scratched into the wall. Inside it were the letters RT *and* BW. Jordan stared at the heart, as if her eyes could burn some truth out of it.

RT, she thought. *That can't be Red Three.*

BW can't be Bad Wolf.

She shook her head. *No, it would have to be BBW because that's how he signed his letters.* She scoured her memory. *Isn't there a Robbie Townsend in that boys' dorm? Didn't he have a crush on Betty Williams last semester?*

That has to be it.

But trying to insist that nothing was wrong seemed like a complete lie. She felt chilled, and she turned around and began to march toward her dormitory. She had the eerie sensation that the Wolf was suddenly right behind her, hidden in that location and once again filming her, materializing out of shadow as soon as she'd turned her back. The nape of her neck burned. A surge of frantic fear came over her and she nearly broke into a sprint. But instead, Jordan forced herself to slow down and walk steadily. *One foot in front of the other,* she told herself. She wanted to sing out in some loud and raucously obscene cadence, like a soldier, but she couldn't find the strength to raise her voice, so she began to whisper in a singsong, "I don't know but I've been told, Eskimo cocks are mighty cold. Left. Right. Left. Right . . ." Her pace, she hoped, was every bit as defiant as the words she couldn't find for herself earlier. But she doubted it was.

Act normal.

Sarah Locksley had joked to herself that this should mean popping some pills and washing them down with warm vodka. *My new normal. Not my old normal.*

Instead, she had spent most of the day relentlessly straightening up her house. She collected debris and placed empty liquor bottles in recycling bins. She vacuumed carpets and washed floors. The laundry ran nearly nonstop for hours, each load carefully folded and placed in her drawers as it was finished. She cleaned every countertop and surface in the kitchen, and switched on the oven's self-cleaning mechanism. The refrigerator was a challenge, but she scrubbed out every bit of spilled milk. Spoiled food was thrown into a trash bag and carted outside. She assaulted the bathrooms with brush, cleanser, and military precision, bending over until her back shouted with pain, but afterward the porcelain and stainless steel glistened. And, in what she truly believed was complete idiocy, she took two plastic garbage bags and went from window to window, door to door, disassembling her *Home Alone* security system. The broken glass spread beneath each entranceway clinked as she swept it up with dustpan and broom.

She couldn't quite bring herself to open windows and air the house out—although she knew she needed to do that. An open window seemed like an invitation to cold air, trouble, and maybe worse.

Nor could Sarah take a feather duster into her husband's study or her daughter's bedroom. Those remained shut. *Normal* could only go so far.

When she'd restored her home to something approximating reasonable, Sarah stepped into her shower and let steaming-hot water run over her, the heat seeping into sore muscles. She stood beneath the stream almost like a statue, unable to move, but not frozen by fatigue as much as turmoil. When she soaped up her hair and body, she felt like her hands were running over the skin of a stranger. It seemed to her that nothing was familiar—not the shape of her breasts, the length of her legs, the tangles in her hair. When she emerged from the shower, she stood naked in front of a mirror, imagining that she was looking at some odd identical twin she had never known, from whom she'd been separated at birth, but who had just moments before suddenly reappeared in her life.

She dressed carefully, choosing a modest pants-and-sweater outfit from the rows of clothes that she'd once worn to work at the elementary school. They were loose-fitting when she had a job, a husband, and a family. Now, with none of those things, her body baggier from the weight loss of depression, they hung on her, and she wondered whether they would ever fit again.

She found her overcoat, brushed a few spots of dust from it, and searched around for her satchel. She double-checked to make sure that her husband's revolver was snugly contained inside. Out loud, she said, "Normal doesn't include being stupid."

She wasn't sure that this statement was accurate.

Sarah stepped outside into weak afternoon sunlight. She could feel her hands twitch, and knew that she was on an edge of fear. She desperately wanted to stop, search up and down the roadway with her eyes, inspect her small world for some telltale sign of the Wolf's presence.

Normal, she thought, *doesn't need to look around nervously and worry about every step outside.*

She felt a shaft of cold within her as she thought that if her husband had only looked in the right direction, perhaps . . .

She shut off that small bit of despair. Instead, she hastily moved to her car and slid behind the wheel, behaving like any person who had someplace to go.

She did. But this was not the sort of trip that would fit into anyone's definition of routine. This trip was to combine the insistently ordinary with the deepest sadness.

Her first stop was the mundane: the local grocery store. She seized a cart from the rack and filled it up with salads, fruit, lean meats, and fish. She purchased bottled water and freshly squeezed juices. Sarah felt a little like a stranger walking through the aisles of healthy foodstuffs. It had been a long time since she'd bought anything to eat that had any nutritional value.

At the floral displays she grabbed two cheap bunches of colorful flowers.

The checkout girl took Sarah's credit card and ran it through the register, which gave Sarah a twinge of embarrassment, because she was sure it would be declined. When it was approved, Sarah was mildly astonished.

She steered her cart and groceries over to her car, keeping her eyes focused on loading, steeling herself against the desire to look about furtively. For the first time in her life she felt a little like a wild animal. The demands of caution and remaining alert to all threats nearly overcame her.

The Wolf won't follow you on this next errand, she thought. *And even if he did, what would he learn?*

Nothing he doesn't already know.

Telling herself to ignore every creeping fear, Sarah stuffed the groceries into her trunk. Then she slid behind the wheel, took a deep breath, and pulled out of the parking lot into traffic.

End-of-the-day drivers ducked in and out of lanes and tailgated her. There is a frustrated energy to commuting time; there's so many people in a hurry to get home that they wind up slowing everyone down. She reminded herself that once she was the same way, at the end of the school day. She would pack up all her classroom items and get behind the wheel and drive rapidly home because that was where her real life was, or at least the part of it that she liked to think of as *real*. Picking up her daughter at day care, fixing dinner, waiting for her husband to come home from fire department headquarters.

Behind her a car honked. She punched down on her gas pedal, knowing that even moving faster wasn't likely to make whoever it was who had decided to be rude any less so.

It took her nearly half an hour to drive to the cemetery. It was located near a large public park so that any city residue dropped away rapidly, giving the last few blocks an almost country feel.

The grave sites were set back on a small sloping plot of land. Streets meandered haphazardly amidst gray headstones. There were pathways that led up to ornate crypts and lurking statues of angels. There was little daylight remaining, and shadows seemed to drop from the oak trees that were scattered about the landscape. Nearly lost in one corner was a small building that Sarah knew housed a backhoe and shovels.

She was alone.

Some of the graves sported dying flowers. Several were adorned with well-worn, tattered American flags. A few had freshly turned dirt. Others were faded by years of weather, the grass around them browned by time. Names, dates, quick sentiments—*beloved, devoted*—adorned some of the headstones. Decades of losses were arrayed quietly before her.

Sarah stopped her car and grasped the two bouquets of flowers.

It has been a long time since you came here, she told herself. *Be brave*.

When she formed this last word in her head, she was uncertain whether she was referring to the Wolf or to the two people who had been stolen from her life. She wished that her husband or daughter would whisper something to her, but there was nothing but cemetery silence in the air.

A little unsteadily, she walked down a pathway running through rows of simple gray monuments guarded by two cherub statues wielding trumpets that played no sound. She could hear her shoes clacking against the black macadam of the path. A part of her wished she were drunk, an equal part of her believed there was no amount of liquor in the world that could overcome her sobriety at that moment.

In her mind, she was working on what she was going to say to her slaughtered family. Words like *I'm sorry* or *I need you both to help me get through this* filled her mouth, as if ready to burst forth. She clutched the bouquets, almost as she had the gun earlier.

Sarah knew how many steps she would walk. She kept her eyes down, head lowered, as if she was afraid to read the names on the gray marble headstone that awaited her. When she knew she was in front of it, she stopped, breathed in sharply, and raised her eyes.

As she did this, she started to speak, almost nonsensically. "I miss you both so much and now someone wants to kill me . . ."

Then, as if someone had drawn a razor blade across her tongue, the weak and flimsy message she had for her dead husband and daughter died in her mouth.

She stared through the encroaching darkness at the headstone. At first, she could only formulate, *There's something wrong.*

She peered at the granite-colored stone. *Graffiti*, she thought at first. A surge of outrage immediately filled her. *This is terrible*, she thought. *What sort of creepy, thoughtless, goddamn stupid teenager would take a can of spray paint and deface a grave? Don't they know they're breaking someone's heart?*

She took a step forward and looked closer. *That's not right.* She realized that she was breathing shallow, quick bursts of air stripped from the rapidly falling darkness.

What should have been the angular "tags" of teenage gangs or the round, bulbous drawings of nicknames were nothing of the sort. Nor were these scratchy, misspelled obscenities hurriedly sprayed across the surface. Sarah stepped forward, as if drawn to the shapes she saw.

They were painted white. They angled across the stone, bisecting each name and the death date. There were four of them.

Sarah had never seen a wolf's paw print before, but she suddenly knew that was precisely what she was staring at.

She dropped the flowers to the sidewalk and ran hard.

19

The stage manager began waving at Karen frantically, pointing at the tattered black curtain that concealed the entrance to the performance apron at Sir Laughs-A-Lot, when he saw her hesitate upon hearing the cell phone in her satchel begin to ring insistently. Her first instinct was that there was some patient emergency that required immediate attention. She grabbed the pocketbook and ignored the manager, although he was urgently whispering, "Come on, Doc. Y'er up. Let's break a leg. Knock 'em out."

She hesitated when she saw that it wasn't her regular cell phone that was ringing. It was the throwaway phone identical to those she had given Red Two and Red Three.

The caller ID read: *Sarah*.

Karen half-reached for the phone as she heard the stage manager—he was usually the bartender at the comedy club—say, "That better be goddamn important. We've got a full house tonight and they are getting real restless."

Karen looked up and saw he was holding back the curtain with one hand and urging her forward with the other. She could just see past him, to where the club owner was standing center stage, introducing her.

"Let's please give a warm Laughs-A-Lot welcome to Doctor K!" the owner was saying as he stepped away from a standing microphone and pointed in her direction.

She took a quick glance down at the phone as it stopped ringing. The display read "*1 new message*." Conflict collided within her. She could hear the stage manager, now in a stage whisper, urging her up and out. At the same time, the phone demanded her attention.

Caught between these two poles, she dropped the phone back into her satchel and grabbed a bottle of water from the stage manager's hand. *The show must go on*, she thought, although she knew perhaps this shoud have been an exception. Karen stepped forward into the floodlights.

She wore a wide, slightly goofy grin, black-framed glasses, and had frizzed out her hair comically. She waved at the audience. She had on her standard comedy-club outfit, which consisted of red high-top sneakers, a black turtleneck sweater, and jeans, topped off by a white clinician's cotton coat and an old, no-longer-functional stethoscope wrapped around her neck like a noose.

A full house, she knew, was actually only fifty or so people at the tiny off-the-beaten-path club. She couldn't see past the glare, but she knew there were couples and foursomes spread about the shadows inside the cavelike interior. A hard-pressed waitstaff hurriedly delivered beer and burgers, trying to get each order filled before she took the stage. She could smell french fries and hear a distant sizzle from the small kitchen.

A smattering of applause greeted her, and she made an elaborate bow. "You know what really bothers me," she said, using a lilt to give her words energy, "is when you write a prescription and say 'Take two of these every day,' and patients immediately double everything . . . because if two are supposed to make them feel better, well, four will probably make them feel a *whole lot* better . . ."

She paused, looked out past the floodlights at the people she couldn't see but knew were there, and smiled. "Of course, nobody here has ever done that . . ." A ripple of slightly self-conscious laugher flowed up toward her.

"I mean . . . does everyone want to become an addict?"

This small insult got a slightly larger response. She could hear a few *"Yeah, why not?"* and *"No kidding!"* exclamations from the audience.

"Of course, that reminds me of an addict I used to know . . ." she continued. Riffing on drugs and acting a little befuddled about the needs of patients was an integral part of her shtick. Whenever she felt uncertain about her humor, she made fun of the things that were the least funny. This invariably warmed the crowd to her. She remembered an old comic taking her aside once, years earlier when she was first trying out some of her routines, and telling her, "You know what isn't funny? A guy on crutches with a cast on his leg. You know what's really fuckin' funny? A guy on crutches with a cast on his leg slipping on the ice and going ass over elbows into the air. That'll get a laugh every time. Everybody loves someone else's over-the-top misfortune. Keep that in mind every second you're up there."

So she did. Her routines made fun of heart attacks and cancer and Ebola virus. Most of the time, it worked.

"So this guy says to me, 'Doc, what's wrong with taking drugs?' And I say back to him, 'Yeah, but dog tranquilizers?' And he kinda smiles and says, 'Me and my dog, we're pretty similar . . .'"

Karen paused. "'Yeah,' I says to him, 'keep snorting that stuff and you'll be wagging your tail a lot *less* . . .'" When she said *tail*, she grabbed her crotch as if imitating a man masturbating.

There was a burst of laughter and some hand-clapping. This was just enough feedback to make Karen relax and feel like she had made enough of an inroad with the audience to be able to finish on a high note. She made a mental point to use that joke, a double entendre: a high note. Part of what she loved about performing was the way standing on stage in front of an audience made her slide thoughts into various compartments, as if her brain were an old apothecary's desk with a hundred different drawers.

She went back to her imaginary addict. "And I tell him, 'You know, you might just find yourself lifting your leg at inappropriate times . . .'"

Another round of laughter filled the room. Part of humor was making the people in that dark room *see* things—in this case a man turning himself into a dog.

"But of course, he says back to me, 'Well, maybe I'll be able to smell the bitches better, too.'" This line, she figured, would make the men in the room clap. It did.

Karen had warmed up, was suddenly feeling confident, had shunted the telephone message that had trailed her onto the stage into some distant, nearly forgotten place, and she took a moment to let the applause surround her. It was like being caressed, she thought.

And then a solitary whistle cut across the noise.

It was a loud, piercing sound. It was not unfamiliar to her. She had heard it before at other shows and ignored it, or joked about it. But this time— the whistle rose steadily in pitch and then abruptly shifted downward—it stopped her cold, because she put a name to it.

Wolf whistle.

She shifted her weight back and forth and took a long gulp from the bottle of water. Her imagination seized—she knew she had to find a joke, but suddenly felt crippled.

All women have heard a wolf whistle. It's nothing more than a common thoughtless way guys have of expressing attraction. It's been around for decades.

Wolf had never meant anything to her before. Now it did. She tried to regain composure. *It's nothing out of the ordinary.* She could hear a part of her scream, *Liar!*

Karen fumbled with the thread of her humor.

"Of course," she said, "the drug companies spend all their time and money researching the wrong problems. I mean, they want to cure herpes and the common cold. But what about a drug that helps women parallel-park?"

A burst of laughter erupted from the darkness.

"Or maybe a drug that cures men of their football addiction? Ladies, we could just slip it into the salsa and cheese nacho dip, and next thing we'd know the game would be off the television and the channel turned to public broadcasting's latest adaptation of *Pride and Prejudice* . . ."

More hoots and giggles.

Karen had started to relax again, to think that the wolf whistle wasn't the Wolf's whistle, when she heard it a second time, blending into the general amusement.

It is, it isn't, she thought, once again trying to grasp hold of the sound. She raised her hand to shade her eyes, trying to see past the floodlights into the audience. But it was just a darkened cavern, filled with indistinct shapes. And then she suddenly thought, *The call from Red Two. It was a warning. He's here. He's just over there past the blinding lights. I could touch him.*

He can touch me.

Karen fought panic. She struggled to keep herself centered and keep up with the comedy patter. She thought, *Make a joke. Say, "Someone must be falling in love . . ." or some such silliness. Make that whistle into something ordinary and benign.*

She couldn't make herself do this. Instead murder overcame her imagination. *Is it happening? Right now? Is he going to kill me in front of all these people?*

Her hands twitched. She gulped again at the water bottle, but it was empty. She was on stage. She had nowhere to hide. A spotlight followed her every move. She wanted to say something that would extricate herself gracefully from the dais. *"Well, I'll be heading back to the ER now."* Then she thought that might trigger the Wolf. If she tried to flee, would he shoot her right then and there? Would he leap up onto the stage like some deranged John Wilkes Booth waving a knife or brandishing a pistol?

She closed her eyes. She was trapped between irrational fears. There was the fear of humiliating herself in front of an audience and the Wolf fear. She swallowed hard. She wondered if she only had seconds left to live.

"Well," she said to the audience, forcing a grin, "that's it for me tonight. Take two aspirin and call me in the morning."

The applause would conceal the shot. So would the darkened room. There would be confusion and panic. Someone would scream, "*Get a doctor!*" But of course, she was the only doctor in the club, and she would be dying on the stage. And in all the tangle of irony, death, and surprise, the Wolf would slip away. She knew this, even if it made no sense. She knew that he had already made his escape plans, and he would be fast on his way to Red Two or Red Three.

Unless they were already killed.

Maybe that was the call, Karen thought. *It said "1 New Message" but maybe the message was, "I'm dead."*

Karen could suddenly see two bodies. Red Two and Red Three, twisted, bloodstained, discarded. It was almost as if she had to step over them to leave the stage.

She stumbled toward the curtain. She knew she should wave at the crowd, which was continuing to applaud, but turning back was impossible. Each stride she took she imagined was her last. Her legs felt weak and unsteady. She expected to hear the sound of a gun firing and she knew that it would be the last sound she ever heard.

When she reached the curtain and let it close behind her, she felt she had never before in her entire life walked as great a distance. For an instant, she gulped at the stale backstage air. She wanted to shrink down and cower in some darkened corner. Then almost as quickly she told herself, *You've got to see!*

Tossing her fake glasses and stethoscope toward her bag, stripping off her white coat, she pushed past the surprised stage manager, the equally astonished owner, and a college-aged man in a tweed jacket and khaki pants who was scheduled to follow her onto the stage. She raced to the side door of the club, which led out to the tables. It had a sign that stated IF OPENED ALARM WILL SOUND, but the security system had been disconnected.

Karen burst through the door.

A few lights in the club had come up—just enough so that she could search the faces in the audience. She did not know what she was looking for. *A single man? Bared wolf's teeth? Look at a crowd of people and pluck the killer out from all of them?*

What she saw was insistently ordinary. More burgers and bottles of beer being distributed. Tables filled with couples. What she heard was a great deal of loud laughter and happily raised voices.

Her eyes swept right and left. She wanted to scream: *"Where are you?"*

"Hey, Doc, you okay?"

She almost jumped into the air. The question had come from the club owner. Karen breathed in slowly. "Yes, yes," she replied.

"I mean, you look like you seen a ghost."

Maybe I did, she thought. *Or maybe I just heard one.*

"No, I'm okay," she said. "I just thought I recognized someone."

"Looks like someone you didn't want to see," the owner said. "You want, I'll get Sam to walk you out to your car after the next guy wraps up." Sam was the burly bartender and stage manager. The assumption behind the offer was a spurned lover or an ex-husband with a grudge.

"I'd like that," she said. She didn't add an explanation.

"Cool. How about a drink to settle those nerves? And hey, your set, it went great tonight. The folks really seemed to like it." The owner gestured toward a waitress.

"Thanks," Karen replied. The waitress hovered near. "Scotch," Karen said. "Neat. And make it a double, with a beer chaser."

"On the house," said the owner as he steered Karen backstage.

It took a few minutes for Karen to be left alone. The stage manager was at the curtain, the owner back on the dais introducing the next act, and the college kid poised to go on. The waitress came and delivered her drinks with the rapidity of someone who knows the tips are somewhere else.

Karen gulped the liquor down, feeling it burn her throat. For a moment she felt dizzy, and she rocked back and forth as if she were already drunk. It took a surge of energy and an inner mantra of *I'm safe now, I'm safe now* before she was able to pluck the cell phone from her satchel. For a few seconds, she stared at the display. Behind her, she could hear the college kid making ribald jokes and the audience hooting in response. *He's good*, she thought. *Better than me.*

She punched buttons on the keypad and held the phone up to her ear. Words tumbled and jolted, skidded, crashed, and screamed. Karen could understand *grave* and *paw prints*, but that was it.

Except for the hysteria. Sobs, groans, panic, and runaway fear. Those came through absolutely clearly.

20

At first Sarah searched the crowd, hoping to spot Karen, but she stopped almost as quickly as she began, because she formulated some crazy notion in her head that if *she* was able to spot Red One, then so could the Wolf, as if he were seated next to her and would merely follow her gaze and know they were both in the stands and somehow manage to kill them simultaneously in front of everyone. So instead, she concentrated on the floor, trying to avoid spending too many moments eyeing Red Three. She picked out a player on the opposing team, gathered her name from the mimeographed programs scattered about the bleachers, and tried to act as if she was connected to some gangly teenager whom she had never seen before.

Once again, she had prepared carefully to go out in public. But this time she had made significant changes.

She had found a cheap jet-black wig left over from a Halloween costume party during happier times, when she'd dressed up as the Uma Thurman character in *Pulp Fiction* and her husband had adopted a black suit and thin tie like John Travolta playing Vincent the hired killer. She remembered the fun they'd had when they had taken to the dance floor and copied the almost painfully slow, exaggerated, slinky motions the movie couple had used to mesmerize audiences. She stuck one of her dead husband's frayed baseball caps on top of the wig.

She hunted around until she found some of her old pregnancy clothing in an old cardboard box, and fastening a small throw pillow around her midsection with shipping tape, she created the appearance of someone perhaps five months along. Some dark sunglasses and an old brown over-sized and out-of-style overcoat that she hadn't used in years completed her disguise. She thought she looked as little like herself as she could manage on short notice.

Sarah did not consider it particularly good, as far as disguises went. She had no idea whether the Wolf would be able to recognize her, especially in a crowd, but she guessed he would, no matter how she altered her appearance. *He'll just smell me*, she thought. She attributed unbelievable powers of detection to the Wolf. She assumed he'd seen her emerge from her house, although she had exited the rear door, scooted around the side, hunched over like a soldier dodging enemy fire to hide her fake pregnancy, and flung herself into her car. She had even carried her overcoat in a plastic garbage bag, so that the style and color were hidden until she put it on when she reached the game. She hadn't been able to spot any out-of-the ordinary cars up and down her street as she peeled out, tires squealing. She had taken the usual elusive steps to avoid being followed.

A large part of her felt this was all foolishness. Trying to hide made no sense. The Wolf, she thought, was everywhere all at once.

Staring out at the basketball court, faking a cheer after a shot dropped through the net, all Sarah could actually see were wolf prints stenciled on the grave headstone. She had tried to examine those prints, but it was difficult for her. It seemed like the Wolf was lurking on the periphery of her existence, waiting for the right moment. *The right moment*, she thought. *What creates the right moment?*

She wedged herself between two couples and tried hard to engage each with banter about the players and the game, so that anyone watching her might think they had all come together that evening to watch. This illusion wasn't hard to create.

Sarah breathed in, waiting for the clock to tick down toward the final buzzer. She closed her eyes and went over what she was supposed to do. It was a haphazard plan, rapidly constructed after calls to Red One and Red Three. Urgency seemed to stalk them in the same way the Wolf did.

The crowd let out mixed sounds of success and failure. The horn sounded, ending the game. People stood, stretching. Sarah saw the two teams lining up to shake hands. It was the moment where the busy-ness of the court transfers into the stands. Each team gave a perfunctory cheer for the other, but Sarah didn't hear this. She was already digging her way through clutches of fans and parents who were jamming the aisles and walkways leading from the bleachers. She kept her head down, dodging people who were putting on jackets and talking animatedly about the game. She hoped that somewhere close, Red One was doing more or less the same.

With a quick glance back over her shoulder, Sarah ducked down a stairwell that led to the locker rooms. A second glance let her know she was alone. She paused, listening for steps behind her, but heard none. There was a distant echo of teenage voices laughing, but they seemed benign and un-Wolf-like. Red Three had told her that down the corridor she would see a door marked LADIES. That was where she was headed. She pushed inside.

Sarah sighed when she realized she was alone. She thought, *The Wolf won't follow me in here.* Again, she knew this was nonsense. A killer bent on murder wouldn't really feel a sense of propriety about entering a women's bathroom. Still, she felt oddly reassured.

There were three stalls to her right, across from some glistening sinks. She went into the farthest. Sarah locked the door behind her and sat down on the toilet to wait. *Fifteen minutes,* Red Three had told her. She checked her wristwatch. Time seemed to pass erratically, as if each minute had some different, odd number of seconds that bore no relation to the regular sixty.

162

* * *

Karen was hunched down in her car, waiting for the first flow of people to emerge through the gymnasium doors. Other than pinning her hair back and throwing on running shoes, she hadn't taken any steps to disguise herself.

Instead, she had arrived in the parking lot outside the gym and stepped out of her car and walked up and down each row of vehicles, staring in at each, making certain they were all empty. This had seemed to her to be just on the near side of crazy behavior, but she felt reassured when she slipped back into her own car.

She had rolled down her window so that she could keep track of the game's progress by listening for the muted cheers from the crowd. She had heard the buzzer signaling the end and known she would have to wait for only a few moments.

The first people through the doors were students. They were laughing as they disappeared into the slippery evening darkness. Then a steadier flow of teenagers, adults, and even some small children began to emerge.

That was her signal to move.

Like a fish swimming against the current, she ducked her head and zigzagged through the exiting crowd. She was the only person battling to get in. That had been her only plan. If the Wolf was behind her, he would create the same commotion she did. She kept looking back over her shoulder to see if there was someone trying to follow her through the knots of people. It did not seem so.

Karen headed toward the same stairwell that Sarah had passed down moments earlier. A few students were walking either up or down, but no Wolf. She found the ladies' room as easily as Sarah. Unconsciously mimicking Red Two's movements, she looked right and left, making sure she was alone. Then she, too, ducked inside.

She let a second of two of silence fill the room before she stage-whispered, "Sarah?"

"I'm right here," came the reply from the stall. Sarah emerged from behind the door and the two women awkwardly embraced.

Karen stepped back and looked at the fake pregnancy outfit and the short black wig and managed a small smile before speaking. "You must have been . . ." Karen started, thinking about the paw prints on the headstones. She stopped, not knowing what word to use. *Scared? Terrified? Upset?*

"Totally freaked," Sarah replied, grimly, even if her choice of words seemed easygoing. "When I called you, I was panicked. But I've gotten hold of myself. Sort of. Still a little shaky. How about you?"

Karen thought about describing being on stage and hearing the wolf whistle and thinking it was the Wolf's whistle, but didn't. She believed that stirring up Sarah's already unsteady emotions couldn't possibly help. *Be the strong one*, she insisted to herself. This admonition was part medical training and part the inability to see what else she could be.

"Have you been keeping time?" she asked.

Sarah nodded. "Maybe fifteen, right about now."

"All right. Let's go."

The two women exited the toilet into the corridor. They were alone, but they could both hear loud teenage voices echoing from not too far away.

"Down and to the right," Sarah said. "That's what Jordan said."

They waited another moment, both of them pivoting right and left. Karen thought it odd, the way they had developed of making sure they weren't being followed. The idea that they were alone in the well-lit cinder-block hallway wasn't reassuring. But neither did they want to see the Wolf, because each knew what that would mean: *The end.*

The girls' locker room was just where Jordan had told them it would be. There were two teenage girls standing outside, jawing with a pair of boys. The girls' hair was damp and their faces flushed, and Sarah recognized them from the game. They stood aside when the two women pushed past them and went into the locker room.

Heat and steam immediately surrounded them. The noise of running water splashed from a shower room. Laughter bounced off the white tile walls loudly.

"Nothing like winning," Sarah said. "Makes other problems disappear."

"Not really," Jordan said, startling the two women. "Or actually, it doesn't make *our* problem disappear," she quickly added, emphasizing the one word with a lowered voice and a shake of her head.

She was only partially dressed, in a skimpy white T-shirt and black bikini underwear. She had a hairbrush in her hand and like the other girls on the team her hair was damp from the shower. Both older women felt a twinge of envy at the easy fitness of the teenager's figure: muscles, flat stomach, narrow hips, and long legs that glistened with a few stray drops of water. Jordan was right at that age where skinny was easy and sensuality seemed to redden her skin like a brisk rub with a towel.

She smiled at Sarah. "I like your costume. Pregnant, right?"

Sarah nodded, then pulled up her sweater to show the pillow taped to her midsection.

"Cool. Probably work on a subway. Help you get a seat," Jordan said.

She slid past Sarah and Karen to her locker and tugged on a pair of faded jeans and a hooded blue sweatshirt from Middlebury College. She smiled and pointed at the school's name. "Prestige school," she said. "Before this past year, I would have gotten in for sure. Now, no way."

"Don't sell yourself short," Karen said with a maternal smile.

"I'm not," Jordan replied. "But I'm a realist."

Karen thought: *No teenager is really a realist.* But she did not say this out loud.

The three women sat on a wooden bench as Jordan slipped on running socks and shoes. She carefully double-knotted the laces, and without looking up at the other two Reds she asked, "What are we supposed to do now?"

Sarah was the first to respond. She pointed at the wig and pillow. "Hide?" she said, using the word as both a statement and a question.

"You mean run away," Jordan replied.

"Yes. Exactly."

Each woman was quiet for a moment, as if measuring the suggestion. Jordan broke the silence.

"If I just go home—and given the way things are at my house, that's not really possible—what makes you think that the Wolf hasn't anticipated that? I mean, we only know he's been watching us for some time. Perhaps he's followed me around my hometown, and that's what he's expecting me to do because it makes sense. Scare a kid . . ."—Jordan gestured to herself—". . . and the kid runs home to mom and pop. Only I can't do that, because my mom and pop are a mess."

Karen shook her head, but answered in a contradictory way. "Maybe we could just each find some friend, visit them . . ."

"And how would we know for how long?" Jordan asked. "I mean, the Wolf doesn't seem to be in any hurry. He probably has a schedule, but we don't have a clue what it is. And eventually, we're going to show up back here—I mean, this is where I go to school and you both live here—and bingo! It starts up all over again. Maybe he's figured on that. Or maybe he *wants* us to run because the more we isolate ourselves the easier it is for him. Or maybe . . ." Jordan stopped.

Karen and Sarah were staring hard at her, and she smiled briefly. "I've been reading a lot about murders," she said. "Not doing my regular home-work. Just studying killers in the library."

"What have you learned?" Sarah asked.

"That we don't have a chance," Jordan replied coldly, as if this were the simplest thing in the entire world and absolutely no big deal whatsoever.

Again the three Reds plummeted into silence. It fell to Karen to break the mood. "I just can't up and leave anyway," Karen said. "I have patients who've scheduled appointments months in advance and . . ."

She stopped. She realized how ridiculous this sounded. There were plenty of other doctors who could take over her practice. She could run. Never look back. The thought made her breathe in and out sharply.

Sarah closed her eyes and rocked back and forth just slightly. "I could go away. Maybe I should. Start over somewhere new. Change my name and find a job and just become someone different. Maybe I could run away and try to hide. It might work."

It felt to her as if someone else was saying these things. Perhaps they made sense. But the idea that she could walk away forever from the two coffins buried so close by hurt her almost as much as the memory of her loss.

Karen must have seen some of this in Sarah's eyes. "That's what the cliché is," she said. "*Start over*. But it's not that easy. And you can't really."

Jordan added, "It's no good anyway," she said. "We like have no clue what the Wolf can and can't do. So even if you managed to slip away and start over, maybe he can follow you. There'd be no way to ever know whether you were safe or not."

She looked at the other two Reds. A quick thought came to her: *We're stronger together.* Then a contradictory thought: *Maybe that's what he imagines we'll think.*

She felt herself shrugging her shoulders at the same time that her hands quivered slightly.

"I think we're each locked here—we stick together, for better or for worse," Jordan added. "I'm guessing the Wolf knows that, and took it into consideration when he chose us. So, really, there's only one answer."

"Which is?" Sarah asked.

"We have to misbehave."

This word made the two older women stop in some confusion.

"What do you mean?"

"We have to *not* act normal." Both Karen and Sarah started to interrupt, but Jordan held up her hand. "I know that's what you said to do, but look, does it really help? No."

She hesitated, and continued. "What are we?" she asked. Then she answered her own question. "We are products of our routines. What makes us feel a little safer? When we drive in circles and wear disguises and imagine that somehow we're fooling the Wolf; and even when we know we're not, it still makes us feel better. What I'm saying is that we each have to figure out how *not* to be ourselves, because the Wolf knows us and has followed us, and"—Jordan jabbed her index finger between her breasts, beating time to her words—"this fucking Little Red Riding Hood doesn't want to just walk blindly into whatever trap he has set."

Karen was astonished at the teenager's muted fury. She was also taken aback by the intelligence of Jordan's idea.

"If the Wolf is waiting for us in the forest, he knows . . ." she started, but Jordan finished.

". . . Then we should be walking in a different forest on a different path."

"Easier said than done," Sarah said. "It's like we're locked into who we are. Jordan, are you going to suddenly skip a basketball game? Karen, you talked about all those patients. They're scheduled. The Wolf has probably scheduled our deaths as well. How do you change who you are and what you do overnight?"

Karen nodded, then said, "Okay. I don't know if it'll work, but we can try. What else can we do?"

Jordan waved her arms around, pointing at the walls of the locker room. While they'd been speaking, the rest of the team had finished showering, dressed, and made their way out, so that now the three were alone in the rows of gray steel lockers. The heat from the showers was starting to dissipate in the humid air around them.

"What?" Sarah asked.

"Have you ever been to my school before?" Jordan asked.

"No."

"What about you, Karen?"

"No."

Jordan continued. "Well, I've never been to the school where you were a teacher, Sarah. And I don't see a doctor in your building, Karen. It makes it all seem completely random, doesn't it? As if the Wolf just picked out three redheads arbitrarily and began his plans. Look, if that's the case, well, then I think we're screwed; all we can do is buy more guns and wait. So that's just crazy thinking. But maybe it isn't random." Jordan was going to continue, but suddenly didn't know what to say.

Karen however, seemed to be trapped in some thought. Sarah started rocking back and forth again. They could hear a shower that some player hadn't quite shut off dripping in the adjacent room.

"We're a triangle," Jordan said. "If we can find the right legs, we can see the connection. I think we've been going the wrong way on this," Jordan said. "It's the mistake everyone who gets stalked makes."

Jordan waved her arms in front of her, slashing through the heavy locker room air. She opened her eyes and faced the other Reds. "We know the Wolf wants us. We have to make him want us so much that he hurries himself into a mistake."

Again Jordan inspected the two other women. She thought they were mature, reasonable, intelligent, and accomplished, all the things that she expected to be someday. *If* she had a *someday*.

"If we were hunting a wolf, what would we do?"

"Get close enough to see him," Karen said.

"Right, and then what?" Jordan asked. It seemed to her most curious: She was acting like the professor, while the others were responding like students. Neither Karen nor Sarah replied, so she answered her own question with a single word. "Ambush."

Sarah quivered, then shrugged. *Why not?* she thought. *I'm half-dead already.* She did not know why, but she burst out in a shrill, humorless laugh, as if she alone had heard some slightly off-color joke that was both funny and offensive. She stood up and reached under her sweater and stripped off her fake pregnancy pillow, tossing all the packing tape she'd used to attach it to her stomach into a nearby wastebasket. Then she unpinned her wig and shook out her hair, so that it flowed freely, a little like lava running down the side of an active volcano.

At about the same moment, the Big Bad Wolf was standing beside his car, staring down at a tire that seemed partially flat. He was just outside of his house, carrying a briefcase with his tape recorder and his notepad and all the questions he'd painstakingly constructed for the Mystery Writers' forensic experts' evening lecture. Afternoon light was fading around him and his first thought was that he would miss the talk because of a bit of bad if not uncommon luck. He kicked at the tire angrily. He bent down and tried to see the nail that had created the slow leak, but he couldn't. It was just as likely that he'd hit one of New England's ever-present potholes and bent the inner tire rim. He knew he'd have to call road service, get them out to change the tire, and waste time the next day getting the damage repaired, and all this would tear him away from what he truly wanted to be doing, which was closing in on the three Reds.

He turned to head back inside, and saw Mrs. Big Bad Wolf standing in the doorway.

"What's the problem, dear?" she asked.

"Flat tire. I'll have to call a garage and—"

She smiled and interrupted him. "Just take my car. I'll call the auto club and wait for them. I don't mind at all and you can still go to your research meeting."

"You absolutely sure you don't mind?" the Big Bad Wolf asked, brightening considerably at the offer. "It's a total pain in the butt, I know . . ."

"Not in the slightest. I was just going to watch television while you were away anyway. I can easily wait for the service guy while I'm watching." She handed him the keys to her car. "Now, take care of my little baby," she said, joking. "You know she doesn't like to go fast on the thruway."

The Big Bad Wolf looked down at his watch. He still had plenty of time. "Well, honey," he said cheerily, "thanks. I'll see you late tonight. Just leave a light on inside and I won't wake you up when I come in."

"You can wake me up. It's okay," she replied.

This was the most routine and commonplace of exchanges, one that a million couples have in some variation every day. It sang of normalcy.

"Here," the Big Bad Wolf added. "Take my keys in case the auto guy needs to start it up." He handed them to his wife without thinking, and got behind the wheel of her little car. He gave her a jaunty wave as he pulled down the driveway.

21

Mrs. Big Bad Wolf watched her car disappear down their little suburban side street. There was a flash of red brake lights at the corner before the vehicle disappeared into the evening. Just as it went out of sight she lifted her hand and made a small half-wave, although she knew her husband wouldn't be looking back in her direction. She was happy to see him go and happier still that she had helped make it possible. Sighing, she stepped back inside their home, walked directly to the kitchen, and dutifully called the auto club, just as she had promised. The dispatcher told her it would be between thirty and forty-five minutes before a tow truck would arrive with someone to change the flat. She hung up the phone. In the living room the television was already playing. She could hear canned laughter and familiar sitcom voices. She put the car keys down on the kitchen countertop and was about to join the characters toiling at Dunder Mifflin or working on the Big Bang Theory when she stopped short.

Car key. Black electronic car door opener with red alarm button. House key attached to a single ring. She recognized those.

Beside them a fourth key. The key to her husband's office.

She stared at that key. She realized that she had never before, not once, held it in her hand. In fact, she couldn't remember ever seeing it, other than during those fleeting moments when her husband stood just outside his office. There were no other doors requiring locks in the entire house. It was, as best she knew, the only key that would open up that particular door. Perhaps he had a spare, hidden somewhere in some drawer, or taped behind a mirror, but she had never seen one and had no idea where he might have concealed it and had never hunted for it despite her constant curiosity about what exactly went on when he was inside working. She lifted her eyes from the key to the office door, looking back and forth as if following the flight of a tennis ball during a match. There was nothing special about the key—a single, silver-coated slab of metal that fit into the dead-bolt lock her husband had installed within a week after their wedding.

"*I need to keep my writing space private,*" he'd told her.

He had said this in an offhand, matter-of-fact manner that fifteen years earlier had seemed to make perfectly reasonable sense. That he needed total isolation to invent plots, scenes, and characters hadn't seemed anything out of the ordinary to her, especially in the first happy weeks of marriage.

She could remember him kneeling beside the door, drill and hardware spread out on the floor beside him, a handyman of secrecy. It had not bothered her in the slightest. *We all need some secrets*, she'd thought during those heady first days.

Except, right at that moment, staring down at the office key, she couldn't immediately recall any of her own that she had hidden from him. Then she told herself to stop being foolish. *Of course you have secrets*, she insisted. *Like when you got so sick and believed you were going to die and you wouldn't tell him how scared you were and how much pain you had. Those were secrets.*

Except she knew he had always understood the truth.

But doubt crept inside her. *Did he?*

Of course he did, she sternly replied to her doubting half. *Remember how attentive he was? Remember how concerned? Remember how he would bring*

172

flowers to the hospital and he would hold your hand and the soft, reassuring tone of voice he always used? He was sweet.

More canned laughter echoed from the living room. Uproarious. Unbridled. Enthusiastic. Irrepressible. Undoubtedly fake laughter, manufactured by a machine.

Without even internally asking herself the crucial question, she answered out loud. "You can't. You just can't."

A rapid argument took place within her. *It's his private space. He'll never know. You can't violate his trust. What's the harm? The two of you share everything. That's what marriage is all about. All you're going to do is read a little bit of the book you know he's writing just for you. A few words, just to get a handle on it. Something to dream about while he works so hard to get it finished.*

The clinching argument wasn't about privacy or curiosity but about love and need, and her own curious obsession: *I know he'd want me to read a few pages. I just know he would. In fact, I'm surprised he hasn't read some to me already.*

This was categorically untrue, and she knew on some level that she wouldn't approach. She would not say the word *liar* to herself. She felt reckless and adventurous, like a child, drawn by uncontrollable fascination, peeping through a bathroom keyhole to see some adult's naked, unsuspecting body. She was excited by the illicit nature of what she was doing, but unable to harness her desire as it mingled with the guilt of seeing something strangely forbidden.

She took the key in her hand and, shaking a little because somewhere within her she knew she was doing something incredibly wrong that she was altogether powerless to stop, went up to the office door.

The key slid effortlessly into the dead-bolt lock. The bolt slid open with a small *click*.

She pushed the door and stood in that transitional space between the two rooms. Light from the kitchen and living room behind her crept forward into the pitch black of the office. She told herself not to hesitate, and reached out and switched on the overhead lamp as she stepped into the room.

For a moment, she shut her eyes as light flooded into the office. Like some better-half conscience, a voice told her to stop: to shut off the lights, step back, keep her eyes closed, slam the door, lock it, and go watch television.

She felt a hot rush of danger. A benign danger that was cooled by curiosity. She told herself, *Just learn a little. It will be your secret.* She smiled, and opened her eyes.

The first thing she saw was a wall covered with different-sized photographs. There were lined 6-by-9 note cards in wildly bright colors—lime green, lavender, yellow—bearing dates and small, pithy observations about location and time beneath the pictures. It looked both terrifically organized and oddly haphazard at the same moment.

She stepped toward the wall. Her eyes centered on a single picture. She saw red hair.

"But that's Doctor Jayson," she whispered out loud.

She stepped closer, peering at another picture. More red hair.

"Jordan?" she asked, although she knew the answer.

She reached out like a blind person to touch one of the pictures. "Who are you?" she demanded of the third picture. It was a redheaded woman standing in an empty, anonymous parking lot on a summer afternoon. She could not see the woman's face very well, as the photograph's subject had buried it into her cupped hands.

She saw sheets of paper with the words *Red One, Red Two,* and *Red Three* and outlines of schedules: *History Class, Academic Building #2, 10:30 MTWTF.* She turned and saw *Patients 830 to 1230 hour break. Frequent lunch spots: Ace Diner. Subway. Fresh Side Salad Store. Return at 130. More patients.*

Another sheet of paper was divided into three sections. Beneath *Red One* was a *Favorite Places* list that had businesses and nightclub addresses. A similar list—though shorter—was provided for *Red Two.* Beneath a picture of Jordan and the identifier *Red Three* was a basketball schedule.

Mrs. Big Bad Wolf stepped back.

She was unsure whether she was speaking out loud or not, but the word *Why?* seemed to reverberate loudly through the room.

This was followed by something clear and whispered: "I don't understand." The photographs seemed slippery and elusive. She couldn't see a reason for them. Not spoken out loud but ricocheting around within her was the weak rationalization: *There's got to be a simple, safe explanation.*

She racked her imagination. Some clear-cut writerly vision of storytelling. Some essential part of the mystery process that she didn't comprehend, but which made utterly perfect and totally reasonable sense to an author. He had to be using real people as models for characters. *That has to be it*, Mrs. Big Bad Wolf insisted. *You just don't get it. You're not the creative sort that understands these complex things.*

But the pictures seemed too explicit and far too provocative. And as she stared, she could tell each was taken from some vantage point that shouted of concealment. From behind a tree. From inside a car through an open window. From around a brick wall. From an upper window in an office building. There was not one picture that even vaguely implied that the subject knew she was being photographed.

A stalker would take these pictures. An obsessed fan or a deranged lover might create this wall of fascination. But she couldn't find these words within her. It was more as if reason and observation had been replaced inside her by some white, burning light and crashing, screeching discordant noise.

No, no, no, Mrs. Big Bad Wolf thought. The word, repeated like some oriental mantra, calmed her a little.

She staggered back, still unsteady but trying to reassure herself with every step, and turned toward the computer. On a corner of the desk next to the printer there was a facedown stack of papers in an 8 ½-by-11 box.

It shouted *novel*.

Mrs. Big Bad Wolf picked up the top sheet and turned it over in her hands.

She read a single line from the top of the page: *Only a fool thinks just of the ending. It's the* process *of killing that incorporates true passion. I can hardly wait for that moment to arrive.*

Her hand shook as she slid the page back onto the pile. For the first time in her marriage, she did not want to read more of her husband's work. Her mind seemed to have gone into a black vacuum that refused to process any information—especially the information that was right in front of her—or to draw conclusions. There were ideas, thoughts, suppositions racing about within her shouting for attention, but she ignored all of the shrieks and cries they made.

"I don't understand," she said out loud. Then she was scared, as if the question would somehow scar the room.

"This just can't be right," she whispered. But she was unsure what *right* was or wasn't.

She looked at the computer. Her fingers shook as she rolled the mouse. A prompt filled a black screen: *Enter Password.*

Mrs. Big Bad Wolf stepped back. A part of her insisted that she could figure out the password—*Maybe it's my name*—but a louder part yelled that she didn't want to open up the portal to the computer because she didn't want to know what she would find there. Carefully, she shut the computer back down. This felt illicit.

Her mind was working rapidly, soaring on tangents that led her nowhere. It was a little like coming across a secret stack of pornographic images that were truly questionable. Images of children. Except these weren't dirty, illegal pictures.

They meant something else.

She turned toward the wall of photographs, but before she could really focus again on what it amounted to, she shut her eyes. If there was something to see, she no longer wanted to see it.

The only thing she could tell herself to do was to retreat slowly, carefully, making certain that she did not disrupt anything so that there was no lingering sign of her intrusion. *Step back out and everything will be as it was just a few minutes ago*, she told herself. But her eyes were drawn to a large red leather-bound scrapbook that dominated a shelf of books, towering over paperback copies of her husband's novels and popular nonfiction accounts that detailed in great degree sensational modern crimes.

The scrapbook was identical to one she had on her bureau. Hers contained wedding pictures and a copy of the invitation and the menu at the small country club where they'd had their modest reception. She suddenly recalled her husband buying the two scrapbooks in a leather goods store on their brief honeymoon. He had given her one and kept the other for himself.

Pictures of our wedding.

She was drawn to it. She reached out, and as if seized by someone else, the scrapbook fell open in front of her.

Her first glance reassured her. No, not the wedding, which would have been a relief, but collections of reviews. *Of course*, she insisted to herself. *Why not?* This made complete sense, and she could feel herself slowly exhaling.

Then she looked a little closer. Intermingled with the reviews were newspaper clippings about prominent murders.

She wanted to shrug. Another *of course*. *Has to be research*, she insisted.

But the newspaper stories seemed to be off-point. She couldn't see the relationship between book reviews and the seemingly unconnected homicides. *There has to be a connection; you just can't see it*, she told herself. There were some grisly, large-type headlines, and grainy pictures of police cars. Names and dates leapt out at her. For another moment, she shut her eyes. When she blinked them open again, she was afraid they were watering.

It was a little like staring at a picture obscured within one of those geometrically designed multicolored artworks that had been popular in the '80s. A trompe l'oeil. There was some image that she couldn't quite recognize, but knew was hidden there.

It had been many years since Mrs. Big Bad Wolf drove recklessly. But that was what she felt: out of control, swerving wildly, tires skidding sickeningly on wet pavement. She seized a blank note card and a pencil from her husband's desk and rapidly wrote down the dates and locations of the newspaper clippings and the names of the murder victims that screamed from the headlines. She took the note card and slipped it inside her shirt, so that it was up against her skin. It felt clammy, like the touch of something dead.

She felt nauseous.

Head spinning, hand quivering, she carefully replaced the scrapbook on its shelf. She returned the pencil to the exact same spot on the desk. She looked around, suddenly frightened that somehow she had touched something, shifted something, and left behind a telltale mark. She had a surge of panic, thinking that her perfume's scent might linger in the closed air of the office. She stepped back toward the door, wildly waving her arms to try to chase any lingering smell out alongside her.

Her eyes took a last look inside, printing the space like a picture in her memory. She shut off the overhead light and slowly closed the office door. Her hands fumbled with the lock and she almost passed out when she heard a loud, blaring noise coming from somewhere close, but from some different world.

She gasped. Electric shock coursed through her body. She dropped the keys to the floor. She staggered backward like someone shot with a gun or struck hard across the face, almost falling. She had to seize the countertop to keep her balance. She could feel sweat on her forehead, and she gasped out a small, terrified gurgle. The noise sounded again.

Car horn.

As promised, the auto service had arrived.

22

Jordan maneuvered along rows of well-worn texts in the school's library. She found many books about the rise of the Ottoman Empire or root causes of the First World War. There were entire shelves devoted to the Reformation and endless volumes assessing the Founding Fathers or the Great Depression. There was precious little about how to avoid being a murder victim.

She felt a little crazy as she wandered up and down the stacks looking for some breezy, cheery title like *So, You Don't Want to Be a Homicide Victim?: Twelve Easy Steps You Can Take at Home to Avoid Becoming Another Statistic*.

Murder as a weight loss program, she imagined.

So far, her research had primarily been concerned with trying to understand famous crimes so she could glean some sort of "anti-information" from them. Her reasoning was simple: If she understood what bad guys did, then perhaps she could avoid making the same mistakes their victims had. She had read about the innocence of Sacco and Vanzetti and the bank-robbing-and-murder sprees of John Dillinger. Billy the Kid and the twenty-one notches on his Colt revolver had fixed her attention, as had Charles Manson, who might not have actually killed anybody, but was regarded as an infamous murderer. She had surveyed the fiction shelves and found some Agatha Christie, which seemed quaint and dated, and some John le Carré, although she felt only slightly like a spy operating in shadowy worlds and didn't think his books could help her. Elmore Leonard might have been more useful, and maybe George Higgins, but she saw they seemed mostly about mobsters in Florida and Boston, and that wasn't really what interested her, because the Big Bad Wolf wasn't some Mafia type or low-rent gang sort. There was even a shelf containing a relentless bunch of books with the word *prey* splashed sensationally and unapologetically across each title page, and though she felt this was what she was trying to avoid becoming, she didn't feel these books would teach her very much.

She took her laptop to a corner of the library where there were small cubicles for students to use preparing term papers or researching English class essays. She did a Google search for *stalking* and came up with over forty million entries in less than a second. She scanned some of these, from what appeared to be government or police organizations. They didn't help either.

Each began with the eminently wise admonition to "limit contact with the obsessive personality." *Great*, she thought. *That's a big goddamn help.* Her problem stemmed from the fact that all the connections between her and the Big Bad Wolf had been his to begin with. It simply wasn't the same as an estranged boyfriend or a deranged classmate or coworker. On the one hand, the Wolf was completely anonymous. On the other, he was so close she could feel hot breath against her neck.

And none of the websites—like none of the books on killing—gave her the slightest idea what to do next.

So, Jordan thought, *you are sort of on your own and not on your own at the same time, because there's always Red One and Red Two.*

She looked across the library. There was an assistant librarian at a desk in the corner and perhaps a half-dozen other students either wandering through the stacks or hunkered down with a pile of books. The assistant librarian was a middle-aged woman bent over a copy of *Cosmopolitan* and obviously killing the last few minutes before she could chase the students from their research and lock up. The students were bookish types who would have been ashamed to sneak some unattributed Wikipedia information into whatever paper they were writing, a practice universally frowned upon by the faculty but regularly employed by almost the entirety of the student body.

She knew the Wolf wasn't there. It made no difference. He had created the impression that he was always close by, as if he was in the next cubicle, smirking behind a stack of research materials as he watched her.

She asked herself, *How can I tell when I'm safe and when I'm not?*

This question reverberated within her. She stood up sharply, pushed all her books aside, slipped her computer into her backpack, and walked quickly out of the library. On the steps, surrounded by early night, she realized that the Wolf could be there. Or could not.

Uncertainty dogged her every stride.

She hunched her shoulders against the chill and headed back to her dormitory. She expected to pass another night neglecting her assignments and tossing fitfully as sleep tortured her.

I can't run away. I can't hide. Just the opposite. I have to get close enough so I can see him clearly.

Dangerous, dangerous, dangerous. The word repeated in her head like an unwanted melody, so much so that she almost missed the sound of her cell phone ringing. She reached first for the throwaway that Karen had given her. But it was her other phone buzzing.

Mom? Dad? she thought, knowing that it wouldn't be.

Sarah was also outside in the early evening, letting cold air flow steadily over her, but not really feeling the chill. *Remarkable*, she thought, *how a little bit of terror keeps you warm.*

She had been unable to remain inside her house. The ever-present television set had failed to distract her. Memories and fears had coalesced into a stew of anxiety, and she had known she had to do something, but was unable to think of what that something might be.

Go to the movies? Ridiculous.

Go out to dinner alone? Don't be stupid.

Head to a local bar to drink? That would be really smart.

So, for lack of any other idea, thinking that it was incredibly foolish to make herself so vulnerable but unable to withstand the buildup of tension within her, she had tossed on a pair of jogging shoes and taken a walk.

Up one block she traveled, down the next, then across a few streets, as haphazardly as possible, with no fixed direction. She had passed a few homes where once she had visited friends and neighbors, but she did not stop. From time to time she had come upon other people, usually out exercising a dog, but on almost every occasion she had hunched up her shoulders and buried her head and neck into her coat and refused to make eye contact. She did not think that some businessman home from work at the office and taking Fido or Spot out for an evening bathroom break would turn into the Big Bad Wolf, but she also knew that this possibility was as likely as any. *Why wouldn't some guy walking his mutt be a killer?* In fact, the only people she discounted were those whose dogs were irrepressible and had that dog-demand and dog-need to greet any stranger on the street with a wag and a sniff. And then, after roughing up the ears and stroking the neck of the third such dog that accosted her despite the apologies and admonitions of its owner, she abruptly asked herself: *Why wouldn't a killer have a friendly dog?*

The idea that *it didn't seem right* hardly comforted her.

She half-hoped the falling night would make her a poor target. The other half within her hoped that the Big Bad Wolf would just seize that moment to end things. It was almost as if resolution was more important than life.

She was unaware of how long she walked. The blocks stretched into miles. The neighborhood changed, then changed again. She turned first one way, then the next, and finally, feet starting to complain with raw blisters, she turned back and limped her way home. By the time she stood outside her home, she was breathing hard and exhausted, which she considered a good thing. Her knees ached a bit and for the first time she felt cold.

She did not immediately enter. Instead, Sarah stood beneath her entranceway light, door key in hand. *Maybe he broke in while I was out, just like he does at Little Red Riding Hood's grandmother's house, so he can wait comfortably inside for me.*

She shrugged and slid the key into the lock. For an instant she felt as if she had exhausted all the fears she could hold within her, the same way there always comes a point when one can cry no more tears. From inside, she suddenly heard her home phone ringing.

No one had called her in months.

Karen had stayed behind long after office hours were finished for the day. The nursing staff, the receptionist, and even the night janitor had all departed. A solitary lamp threw shadows against the wall.

She remained at her desk, deep in erratic thoughts.

That she was always scared was a given. *But how scared should I be?* Like the "pain" scale on the wall of her office, she thought she should be able to rate her fear. *Right now, I'm at 8. In the comedy club I was at 9. I wonder what 10 will feel like.*

Instead, she started to repeat over and over, "Red One, Red One, Red One," in a low, raspy, but singsong voice that sounded like she was developing a common cold, when she knew that it was more tension that had stripped her throat of melody.

She looked up at the ceiling and realized that the words sounded eerily similar to the little boy's refrain of *"Redrum, redrum, redrum"* from the Stanley Kubrick adaptation of Stephen King's novel *The Shining.*

So, Karen tried to run the two together. "Red One, *redrum,*" she said out loud.

Karen had just given herself an inner push, trying to energize weakened muscles and frayed tendons into pulling together to get up and head home, when her desktop phone rang.

Her first instinct was to ignore it. Whatever inquiry from whatever patient could go to the answering service, who would inform the caller to dial 911 if it was life-threatening or else to call back during regular office hours.

But, hell, you're here, she told herself. *This is your job. Someone's sick. Answer the damn phone and help them.* She reached out and picked up the receiver and answered, "Medical offices. Doctor Jayson speaking."

She heard nothing but silence on the other end.

The absence of sound can be far worse than any scream.

Red One froze at her desk.

A few minutes later . . .

Red Two nearly lost her balance and had to slam back against a wall to keep from falling to the floor.

A few minutes later . . .

Red Three stood stock still as darkness flooded around her.

None heard anything other than breathing for the first few seconds. Each was nearly overcome with the desire to hang up or throw the phone across the room or into the night or rip it from the wall socket. They did not do any of these things, although Red Three cocked her arm and nearly let loose, before slowly returning her cell phone to her ear.

Each Red waited for the person on the other end to either say something or hang up. The time seemed fierce, relentless.

Each truly expected something frightening, a disembodied cold voice that said, "*Soon,*" or "*I'm coming for you,*" or even some demonic laugh right out of a Hollywood B movie.

But none of these words or noises came. The quiet merely persisted, as if swelling in timbre and reaching a crescendo, like an orchestra gathering for the final symphonic notes.

Then, abruptly, it was gone.

Red One slowly returned the phone to its cradle on her desk. Red Two did the same. Red Three slid her phone back into her pack. But before they stepped away, they all did the same thing: They checked the caller ID on their phones. None allowed even the vaguest hope that this number would lead anywhere near the Big Bad Wolf.

23

Mrs. Big Bad Wolf lay crumpled in bed like a discarded piece of scratch paper. It was shortly after the sun had come up, and she stared across twisted sheets and pillows at her husband, who slept peacefully beside her. She listened to the steady, even sounds of his breathing and knew from long experience that his eyes would flutter open just as the clock on the bureau reached 7 a.m. He was utterly consistent in this and had been throughout the years of their marriage, regardless of how late he'd tucked himself into bed the night before. She knew that he would stretch by the side of the bed, run his fingers through his thinning hair, shake a little like a lazy dog roused from slumber, and then pad across the bedroom to the bathroom. He might complain about morning joint stiffness and arthritis. She could count the seconds before she would hear the water running in the shower and the toilet flushing.

This morning everything would be precisely the same.

Except it wasn't.

Mrs. Big Bad Wolf assessed every crease in her sleeping husband's face, counted the dark brown age spots on his hands, and noted the gray hairs in his bushy eyebrows. Each item in her husband-inventory seemed as familiar as the weak morning sunlight.

She could feel an argument bubbling up within her: *You know this man better than you know anyone other than yourself* versus *Who is he, really?*

She had slept precious few hours and felt the nasty sort of exhaustion born of tossing and turning throughout the small hours. And when she had managed to sleep, her dreams had been remorseless and unsettled, like childhood nightmares. This was something she had not experienced since the days of her heart troubles, when fears would shake her night. A part of her wanted very badly to rest and forget, but it was overwhelmed by too many questions, none of which she could ask out loud.

The night before—after she had violated her husband's work space— she had stared blankly at a succession of favorite television shows that failed to make even the slightest dent in her worries. She had shut off the television and turned off all the lights and sat in her usual seat in the pitch dark until she saw the headlights of her car reflecting off the white living room walls. Then she had purposely hurried to bed. Normally, no matter how tired she was, she would have stayed up to ask him about the forensics lecture. Not this night. She had feigned sleep when he'd quietly snuck into the bedroom and slid into bed beside her. She had felt cold, wondering whether this was a stranger who slipped in next to her. Once upon a time, he might have stroked her arm or her breast to awaken her with desire, but those days were well past.

What did you see in his office?

This question echoed within her. It had seemed loud through the dark of night, and only softened slightly as the dawn arose through the bedroom window.

I don't know.

She wondered if this was a lie. *Maybe I do know.*

Simple, benign explanations warred with dark, dire interpretations. She felt as if she were standing in a square in some foreign country trying to get directions. Every sign was in letters that she couldn't read, every passerby spoke some language she couldn't comprehend.

"Hey, good morning!"

The Big Bad Wolf was stirring.

She thought her voice would quaver, but it did not. *Ask the obvious*, she told herself: *Are you a killer?*

But she did not.

She thought her voice was weak and reedy when she asked, "How was the lecture? I tried to stay up for you, but just crumped out before you got back . . ."

"Oh, fascinating. The state police guy was really pretty clever and funny, and damn smart. I learned a lot. Got in late."

What did you learn? Did you learn how to—

She stopped. The questions frightened her.

She watched him roll from the bed and cross the room.

Call the police. Call the local district attorney. Call someone. Who?

"Hey, I noticed we're almost out of toothpaste," he said.

Normal, she thought. *Nothing has changed.*

This falsehood made her feel significantly better. She decided to consider what she would make for his breakfast, instead of wondering whether she had stumbled upon some sick secret. But she wasn't very confident that a decision about eggs or pancakes would hold much sway over *Is your husband a killer?* for very long.

By the time she arrived at work, Mrs. Big Bad Wolf was unsure whether she completely wanted answers to the questions that her transgression had created. What she wanted was to rewind time as if it were a videotape— return to the moment when she had realized she held the key to her husband's writing room and decided to sneak inside. A part of her was ashamed that she had lied to him. Another part was simply confused.

The first thing she did was go to the black steel cabinet that contained all the student records and pull out Jordan's file.

On the inside jacket was the official school picture of Jordan taken at the beginning of the fall term. It reminded Mrs. Big Bad Wolf of pictures taken by the police: Front view. *Turn*. Right-side profile. *Turn*. Left-side profile. All that was missing was the placard with identifying numbers held beneath the chin.

She flipped past the photographs and pored over the details contained within the folder. Mrs. Big Bad Wolf had been a secretary in the private school for far too many years not to understand the patterns delineated by the documents on file. She believed they were boringly typical. She had a short conversation with herself: *The kids always think all their problems are really special. They're not. What's next? Jordan experiments with sex. Jordan starts smoking weed or abusing a classmate's prescription for* Ritalin. *Jordan breaks some school rule in a spectacularly obvious fashion and gets kicked out.*

But what she couldn't see was anything that connected her husband to Jordan.

And more: *Why her? Why would she be a target, either for killing or for modeling a character in a book after?*

Thoughts like this seemed to crash through Mrs. Big Bad Wolf's thinking, out of control, spastic.

She found herself staring into the many sheets of Jordan's file with an unbridled anger. She could feel heat rushing through her.

What about you is so goddamn special that my husband has your fucking picture on his wall?

This question screamed inside her.

And, in the same moment, she realized she hated Jordan. It was a real, fierce, boiling-jealous hatred. She could no more have said why she felt this as she could have related what she was going to do about it. Mrs. Big Bad Wolf closed up the teenager's file, slapping it shut on her desk.

This left her doctor and some other unknown woman to worry about. *Why them?*

She reached down into her pocketbook and pulled out the piece of paper on which she'd scribbled the names and dates of her husband's books and the seemingly disconnected murder cases that he'd seen fit to clip from newsprint and store in his leather album.

She realized she had some research to do. She didn't know how much time she had to do this, but she knew she had to hurry.

*   *   *

In his office that morning, the Wolf happily transcribed his notes from the lecture. He was also pleased with the calls he'd made.

He wrote: *Sometimes the loudest noise you can make is no noise at all.*

The cell phone he'd used to call each of the three Reds had been purchased with cash at a small electronics store—one that he'd made certain had no security cameras. After stopping alongside a highway and making the calls, he'd removed the memory chip and smashed the phone beneath his heel. Part had been discarded in a Dumpster outside a rest area. The remainder had been tossed into a small river not far from where the lecture was held. One of the things the Wolf enjoyed most about the science of murder was the preparation in anticipating every small detail of dying.

The key thing, he typed furiously, *is to make sure that you've established the correct level of terror. Fear in your victims—whether it's caused in a few seconds of realization panic or by a slow buildup of uncontrollable anxiety—is what causes them to make immense mistakes and what underscores your equally immense excitement. They stumble and trip and expose themselves while trying to flee or hide. Happens every time. Ever seen one of those teenage "slasher" movies? Every direction they turn either Jason or Freddy Krueger or the Texas guy with the face mask and the chain saw has anticipated their move and is waiting for them. What the victims don't get is that the actions caused by their fear have made them infinitely more vulnerable. When they run amok, they open the door to someone more familiar with the terrain to exploit their fright. Arguing that* Friday the 13th Part One Zillion *has it just absolutely right seems a little crazy—but it isn't really. Remember Little Red Riding Hood? The Wolf knows every inch of the territory with an intimacy she can't imagine. Those movies are no different. It is into those gaps created by unplanned fear that the really sophisticated killer must adventure. Some of the richest moments in the killing experience come from those places, even if they are short in duration.*

Every second becomes precious.

The best killer owns time.

The Big Bad Wolf hesitated, fingers above the keyboard. He could feel inexorable progress in the words that flowed onto the computer screen and the steady buildup of pages in a box at his elbow.

Weapons. Time to select each weapon.

Red One's death would be different from Red Two's. And neither of the first two would be the same as Red Three's.

Three random and seemingly unconnected murders. Everything he'd learned from speaking with cops, defense attorneys, and prosecutors, last night's lecture, and poring over popular literature, both fiction and nonfiction, had informed him that on the day the three Reds died, it had to seem like just so many unhappy coincidences. There would automatically be three separate investigative teams working three obviously unique homicides, in different parts of the county. If the authorities did take the time to speak to each other, they would see a wealth of contrasts, not three killings that were linked together. Each would have its own special *whodunit* nature. Each would be designed to stand alone—when the truth was something far different. That way, he truly believed, when his book arrived on the stands filled with details and truths that only a true master criminal could know, fascination in the public eye would redouble.

The publicity surrounding the embarrassment of the local police would catapult the book to the top of the best-seller lists. He was totally confident about this. The Three Reds would not only satisfy every sophisticated murderous urge he felt, they would bring him a lot of money.

Money he knew that some publisher would happily deposit into a blind anonymous offshore banking account.

Knives. Guns. Razors. Ropes. His own large hands.

There was a wealth of means at his disposal. It was simply a matter of matching the right style to the right Red. *This*, he thought, *was nothing unusual for murder mystery novelists. It was what they routinely did with characters and plots.*

He smiled and actually laughed out loud, before bending back to the design work that so enthralled him. He thought of himself as an architect. He believed that every line he drew was precise.

24

Oddly, it was Red Two who fielded the phone call of silence and reacted calmly. Sarah surprised herself. Every other contact with the Big Bad Wolf threw her into a frantic, gun-waving, panicky response, and yet this time, as ominous and threatening as the quiet on the other end of the line had been, it moved her into a place far different. She had felt cold, but not the chill of fear as much as the ice of a decision being thrust upon her. She suddenly knew exactly what she had to do. This made her feel almost warm and comfortable.

Red One, on the other hand, had burst into tears.

The silence seemed to shout *incompetence* to her. Her entire life had been devoted to figuring out the answers to complicated questions, and now, no matter what she did, the answer eluded her. Scream obscenities? Scream defiance? Scream some phony show of strength? So as soon as the Big Bad Wolf disappeared from the black opposite end of the line, she set her phone down on the desk in front of her and allowed herself the release of tears. They streamed down her cheeks accompanied by gasps and sobs and even a low moan of despair. Karen gave in to the unbridled, unstoppable flood of emotion, rocking back and forth in her seat, her arms clenched tightly around her, chest heaving in agony. She was unsure how long she tied herself into knots. But like a small child crying over a missing puppy, eventually she choked back her tears and was able to fight her way to normal breathing, even if she had absolutely no idea what to do next. Her only desire was to speak with the other two Reds because, as different as they were from her, they were the only people on the entire earth who could understand what she was going through. Except, she realized, perhaps the Big Bad Wolf.

Red Three had been overwhelmed by rage.

Sleep eluded her after the call, and she spent much of the night unsuccessfully reexamining the Big Bad Wolf's YouTube video, trying to find some hidden clue that would help her fight back. At 3 a.m. she finally crawled into her bed and pulled the covers up over her head like a child half her age, afraid of the dark. But underneath the blankets she sweated, teeth clenched. Eventually she threw off all the covers and lay rigid, like a corpse, staring up at the ceiling. When her alarm sounded, she arose feeling filthy, a sensation that hot water and shower suds failed to remove. As she walked to class that morning, she stumbled and nearly fell when she passed the spot where she had been standing the night before when the phone call of silence came. It was as if she'd been tripped by short-term memory, and she kicked at a spot in the pathway as though it was to blame for her near-tumble.

Her first class that morning was advanced Spanish. Mrs. Garcia, the teacher, had grown up in Barcelona, so reversing her skills to teach U.S. high schoolers wasn't much of a challenge. She was a thickset, dark-haired woman, with a cackling laugh and unabashed enthusiasm for anything that was even vaguely connected to her native country. She showed films like *Pan's Labyrinth* or *The Secret in Their Eyes* and assigned books from Cervantes to Gabriel García Márquez, even when she doubted the students understood very much. If someone mentioned art in the class, she almost invariably launched into a rhapsodic description of Madrid's Prado and its famous Goya and Hieronymus Bosch paintings. Jordan was just scraping by in the class, but still, Jordan liked Mrs. Garcia immensely, because she was neither parent nor administrator and didn't try to act like she had all the answers to Jordan's problems.

This morning Jordan took her usual seat near the back, adjacent to a window, so she could look outside and watch blackbirds roost in a nearby tree. She remained completely distracted, playing over in her memory every aspect of the silent phone call. If there had been words or even guttural noises, heavy breathing, whistling, or the slapping sounds of some man playing with himself, she could have interpreted these and formed some sort of picture in her mind. But the absence of noise left her staring at a blank canvas.

She clenched her hands into fists, placed them just beneath her breasts, and pushed them together, as if fighting with herself.

"Jordan?"

Her knuckles grew white. She wanted to strike something.

"*Senorita Jordan?*"

Anger covered her face like a mask.

"*Senorita Jordan, que pasa?*"

It was the tittering of other students that brought her back to the classroom. She looked around wildly, facing the grins and low, mocking laughter. She had no idea what was happening, until she looked to the front and saw Mrs. Garcia in front of the blackboard staring directly at her. Jordan realized instantly that she'd been asked a question and hadn't responded.

"I'm sorry . . ." she stammered.

"*En español, por favor, Jordan.*"

"I don't know . . ."

"*No estabas escuchando?*"

"Yes, I was listening, I just . . ." She stopped mid-lie.

"*Te pasa algo?*"

"No, Mrs. Garcia. Nothing's wrong." This was another lie, and she knew both the teacher and the other students knew it.

"*Bueno. En español, por favor, Jordan,*" Mrs. Garcia repeated. "*Cuál es el problema?*"

"There's no problem. I was not . . ." She stopped, seeing that she was about to contradict herself. She understood she was supposed to reply in Spanish, but the words were just slightly out of reach. Phrases, sentences, snippets of passages from books, dialogue from movies, all in melodic Spanish, flooded into Jordan's head. She searched desperately for the right combination with which to answer her teacher's questions.

Mrs. Garcia hesitated. This pause allowed a couple of the other teenage girls in the class to whisper something to each other. Jordan could not quite hear what they said, but she knew it was something cutting.

She could not help herself. Standing up, she spun toward the other girls. She could see half-taunting grins in their faces. To the girl closest to her she snarled, "*Pinche puta idiota!*"

The girl recoiled. Jordan wondered whether anyone had ever called her a *fucking idiot bitch* in any language.

"Jordan!" Mrs. Garcia broke in.

But this made no difference to Jordan, who felt days of fury released within her. "*Besa mi culo, puta!*" she insulted another girl. *Kiss my ass, bitch.*

One of the boys in the class half-rose, as if to come to the defense of the insulted girl, but Jordan pulled out the most common of all Spanish insults and one that she was sure the boy would know. In fact, they would all know it, she told herself.

"*Chinga tu madre!*" Jordan blurted out, pointing at the boy's chest.

"Jordan, that's enough!" Mrs. Garcia had slipped into furious English. She rarely did this.

Jordan could feel every eye in the room on her. She threw her head back, defiant, and was about to direct another insult at the class. She remembered an old insult from one of the books they had read earlier in the semester: *El burro sabe más que tu . . . The donkey knows more than you.* She was about to shout this one out, but hesitated.

"You can either leave or stay—your choice, Jordan," Mrs. Garcia said in a slow, furious tone. "But either way, you will immediately cease what you are doing."

The command demanded silence in the class. Whispers, undercover laughter, muffled obscenities all stopped.

Jordan reached down and started to collect her things. She had this vision of giving the finger to all the kids in the class, walking out, and finding some isolated, bucolic spot where she could be alone and patiently wait for her killer to find her and put an end to everything. But partway through this dramatic exit, she stopped. She looked up at Mrs. Garcia, whose red face had dimmed, and who now looked merely sad.

Jordan took a deep breath. "No," she said suddenly. "*Ésta es mi clase favorita.*" She sat down abruptly.

Another silence riveted the classroom. After a long pause, Mrs. Garcia cleared her throat, looked sadly again at Jordan, and muttered, "*Bueno,*" before continuing with the day's lesson.

Jordan sat back down in her seat and resumed staring out the window. She didn't want to make eye contact with any of her fellow students. Instead she thought:

Big—that was *grande*.

Bad—that was *malo*.

Wolf—that was *lobo*.

She put them together in her head. *Grande malo lobo*. It had a nice rhythm to it. Spanish was like that, she thought. Every phrase sounded like it belonged in a song. Jordan sighed and stiffened, still refusing to turn and have any contact with her classmates. She felt like a piece of radioactive waste. She was glowing, dangerous, and no one could touch her.

When the class ended, Jordan waited for the others to leave. Mrs. Garcia had taken a seat behind her desk at the front. She gestured for Jordan to approach.

"I'm sorry, Mrs. G," Jordan said.

The woman nodded. "I know you're having a tough time, Jordan. Is there any way I can help?"

Do you have a gun? Can you shoot straight? "No. But thank you."

The teacher looked disappointed, but managed a small smile. "You will let me know if you think I can. Even if it's just to talk things over. Any time. Any day. Any reason. Okay?"

Are you a killer or just a Spanish teacher? Can you kill a man who wants to kill me? "Okay, Mrs. G. Thanks."

Jordan slung her backpack over her shoulder and left the classroom. She hadn't gone far when she heard a buzzing noise, which she recognized as the throwaway phone that Red One had given her. She ducked into a women's toilet and found an empty stall before removing the phone and staring at the screen.

It was a text from Red Two.

Meet tonite. Talk. Important.

She was about to reply to this, when a second text came in, from Red One.

Pickup pizza place 7.

She texted both back: *OK.*

She wanted to add *If we're still alive at 7 tonight.* She didn't.

Then Jordan headed off to English class. The assignment that day was Hemingway's "A Clean, Well-lighted Place." She had read the story through twice, but decided that if her teacher asked her about it, she would pretend she hadn't even looked at it.

What she had liked most was the Spanish waiter in the story. The older one who was willing to keep the bar open for the lonely ancient man, not the young one in a hurry to get home to his wife.

Nada y pues nada y pues nada.

She knew exactly what the waiter meant with every word, and it didn't need any translation.

25

"This was the best idea I could come up with on short notice," Red One said. "It seems like a safe place."

A safe place was a concept that seemed alien, except that when they were together, somehow the threat they all shared seemed diminished by division: *Terror divided by three equals what?*

The three Reds were standing on a dark and narrow side street in a cone of wan light just outside the door of the Goddess Bookshop, away from the more frequented parts of the small city. Mainly women—various ages, varied shapes, including a few hand in hand with toddlers or pushing strollers—were entering the small store. The bookshop featured shelves filled with new-age novels, works on necromancy and female health issues, along with the occasional how-to volume on tarot card reading or predicting by astrological sign.

This night an out-of-town author was coming in for a discussion of her latest novel and rows of folding chairs had been set up throughout the modest space, close to a small podium. There was a large poster of the woman: She was between Red One and Red Two in age and wore her long black hair in what Jordan considered vampire style—straight down, obscuring some of her features to give herself a mysterious although not particularly subtle look. The writer also sported an all-black outfit—boots, slacks, silk shirt, and thick woolen cape—distinguished only by a single large necklace that featured some heavy mystical sign encrusted with sparkling stones. Copies of her book were displayed in tall stacks right inside the doors. The poster indicated that it was part of an ongoing series. This particular novel was titled *The Return of the She-Killer* and featured an exaggerated cartoonlike drawing of a Valkyrie warrior maiden on the jacket, gleaming sword drawn and battling against a squad of overmuscled yet clearly overmatched horned, helmeted Viking types. Dragons flew in the jacket background.

Karen led the other two Reds inside and steered them to some seats off to the side of the makeshift podium, where they would be able to see both the speaker and anyone entering the store. They settled into the uncomfortable steel chairs and each, without saying anything to the others, began to assess the face of everyone joining the gathering.

There were only four men in the crowd. Each looked slightly uncomfortable in a different way. The three Reds watched them furtively, looking for some telltale sign that might suggest they were looking at the Big Bad Wolf.

One man was small, wiry, with a mouselike furtiveness—but he had come in with a woman twice his size and a young daughter, whom he spent much time trying to keep from squirming in her seat. Another was a burly, bearded sort, not unlike the men on the author's book jacket. He had a lumberjack's build and sported a red-checked woolen jacket. But he had entered accompanied by a pink-haired, multiple-pierced young woman wearing exaggerated clothing similar to the author's, and she had dutifully filled the man's arms with copies of what appeared to be other books in the series and apparently tasked him with getting signatures on each. He had a beaten-dog look to him. The other two men looked more academic—thick glasses, tweed suit coats, and corduroy trousers—and both displayed their discomfort at being dragged along to the reading in their body language. Each man sat with his arms folded, slouched in a seat, bored look on his face beside a woman perched on the edge of her chair, eyes glowing, pitched forward, eagerly hanging on every word.

None of these men seemed even moderately murderous in any fashion.

This meant little to the three Reds. They were each alert to *any* possibility —although none of them knew exactly what to look for. *I can spot a disease that might kill,* Karen thought. *I can see it in a blood test or on an X ray. I don't know if I can spot a killer.*

Jordan's look burrowed into each of the four men in the audience. She was more confident. *If you're here, I'm going to know it,* she said to the Wolf that she had created in her mind's eye. She was too young to ask herself the crippling question *How?* She kept trying to fix each of the men with a fierce eye-to-eye, but even in their discomfort they all seemed more interested in the speaker.

Sarah, conversely, kept her gaze sliding between the men. She had no belief that she would know the Big Bad Wolf even if he were standing right next to her, a bloody knife in his hand and a large sign hanging around his neck. She smiled. This made no difference to her any longer.

Each kept their eyes sweeping over the gathering like sentries on duty even as the bookstore owner gushed her introduction of the author, who stepped to the platform amidst enthusiastic applause.

"My books are *all* about *female* empowerment," the writer began with expected emphasis.

That was the point at which each of the Reds stopped paying the slightest bit of attention to what they heard.

The speech lasted just shy of an hour and there was a predictable series of questions afterward, ranging from the specifics of one warrior-maiden's murderous foibles to the more general complaints about the lack of mainstream publishing energy that went into books with "women's themes." The session was generally humorless.

Karen in particular wanted it all to end. She shifted about on the steel chair, desperate to turn to Red Two and ask her, *"What's so urgent that we had to meet tonight? What's happened?"*

Other than the phone call, she thought. That had happened to all of them. A part of Karen was angry. She was exhausted both by the torture of worry and the pain of uncertainty, and she wanted it all to stop. But she wasn't willing to acknowledge to herself that one way of its all coming to a halt was the Big Bad Wolf's success.

The writer finished and basked in applause. There was a flurry of bookstore-worker activity as the author sat down behind a nearby desk, flourished a large pen, and started to sign books. On another table chocolate brownies, hummus and chips, and small plastic glasses of very cheap white and red wine were being served to those in the audience not gathering in line to fawn over the writer.

Sarah motioned toward the table. She got a stale brownie and gestured for Karen and Jordan to accompany her away from the signing and the cash register and the food table. In the midst of all the people, the three Reds were alone.

They stood in front of a wall of books on subjects ranging from abortion to voting rights. Their eyes were on the books—but the conversation was exclusively on something else.

Sarah started with a small, coy laugh. "Well, if the damn Wolf could sit through all that crap . . ." she said, letting her voice trail off. Even Jordan, who always seemed so intense, forced a smile.

Sarah shook her head. "Anyone have any doubt who that was on the phone last night?"

Again there was silence.

"Do you both feel like he's getting closer and closer?" Sarah asked.

There was no need to respond to this question.

"He could go on doing what he's doing forever," Jordan said. "Maybe that's what he likes."

"I don't think so," Sarah replied. "I mean, sure, he has to love what he's doing. But I think he loves something bigger more." They all knew what *bigger* meant.

All three women kept their eyes straight ahead, as if the titles and book jackets on the shelves in front of them might have an answer.

Sarah continued, "The more I think about it, the more it's like being in a classroom. We're all learning about murder, aren't we? You know, I spent a lot of time in classes teaching. And one thing I know: When something happens that interrupts the class, it ruins every lesson plan you've made. Every bit of design you had for that day's teaching just disappears.

Her voice, as eager as it was, seemed to trail off into some memory. Jordan imagined that Sarah had suddenly remembered what that "interruption" had been.

"A disruption that's small—well, you deal with that quickly and effectively. Send an unruly student to the principal's office; a little firmness restores order in the class. Get back to teaching."

Jordan knew exactly what she was talking about. She had, after all, been that *unruly student* earlier in the day.

"But sometimes there are disruptions that you can't handle easily. Where everything just explodes all at once."

"What happens then?" Karen asked.

"All your planning just goes straight to hell."

"So," Jordan said. "What are you saying?"

"We're in his classroom. We have to disrupt that chain of plans he has for us. Break his system. Throw the goddamn proverbial monkey wrench into whatever the hell it is he's designed to happen to each of us."

Karen nodded, but whispered, "Sounds nice. But far easier said than done."

"No," Sarah said. She reached out and grabbed Karen's wrist, pulling her a little closer. "I know how to screw it all up for him. Fuck up the Big Bad Wolf and what he has in mind for us totally and completely." The obscenity felt honeylike rolling off her tongue.

"How?" Jordan blurted out. She was both confused and suddenly hopeful. Just the thought of *doing* something rather than waiting for something to be done to her was encouraging.

Sarah's eyes abruptly started to glisten with tears at the same time that her mouth widened into a grin. She reached up and stroked Jordan's cheek, a surprising act of affection toward someone barely more than a stranger. "One of us has to die," she said.

The others looked shocked. Karen gasped and tried to take a step back, only to be stopped by Sarah's grip, tightening around her arm and pulling her close. Sarah shook her head.

"No," she replied to the unasked question. "It's me."

26

Mrs. Big Bad Wolf discovered rapidly that there is only so much one can find out about specific crimes sitting at a desk and traveling through the Internet. She received even less electronic help unraveling the mystery of the man she loved.

Being an administrative secretary and devoted to routine and order, she made a spreadsheet to keep her inquiries organized. Four books. Four murders. Then marriage. She placed publication and homicide dates at the top of the page. She made subcategories of scenes and characters from the books and contrasted these with actual victims and homicide locations. She listed murder weapons used in real life versus what she had read on the pages of her husband's novels. She collected every small detail she could glean from the diverse newspaper articles that came up on her computer screen and reexamined it like some sort of extremely anxious literary critic. The printer by her desk whirred as she searched doggedly for patterns, for similarities or any shared aspect between books and murders that would lead her down the route to understanding.

It was hard work.

She chewed pencil eraser ends and sucked on hard-candy mints, looking over her shoulder to make sure no one could see what she was doing, even though she knew no one else was in the office. The dean had fortunately chosen that week to go to an academic conference in New York City. He had left behind precious few tasks for her to finish, so she was able to drive herself with a feverishness that paralleled her racing emotions.

Mid-morning a sophomore boy came by seeking information about a summer language program abroad. She quickly shooed him away with a fast lie, claiming she didn't know anything about any such program, even though there was a large brochure describing everything about it in her top drawer.

A little later, right before she would ordinarily have taken her midday break, two senior girls showed up in her doorway needing the dean's permission for an overnight college visit. This was a standard ruse designed not so much to assess a future school as to meet with a couple of boys who had graduated the year before. Mrs. Big Bad Wolf dismissed the pair with a harsh, sarcastic snort and two simple, embarrassing questions: "Do you think you're the first students clever enough to think up this scheme?" and "Do your parents know about this proposed adventure?"

She skipped lunch. Ordinarily she would have been famished, but this day anxiety filled her stomach.

As the workday dwindled into afternoon, she realized that whatever truth her efforts might uncover, it was mired in some sort of swamp. She could see some elements of books and crimes that seemed to match, and others that didn't. A knife-wielding killer in one book seemed to eerily mimic behaviors described by news accounts. A young prostitute discovered in a fictional alley seemed similar to a prostitute who was abandoned street-side in one real city.

It occurred to Mrs. Big Bad Wolf that she was slipping across thin ice. Anything she uncovered just might be the same, but at the same time, it might be different. She told herself to be precise. She told herself to be concrete. She told herself to be analytical.

In two of the murders she'd inspected, men had actually been convicted of the crimes and were serving hard time. In the two others, police had filed the killings into "cold case" categories, which, as she knew from watching reality television shows, were only periodically looked at by a detective here or there. If some new piece of evidence magically arose, it might lead to an arrest amidst trumpets and fanfare, but she was smart enough to know that these infrequent made-for-Hollywood successes obscured the vast majority of real-life failures.

Mrs. Big Bad Wolf was stymied.

When she had seen that two of the killings selected by her husband had resulted in convictions, she felt her heart soar and her pulse rate diminish and she whispered to herself, "See, I told you so. It's no big deal. Nothing to worry about." But the fact that two murders hadn't been resolved troubled her. And she was further disturbed because one of the men convicted of a killing had given a lengthy jailhouse interview to a reporter persuasively insisting on his innocence and claiming the case against him was totally circumstantial; and the other, according to a much smaller story in a smaller newspaper, had agreed to be represented by the New York City–based Innocence Project, which specialized in overturning false convictions by presenting newly discovered DNA evidence.

She hated the word *circumstantial*. Perhaps it had been good enough in a courtroom. But for her it asked more questions than it answered. What frightened her was the idea that few people in the world were better at creating circumstances than her husband. *That's what a writer does,* she thought.

She argued inwardly: *But he does this to make his books smart and seem authentic. No more. No less. No ulterior motive.*

Mrs. Big Bad Wolf gripped her desk as if the earth were threatening to shake beneath her. She stared at the newspaper article that filled her computer screen. A particularly gory killing: knives, dismemberment, and blood.

She burst out, suddenly not caring if anyone overheard her, "Just where the hell else would he get the right details he needs for his books?" This seemed like a reasonable question to her, and she abruptly slumped back. She idly reached out and typed a new entry in her spreadsheet.

It was the date she'd met her husband-to-be.

Rocking in her chair, she began to hum to herself snatches of dated Top 40 love songs from the '80s. At the same time Mrs. Big Bad Wolf tried to picture the four real-life murders. The music she felt buzzing on her lips contradicted the images she created in her imagination of abandoned bodies strewn about isolated country locations and blood-spattered clothing.

She could see blond, matted hair and smell decomposing flesh. She closed her eyes and, instead of delving deeper into mental murder pictures, abruptly recalled walking up the steps of her local library to hear a lecture on a warm, late spring evening. She remembered it was the first time that season cricket sounds had filled the air. She did not know why she recalled that detail, but it blended with a memory of taking a seat near the front.

I was alone up until that night.

Following the speech at the library, she'd shouldered past several other women who were trying to talk to the Big Bad Wolf. She remembered how he'd smiled. She had been a little embarrassed; she was rarely that aggressive in social situations.

"So, do you like murder mysteries?" he had asked her as he sipped lukewarm coffee and munched on stale chocolate chip cookies.

"I love murder mysteries," she had replied. "I live for murder mysteries." These words had surprised her. "Especially yours."

He had smiled, laughed out loud, and made a small Asian bow of thanks. Then he steered their conversation into a discussion about pulp writers like Jim Thompson and contrasted him against the newer crop of procedural-heavy authors like Patricia Cornwell or Linda Fairstein. They'd bonded over affection for the old noir books. *The Killer Inside Me*, they'd agreed, was a far superior read to anything on the current market.

Mrs. Big Bad Wolf's eyes shot open and she bolted upright in her seat. She tried hard to remember which of them had brought up that title first.

It seemed suddenly important, far more important than remembering the cricket sounds, but she couldn't instantly recall who said what. This astonished her. She thought that entire first conversation was printed in her memory. She wondered if twenty-four hours earlier she could have recited everything they had said to each other that night, word for word, sentence for sentence, like an actor recalling some famous Shakespearean soliloquy.

She had a pencil in her hand, and she snapped it in two. For a second she stared down at the splintered twin shards of yellow wood and lead. Then she went back to her task, even though it made her unspeakably sad.

The Big Bad Wolf thought, *Nothing focuses the mind like death.*

This was as true for the ninety-five-year-old pensioner living out his days in a nursing home as it was for the nurses watching over tiny premature babies in a pediatric intensive care unit. A teenager who'd had too much to drink sobered suddenly in the split second he lost control of his father's car on a wet roadway and caught a flash of the thick tree trunk he was about to hit. The same was true for the daydreaming soldier ducking against a dusty wall as automatic-weapons fire exploded in the air around him.

So he imagined that Red One, Red Two, and Red Three were entering into the same heightened state of awareness. He wrote: *There is a curious symbiosis between killer and intended victim. We each take the same test, with the same answers to the same questions. The difference is that one of us emerges stronger. The other doesn't emerge at all.*

In many primitive cultures, warriors believed that they absorbed the strength and capabilities of the enemies they vanquished. This could be achieved by devouring an enemy's heart or merely, like David conquering the clumsy Goliath, cutting the poor dumb fool's head off.

Our military today is too "sophisticated" to believe in such mythology. Too bad. It was true in the past. It's true today.

The modern killer is like a warrior of old. Every success makes him stronger. He may not have to eat anyone's brains or heart or make a sandwich out of a vanquished victim's genitals. But he achieves the same effect without dinner.

The Wolf stood up from his desk, pushed his chair back, and punched the air like a shadow boxer. He reached down and plucked the stack of printouts from the box where he kept them, and he fanned them in the air as if his thumb could accurately measure the number of pages. He was convinced that his latest chapters, describing the special way he'd terrorized each Red, would rivet readers. He knew instinctively that *his* fascination would be shared by anyone reading the pages. He understood that readers' obsession with him would mirror his obsession with each Red.

They will want to know how the Reds die, just as much as I want to kill. They will want to be standing right beside me, experiencing the moment precisely the same way I do.

Murder would make him rich. *In more ways than one,* he thought. He could feel energy coursing through his body. If it hadn't been miserable and wet outside, he probably would have dug out some old running shoes and sweat clothes and gone jogging. It had been many years since he'd actually exercised, but he could feel the need surging through him. Then he laughed out loud.

"That's not what you're feeling," he said out loud.

It's closeness, he told himself. He was very close to accomplishing so much. For an instant, he no longer felt old. He no longer felt ignored.

He felt unbridled strength.

The Big Bad Wolf looked at his watch. His wife would be home soon. Dinner routine followed by television routine and then bed routine. He did a quick calculation in his head. *Just enough time for a quick drive-by,* he thought. *But whom shall I go see?* Red Three was not a good choice; he didn't want to accidentally pass his wife coming home from their school. She'd want to know why he was going the wrong direction at the end of the day. Red One was probably still in her office seeing patients. She typically worked late several weekdays, and this was one of them. *She's too damn dedicated, even when she's about to die.* He didn't want to have to hang outside the medical building waiting to catch a glimpse of her as she went to her car.

The Wolf smiled. *So it'll be Red Two.* He knew she was the one with the least ability to move about. She was tethered to her house by uncontrolled emotions. *Poor gal*, he thought. *She's probably going to welcome death, even more than the others.*

He closed up his computer. *In fact, she'll probably thank me when we have our special get-together*, he told himself.

She knew it was time for her to leave the office as the workday hastened to a close, but Mrs. Big Bad Wolf lingered. She had learned much and little. She had accumulated facts that merely created more fictions. She was filled with doubt and uncertainty, and her stomach clenched with confusion.

She thought, *If only I could get one piece of clarity, I could build off that.* What she wanted was just a simple and neat understanding: *He's a killer.* Or perhaps, *He's not a killer. He's just a writer who steals details from real life. Like every other writer.*

She looked up at the clock on the wall as if the time might provide some sort of concrete foundation. Then she reached out her hand and picked up the telephone. She had written down a name collected from a news story and coupled it with a number easily obtained over the Internet. Her fingers shook only slightly as she dialed.

"Detective bureau," a crisp voice answered.

"Yes. Good evening. I'm trying to reach a Detective Martin Young," Mrs. Big Bad Wolf replied swiftly.

"Is this an emergency?"

"No. It concerns an old case of his."

"You have some information for him?"

"That's correct."

This affirmation was a lie. She *needed* information.

"Detective Young should be in within a half hour. He's on the early night shift this week. You want me to have him call you?"

"Does he have a direct line?"

"I'll give you that number. I'd wait at least forty-five minutes."

Mrs. Big Bad Wolf wrote down the number and began to wait.

She continued to watch the clock. She had always thought that when someone stared at a second hand sweeping around a clock face, it made things seem longer and slower. To her surprise the opposite was true. Her imagination filled with twisted thoughts and unsettling scenes. Minutes jumped by, until she felt she could try Detective Young again. She dialed his extension.

A different gruff voice answered, "This is Detective Martin Young."

"Good evening," Mrs. Big Bad Wolf said. "My name is Jones," she lied. "I'm a teacher in a private New England school." This was less of a lie.

"How can I help you?"

Mrs. Big Bad Wolf took a breath and continued with the tale she had decided to tell. It was a reasonable falsehood, she believed, and one that the cop would readily swallow. "We have a student in a senior-year current events class who has written a paper about a crime that took place in her hometown some years back. Your name is mentioned. I just want to be sure that the student has things accurately before giving her a grade."

"What sort of paper?" the detective asked.

"Well," Mrs. Big Bad Wolf continued, "the assignment was to write about a crime."

"Sounds like a pretty odd assignment."

Mrs. Big Bad Wolf faked a laugh.

"Well, you know, with kids these days, we work really hard to come up with tests and papers that they can't plagiarize from the Internet or buy from some term-paper service. Do you have children, Detective?"

"Yeah, but they're off in college now. And you're right. They're probably buying tomorrow's assignment with one of my credit cards."

"Well, then you know what I mean."

The detective half-snorted and half-laughed in agreement. "So, what's the case?" he asked.

Mrs. Big Bad Wolf shuddered as she read a name off her spreadsheet.

The detective let out a long sigh. "Ah, man, one of my most frustrating failures," he said. "You never forget those. And you say your student wrote about that one? She can't have been more than a baby when it happened."

"Apparently it happened not far from where she lived and her family talked about it growing up. Made a distinct impression on her."

"Well, that's not surprising. Eighth-grade kid disappears on the way home from school. It happens, but usually someplace else, if you know what I mean. We're not the big city here. Anyway, hell, all the people in that neighborhood were terrified. Neighborhood watches got formed. Parents started escorting kids to and from all the local schools. There were meetings in every community center—you know, the "What can we do?" type of gabfest. Problem was, me and all the other detectives were pretty stymied, what with no witnesses and no body. Of course, when some hunter found the bones in the woods three years later it terrified everybody all over again."

"And suspects?" she asked, trying to control her voice.

"A name here. A name there. We took a good look at the people familiar with the girl's route home and every registered sex offender within miles. But we never had a case."

"And now?"

"And now it's history."

Mrs. Big Bad Wolf shuddered as she hung up the phone. *A missing eighth-grade girl. Dead in the woods.* She paused. *Missing in a small city that she knew her husband had once lived in nearby.* She tried to take down some notes, but it was hard, because her hand shook uncontrollably. *Nearby is not the same as murder,* she told herself. She wasn't sure whether this was true.

The Big Bad Wolf drove by the house slowly, stealing glances at the windows, hoping to catch a quick glimpse of Red Two. No luck. He accelerated and went around the block.

Just one time more, he told himself. *Maybe you'll get lucky.* He knew he had to be disciplined. A car rolling past a house more than twice would surely be noticed. Two times was the maximum. That way he looked like someone who had accidentally missed an address and was retracing his path. He grimaced as he steered the car down Red Two's street for the second pass. He could feel his heart rate increase and a drop of sweat gather beneath his arms. He wanted to laugh out loud. *Like a forlorn teenager in love,* he told himself, moving slowly, deliberately, staring at dark windows.

* * *

Red Two sat at her kitchen table. She had a sheet of pink flowered stationery in front of her and she tightly gripped a pen. Night was creeping into the house, but she didn't stand and turn on the lights, preferring to work in the shadows.

Sarah carefully chose each word on the page. *When you're writing for the very last time, make it all count.* The page filled up slowly. Sad words about her husband. Tormented words about their child. Tortured words about her loss.

But she held back all the angry words about the man who wanted to kill her, but whom she intended to cheat.

27

Red One held a very short list in her hand. *Do this. Then do that.*

Karen had absolutely no confidence that even a small part of their plan would work and total confidence that it would all work. She ricocheted between contradictory doubts and beliefs like a stray gunshot deflecting off a shiny steel surface.

She was seated behind the wheel of a rental car, a nondescript gray Chevrolet four-door that she had sent her nurse out earlier that day to bring back for her. She had traded keys with the same nurse, before asking the young woman to head out on some made-up errand driving Karen's car.

The nurse had been mildly surprised, especially when Karen had dressed her in her own overcoat and had pulled a knit woolen cap down over her blond hair. Nurses were accustomed to grudgingly following directions from doctors, regardless of how crazy, dumb, or mysterious these directions might appear to be, and the nurse had seemed satisfied with the cryptic explanation: "I think this guy I had a bad breakup with has been watching me, and I'd like to avoid some ugly confrontation." Her nurse had much experience with her own never-ending series of bad boyfriends, so this all seemed to make some sort of bizarre sense to her.

She had readily taken off in Karen's car in the opposite direction—letting Karen sneak from her office undetected, or so she hoped. She had assigned superhuman capabilities to the Big Bad Wolf. He didn't need sleep, food, or drink. He could render himself invisible or soar in the air above like a hawk hunting for prey. He could follow her scent like the Wolf he was, picking up Karen's odors on the barest of breezes.

But this evening she hoped he would be following the wrong person.

She looked out through steamed-up windows at the world around her and reassured herself: *You are alone*. The rental car was parked on a gloomy, deserted street, not far from some decrepit warehouses that had once housed mills and manufacturing businesses but now sported boarded-up windows, chain-link fences, and rusty barbed wire stretched over doorways. Swathes of graffiti marred the walls. It had been nearly half an hour since any other vehicle drove past, and no one had wandered down the cracked and crumbling sidewalk. It was a sad, lonely, and abandoned part of the small city, unsettling in the growing shadows. It looked like a Hollywood set for a murder; the faded redbrick of the adjacent buildings was stained with grime and cold rain spat heartlessly at the black macadam. A yellow streetlight did little to dispel the growing dark. Karen was parked in a spot that cried out *abandoned and forgotten*, as if some disease had carved all the life away. It was the type of place where nothing good seemed possible.

But it was the best spot for what she had to do.

She looked at her watch. For an instant, she was nearly overcome with a shapeless sadness. She did not form the words *It's happening now* in her head, but she could feel her pulse quicken.

Sarah pulled her car into a bus stop no-parking zone and cavalierly made sure that she was illegally blocking the space.

For a moment she closed her eyes, afraid to look out the window. It was the first time she had been to the juncture of roads that had crushed her life so abruptly.

But, just as surely, she knew it was the only place to leave what she intended to leave behind. The location would speak as loudly as any final message she could write. Quickly, keeping her head bowed and her back to the intersection, she slid from behind the wheel and moved just beyond the clear Plexiglas hut where folks waited in bad weather for the bus to arrive. It was empty, as she hoped it would be.

On the opposite side of the sidewalk behind the bus stop there was a large oak tree, which provided a bit more shelter and shade in the summer. Sarah looked at the barren branches and thought, *They would have bloomed fully by that day. Lots of green leaves. They would have rustled in the breeze. It's a nice sound that quietly reminds people of the fine days to come.*

Sarah was carrying a large satchel. She tugged out a small hammer and some nails as she walked up to the tree trunk. She took a determined, workman's stance and removed an 8-by-10 glossy picture of her husband, herself, and their daughter, taken about a year before the fatal accident. She had carefully covered it with plastic see-through wrap to protect it from the drizzle that fell around her.

She nailed the picture to the tree trunk. Eye height.

Working rapidly, she took a large pink envelope from her purse. This was encased in a waterproof clear plastic bag. She nailed this directly beneath the picture, using two nails to make sure it wouldn't fall to the ground. The hammering noise was like pistol shots fading into the evening gloom.

The outside of the envelope had a simple message written in large letters and strident red ink: GIVE THIS TO THE POLICE.

Not very polite, she thought. *Not even a please or a thank you.* She turned and stole a look toward the intersection. She stopped suddenly, as if hypnotized, breath coming in short, sharp gasps. *They were coming that way. The fuel truck was speeding through the stop. They were probably laughing when it happened. Maybe he was singing. He always liked to sing in the car to our daughter. It was silly and he would make up the words to songs, but she would giggle helplessly because no one in the entire world could possibly be as funny as her daddy.* Sarah choked. She could hear the screech of tires and the terrible sound of impact and metal twisting. It was an explosion of memory and her hands shook and she could not help herself; it was as if all the muscles in her body had been suddenly sliced through. She fell to her knees like a supplicant in a church, staring at the place where all her hopes had died.

Her hands involuntarily lifted up and covered her face. For a moment she held them there, as if playing the child's game of peekaboo. She had the terrible thought she would never be able to move, ever again.

At the same moment, she could hear a firm voice she didn't immediately recognize yelling within her: "*Do it, Sarah, do it now!*"

It took every bit of effort to stand. She could feel her pulse racing. Her legs were still weak. She knew her face was heart-attack pale.

First she took one step, then another, as she turned her back on all her sorrows. She stumbled at first, drunkenly putting one foot in front of the other and picking up momentum.

Then Sarah ran.

Near panic, filled with fear, but increasing speed with every stride and understanding that she had no other route, Sarah raced into the growing darkness.

One block flew by her, followed by a second. Sarah didn't try to pace herself; she sprinted. She could barely see the buildings she swept by.

Find the river, she thought.

Running desperately hard, trying to leave all memories behind, she dashed forward. The sidewalk narrowed slightly on the approach to the bridge, but she pounded to the top. Then she stopped, gasping for breath.

The bridge had four lanes of roadway and stretched across a portion of the river just beneath Western Falls. There was a treatment plant nearby which used the natural flow of the river to help cleanse sewage. The water was dark, fast, turbulent, and dangerous; more than one fisherman working the stretch above had slipped and died in the powerful currents created both by the demands of the plant and the twenty-foot drop forged by nature and helped by turn-of-the century engineers. But the plant barely worked anymore and the industries that had sprung up nearby had closed, so now the only thing that seemed to have life were the black, rain-choked, swirling waters.

Even the small fence supposed to keep people from getting too close to danger was in disrepair. A faded yellow sign warned passersby of the risks. Not many people used the footpath by the bridge. She stripped off her overcoat and let it sink, crumpled up, to the ground. She felt a sudden chill against her neck.

It was a fine place for someone consumed by despair to die.

Sarah bent over, trying to catch her breath. She looked up suddenly. *Soon*, she thought. *Any second now, Red Two*.

Fourteen points, eight boards, a pair of assists, and we won by eleven.

Red Three had taken her customary seat alone in the back of the school's van. Even with her solid, nearly spectacular contribution to the team's victory, she was still left alone on the road trip. There had been a few perfunctory "good game" and "way to go" hand-slapping reactions in the immediate aftermath, but by the time the steam from the showers in the away-girls locker room had dissipated and the last brush had been drawn through wet curls, Jordan was back to her routine outcast status, which was what she had counted on.

She sat with her face pressed up against the glass in the window by the back row. It was cool against her forehead, but she felt hot and sweaty. The other girls on the team were lost in various conversations. The coach was driving and the assistant coach was in the front seat.

Jordan had played at this other school a half-dozen times since making the varsity. She knew the route the van would travel back to her school. She knew how long it would take and what streets they would pass.

She had adopted a forlorn, lost look, as if her thoughts were elsewhere, when they were actually riveted on what she could see outside. *At the stoplight, we'll take a right. Five minutes. Maybe less.*

She could feel her body tighten with tension. The muscles on her arms were taut, and her legs seemed like rubber bands being pulled to breaking. It was like the locker room anxiety before the start of a big game.

It's up to you. It's always been up to you. Doubt crept into her, settling alongside fear. *He'll never stop. Not until we're all dead.*

Jordan tore her eyes away from the window. The coach was driving slowly and cautiously, because the unwieldy van was hard to handle on the slick highways. The assistant was going over the stat sheet from the game, using the light from the dashboard to read off numbers. Her teammates were continuing to talk about boys and parties and classes and tests and music and assignments and all the usual stuff that occupies teens—talk about nothing and everything, all at once.

She returned her gaze to the window. *We go left, then past the apartments and the bodega where they probably sell under-the-counter drugs along with overpriced foodstuffs. There's a stop sign, which he will only pause at, because this shortcut takes us through a bad part of the city and he's got a van filled with rich white girls and that's potentially a bad combination. So he'll accelerate a little, even in the bad weather, right up the street past the empty warehouses and onto the bridge.*

She gritted her teeth. It was a little like Jordan could see it all happening seconds before it did. She could feel the Big Bad Wolf's presence, just as if he were seated beside her, breathing heavily into her ear.

The engine sound increased as the van picked up speed. *Now!* Jordan told herself. *Do it now!*

She took a huge deep breath and then let loose with an immense, terrified, full-throated panicky scream that exploded in the confined van.

Sarah took one last look down the roadway, then vaulted the fence.

She hesitated above the black, swirling waters. *Goodbye to everything, Red Two*, she told herself.

The van swerved wildly across an empty lane, the driver-coach almost losing control at the piercing shriek from the back. Jordan had pushed partway onto her feet and was pointing furiously out the window into the creeping blackness of falling night, her arms waving wildly.

"She jumped! She jumped! Help! Help! Oh my God! The lady, she was standing there by the bridge, I saw her jump!"

The coach wrestled the van to a stop and managed to throw on his emergency flashers. "Everybody stay where you are!" he shouted. The assistant coach was struggling with his seat belt and trying to open his door. He yelled, "Someone call 911!" as he went through the door and ran to the concrete barrier by the side of the bridge to search the pounding ink-sweep of water. The other girls were all shouting incomprehensibly, craning their heads in the direction Jordan pointed, a cacophony of fear and panic. One had grabbed a cell phone from a backpack and was furiously dialing for help. Jordan abruptly slumped down, head still pressed against the glass, moaning and starting to sob uncontrollably, deep, guttural sounds of despair mingling with, "I saw it. Jesus Christ. I saw it. She jumped, she jumped. I saw her jump . . ."

28

Mrs. Big Bad Wolf was oddly familiar with the turbulent emotions swirling around within her. She had been through illness that had threatened to steal her life, she had experienced the clammy belief that her body was about to betray her, and she had once before faced up to the idea that imminent death awaited her.

And she had survived. But she was not sure she could survive what awaited her now. She wondered: *Can the truth kill me?*

She knew the answer to that question: *Of course it can.*

Her head filled with furious admonitions. *Dumb. Dumb. Dumb. You should never have opened that office door. Before you did that stupid thing, you were happy. Never open a locked door. Never.*

Across the room, the Big Bad Wolf was shuffling through the day's mail, discarding just about everything into the plastic bin they used for recycling, grimacing at the occasional bill that appeared in the midst of flyers, catalogues, and letters marked "Important" which were only false come-ons for new credit cards or requests for donations to political parties or causes. Mrs. Big Bad Wolf noticed that her husband kept a few of these;

she knew that he made small contributions to cancer and heart research. These were a few dollars here or there, donations that prompted him to joke, "I'm just trying to make sure we get into heaven."

She was unsure whether heaven was any longer a possibility for either of them.

"So, shall we watch some television?" the Wolf asked as he finished with a flourish, tossing the last useless letter into the trash.

The answer, Mrs. Big Bad Wolf knew, was routinely *yes*, followed by their taking their usual seats and flipping through the usual channels to find the usual shows. There was something wondrously reassuring, almost seductive, in the idea that she could simply say *yes* and shuffle back into the way things had been. With popcorn.

She was torn. A large part of her insisted that she just keep her mouth shut and let everything slide inexorably back into the life that made her so happy. But a small portion of her acknowledged that nothing in the world was as crippling as uncertainty. She had been through that with disease, and now she wondered whether she could ever take her husband's hand and hold it in her own again without frightening, lingering doubts.

While this debate raged within her, making her almost dizzy with anxiety, she heard herself say, "We have to talk about something."

It was a little like someone else had entered the room and some other Mrs. Big Bad Wolf was speaking out loud, in an overdramatic, theatrically ominous tone of voice. She wanted to shout at this intruder, "*You keep your mouth shut!*" and "*How dare you come between my husband and me?*"

The Big Bad Wolf turned slowly toward her.

"Talk?" he asked.

"Yes."

"Is there something wrong? Are you feeling bad? Do I need to take you to the doctor?"

"No. I'm fine."

"Well, that's a relief. Is there some problem at work?"

"No."

"Well, okay. Let's talk. It's something else, I guess. So what's on your mind?" He didn't sound anything other than mildly bemused. He gave a little shrug and gestured toward her as if inviting her to continue.

Mrs. Big Bad Wolf wondered what her face looked like. Was she pale? Was it furrowed with fears? Did her lip tremble? Did her eye twitch? Why couldn't he see the distress that she knew she was wearing like a loud and colorful suit of clothes?

She felt unable to breathe. She wondered if she would fall to the floor choking. "I . . ." she stopped.

"Yes. You what?" he responded. The Wolf still seemed oblivious to the hot-iron agony that encased his wife.

"I read what you're writing," she said.

The grin on her husband's face faded quickly. "What?"

"You left the keys to your office when we switched cars the other night. I went in and read some of the pages by your computer."

"My new book," he said.

She nodded.

"You were not supposed to do that," the Wolf said. The timbre of his voice had changed. The amused tone had been replaced by an even, flat sound, like a single dissonant note on an out-of-tune piano played over and over. She had expected him to cry out in outrage and anger. The equanimity in his voice frightened her. "My office, what I'm working on, that belongs to me. It's private. I'm not ready to show it to anyone. Even you."

Mrs. Big Bad Wolf wanted to say, "*Forgive me*" or "*I'm sorry. I won't do it again.*" She was suddenly confused. She was unsure who had done the worse thing: herself, for violating her husband's space and work, or him—because he might be a killer.

But she swallowed all her apologies like sour-tasting milk. "Are you going to kill them?" she asked. She could not believe she was asking that question. It was beyond blunt. If he replied *yes* what would that mean for her? If he said *no* how could she believe him?

It never occurred to her that she might be putting herself at risk merely by asking.

He smiled. "What do you think I'm going to do?" he said. The timbre in his voice had changed again. Now he spoke like someone going over a grocery list.

"I think you intend to kill them. I don't understand why."

"You might get that impression from what you read," he replied.

"There are three . . ." She'd started a question, but stopped, unsure what the question should be.

"Yes. Three. It's a unique situation," he replied to something she had not asked.

"Doctor Jayson and that girl at my school, Jordan—"

"And one other," he said, interrupting. "Her name is Sarah. You don't know her. But she's special. They are all very special."

This word *special* seemed to be wrong, she thought, but she could not say how or why. She shook her head. "I don't understand," she said. "I don't understand at all."

"How much did you read?" he asked.

Mrs. Big Bad Wolf hesitated. The conversation wasn't going as she'd thought it would. She had confronted her husband and asked him if he was a killer, and this should have made everything clear, but instead they were talking about words.

"Just a little," she said. "Maybe a page or two."

"Is that all?"

"Yes." Mrs. Big Bad Wolf knew this was the truth, but it felt like a lie.

"So you don't really know what the book is about, do you? Or what I'm trying to achieve in what context. If I asked you about plot, or characters, or style, you couldn't really answer, could you?"

Mrs. Big Bad Wolf shook her head. She wanted to cry. "It's about killing."

"All my books are about killing. That's what mystery and thriller writers do. I thought you liked them."

This comment, maybe even intended as a criticism, struck home. "Of course I like them. You know that," she said. It sounded like a plea coming out of her mouth. What she wanted to say was, "*Those books are what brought us together. Those books saved my life.*"

"But you only read, what did you say, a couple of pages? And you think you know what's in the book?"

"No, no, of course not."

"You realize there are several hundred pages that you didn't read in that manuscript?"

"Yes."

"If you picked up a spy novel by, oh, say John le Carré, and read two or three random pages from somewhere in the middle, do you think you could tell me what the book was about?"

"No."

"Do you even know whether my book is in the first or third person?"

"It seemed like the first person. You were talking about murder—"

He interrupted. "Me? Or my character?"

She wanted to cry again. She wanted to sob and toss herself down on the floor because she didn't know the answer. A part of her feared *you* and a part of her pleaded for *your character*. All she managed was, "I don't know." The words came out in a half-wail.

"Don't you trust me?" he asked.

Tears finally started to well up in Mrs. Big Bad Wolf's eyes. "Of course I do," she said.

"And don't you love me?" he asked.

This question pierced her. "Yes, yes," she choked. "You know I do . . ."

"Then I don't see what the problem is," he said.

Mrs. Big Bad Wolf's head spun. Nothing was happening the way she thought it should. "The pictures on the wall. The schedules. Diagrams. And then the words I read . . ."

He smiled, benignly. "When you put it all together it made you envision one thing . . ." She nodded. ". . . But the truth could be something totally different."

Her head bounced up and down in agreement.

"So," he continued, speaking softly, almost with the same simple tone and terms one would use with a child, "everything you saw made you worried, right?"

"Yes."

He leaned back in his seat. "But I'm a writer," he said, layering a grin across his face. "And sometimes to let loose creativity you have to invent something real. Something that seems like it is happening right in front of you. Something more real than real, I suppose. That's a good way of putting it. That's the process. Don't you think that's true?"

Again she was afraid she would choke. "I guess so," Mrs. Big Bad Wolf said slowly. She rubbed some of the tears out of the corners of her eyes. "I want to believe—" she started, but she stopped abruptly. She took another deep breath. She felt like she was underwater.

"Think of the great writers—Hemingway, Faulkner, Dostoyevsky, Dickens—or the writers today we kind of like, John Grisham and Michael Connolly and Thomas Harris. You think they're any different?"

"No," she said hesitantly.

"I mean, how do you invent a Raskolnikov or a Hannibal Lecter if you don't crawl into their skin completely? Think like them. Act like them. Let them become a part of you."

The Big Bad Wolf didn't sound like he wanted an answer to his question. His wife felt tossed back and forth by uncertainty. What had seemed so obvious and terrifying after she violated her way into the office now seemed to be something different. When she read his work in progress, had she come to it already suspicious, or naïve and innocent?

She suddenly remembered sitting in a stark, sterile doctor's office listening to complicated treatment plans and therapeutic programs but only really hearing about the low odds of living. This entire conversation seemed to her to be the same. She was having difficulty hearing anything that didn't reassure her, but everything just seemed to make things more complex. At the same time, however, Mrs. Big Bad Wolf grasped at threads of certainty. A single, terrified voice shrieked within her, and she finally gave in and asked the blunt question. "Have you killed anyone?"

She wished she could turn this question into a demand, like a television prosecutor filled with righteous fury and insistence on the truth, but she felt herself melting. It was so easy to be harsh and firm over at the school with all the stupid requests from overprivileged and selfish teenagers. Being tough with them wasn't a challenge. This was different.

"Do you think I've killed someone?" he asked. Every time he turned her questions back on her, she weakened. It was a little like standing in front of a fun-house mirror, watching her body turn wide and fat, then elongated and thin, and knowing that wasn't what she really looked like, only afraid that she would somehow be trapped by the distorted mirror image and that would become her—misshapen, freakish. Unsteadily, Mrs. Big Bad Wolf rose, walked across to where she had left her satchel, and pulled from it sheaves of paper. She grasped all the printouts and spreadsheets that she had compiled that day.

Her hand shook as she held them, and she stared down and was suddenly confused. She had placed them in careful order when she left her office. They were organized and arranged by time and date and detail, as if proving some point all by themselves. But it seemed to Mrs. Big Bad Wolf that somehow now they were in complete disarray, a disjointed and tangled mess that added up into nothing.

"What's all that?" the Big Bad Wolf abruptly asked. Again edginess had slid into his voice.

"Why did you keep newspaper clips of these crimes?" she inquired, trying to ask a sensible question, one that would help bring clarity.

"Research," he answered quickly, cutting his words off sharply. "Based novels on real life. Kept clips. To remind me of the techniques that worked." He looked directly at her. "So, not only did you read my new book, but you looked at my private scrapbooks as well."

She felt like she was being cross-examined. She couldn't bring herself to utter the word *yes*, so instead she just nodded.

"What else?" he asked.

She shook her head.

He asked again. "What else?"

"That's all," she said. The words scratched her throat as they emerged.

"But that's *not* all, is it?"

Now tears truly began to scorch her cheeks. She wanted to give in to despair. "I tried to check," she moaned. She didn't need to say *what* she had tried to check.

"Check? How?"

"I called a detective connected to this case."

She handed him a clip from a newspaper. In low-rent-newspaper language, it described an unfathomable terror. Snatched from the earth and killed. This was a case that went beyond nightmare, and Mrs. Big Bad Wolf twitched slightly as her hand brushed against his. She thought she was trapped somewhere between the sterility of the news story and the utter terrible truth of the missing girl's last minutes. Mrs. Big Bad Wolf looked at her husband as his eyes drifted over the newspaper story. She expected him to burst out in self-righteous rage, except she wasn't sure why he would react that way. Or any way.

The Wolf glanced at the pages and then shrugged. He handed them back to his wife. "What did he tell you?"

"Not much. It's a cold case. Filed away. He doesn't expect any sort of a breakthrough."

"That's what I would have expected. If you'd asked me, I could have told you that. You know, you probably spoke to the same detective I spoke with years ago, back when I was writing the book."

This had not occurred to Mrs. Big Bad Wolf.

"You remember, in my book, the girl is a seventh grader. She's blond and came from a broken home." Now the Big Bad Wolf was speaking like a teacher in a class for particularly stupid children. "But see, in the picture here, the victim is older and dark-haired and came from a large family."

Mrs. Big Bad Wolf shuddered. *Of course. You should have remembered that. It's all different.*

The Big Bad Wolf folded his arms in front of him. "I thought we always trusted each other," he said. "When you were sick, didn't you trust me to help take care of you?"

"Yes," she mumbled.

"Since the very day we met, haven't we always had a special, I don't know, something?"

"Yes, yes, yes," she said. It felt like she was begging.

"We have always been partners, haven't we? What's the silly word the kids like to use today? *Soul mates*. That's it. Two words, actually. Right from that first minute, you knew you were put on this earth for me, and I knew that I was here for you . . ."

Softly spoken *yeses* poured from Mrs. Big Bad Wolf's lips.

The Big Bad Wolf smiled. "Then I don't understand," he said. "What are you so worried about?"

"The others . . ." she started to say.

"Which?"

"Before we married. Before we met."

"Other women?"

"No, no, no . . ."

"Well, what others?" He was using a soft voice. Words seemed to float in the air between them, cloudlike.

"The women in the news stories."

"You mean the real-life cases I used for my fictional books?"

"Yes."

"What about them?"

"Did you kill them? And then write about them?"

The Big Bad Wolf hesitated. He pointed toward the living room couch, waving his hand for his wife to take her customary seat. She let the question reverberate in the house like a distant thunderclap diminishing amidst pounding rain. As she seated herself uncomfortably, the Wolf plopped down in the armchair he usually occupied through the evening. He leaned back like he was relaxing, but he looked up at the ceiling as if seeking guidance from above. "Doesn't it make more sense to read about them and then write about them?" he finally asked, dropping his eyes to fix on hers.

Mrs. Big Bad Wolf was trying to organize her thoughts, measuring dates of deaths against publication dates, adding in the time it took to write, the lag time between completion and publication—all the mathematical factors involved. She could not understand why dates she thought were etched clearly into her memory now seemed faded and unreadable.

"Do you really think I killed someone? Anyone? Do you think that's me?"

She was unsure. Part of her wanted to say *yes*. But another part did not. She found herself moving forward involuntarily, so that she was perched on the very edge of the couch, almost ready to slip to the floor. She felt ill, nauseous; her head reeled and she could feel unconnected pain throughout her entire body. Her heartbeat was pounding—she could feel it in her chest, pushing furiously against her breast—and her temples pounded with a sudden, vicious headache. She was thirsty, her throat was parched, and she suddenly thought, *If he tells me the truth, would he have to kill me?*

Maybe that would be better.

"Of course not," she said.

The Big Bad Wolf softened his gaze and looked at his wife in the same way that a child might look at a baby kitten. His mind was churning, part congratulatory, part racing ahead with new plans. In the first place, he felt the conversation had gone exactly the way he'd expected it to. He hadn't known *when* his wife was going to stumble on his reality, but he had known it would happen, and many times, alone in his office, or perched in some vantage point watching one of the three Reds, he had played out what she would say and how he would respond. And he was pleased with the way he'd limited the lies. That was an important consideration, he believed. Always tell as much truth as you can, so that the lies are far less recognizable.

But beyond his sense of satisfaction for having successfully prepared for that moment, he was accelerating his next steps. *Write a chapter entitled* Maintaining the Right Disguise, he said to himself. *The key to any successful murder is creating the proper hiding place. It makes no sense to be a loner, to be isolated, driven and reeking of wrongdoing to the first cop that comes sniffing around. The best killers appear to the naked eye to be something much different. No one will ever say about him,* "He seemed like he was up to no good." *No. About the Big Bad Wolf, they will say,* "We had no idea he was so special.

He seemed so ordinary. But he wasn't, was he? We had no idea he was so great." *That's what they will say about me.*

He looked over at his wife. He could see all the troubles and doubts that still echoed within her as if they were flashes of light shooting from her eyes. The Big Bad Wolf reached over and took her hand. It was still trembling.

"I think I've been far too private about my work," he said. "Far, far too private," he emphasized. "You know me so well," he continued, "I think it would make much more sense if you were involved a bit more. You know so much about writing and you love words so much, and perhaps it would be an advantage if you helped out a bit. I mean, you've always been my biggest fan. Maybe you should be a bit of a *helper* on this book as well. Maybe you should be like a production assistant, or my de facto editor."

He saw his wife lift her head slightly. His tenderness had a distinct impact. "Dry your tears," he said, reaching across and plucking a tissue from a side table, then sympathetically dabbing it at the corner of her eyes.

Mrs. Big Bad Wolf nodded. She managed to meet his smile with one of her own. "But I'm not sure what I can do—" she started, but he waved a hand in the space between them, cutting her off.

"I will figure out something," he said.

He lifted himself up from his customary seat and sat down beside her. "I'm glad we had this talk," he said. "I want to make you feel better, and I know when you worry so much it's not good for your heart."

"I was so . . ." again her words trailed off.

Afraid? Worried? Concerned? Well, you had every right to be. He laughed and gave her shoulders a squeeze, leaving his arm draped loosely around her as if they were a pair of preteens at their first movie theater date. "It's hard living with a writer," he said.

Mrs. Big Bad Wolf's head bounced up and down.

"Okay," the Big Bad Wolf said, grinning. "So, you will help me kill them?" he said, surrounding *kill* with quotation marks. *One more lie*, he thought. *And then we can watch television.*

Mrs. Big Bad Wolf nodded.

"Fictionally, of course," the Wolf added with a happy laugh.

29

The sergeant who took her statement thought Red Three was on the verge of hysteria, but he was a twenty-year veteran of the force, with two fourteen-year-old twin daughters at home, and so he was accustomed to sorting through the high-pitched noise that stressed teenagers used for language, although secretly he wished they all had a volume switch that he could just dial down a little.

He wrote down in his notebook phrases like *I saw her jump* and *She disappeared over the edge* and *One second she was standing there and the next she was just gone* that Jordan had ripped from between sobs. He tried to get her to give him an accurate description of the woman she saw throw herself from the bridge, but Jordan was limited to a wild-eyed, arms-waving *Dark clothes, hat, medium height, mid-thirties.*

The cop interviewed the coach, the assistant coach, and all the other players and dutifully listed everyone's cell phone number. None had seen what Jordan saw. They all had reasonable explanations for why their attention was elsewhere.

He offered to call for an ambulance, as he feared that Jordan, who continued to alternate between tears and a kind of icy, withdrawn, flat look, was going into shock. Indeed, the cop believed that the reaction the teenager had was the most compelling evidence of a bridge suicide. *She saw some damn thing*, he thought.

None of the other officers in the half-dozen patrol cars spread out across the bridge had come up with much of anything other than an abandoned jacket. The flashing red and blue lights of the patrol vehicles reflected off the damp roadway, and made it difficult for the officers searching up and down the narrow walkway to find any evidence. High-powered flashlights carved out small slices of black surface when shone down on the rushing waters. Eyeball examinations of the area found few signs of suicide; there was a telltale muddy footprint of a woman's-sized running shoe at the beginning of the bridge's footpath, and there was a scuff mark in the cement where Jordan said the mystery woman launched over the edge.

But the overall lack of overt indications of death didn't surprise the policeman. This wasn't the first time he had been called to the bridge for a reported suicide. It was a preferred spot. There was plenty of leftover despair in the small, fading mill town, where manufacturing jobs had been replaced by illicit drugs. He—like many of his neighbors in the town—knew that the strong currents would sweep a body downstream, maybe toward the treatment plant, possibly over the falls. The force of the unforgiving waters might carry it miles down the river. It was also possible that the body was hung up on the debris that littered the river bottom. It had sometimes taken weeks for authorities to recover bodies that went in at that spot, and there were some that were never found.

He was already writing his report in his head to leave for the morning detective crew. It would be their problem to follow up. Find a name. Notify next of kin. The fact that there seemed no ready proof available to the cop didn't mean that it hadn't happened. He just wanted to finish his part of the case. Police divers and a boat crew would wait until daylight before they started with their hunt for the body. *They won't be happy when they get this order*, he thought. It was dark and dangerous work in ink-colored waters, and likely to be completely futile.

Better chance that body will show up by accident. Maybe a fisherman will snag it one day this summer. That would be some surprise to reel in.

He placed a hand on Jordan's shoulder. "Would you like me to call an ambulance, have the EMTs check you out?" he asked her gently, switching from cop tone of voice to father.

Jordan shook her head. "I'm okay," she replied.

Her coach interjected, "We have support staff at the school who can help her if she needs it. Trauma specialists."

The cop slowly nodded. This sounded like snobbery to him. "You sure?" he asked again, directing his question to Jordan. He didn't like the coach, who seemed a little put out by the whole event. *Like it's some big inconvenience some woman killed herself as you happened by*, the cop said to himself. "Easy for me to call," he added to Jordan, who was wiping her eyes with the back of her hand and whose rapid-fire breathing seemed to be slowing to normal. He didn't mind making the coach wait longer on the bridge in the cold drizzle, and in his experience the EMTs were far better at dealing with sudden shock than just about anyone else.

"Thanks," Jordan said. Her voice seemed a little stronger. "But I'm okay. I just want to go back to my dorm."

The cop shrugged. It was always tempting to see anyone ordinary and young caught up in any sort of police event through the eyes of his own kids, but his years of police work had given him a thick skin and a crusty exterior. He had his statements. He had contact numbers for everyone in the van. He had ordered other patrolmen to continue to fruitlessly investigate the area.

He'd done all he could that evening.

The cop saw the coach dialing a number on his cell phone. "Who you calling?" he demanded.

"School heads," the coach replied. "They will want to know why we're late. Need to keep the dining hall open. And they'll arrange for someone to speak with Jordan tonight, if necessary."

The cop thought this was actually the coach making sure he wouldn't be blamed for getting back to campus late.

"Well," he said, "all of you are free to go. If there's any need for a follow-up, someone will be in touch."

"You will have to contact the dean's office if you want to talk to any of the kids," the coach said.

"Really?" the policeman said. He didn't add, "*The hell we will,*" which was what he thought. He just let the skeptical tone he used with the single word convey that impression.

He watched the team climb back into the van. Some of the girls still seemed upset, and were holding hands or hugging each other. He noticed that no one threw an arm around Jordan.

The cop took note that Jordan made her way to the back of the van and that she sat alone.

He gave her a little friendly wave, which wasn't very professional, but which came naturally to him. He was pleased when he saw a flitting smile on Jordan's face, and a shy return wave.

Damn, kids can be cruel, he thought. He knew he wouldn't get home before his own daughters had gone to bed, but he decided then that he would look in on them and maybe just spend a few minutes watching their sleeping faces. He knew his wife would understand why he needed to do this without asking any questions.

It was not until early the following morning that the detectives assigned to complete the suicide investigation received a call from two clerks who worked in a local motor vehicle registry office. They had been waiting at the bus stop and spotted the letter Red Two had nailed to the tree, and had obeyed the message and called the police. They were smart enough not to touch anything, and they were dedicated enough to wait for a detective to arrive and take possession of the letter and the photograph, even though this made the clerks late for work.

At more or less the same time, Red One was seated across from a woman just a little younger than her, but twice her size. The woman wore close-cropped hair and had massive arms and girth to match. One ear was riddled with at least a half-dozen earrings, and the edge of a tattoo peeked out from beneath her blouse. She was the sort of woman who gave off the impression that she rode a Harley-Davidson chopper to work and that for fun she challenged lumberjacks to arm-wrestling contests, which she rarely lost. Karen was astonished, however, by the soft tone of voice the woman used.

"Here's what we can do," the woman said. "We can protect your friend. We can protect her children. We can provide a safe place for them to transition to a new life. We can assist them with social work advice and legal help as they adjust. We can set them all up with therapists as well, because a number of really prominent local psychiatrists volunteer their time here. We can really help them get started anew."

"Yes?" Karen said, because she heard *but* attached to the end.

"Nothing is foolproof," the woman said.

A distant sound of children laughing penetrated the walls. Karen guessed it came from an upstairs day-care center.

"What do you mean?" Karen asked.

The woman leaned back in her desk chair, rocking backward as if relaxing, but keeping her gaze fixed directly on Karen's face, measuring it for reactions.

"I'm required by law to say that."

"But there's more, right?" Karen asked.

The huge woman sighed.

"Here at Safe Space we are three city blocks from the police station. It is manned around-the-clock, all year. Response time from there to our front door, following a 911 call, is less than ninety seconds. We have an arrangement with the police—there's a code word that the entire staff and all our clients learn—that means that some man has shown up and means to do something violent, so the police respond in force, weapons drawn. We put this in place after an incident last year. Perhaps you remember it?"

Karen did. Headlines and breathless news reports spread over several days. A man, his estranged wife, two children aged six and eight, and three policemen. When the shooting stopped, the wife and one of the officers were dead and one of the children was seriously wounded. The estranged husband tried to kill himself, but had expended all the bullets in his revolver, so he knelt on the sidewalk, gun in mouth, pulling the trigger and clicking uselessly on empty chambers until he was handcuffed and taken away. The case was still in the court system. The man was now claiming temporary insanity.

"My friend is worried about her husband's tendency to violence," Karen said. Then she shook her head. "That makes it sound like a common cold. The man is a flat-out savage. He's beaten her badly, time and again. Broken bones and black eyes. He's threatened to kill her. She has nowhere else to turn."

"That's why we're here," the huge woman said. Karen could sense anger within her words, directed toward some anonymous man. In this case a fictional man. The story Karen had made up involved a friend, two little children, an abusive husband, and the wife's plan to run away before he killed her. Karen had taken common truths and rolled them together. She knew the director of Safe Space wouldn't ask too many questions.

"So, it would be three—your friend and the children . . ."

"I think the children can be sent to family where they will be safe. But the husband will pursue my friend right to the edge of the world and off it, if he has to. He's obsessed and crazy."

"I don't know if separating—"

"He doesn't care about the kids. They're not his anyway, so they are just in the way of whatever he's going to do. It's my friend who is in danger."

"I see. And is he armed?"

"I don't know. I would assume so."

Karen wondered just what sorts of weapons the Big Bad Wolf had handy. Handguns. Rifles. Swords. Knives. Bombs. Bows and arrows. Poisons. Rocks and sharpened sticks. His hands. Razor blades. All were potentially lethal. Any might be what he was intending to use on the three Reds.

"How about your friend? Is she armed?"

Karen pictured Red Two's gun. She wondered if she could figure out how to load it, aim it, and fire it. She did not even dare contemplate the *killing* part of the equation.

"No," she lied.

The director paused. "I'm not supposed to say this," she said. She lowered her voice almost to a whisper, leaning forward. "But I won't allow another incident like the one last year."

She raised her hand and placed a large semiautomatic pistol on the desk. It was black and heartless. Karen stared at it for a moment and then nodded. "That makes me feel substantially better," she said with a small laugh.

The woman removed the pistol to her desk drawer. "I take combat classes at the gun range."

"A wise hobby."

"I've become an expert shot."

"That's reassuring."

"When will you be bringing your friend in?"

"Soon," Karen said. "Very soon."

"Intake is round-the-clock. Any time is the right time. Two in the afternoon. Two in the morning. Do you understand?"

"Yes."

"I will tell the staff to expect a new guest at potentially any time."

"That would be most helpful."

Karen gathered her things. She sensed the interview was at an end, but the director had one final question.

The director looked at her closely. "It is a *friend* we're talking about, isn't it?"

Red One had one more stop to make before going to her office for the remainder of the day. It was a place she'd been many times before but that, even with her medical training and experience, she found too sad for words.

One of the things she'd always noticed about the hospice center at the retirement home was that the lights in the entranceway were bright, harsh, fluorescent, and unforgiving, but as one worked his or her way deeper into the building, they softened, the shadows grew larger, and the white walls turned to shades of yellowish gray. The building itself seemed to reflect dying.

Bagpipes, she remembered from her last visit.

The hospice nurses were a little surprised to see Karen. They hadn't called her. "Just checking on some old paperwork," Karen said breezily as she swept past the desks where the nurses hung out when they took momentary breaks from the relentless dying that filled the rooms. She knew that explanation was more than enough to give her privacy.

She went into a small side room with a copying machine, a coffeemaker on a table, and three large black steel filing cabinets. It did not take her long to find the manila file that she needed.

She took this back to her desk and opened up the computer, adjusting it in front of her. For an instant, she was tempted by the stale package of cigarettes in the top drawer, waiting for her. She realized that she hadn't had a smoke in days. *Good for you, Mr. Big Bad Wolf*, she thought. *Maybe you've helped me finally kick the habit. So when you kill me you'll be saving me from a really nasty end. Can't thank you enough.*

Cancer was what she was looking for in the file. Not exactly the disease. But it was what killed the person whose file she spread out on her desk.

Cynthia Harrison. *A common enough name*, Karen thought. *That's good. Thirty-eight years old. Young for breast cancer. That was sad. But just three years older than Red Two.*

A husband. No children. *Probably that's how she found out the bad news: when she couldn't conceive. They started to run some routine fertility tests and troubling indications showed up in the results. Then it would have been a rapid treadmill of doctors, treatments, and never-ending pain.*

Cynthia was in hospice for just three weeks, following unsuccessful radiation that was followed by equally unsuccessful surgery. *They sent her here because it's the least expensive place to die. If she'd stayed in the hospital it would have cost thousands. And they knew she had just long enough for folks to make the right arrangements.*

She checked the funeral home information and saw which of her colleagues had signed the death certificate. It was the surgeon. *He probably wanted to sign and forget about his failure*. She wrote all the necessary information down on a pad of paper, all Cynthia Harrison's vital statistics: Date of birth. Place of birth. Last address. Profession. Next of kin. Social security number. Relevant medical history. Height. Weight. Eye color. Hair color. Karen parsed every detail she could from the extensive hospice file.

After she closed the paper file, she found all of Cynthia Harrison's computer entries in the hospice archive. These she moved to the *trash* bin. Then she electronically emptied the *trash*. She knew that someone skilled would be able to find it all, if driven to do so. But she doubted anyone would be.

Then she walked down the hallway to one of the nursing stations. It was a simple matter of finding a red-colored *Danger! Infectious Medical Waste* plastic bag and a large sealed container where needles, used sample cups, and anything that might have picked up some powerful virus or deadly bacteria were tossed.

"Sorry, Cynthia," she whispered. "I wish I'd known you." *Except now I do*, Karen finished the thought. She rolled up the entire file tightly and snugged it into the plastic bag, sealing the top carefully before dropping it into the closed bin designed for the sole purpose of keeping everyone safe.

Red Two danced.

She waltzed with an invisible partner. She tangoed to sexy electric beats. She bowed across the room to empty space, as if following the stately steps of an elaborate Elizabethan galliard. When the music changed, she started to twitch and shake as if on a modern dance floor. *Dancing with the Stars*, she thought. *No, Dancing with the Wolf.* She mimicked ridiculous '60s dances like the Frug and the Watusi that she remembered her parents demonstrating at silly moments. At one point, she even launched into the Macarena, gyrating her hips suggestively. Eventually, as exhaustion crept into her steps, she became balletic, moving her arms above her head slowly and spinning about. *Swan Lake*, she hoped. She had seen a performance as a teenager. Stirring. Beautiful. It was the sort of magical memory that an impressionable fifteen-year-old girl never forgets. Once she'd expected to take her daughter to see a similar show. No longer. In the small world of the basement, she lifted her arms above her head and tried to raise herself up on her toes, like the dancer playing a white swan would, but it was impossible.

Her music was contradictory. None of the songs that filled her head matched her movements. Rock and roll wasn't like square dancing, even if that was what she did.

Red Three had left her an iPod with several playlists designated *Waiting Music*. She did not recognize all the performers—she had never heard of David Wax Museum or The Iguanas and had no idea who someone named Silina Musango was or who made up a group called The Gourds. But the music Red Three had selected for her was irrepressible, enthusiastic, uplifting, and she appreciated the joyous rhythms and the wild energy incorporated in every song.

Red Three was trying to help, Sarah realized. *Damn thoughtful of her. She knew that after I killed myself, I'd be isolated and a little crazy.*

Smart girl.

Red Three had created another playlist, but Sarah didn't listen to this one, because she didn't think the time was yet right. She knew it would have far different sounds and selections. This playlist was titled *Killing Music*.

When fatigue finally overcame her, Sarah pulled out her earphones and slumped to the cement floor of Red One's basement. It was cool beneath her cheek. She knew she was making herself filthy. Dust and grime were everywhere, and she could feel sweat streaking her forehead and dripping from her chin, but she did not care. The air was hot and thick as a result of the furnace in the corner having kicked on to heat the house. There wasn't a window, so she could not look outside. She knew only that she was hidden and that even if the Big Bad Wolf were parked outside watching the front door, he wouldn't be able to see her. A part of her thought that if she shut off the single overhead bulb that filled the room with weak light, it might be the same black turbulence as the river waters that she'd faked diving into.

The night before, when she'd run through the growing nighttime to where she knew Red One was waiting for her, she'd imagined Red Three's piercing scream. *I bet it convinced everyone.*

She curled up into a ball.

Sarah died last night, she thought. *Suicide note and "Goodbye, I'm gone forever." They will bury me beside my husband and my daughter. Except it won't be me. It will be an empty coffin.*

She knew she was destined to become someone new. She wasn't at all certain she liked this. But until she was reborn, she would only be Red Two.

A deadly Red Two, she told herself. *A homicidal Red Two.* A cold chill of ferocity slid through her, surging up against uncontrollable rage.

But then she abruptly gave in to all the emotions reverberating within her and sobbed uncontrollably on the floor as she cradled not a picture of her dead family, but the .357 Colt Magnum.

30

The Big Bad Wolf gasped once, then shouted out an incomprehensible torrent of curses. He spun about and had to restrain himself from punching the kitchen wall. Instead, he crushed the local news section of the daily newspaper in his fists and closed his eyes as if someone were drawing fingernails across a blackboard making a scratching sound that assaulted every nerve end in his body. Beneath his fingers was a headline on a short article: *Former Schoolteacher a Suspected Suicide*.

"No, goddamnit! No!" he bellowed in sudden, uncontrollable rage.

Bright light reflected off the river surface. The rain had finally stopped and the weather had warmed slightly. The wind had dropped and the morning sun had risen into a wide, cloudless blue sky. A small crowd was gathered on the bridge, leaning up against the low concrete barrier and watching the activity below. A news crew seemed bored, their shoulder-held camera lying uselessly against the wheel of their panel truck. Cars on the bridge slowed down as they gawked at the activity before speeding away. Three Hispanic women, each pushing a baby-filled stroller, had paused and were talking rapidly and gesticulating toward the flat black water surface. One woman crossed herself three times rapidly. The Big Bad Wolf slid in beside a pair of men not much older than him. He knew they would both be observant and filled with opinions readily shared. They were smoking, letting wisps of cigarette smoke pungently fill the still air.

"I tell yah, they ain't gonna find nothin'," one man said confidently, although he hadn't been asked a question. He wore a tattered gray overcoat and a crumpled brown felt fedora that was snugged down tight on a weather-beaten forehead. He shaded his eyes against the morning glare.

"Man, I wouldn't go in there," said his companion. "Not even with a safety line."

"You know, they ought to post no-swimming signs all over the place."

"Yeah, except they ain't looking for no swimmer."

The two men grunted in agreement.

Poised thirty yards from the bridge buttresses were two small aluminum outboards. A pair of policemen in black wet suits and wearing twin aluminum air tanks were taking turns slipping into the river, while others held ropes and maneuvered the boats against the strong currents.

The Wolf watched carefully. There was something hypnotizing in the way a diver would disappear, leaving a trail of air bubbles and a slight disturbance on the water surface, only to emerge within a few moments, struggling against the powerful flow of the river. He could see frustration and exhaustion as the divers were pulled from the water and the boats moved to a different position. *A grid search*, the Big Bad Wolf thought. *Standard police technique: Divide the area into manageable segments and inspect each before moving to the next.*

"Have they come up with anything at all?" he asked the two old men, who clearly had been watching all morning. He used a carefully chosen tone of idle curiosity.

"Some crap. Like a kid-sized jacket or something. That got 'em all excited for a while and both guys went under for maybe fifteen minutes. But nothing else. So now they're moving back and forth. Maybe trying to get lucky."

"I sometimes fish that stretch," his companion said. "But no one is dumb enough to go near the river until after it comes down in the summer. At least no one who wants to live." This old man was wearing a navy baseball cap adorned with the name of the USS *Oriskany*, a retired Vietnam-era carrier that had been sunk to make an artificial reef. The cap had a frayed peak. The Wolf noticed that his hands were scarred and gnarled, like the roots of an ancient oak.

"I tell yah, they ain't gonna find nothin'," the other man said again. "They're just wasting our tax dollars out there. They buy up all that fancy diving equipment and never get much chance to use it."

"They'll give up soon enough," Baseball Hat said to Fedora.

The Big Bad Wolf decided to keep watching. But he thought the old man was probably right.

They ain't gonna find nothin'.

Maybe, he thought, *because there's nothing to find.*

He just wasn't sure, which irritated him no end. He knew certainty was the lifeblood of murder. Small details and accurate assessments. He sometimes considered himself to be an accountant of killing. This was one of those moments where attention to minutiae was critical. *It's like doing a tax return of death.*

Maybe I have killed her, he thought. Certainly the intense pressure he'd brought to bear was enough to drive someone to take her own life. *If you know you're about to be murdered, wouldn't you elect to kill yourself?* That made a certain amount of sense. He thought of prisoners awaiting execution who hang themselves in their cells, or people who receive a diagnosis of a terminal illness. He had a vision of doomed financial brokers and office workers throwing themselves from the Twin Towers on 9/11. *The uncertainty of awaiting death can be far worse than the pain of suicide.* And he knew that Red Two was the weakest of the three Reds. If she had tossed herself into the river, well, that was *almost* as good as choking her to death himself. For a moment he could feel pressure in his hands, as if they were wrapped around Red Two's neck and he was actually throttling her beneath him.

Certainly worth putting a notch on the gun, he told himself, thinking like some old Western gunslinger.

Death is like the truth. It answers questions.

He made a mental note to put that in his next chapter. Perhaps he could legitimately claim her murder alongside the two others. He considered this possibility and realized that his earlier anger just might have been misplaced. *Readers will be intrigued by the thought that I could drive her to take her own life. It will be shocking. Like all those people slowing down on the bridge to see if they can spot something, readers will need to see what happens next. It will make them more anxious for Red One and Red Three. And that will make the last days for the remaining Reds a little easier to manage, with one less stop along the road to death.*

Like a journalist collecting elements for a story on deadline, the Big Bad Wolf looked around. He took in the policemen working in the river, he counted the people watching from the bridge, he noted the news crew packing up their cameras and sound equipment and readying to leave for some bigger and better photo op. This made him smile. *They don't know it*, he thought, *but this is the best damn story around. By far.*

But this story is all mine.

The Wolf decided he would give the river searchers another half hour to pluck Red Two from the black currents, but no longer. He settled in and waited for answers that he didn't really expect to get from his perch above the waters.

The dean stood in his doorway and half-smiled at Mrs. Big Bad Wolf. He seemed troubled, as evidenced both in his soft tone of voice and his hunched-over posture. "Did you read the report from the girls' basketball coach? They had some trip back to school," he said, shaking his head.

On her computer screen, Mrs. Big Bad Wolf began reading a copy of a single-page account that the coach had e-mailed to the dean. It was short on description, just a brief recitation of the reasons for their delay getting back after a victory. She had the distinct impression the coach would have preferred to write about the win, not the aftermath. Nothing in the coach's report indicated that the suicide victim Jordan saw had red hair. Or that Jordan knew the victim. Or that they were connected in any way.

She nodded her head to the dean to let him know she was finished reading.

"Will you send a text and a follow-up e-mail to Jordan Ellis's history teacher—that's where she's in class next period. Ask him to tell her to come to my office before lunch."

"Will do," Mrs. Big Bad Wolf replied cheerily.

The dean thought for a second, then said, "Tell him she's required to be here."

She typed out the messages. After sending them, she punched up Jordan's schedule on her screen. Then she glanced at the clock on the wall, and guessed that Jordan would walk through the office door at eleven.

She was off by two minutes.

Jordan seemed hurried, distracted. Mrs. Big Bad Wolf put on her most sympathetic look and used her most understanding voice. "Oh, dear, that must have been simply terrible last night. I can't imagine how frightened you must have been. It must have been awful for you. And so sad."

"I'm fine," Jordan said briskly. "Is he in?" She gestured toward the inner office.

"He's expecting you, dear. Go right in."

Mrs. Big Bad Wolf felt a quickening in her heartbeat. She had not realized how exciting it would be for her to find herself close to Jordan—knowing that she was a literary model for a murder victim. She suddenly felt alive, as if caught up in a swirling confection of secrets. Jordan's sullen responses and slouching, contemptuous attitude made Mrs. Big Bad Wolf imperceptibly nod her head in total comprehension. *She's perfect*, she thought. *No wonder he chose her.* She could suddenly see hundreds of reasons to kill Jordan.

Kill her, Mrs. Big Bad Wolf thought. *On the page.* Her hands trembled slightly, quivering with a delicious sort of intrigue. *It's like being caught up in my own private novel.* Mrs. Big Bad Wolf felt herself sliding, as if slipping into some world where what was real and what was fiction were no longer different. It was like descending into a warm and soothing bath.

Jordan strode past her desk, and Mrs. Big Bad Wolf watched her from behind. She could suddenly see arrogance and selfishness and teenage isolation and nastiness all wrapped up in Jordan's every step.

Her breathing was shallow, and she wanted to burst out in a laugh. It was a little like being let in on a huge, wonderful secret. She could suddenly imagine the entirety of the writing process, turning a self-centered, privileged young woman into a character in a book. Just like being present at the Creation, she thought, although she admitted that was overstating matters slightly.

She suddenly rose up and trailed Jordan into the dean's office. As Jordan slipped into the chair across from the dean, Mrs. Big Bad Wolf cheerily said, "Don't forget about the phone meeting with the trustees." This phone session was not until later, but it gave her an excuse to leave the office door ajar, which she guessed neither the dean nor Jordan would notice.

A production assistant, she thought. *A good production assistant listens to everything. I'm a lot more than just a secretary.*

Mrs. Big Bad Wolf returned to her desk and craned her head to listen, arranging a pad of paper on the desk in front of her to take notes.

The first thing she overheard was: "Look, I'm okay. I don't need to speak with anyone, especially some touchy-feely psychologist. I'm fine." Jordan's voice seemed angry and filled with contempt.

"I understand, Jordan," the dean replied slowly, "but these sorts of traumatic incidents have concealed impacts. Seeing a woman kill herself the way you did can't just be shrugged off."

"I'm okay," Jordan stubbornly repeated. She was desperate to get out of the office. Every second she spent distracted from the real threat was potentially dangerous. She knew the only respite she had from the Big Bad Wolf were her moments on the basketball court, when she could lose herself in exertion. She wanted to scream at the dean, *Do you know that I'm doing something far more goddamn important than any class or any*

247

meeting with a shrink or anything you can imagine in your closed little private school mind?

She said none of this. Instead she could feel tension within her tightening like a knot and she knew she had to say the right thing to get out and get back to the more serious business of avoiding being murdered.

"Well, yes, I believe so," the dean continued. "And I'll take your word for it. But still I'm insisting that you speak with someone. If you do that and the doctor signs off, says all is okay, then so be it. But I want a professional involved. Did you sleep any last night?"

"Yes. Eight hours. Slept like a baby," Jordan trotted out the cliché, not actually imagining that the dean would believe her.

He shook his head. "I doubt that, Jordan," he said. He didn't add *Why do you lie to me?* although that was what went through his head. He handed her a piece of paper. "Six o'clock. This evening at Student Health Services. They will be expecting you."

"All right, all right, I'll go, if that's what you want," Jordan said.

"That's what I want," the dean replied. "But it should also be what you want." He tried to say this in a softer, more understanding tone.

"Can I go now?"

"Yes." The dean sighed. "Six p.m. sharp. And fail to show up and we'll just be back here tomorrow morning, doing all this all over again, except this time someone will escort you to the appointment."

Jordan stuffed the appointment slip into her backpack. She rose and exited without saying anything else. The dean watched her leave, thinking he had never seen anyone as determined to throw away every opportunity as Jordan.

Outside his office, Mrs. Big Bad Wolf hurried to jot down everything she had heard. *Six p.m. Student Health Services.* She looked up as Jordan swept by her, then reached for her telephone. The teenager hadn't even looked in her direction.

31

Outside the window Jordan could see nothing except growing darkness. Her angle through the glass showed empty playing fields blending into distant stands of trees that marked the beginning of undeveloped conservation land. This was typical of private schools in New England: They favored the woody, isolated, forest look that gave visitors the impression that there were no distractions from the world of studying, sports, and the arts that was cultivated at the school. Jordan knew that in other directions there were bright lights, loud music, and all the typical sorts of trouble that teenagers routinely found.

She waited patiently for the psychologist seated at a desk across from her to finish a conversation with a local psychiatrist who specialized in pharmacological solutions to teenage angst. They were discussing a prescription for Ritalin, the preferred drug to deal with ADHD. The psychologist, a frowsy, angular young woman probably only about ten years Jordan's senior but trying hard to look more mature, was being careful not to use any names, because Jordan was present. The issue appeared to be a refill order that shouldn't have been necessary. Jordan knew exactly why this anonymous student had run out of Ritalin early: because he had sold some or had some stolen, or maybe both. It was a favorite party drug.

Fun for some, she thought, *and now the kid can't concentrate enough to get his history term paper finished.* She wanted to laugh at the dilemma, and the pathetic way the student had tried to talk the psychologist into getting more pills. Jordan knew the school monitored the number of pills each student was supposed to have on hand at any given time: just enough for a once-a-day respite from distraction.

The psychologist gestured in the air as if to make a point and then, with the phone still to her ear, waved in Jordan's direction, a *just a minute* motion that turned Jordan back to the window. She could just make out her reflection in a corner of the pane—pale, as if the image was of some different Jordan. *That's Red Three, not Jordan*, she decided.

In that moment, Jordan wondered whether the Big Bad Wolf had electronically visited the YouTube entry for Red Two. It had not taken Jordan long to post two messages on the website: *RIP Red Two* and *We will miss you, your friends 1 and 3*.

She didn't know if he would see them. But she thought they were a nice touch.

The psychologist hung up the phone with a chorus of *"Okay, okay, okay"* before slumping back. She smiled. "So, Jordan, tell me about what you saw last night."

She doesn't waste any time, Jordan thought. "Maybe if I had a prescription for Ritalin . . ." Jordan began.

The psychologist managed a laugh. "That was a pretty predictable conversation, wasn't it?"

Jordan nodded.

"But unsuccessfully trying to talk the staff out of a class two substance isn't the same as seeing a woman kill herself," the psychologist said.

Straight to the point, Jordan thought again. "We were driving back to school after the game. I was the only one staring out the window. I spotted the woman climb up on the bridge barrier and saw her jump. Then I screamed. Just a natural reaction, I guess."

The psychologist bent forward, expecting more.

Jordan shrugged. "It wasn't like I killed her."

But now she's free, Jordan thought. It was a little like seeing someone else get a gift that she particularly wanted. She envied Red Two.

Jordan shifted in her seat. The psychologist was asking more questions, probing feelings, impressions. It was inevitable that she would try to steer this conversation into some discussion about her parents, her grades, and her bad attitude. Jordan waited for this to land in front of her, replying as succinctly as she could. She just wanted to get out of the psychologist's room with as little damage as possible and get back to the task of saving her life. She was willing to say anything, behave any way, or act as appropriately as she possibly could to achieve that result.

Nothing I say here means anything. For a moment she considered telling the psychologist everything. The letters. The video. All about becoming Red Three. It was like telling herself a joke, and she had to stifle a smile.

And what will she do? She will think I'm crazy. Or maybe she will call the dean. He's a well-meaning idiot and he'll call the police. More well-meaning idiots. And then the Big Bad Wolf will just disappear into the woods and wait until I'm on my own again, and he's free to do whatever he wants. Maybe I'll get a year or two and then I'll be Red Three all over again. And I know what he will do then.

Jordan could hear herself replying to the psychologist's questions, but barely paid any attention to what she was saying. The words coming out from between her lips were flimsy and had no real connection to what was happening to her. She believed the real forged iron and steel was within her, safely stored away for the time being, being held back for when she truly needed it. *That will be soon enough. The Big Bad Wolf is our problem,* she told herself. *And we're going to solve it ourselves.*

She smiled at the psychologist, idly wondering whether a smile was actually the right bit of performance, thinking that perhaps the fastest way out of the office and the meeting was to concede some small bit of trauma, so that the shrink would have something to write in a report to send to the dean and everyone would think they were doing their job.

Jordan considered this for a moment and said, "I'm a little afraid of having some really bad nightmares. I mean, I can see that poor woman as she jumped. It was so sad. I would hate to be that sad myself."

The psychologist nodded. She wrote something down on a pad of paper. *Sleeping pills,* Jordan thought. *She's going to give me a prescription for sleeping pills. But just a couple so I can't kill myself.*

There was a single weak light over the entrance to Health Services, and Jordan paused for an instant as she exited to survey the nighttime stretching in front of her. The Health Services building was tucked off on a side street in one of the less-frequented parts of the campus, so Jordan realized that she would have to pass through a great deal of darkness before reaching a spot where other students were likely to be walking the pathways.

Hunching her shoulders against a wind that had picked up, she hurried forward.

She had not traveled more than a half-dozen strides when she saw the figure in the shadows, right where a large oak tree brushed up against the back of one of the now-empty classroom buildings. It was like seeing a ghost. Jordan nearly stumbled and fell. She had the sensation of her heart stopping, then starting again, all in the same microsecond.

The figure was dressed in black. A scarf and hat obscured his face. The only feature that seemed to glow with life were his eyes.

She lifted a hand, sweeping it through the nighttime in front of her, as if she could erase the vision. The figure remained still, watching her. Slowly, she saw the man raise his hand and point directly at her. The voice seemed muffled, as if the breeze had steered it toward her from a dozen different directions.

"Hello, Red Three."

A part of her was riveted in place. A part was panicked, as if it had broken loose from some mooring inside her. She wanted to break into a run, but her feet felt mired in the ground. It was as if fear had bisected her body and that, like droplets of mercury hitting a floor and scattering, parts of Jordan were spreading in different directions. Jordan felt conflicting commands racing through her head, all out of control. She felt weakness in her knees spreading infection-like through her body and she thought she might crumple to the ground and crawl into a fetal position and just wait. *It's happening now* ran through her head, followed by *He's going to kill me now!*

As if struck, Jordan staggered back.

The figure seemed to melt into the thick black trunk of the tree. It was as if Jordan could no longer focus her eyes, could no longer differentiate between human form and shadow. Involuntarily, she raised both arms and held them out in front of her face, as if to ward off a blow.

There was a strange sound surrounding her that she couldn't recognize at first, and then she understood it was her own breathing—shallow, raspy, and devolving into a childlike whimper.

She looked around wildly, thinking, *Someone help me*, but she couldn't form these words with her tongue and lips and scream them out. There was nothing except darkness and silence.

When she returned her eyes to the figure, it was gone. Like an act in a magician's stage show, it had disappeared into shadow.

Run now, she shouted to herself.

She turned away from where she had seen the figure and launched herself forward. She was an athlete, and she was fast. She wasn't burdened by a backpack jammed with books or a prom queen's high heels; there was no ice on the pathways. Her stride lengthened, her feet striking the black macadam of the path with slapping sounds that were like gunshots echoing from far away. She pumped her arms and sprinted, desperation driving her speed, and the only thing she could think was that it wasn't going to be fast enough. She could feel the Wolf behind her, closing the distance, jaws snapping at her heels, teeth reaching for her.

The sensation that she had only seconds left to live crushed her and she wanted to cry out that it was unfair, she wanted to live, she didn't want to die there, that night, at a school she hated, surrounded by people who weren't her friends. She gasped out the words *Mother, help me!* even though she did not want her mother's help, because her mother never helped anyone other than herself. She felt like a small child, little more than a baby, helpless and defenseless, panicked and afraid of dark and thunder and lightning, though the world around her was still and calm.

Just at the second she felt a hand seizing her from behind, Jordan stumbled. The world seemed to spin about, and she was tossed down, sprawling like a skater who loses an edge. She threw her hands out to brace her fall and let out a small scream. The hard path surface scraped her palms painfully as she banged her knee. Pain shot through her, and she was momentarily dazed. She was prone on the cold ground, but she had the presence of mind to roll over and kick out at the Wolf that she knew had nipped at her heels, sending her into the tailspin. She could hear her shrieks, "Get away! Get away!" as if they were coming from some other place. Everything seemed disjointed, disconnected, unreal and alien.

She fought back. Tears filled her eyes. She punched and battled, using every muscle, tendons stretched to breaking, smashing out against the darkness that threatened her. She could feel her hands showering blows against fur, flesh, and sharp bared teeth that tore at her; she could feel spittle and hot blood flying into her face, preventing her from seeing clearly. She felt herself being grabbed and lifted up, and she scratched and clawed, using every fiber of her being because she wasn't willing to die right there. She fought as hard as she could.

Against nothing.

It took seconds that seemed much longer than any space of time Jordan had ever experienced—even the end of a close game, where tension and time coalesced to make everything seem to speed up or slow down, as if the rules of nature had been suspended—or Jordan to realize: *I'm all alone.*

No Wolf.

No killer.

No dying.

At least not yet.

Jordan lay back, spread-eagled on the cold ground. She could feel heat rushing from her body. She stared up into the black night sky and saw stars blinking into light. She shut her eyes and listened. Familiar sounds crowded her ears: a distant car accelerating, noisy students from a dormitory, a few chords on an electric guitar accompanied by the belching notes of a saxophone. She squeezed her eyes tight, before they suddenly shot open.

Footsteps.

She gasped again and sat up. She looked right, then left, her head swiveling back and forth.

No one. "But I heard him . . ." she whispered, as if arguing with herself. Red Three thought one thing. Jordan Ellis thought another.

She listened hard, and imagined she heard a fading, distant wolf's howl—unmistakable . . . impossible. She knew it had to be a hallucination, but it seemed real. It was a little like being trapped in a different era, in a different world, where predators maneuvered freely after the sun set. She knew she was a part of modern life, with all the lights and energy of progress, but the forlorn cry she heard clearly belonged to a far different time. It both existed and didn't exist.

Jordan scrambled to her feet. Her jeans were ripped and she could feel sticky blood on her palms and her knee. She urgently searched the shadows around her for another sight of the Big Bad Wolf.

But nothing except shades of black greeted her.

Feeling panic slide away from her, and urgency replace it, Jordan started to run again. Though this run was at a more controlled pace, she knew that she had to get back to somewhere bright as quickly as she could.

When the cell phone rang in her purse, Red One was standing at the top of the stairs leading to her basement carrying a tray with a salad and a ham sandwich and a bottle of water. She had called out to Red Two, who was waiting for her below, out of sight, concealed from any prying eyes.

She set the tray down and tore the phone from the satchel.

"Yes? Jordan?" Karen said.

"He was here, he was right here, he was waiting for me and he chased me—at least, I think he did—but I got away. Or maybe, I don't know . . ." Jordan spoke in a rush, her excited words barely understandable. Then the teenager's voice trailed off into silent confusion.

The physician of rationality took over. "What exactly did you see?"

"I was at Health Services. They made me go see a shrink because they thought I'd be traumatized after reporting Sarah's suicide . . ."

"Except you knew—"

"Yes, of course, I knew she was okay, that was the plan, but when I came out, there was a man in the shadows, I saw him, but then he wasn't there . . ."

"Are you sure?"

Red Three hesitated. Jordan wasn't at all sure of anything. Fear, she understood, creates confusion. So she wasn't completely honest.

"Yes. I'm sure. Pretty sure. He spoke to me. I heard him call me Red Three. At least, I think I heard that."

"How could he have known you were at Health Services?"

"I don't know. Maybe he'd been following me earlier, and I didn't notice and he just waited outside."

"Okay," Karen responded slowly.

"Karen," Jordan said abruptly.

"Yes?"

"I feel so alone."

Karen wanted to say something reassuring, but did not know any words that would help. Instead her mind was churning with ideas. "You're sure as you can be that it was him?"

"Yes. As sure as I can be."

"You're not alone. We're all in this together," Karen said, although she didn't completely believe this. "Look, Jordan, hang in there. I'll call you back later." She closed the phone and looked at Sarah.

"Grab your things," she said, with a sea captain's brisk decisiveness. "We have a couple of free minutes. The Wolf was out stalking Jordan, so we know he's not outside here right now. We've got to move."

"Is she okay? Should we go see her?"

"She was scared. But she'll be okay, I think. We have to stick to the plan. He can't know you're alive. We have to keep you hidden. It's the only way."

Sarah nodded. All she had was a small duffel bag with some spare clothing that Karen had loaned her, Karen's comedy-club laptop computer, and some sheets of paper filled with information about a dead woman named Cynthia Harrison. The bag also held her dead husband's gun. That gun was the only part of Sarah Locksley's former life that remained intact.

Moving as quickly as they could, each understanding that something had happened that night that should scare them, the two women burst from the house and hurried across the yard to Karen's car. Karen jammed the key into the ignition and spun the tires in her dirt-and-gravel drive as she accelerated.

"They're expecting you at any time," she said. "And he won't know where to look anymore, even if he does suspect something. At least you'll be safe while we do what we have to do."

Neither Red One nor Red Two actually believed that statement in its entirety. Maybe, both thought, there were small parts of their lives that might be safe.

But not the whole.

The front door closed with a thud. She heard a jacket being tossed on a hook and boots being shoved into a closet.

"Hi, dear. Sorry I'm late."

"That's okay. Dinner will be ready in a couple of minutes."

"I just want to take down a few notes, then I'll be out."

"How did it go?"

"Totally cool. Just totally cool. She went to the appointment like you said she would. I saw her go inside. It was great. I mean really great. Just the sort of scene that will really help the book. I just wish I'd been able to go into the office with her so I could have listened in. But I can make that part up, no problem. Getting teenage language right on the page is a challenge: hell, it has been since J. D. Salinger sort of defined the entire genre. But these little details are what make the story come alive when I put it all together. I really owe you one."

Mrs. Big Bad Wolf felt a surge of pleasure. She had been unsure whether her husband would want to know about the meeting or not when she had called him. Now she felt like she was truly a part of the creative process.

"That's what I'd hoped. That's why I called. So, if you owe me a favor, maybe you'll do the dishes tonight?"

The Wolf kissed his wife on the cheek, then pinched her rear end, making her squeal a little with pleasure and slap at his hand with mock indignation. "Yes. Absolutely." Both of them laughed. "I'll just jot down some ideas for the next chapter, wash up, and I'll be ready to eat. I'm completely starved."

The Wolf was surprised at just how hungry he was. Coming that close to Red Three—even if only for a few seconds—had made him ravenous. He felt a parallel sense of desire; it was all he could do not to grab his wife and rip her clothing off. He marveled at the intensity of his feelings. *Passion and death go hand in hand*, he realized.

"Will you let me read some more soon?"

He grinned. "Soon. When I get a little closer to the end."

He turned to leave, but paused momentarily before going to his office. He looked back at Mrs. Big Bad Wolf standing in front of the stove, stirring rice that was simmering in a pot. She was humming something, and he tried to pick out the tune. It seemed familiar, and he was on the precipice of recognition; he only needed to hear a few more notes. For an instant he glanced around. He could see the table fixed with two place settings, and he could smell chicken baking in the oven. He reveled in the almost overwhelming ordinariness of it all. *This is what makes killing special*, he realized. *One minute you are seated in the cockpit just going through your routine, totally mundane, done-them-a-million-times preflight checks, and the next you are hurtling down the runway, picking up speed and momentum, and taking off, into something utterly different every time. You set yourself free of all earthly bounds.*

Mrs. Big Bad Wolf tapped the edge of the simmering pot with the large wooden spoon in her hand. Like a drummer trying to capture an elusive beat, she realized that the rhythm of her life had changed in a mysterious and quite pleasant way. *Writing, killing, and love*, she thought. *They are all in their own way the exact same thing, just different stitches in the same fabric.* She slapped the edge of the pot with the spoon handle in a familiar sequence: *boom, pa boom, pa boom boom,* the famous bass line to Buddy Holly's "Not Fade Away."

32

For the next few days, the Big Bad Wolf watched every news show, read every word in the local papers, even tuned in to local radio hoping to hear some stray commentary in an effort to uncover the whereabouts of Red Two. He dutifully made a point of driving past the suicide location frequently, to see if the police had recovered her body. He was annoyed when they apparently gave up the search. It did not mean she wasn't at the bottom of the river. He just didn't know for certain. He cursed the cops, and thought they were incompetent. He needed answers and they were supposed to provide them.

Two evenings after he followed Red Three out of the Health Services building—which had been a delicious high point—he spent a frustrating hour walking in Red Two's neighborhood. The lights were off in her home and had been since the night she allegedly jumped, and he could see no sign of life whatsoever except for a bouquet of white flowers that someone had placed up against the front door. The flowers were already beginning to wilt.

Pausing on the street outside her house, he realized that he no longer had to conceal his presence from her. She was gone, that was clear.

He felt angry and cheated.

The night before, he had stolen from his wife's side and locked himself in his office. He'd double- and triple-checked his extensive dossier on Red Two. Nothing in his research suggested anyone—distant family or casual friends—who would have taken her in and hidden her from him. He chastised himself, imagining that he'd somehow missed some connection.

But then he remembered the grave site with the two names on it, which was now awaiting a third. Those two names were primary reasons why she had been singled out as Red Two in the first place. *She would never, not ever, leave them behind. She couldn't. There were only two ways for her to join them: me, or that damn bridge over that damn river.*

It was painful for the Big Bad Wolf. He'd believed he'd been smart enough to take her just to the brink of wanting to kill herself, so that when he arrived at her side, she would almost appreciatively accept death.

He knew this presented a writing challenge. His readers would want to know every step he'd performed. They'd want to experience the tension and face the same choice that Red Two did. Die one way. Or die another.

Always think of the readers, he reminded himself.

He made his usual checks on Red One. She seemed to be sticking to her routine, just as he'd suspected she would. As scared as she might be by Red Two's death, Red One seemed to find safety in continuing to maintain a normal front. She was no longer haunting the comedy clubs, or even sneaking a smoke in a parking lot. *Too frightened to even indulge an addiction,* he thought. She arrived at work early and stayed late, then drove directly home. This pleased him. And he did not think that Red Three would run away. *That's one of the great mysteries of killing,* he thought, as he stared in at Red Two's dark house. *The rational part of us thinks we would flee, hide, turn to our friends for help, and somehow take steps to keep ourselves safe. But we never do. As the distance narrows between hunter and hunted, one half of the equation becomes more focused, more skilled, and far more determined, while the other half becomes more crippled and less able to think clearly. Her world grows smaller and smaller.*

He thought of Discovery Channel videos of lions chasing antelopes, or wolves like him stalking caribou. The hunted race back and forth wildly, panicked, out of control. The hunter remains single-minded in its approach, cutting off all avenues of flight. Determined. Direct. He didn't think he was any different. He needed to emphasize that point in the book.

He had an odd thought: *Male lions let the females do the hunting, but they are the first to eat the kill.* He wondered if wolves were the same. *Not likely. We're not lazy.*

The Wolf stole a last glance at Red Two's house. He doubted he would return there again—and then, in the same moment, had the sensation that he could barely tear himself away. He reimagined the pleasure that rolling past Red Two's house had given him, spying on her over weeks and months. He had a hard time thinking that phase was finished. It was time for him to head home, but he couldn't shake the sensation that something was incomplete. He hoped that killing Red One and Red Three would give him the satisfaction he craved. But for the first time he was worried. His feet dragged like an old man's against the sidewalk and the spring in his step felt diminished. He mumbled to himself as he made his way back to his car, "You work so damn hard, and then something comes along and screws it all up."

He told himself to not be so hard on himself. Everything else was going according to plan. He misquoted the poet out loud, "Ah, the best-laid plans of mice and men often go astray."

The Big Bad Wolf snorted and laughed. *Flexibility*, he believed. He needed to write some pages on the necessity of flexibility. *Be prepared for the unexpected. No matter how things are falling into place, always be ready for sudden changes. Like a jump from a bridge.*

When he got to his car, he slumped behind the wheel as if exhausted. "We are down to days now," he said out loud. He liked the forcefulness in his voice. As he put the car in gear, he began to consider weapons and locations. He thought that he should divide his manuscript into two sections: *The Hunt* and *The Kill*.

* * *

Karen sat primly across from the funeral director.

"This is an unusual request," he said haltingly, "but not impossible."

The office had an appropriately somber tone, with lots of dark wood and shaded windows that prevented too much light from slipping in. The funeral director was a bald-headed, stocky man with pudgy fingers, and seemed like a friendly sort even with his somber black suit. *A firm handshake, a warm smile, and an enthusiastic voice when death is the subject*, she realized. She had expected a cliché, a tall and cadaverous, deep-voiced Uriah Heep of a man.

"Just a small gathering," Karen said. "I'm afraid since the accident that left her widowed, Sarah really let almost all her relationships drop. She was very isolated and alone. But that doesn't mean there aren't some of her friends left who want to pay their respects. Maybe some of the teachers where she worked, or some of her late husband's coworkers in the fire department."

"Yes, that makes sense," the funeral director said. "And family?"

"Unfortunately, very spread out. She was an only child and her parents have passed away," Karen lied. "And her cousins are unwilling to accept the reality of her death. Or maybe they just don't care."

Karen avoided the word *suicide*, as she knew the funeral director would.

"That is most unfortunate," he said, but his tone suggested the opposite, that it made matters much easier.

"I thought of doing this at my house—you know," Karen continued, "just a little private gathering to speak our affection for the deceased—but that seemed too informal." She knew he wouldn't like this suggestion.

"No, no, either a church or in one of our smaller venues is much better. I have found that often people whose friendships seemed to have been dropped would be surprised by the strength of the turnout."

That is, they would be surprised if they weren't dead, Karen thought. She nodded. "So true," she said. *And at my house there would be no fee.* "So can you show me the rooms you have available?"

"Of course," the director said with a smile. "And let me just bring my schedule book as well."

He led Karen down a narrow, thickly carpeted hallway painted in somber off-whites. Outside a set of double doors with a plaque that read THE ETERNAL PEACE ROOM, he paused. "No casket?"

"No," Karen said. "The police have yet to recover her body—if they ever will. I thought just flower arrangements around a montage of photographs."

He nodded. "Ah, that would be lovely."

Karen had the impression she could have said, "I want to show homemade pornographic films," and he would have replied, "That would be lovely."

The director held the door open for her.

It was a small room, with seats for about fifty. There were speakers mounted into the walls softly playing funereal organ music. In the corners there were vases for flowers. It seemed distinctly artificial and soulless. Karen thought it looked ideal. "Oh, this is nice," she said, while secretly thinking that if the Wolf managed to kill her, she could imagine no worse place to lie in state. *Christ, I hope if he wins, someone takes my dead body and puts it up on a stage and gets every comic in the county to come by and make the worst, most outrageous, most offensive jokes they possibly can over me so that everyone can have a good laugh at my expense.* "Those are nice curtains," she said, pointing at the back of the room. They were fake silk.

"Yes," the director said. "They lead to a small room. Sometimes family, you know, need some extra privacy."

"Of course," Karen said. She thought they would be perfect for what she had in mind.

Just like the Big Bad Wolf, Red Three was thinking about weapons as the van from her school pulled into the parking lot at the mall.

"All right, just two hours. Check your watches now," the junior faculty member announced as he opened the door for the dozen students packed into the vehicle. "And stay together. Buddy up. And no one get into any trouble."

The school routinely ferried students over to the mall on shopping trips. Jordan had very rarely signed up for any of these excursions. She did not particularly like the bright lights and canned music that filled the place, nor did she enjoy window-shopping or trying on what passed for cheap teenage fashion.

The junior faculty member—a young man in his early thirties who taught geography—would get himself an overpriced cup of coffee and find a spot in the food court where he could read while waiting for the two hours to be up. He was there primarily to make sure heads were counted and no school or mall rules were broken.

Jordan fully intended to break a major rule.

She had in her pocket one of Red One's credit cards, and specific instructions about what to purchase. She was pressed for time—not only because the junior faculty member had put a deadline on the mall visit, but because Jordan knew that later that evening Karen would call credit card security, tell them the card had been lost or stolen, and cancel the account.

Her first stop was an electronics store. The video recorder that the salesman was eager to sell her was slightly larger than a cell phone and could be operated with one hand. It had a wide-angle-lens attachment, which Jordan believed would be helpful. Red One's credit card was rapidly accepted.

Jordan's next task was something that she had not discussed with Karen. She felt a little guilty as she stepped into the clothing store. It was a higher-end type of place, catering to young professionals. She went directly to shelves of overpriced cashmere sweaters and selected a black turtleneck that she liked in her own size. She took this to the checkout counter, where a girl hardly older than she was behind the register.

"It's a gift for my mother," Jordan said with a fake smile.

The register girl ran the credit card and asked, "Would you like a box to put it in?"

"Yes," Jordan replied. She had been counting on this small detail, that stores in the mall didn't box items up themselves any longer. Now they just put a folded cardboard box and the sweater in a paper bag adorned with the shop's logo.

Jordan signed the receipt with a scrawl that imitated Karen's name. She glanced at her watch. She needed to hurry.

At a paper goods store, she purchased a birthday card, some gaudy silver wrapping paper, and tape. Then she marched to a large chain store that specialized in sporting goods. Surrounded by Nike, Adidas, Under Armour T-shirts, sweat clothes, and manikins modeling the latest in running gear, Jordan went directly to the section marked *Hunting and Fishing*. A middle-aged salesman was lurking amidst camouflage clothing, fishing rods, lures, life jackets, and paddling helmets.

"Hi," Jordan said briskly. "Can you help me?"

The salesman looked up from putting the price tags on bows and arrows, and Jordan could tell that he immediately dismissed her. Teenagers were usually over in the section with running shoes or looking for headphones for an iPod.

"My dad is a big hunter and fisher person," Jordan said with a laugh. "I want to get him something for his birthday."

"Well, what sort of gift?" the salesman asked.

"He really likes to bring fresh fish home for dinner," she replied. "He has a boat that he takes out."

Jordan's father was an executive at a Wall Street investment firm. As far as she could tell, he had never spent a night outdoors, and he avoided leaving his office for anything more rustic than a two-martini business lunch at a French restaurant. She pointed at a display. "What about something like that? Do you think he'd use one of those?"

The salesman followed her eyes. "Well," he said, "no fisherman who likes to bring his catch home would be caught without one. These are really good. Top of the line. A little pricey, but I bet he'd enjoy it."

Jordan nodded. "That's what I'll get, then."

The salesman took the eight-inch filleting knife down from the display. "These are Swedish and come with a lifetime sharpness guarantee."

Jordan admired the narrow curved blade and black grip. *Like a razor*, she thought.

She did not have much time left before the junior faculty member would start collecting all the students for the ride back to the school, so she hurried to the second-floor ladies' room, which she guessed would be more private than the larger toilets near the food stations. She burst in, and to her relief, she was alone.

She took the filleting knife out of its plastic packaging and removed the blade from its leather sheath. She took a single sheet of tissue and sliced it easily. Then she brandished the knife in the air, like a swordsman. *That will do*, she thought. Then she carefully slid it within the folds of the black turtleneck. This she placed in the box they had given her at the store. Working as quickly as she could, Jordan then took some of the brightly colored paper and ribbon and wrapped the package up, taping every crease shut. She took the birthday greetings card and wrote "Happy Birthday Mom! Hope it fits! Love Jordan" inside the card. She put this in an envelope and taped it all to the package.

The school did not allow students to own weapons of any type, but Jordan knew she needed one. She had no intention of sending the sweater to her mother, whose birthday was many months distant anyway. But no junior faculty member would ask her to unwrap such a package, and even if he did, he would just glance at the sweater inside and not feel within its folds for anything else.

Jordan wondered whether the Wolf was as good a smuggler as she was.

She tried to create the sensation of driving the filleting knife between his ribs into his heart. *Drive it up under his chest bone*, she thought. *Be relentless. Get all your weight behind it and every bit of strength you can summon and don't hesitate. Kill him before he kills you.* The idea of surprising the Big Bad Wolf with a weapon as deadly as the filleting knife gave her a sense of safety, although the Wolf was *always* ill-prepared and at her mercy when she pictured the confrontation in her head. And the Wolf never had a gun or a knife or any other weapon of his own when she envisioned their face-to-face meeting.

Jordan couldn't quite piece together how she'd gain the upper hand. She just knew she had to find a way.

One of the first things Sarah noticed about Safe Space was that some of the laws that people commonly took for granted were wildly ignored there. She liked this. She fully expected to ignore some other laws in the days to come.

For example, when she hunched over the laptop computer and started to construct a new identity out of the Cynthia Harrison information that Red One had provided, she thought she would have to keep what she was doing secret—only to find out that the staff at the women's center were experts at creating an entirely new person out of electronic vapors.

It was not the first time, the center's director told her, that the easiest course of action for an abused and beaten woman was to simply become someone different. The local police knew about this sideline at the center, and did nothing to stop it. There was an agreement that as long as a woman was trying to avoid becoming a victim, the cops would look the other way.

Hiding was the center's primary purpose.

Protection was the second.

In short order, they had helped her get a copy of the dead woman's birth certificate from the small town where Cynthia Harrison was born, which they subsequently managed to get illegally notarized, making it wonderfully and magically official. A new social security card was applied for and a replacement driver's license was put in process through a dizzying bit of computer legerdemain. A bank account at a large national bank—nothing local that might be traced—was established with some cash that Karen had given her.

Sarah was disappearing. In her place a new Cynthia was taking shape.

When Karen dropped her off, Sarah had been welcomed with hugs and encouragement. Before she was shown to a small, functional, and sunlit room on the third floor of the old Victorian house, the director asked her some pointed questions about how dangerous her husband might be.

Sarah said nothing about Red One, Red Two, and Red Three. She made no mention of the Big Bad Wolf. She stuck to the outline of the story that Karen had invented: beaten and stalked. The director asked, "Are you armed?"

Her first instinct had been to lie about the gun in her bag. But she was lying about so many other things that this additional falsehood seemed distinctly wrong, and so she answered, "I stole a handgun."

"Let me see it," the director said.

Sarah had produced the weapon, handing it over butt-first. The director cracked the cylinder expertly and removed the bullets. She held these in her hand, caressing the burnished bronze of the shells before reloading the revolver, sighting once down the barrel, saying "Bang!" under her breath, and handing it back to Sarah.

"That's quite a weapon," she said.

"I've never fired it," Sarah responded.

"Well, we can do something about that," the director continued. "But we're always concerned about the children staying here with their mothers. Don't want an accident. And the kids, the older ones—you know: eight, nine, ten—they might be tempted because they're so scared of the men that might show up."

Then she reached into her desk, removed a trigger lock, and gave this to Sarah. "The combination is seven-six-seven," she told Sarah. "It's easy to remember: It's the numeric equivalent to SOS on a telephone."

The director had smiled. "I'm going to teach you how to use that," she said. "Far better to know what to do and not have to than to not know what to do when you absolutely need to."

Sarah thought at that moment that for all the time she had remaining as Red Two, she would keep exactly that thought in mind.

33

Back door. Flowerpot. Spare key.

Karen had parked a block from Sarah's empty house, waited for night to drop around her, and then walked two additional blocks in the wrong direction, frequently looking over her shoulder. She realized that merely by her being in Red Two's neighborhood, her destination was patently obvious. Her feelings were typical of the crazy-making behavior that the Wolf had installed in all of them: *Walk the wrong direction. Imagine a killer outside your window. Hear things. See things. Don't trust anything, because if you let your guard down you are going to die. And you might just get killed anyway.*

Karen stopped on the street and breathed in slowly. She had a small backpack on her shoulder. The scientific part of her considered the depth of fear and disruption in the lives of each of the three Reds. *I can't be a doctor or a comic. Sarah can't be a widow. Jordan can't be a normal teenager, if there is such a thing.* She was almost overcome by the notion that everyone faces some end someday, but it is the uncertainty of how it'll arrive that keeps people chugging along. Change that equation—inject a fatal disease or a sudden accident or a faceless murderer into the algorithm of dying—and nothing is exactly the same again.

She turned sharply and headed down the street that ran behind Sarah's house.

"The neighbors in back have navy-blue shutters on their front windows and a door painted bright red. The house is shiny white. It's all very patriotic and they light it up at night. There's no fence in front—you can just walk into the backyard. In the rear, over in the northeast corner, there's a kid's wooden jungle gym. You climb halfway up the ladder and from there you'll be able to jump the chain-link barrier that separates my place from theirs. There's a tree at the edge of the property. Hide there for a minute and then head to the back stoop. No one will see you."

Sarah's instructions were explicit, a schoolteacher's organized, well-thought-out plan: *Do this. Do that. Class, pay attention!* Karen kept her head down, sneaking glances at the houses on the street, looking for the red, white, and blue. When she spotted it, she stuck close to the side of the house and ducked into the backyard.

She was moving as fast as she could. She saw the jungle gym and sprinted toward it. In the distance she could hear a dog bark—*At least it's not a wolf's howl,* she thought—and just as Sarah had told her, she climbed midway up the ladder. The structure swayed a little as she reached out with her right foot for the top of the chain-link fence, and then, with a push, launched herself over.

Karen landed, pitching forward awkwardly onto the damp grass behind Red Two's dark home. She scrambled over to the base of the tree where Sarah had told her to hide and waited until her breathing slowed. The adrenaline rushing through her ears sounded like a waterfall, and it took a few minutes for her to be quiet enough to pick out night noises: A car several blocks away. A far distant siren. More dogs, but not enough sound to make anyone imagine they were truly alarmed.

Wait.

She listened for muffled footsteps. She craned her ears toward any noise that might be a man following in her path.

Nothing.

What she needed from Red Two's house was not complicated. If she had been thinking correctly, she would have told Sarah to bring some with her when she faked her suicide. But Karen hadn't been that wise, and now she had to get them herself.

She had considered simply walking up to the front and letting herself in, not caring whether the Wolf saw her or not. But this bit of bravado had seemed wrong. *Secrecy is better*, she told herself, although *why* eluded her.

Back door. Flowerpot. Spare key. Karen scrambled to her feet, hunched over, and ran forward.

At the steps leading into the house, she dug her hands into the cold dirt of the flowerpot. It took seconds to find the key, wipe it clean, and get to the door. In the darkness, she fumbled a bit thrusting it into the lock. She heard the dead bolt click open, and slipped inside.

Shadows filled the house. There was ambient light from a streetlamp outside, but this did little to make the scene anything less than minor variations on black. Karen had sensibly bought a small flashlight with her—she wasn't turning on any lights—and like a burglar, she crept through the hallways, her small lamp making pinpricks of light when she swept it back and forth.

The house seemed stuffy with death. She could see the limp light from her flashlight quiver in her hand. Sarah had told her where to look, but she still felt like she was walking across some alien landscape and that if she made any noise at all, it would awaken the sleeping ghosts surrounding her.

Tugging the backpack from her shoulder, Karen began to collect the few items she needed. She moved from room to room, avoiding the dead husband's study and the dead daughter's bedroom, just as Sarah had instructed her. A framed portrait from a hallway, a photograph stuck to a refrigerator door with a magnet—Karen gathered pictures for a montage. *She has to seem dead. The pictures have to underscore a different time, when Sarah was vibrant with hope. The contrast is important.*

She was nearly finished, just looking for a final family photograph that Sarah had told her was on the wall in her bedroom, when she suddenly thought she heard a noise coming from the front.

She could not have said what the noise was. It might have been a scraping sound, perhaps a rustle of papers. Maybe the wind, but she couldn't recall feeling any when she had approached the back. Her first, terrifying impression was that someone was now in the house with her.

Not someone. Him.

He will kill me here.

This didn't make sense to Karen. Sarah *should die here. It's* her *home.* This also didn't make sense.

Karen froze as she clicked off her flashlight. She thought every short breath she stole from the night was loud, blaring. She listened. *Nothing.*

Your ears are playing tricks on you.

Still, she seized the last portrait from the wall and stuffed it into the backpack as quickly as possible. She thought just the sound of the zipper closing the pack was loud and raucous.

She pivoted back to the door. *No, he's out there. Waiting for me.* She tried to tell herself she was completely crazy: *So this is what insanity feels like.*

It took an immense amount of strength for Karen to hurl herself through the door. She nearly stumbled and fell on the stairs. She raced for the back fence, expecting to fall at any point, and surprised herself that she was able to grab the top and scramble over. The chain link seemed to snatch at her, like so many desperate fingers clinging to her clothes.

A light went on in the red, white, and blue house.

She ignored it and ran into the welcoming night, heading toward her car.

For the second time that night, Karen's hands shook. She fumbled the car keys to the floor and cursed loudly as she reached down and groped around before finding them.

It was several minutes, and several miles, before she could feel her racing heart slow down. She imagined herself to be like a deer that has outrun a pack of wild dogs. She wanted to huddle in some safe, dark spot until she regained her composure.

A car zipped past her. She fought off the impulse to swerve crazily, as if the other car had come too close. She shook her head, trying to dislodge every fear that choked her.

She was letting thoughts just roll around wildly within her, when suddenly her cell phone rang. Again, she nearly swerved. The ringing clawed at her, and she reached out, almost losing her grip on the steering wheel. It was not the special cell with the number only Jordan and Sarah had. It was her regular phone. She seized it from the passenger seat.

A medical emergency, was her first and only thought.

"Doctor Jayson?" A crisp, authoritative voice.

"Speaking."

'This is Alpha Security. Are you at home?"

Karen was confused. Then she remembered the alarm system that she'd installed in her house after the Big Bad Wolf's first letter, and the expensive monitoring plan she'd purchased. "No. I'm on the road. What seems to be the problem?"

"Your system shows an intrusion. You are not at home currently?"

"No, damn it, I told you. What sort of intrusion?"

"Protocol requires me to tell you not to return to the home before I am able to contact the local police, so that they can meet you at your house. If there is a burglary in progress, we do not want you surprising some criminal. That's the police's job."

Karen tried to respond, but choked on each word.

A police car was waiting at the turn into her driveway. A young cop was standing beside the driver's-side door, waiting for her. He was slouched against his vehicle, and didn't give off any appearance of urgency.

"This is my home," Karen said, rolling down the window. "What's happening?"

"Do you have some identification, please," the cop responded.

She produced her driver's license. He took it from her, seemingly not noticing her quivering hand, looked at it, measured her face against the picture on the card before handing it back.

"We've already checked the house," he said. "There's another cruiser up there. Will you follow me, please?" This question was spoken like a command.

Karen did as she was told. The police car in front of her garage was occupied by two officers, one of whom was an edgy young woman who kept her hand on the butt of her holstered 9 mm pistol. The other was a substantially older man, slightly potbellied, with gray tufts of hair that protruded beneath his cap.

Karen felt her knees go weak as she exited her car. She was afraid she was going to stumble and fall on her face, or that her voice was going to crack with fear.

"Hello, Doctor," the old cop said, cheerily. "You were lucky you didn't come home early."

"Lucky?" Karen asked. It was all she could do to squeeze out the single word.

"Let me show you."

He led Karen past the front door—which was wide open—to an adjacent window. It was broken, with glass shards fanned out on the floor inside.

'That's where he got in," the cop said. "Then when the phone rang—that's what the security company does: They call your house, and if you answer they ask for a code, and if there's no response within six rings, they call us—anyway, phone rings, burglar sees the caller ID, panics, maybe grabs something, sprints out the front door, and heads off into the woods, or off to wherever he's parked his car. It took us a few minutes to get here, but he was long gone, and—"

"How many minutes?" Karen interrupted. Her voice seemed pale, as if her words had somehow lost their color.

"Maybe five. Ten at the very most. We were fast. One of our guys was just a couple of miles up the main road, looking for speeders. He got turned around, hit his lights and siren, and got up here quick."

Karen nodded.

"I already called a window guy. Hope you don't mind. We keep some names on file at headquarters of guys who will come straight out, day and night . . ."

"No that's fine."

"He'll be here any minute. Fix up the broken glass. Get your alarm system back online. But while we're waiting, we'd like you to just check out the house, see what was taken before the bad guy ran. The insurance people, you know. They want as much in the police report as possible when you make your claim."

Again Karen nodded. She couldn't think of anything to say. Her imagination was crowded with too many possibilities:

It was the Wolf.

No, it was too clumsy. He would be sophisticated. Clever.

Why would someone else break in? It can't be a coincidence.

Did he come to kill me?

She didn't know what to say to the policeman. Instead, she just walked slowly through her house, searching for some sign that something was missing. But other than the glass spread about beneath the broken window, she could see nothing. It was almost as if whoever it was had broken the window, jackknifed into her house, and made an immediate turn and exited. *That can't be the Wolf,* she told herself. *He would want something. And the Wolf would have known I wasn't here.*

With the cop hovering over her shoulder, she went into every room, checked every closet, opened every door, and switched on every light. Nothing was missing. This merely confused her more.

Midway through her survey, a middle-aged man from Smith 24-Hour Glass Repair showed up and rapidly began work on her window. The repairman had greeted the cops as if they were relatives, which Karen guessed might be the case.

"Anything?" the gray-haired cop asked.

"No. Everything still seems to be in place."

"Keep looking," the cop said. "Sometimes it's not so obvious, like a wide-screen TV ripped from the wall mount. Do you keep cash or jewelry around?"

Karen searched through drawers in her bedroom bureau. Her meager collection of earrings and necklaces was where she had left it that morning.

"Nothing missing," she said. She knew she should feel reassured, but instead she felt queasy, nauseous.

"Lucky. I guess that alarm system did its job. We've had a number of break-ins in this part of town. Snatch and grab mainly."

Karen did not feel lucky. She continued to survey her house. Something still seemed wrong, and it took her a second to realize that Martin and Lewis were nowhere to be seen. "I have two cats . . ." she started.

The cop glanced around. "Live alone, ought to have a big, mean dog."

"I know that. But they're not here," she replied. "They're inside cats—you know, don't really go out."

The cop shrugged. "They probably took off fast as hell out the front door right behind the bad guy, just as scared as he was. My guess is they're hiding in some bush someplace close by. Put out a bowl of food on the rear deck after we leave; they'll be back soon enough. Cats, you know, they can take care of themselves pretty good. I wouldn't worry. They'll show up when they get hungry or it gets too cold. But I'll put it in my report anyways."

Karen thought she should call for Martin and Lewis. But she knew they wouldn't come. Not because they wouldn't obey her summons. Because she was absolutely, 100 percent completely certain they were dead.

34

The Big Bad Wolf held a nine-inch hunting knife in his hand, balancing it on his palm. It had a satisfying weight—not too heavy to be unwieldy, but not so light that it couldn't be used to cut through skin, muscle, tendons, and even bone. He placed his thumb against the serrated blade but stopped himself from the temptation of drawing it across the razor-sharp edge. Instead, he moved his index finger to the flat side and gently stroked the length of the knife, reaching the tip and stopping. After a moment, he scraped at a little dried blood near the handle, before reaching below his desk, bringing out a spray bottle of disinfecting kitchen cleaner, liberally applying it to the entirety of the knife, and then carefully wiping every surface to destroy any lingering DNA.

"You don't want to be mixing cats' blood with Reds' blood," he said out loud. But this was spoken barely above a whisper, because he didn't want Mrs. Big Bad Wolf overhearing anything. And, he reminded himself, she would definitely not have approved of killing cute little pussycats, even if he had told her it was essential to the overall plan. *She might be unsure about murder, but not about cat killing.*

They hadn't even clawed him. He wondered for a moment what their names were. That was a detail that should have shown up in his research on Red One's life. He hated slippage.

Be meticulous.

The details of death need to be measured out, anticipated, designed to the absolute second. The documentation needs to be equally precise. The descriptions you write need to be pitch-perfect.

"Don't forget," he said, "you are also a journalist."

He was in his office, surrounded by his pictures, his words, his plans, and his books.

"We have arrived at the end game," he said, this time pivoting to the wall of pictures and addressing each Red. He pointed the knife at the images. He wanted to do a Muhammad Ali I-Am-the-Greatest! victory dance, but fought off the urge, because nothing was truly finished yet.

The Wolf brandished the blade once more in the air, slicing fantasy throats before lowering it to his desktop. Then he gave his desk chair a little push so that he spun about and wheeled over to his bookcase. He pulled out several volumes: the late John Gardner's *On Becoming a Novelist*, Alice LaPlante's *The Making of a Story*, Stephen King's *On Writing: A Memoir of the Craft*. He placed these books beside the copy of Strunk and White's *The Elements of Style* that he kept handy at all times. He smiled and thought, *Some crazy killers read the Bible or the Koran to find scriptural justification and guidance. They believe there are messages in every holy word, meant just for their own ears. But writers believe Strunk and White is the de facto bible of their craft. And I prefer John Gardner because his advice is so thoughtful, although he was a little crazy himself. Or maybe he was just eccentric—he rode a Harley-Davidson, lived in the wilds of upstate New York, and wore his silver hair down to his shoulders—that he seemed crazy at times.*

Just like me.

He moved the knife over beside the books as if they were coupled.

Then he wrote:

A knife is both a wonderful and a poor choice for a murder weapon. On the one hand, it provides the intimacy that the killing experience requires.

Psychologists and low-rent Freudians believe that it represents some sort of penis substitute, but obviously that oversimplifies matters significantly. What it does is bring the necessary proximity to murder, so that there are no barriers in that final moment between killer and victim, which is the nectar we all drink. It links us beyond partners, beyond twins, and beyond lovers.

On the other hand, it is damn messy.

Blood is both a killer's desire and his enemy. It spurts uncontrollably. It flows quickly. It seeps into unwanted spots—like the soles of one's shoes, or the cuff of one's shirt—and leaves little microscopic reminders of the killing moment that some stodgy cop with a microscope can actually find in a later investigation. This makes it the most dangerous substance to come in contact with.

One of the best theories about the infamous 1892 Fall River murders done by Lizzie Borden—"Lizzie Borden took an axe and gave her mother forty whacks, When she saw what she had done, she gave her father forty-one . . ."— is that she stripped naked to murder her parents and after she had finished, she bathed and dressed herself, so when the authorities showed up there was nothing incriminating about her.

Except, naturally, the two dead bodies in the house.

You can't be taking anything away from a murder site—like an article of clothes or a lock of hair—that you are not 100 percent certain about, and you have to know every second that this item might bring about your eventual downfall.

He stopped, his fingers above the keyboard, and thought: *I'm not like so many cheap killers; I don't need a gory souvenir. I have my memories and all those nicely detailed newspaper articles. They're like reviews of my work. Good reviews. Positive reviews. Ecstatic, super, praise-worthy reviews. The kinds of reviews that get four stars.*

He bent again to his writing:

Risk, of course, is always enticing and blood is always a risk. A proper killer needs to understand the narcotic, addictive quality it has on the soul. You can't ignore it, but nor can you be enslaved by it.

But managed risk is the best.

Balance is important. Shooting someone with a gun, or even an antique bow and arrow, gives one the necessary distance to remove many of these subtle threats to detection at the same time that it increases other pitfalls that can lead to detection. Did you steal that gun? Are there fingerprints on the bullet casings? But my antipathy toward guns is different: I hate separation. Every step back from your Red diminishes the sensation. You categorically do not want to walk away from a carefully plotted murder with a sense of incompletion and frustration.

So, the careful killer anticipates problems and takes steps to avoid them. Sees that with every choice come issues. Surgical gloves, for example. You want to use a knife? Good choice, but not one without dangers. Those gloves are a must-have bit of paraphernalia.

He balanced thoughts. *It will be the knife. Just as the Wolf relies on his teeth and claws, my knife will achieve the same. There won't be anything anonymous when they see that blade.*

For a few minutes, he worried over his words. He was concerned that his tone was a little too familiar and that he spoke a little too directly to his planned readership. He wondered for an instant whether he should redo the most recent passages. John Gardner in particular, and Stephen King as well, went on at length about careful planning and the value in rewriting. But he also didn't want to overwork the spontaneity out of his manuscript. *That's what will bring the readers into the bookstores*, he thought. *They will know they are with me every step of the way.*

The same as Red One and Red Three.

He quickly spun away from his desk, scooted across to his bookcase, and ran a finger up and down the spines of the books collected there. On the third shelf, he found what he was searching for: the late newspaper columnist Tom Wicker's account of the uprising and takeover of Attica Correctional Facility, *A Time to Die*. He scoured the opening pages with his eyes until he found the passage he wanted. It was the author's lament that despite acclaim as a reporter and writer, in his own eyes he had done little to "signify" his life.

He laughed out loud. *That's not going to be my problem.* He turned back to his computer, hunching over, writing feverishly.

I have studied. I have inspected. I have watched. A killer is like a psychologist and like a lover. One must know one's target intimately. Red One is most vulnerable in the space between her front door and her car. Night is better than morning because when she comes home she is scared of what awaits her inside. She doesn't focus on the distance between her car—safety—and her front door— possible safety, potential threat. That was a side benefit of my little break-in. It forces her to concentrate on what might be within her walls waiting. As in the story of Little Red Riding Hood, she will expect me inside. The distance between the car and the front door is less than twenty feet. There is a bright light by the front door, which comes on before she arrives in the dark. She has the whole house on a timer. Remember that detail. If I break that outside light to give myself extra cover, she will be suspicious. Perhaps she won't get out, she'll turn her car around and flee. No, even though it lessens the numbers of shadows I can hide in, I have to leave it shining brightly.

He stopped writing and reminded himself: *The Wolf will come at her from the woods. She will not see me coming.*

The biggest problem, he thought, *is really the length of time between murders.*

He picked up where he had left off:

Red Three's most vulnerable moment is in the evening as well, when she walks alone across campus. But her second most vulnerable time is on Tuesday mornings. She does not have a class until 9:45. The other members of her dormitory have first-period classes that begin an hour earlier. So Tuesdays, my little Red Three likes to sleep in a little later and does not realize she is alone in that old house, because Ms. Rodriguez, the dorm parent, has early morning faculty commitments those days.

Red Three gets up slowly and idly heads to the shower down the hallway with her toothbrush and some shampoo, not really awake, wiping the sleep from her eyes without any idea what might be waiting for her there.

He smiled and nodded. He said to himself, "So it will have to be a Tuesday: Red Three in the morning and Red One in the evening."

The Big Bad Wolf liked that, even though it should have been morning, evening, and night. *I would have gone for Red Two after midnight.* But there was nothing he could do about that.

He saw the obvious problem: *What if Red One learns of Red Three's murder? Then she will know that this is her last day. She will know that she is only minutes away from her own death.*

That space of time between murders—there's the dilemma.

So, it must seem to the outside world that Red Three isn't dead. Only strangely absent. From class. From basketball. From meals. Not absent from life, which is what will be accurate.

He picked up Strunk and White from his desktop. *They always argue for brevity and directness. The same is true for killing.*

The Big Bad Wolf turned back to his computer.

Red Three gets more beautiful every day. Her body becomes more lithe, more limber as she approaches womanhood. She is the one about to be cheated the very most.

Red One is the opposite. She ages just infinitesimally with each passing hour. She grays and knows her dying is right around the next minute and it wears on her figure, just as it gnaws on her heart.

The Wolf worked a little more before deciding to print out a few pages. He wished he were a poet, so he could more eloquently describe his two remaining victims. He was a little saddened when he thought of Red Two. *This will be hard,* he told himself, *but you will have to write her epitaph in a chapter of its own.* He nodded, quickly typed in some notes on a file he decided to call "Red Two's Last Will and Testament," and before shutting down the chapter he was working on wondered whether there was any need left to encrypt his files. He thought he no longer had anything to fear from Mrs. Big Bad Wolf. He imagined he'd *never* had anything to fear from her. She loved him. He loved her. The rest was all just part of life together.

While he was thinking these things, he idly flicked over to the Internet. He passed over the usual deluge of daily come-ons he received from *Writer's Digest* and *Script* and other places urging him to sign up and spend some money, because through "webinars" or access to DVDs featuring all the tricks of the writing trade he could get published or optioned or taken step-by-step and dollar-by-dollar through all the elements necessary to create his own e-book. Instead the Big Bad Wolf went to the website of a local news station to try to get a seven-day weather forecast. He knew a steady and cold rain would be best for his Tuesday plan. But before he could check the weather, he saw a brief teaser headline on a news digest that caught his eye:

Memorial Service Planned for Teacher Saturday

35

Red Two asked herself, *What should you say about your own death? Or, maybe, what would you like someone else to say? Was I a good person? Maybe not.*

Sarah struggled with the ideas that flooded her head. She felt trapped between life and death. The muffled sounds of gunfire were like distant thunderclaps, penetrating the thick ear protectors she wore. In the booth next to her, the Safe Space director was banging out quick shots from a Glock 9 mm, filling the air with angry explosions. Sarah lifted her dead husband's weapon, held it out steadily with both hands the way she had been shown, and aimed down the sight at the black cartoon of a fierce man grasping a large knife, wearing a snarl and a scar, and painted with a target in his chest. She pulled the trigger three times. She doubted if the target looked much like the Big Bad Wolf.

The recoil sent shock waves through her arms, but she was privately pleased that it didn't make her stagger back or fall to the ground as she'd expected.

She looked up, squinting down the firing range. She could see that two shots had landed just outside the target, but a third had torn the paper dead center. She didn't know whether this was the first shot or the last, but she was pleased that at least one would have proved fatal.

"Attagirl," the director said, leaning around a small partition that separated the shooting galleries. "Try to get a handle on how the weapon will pull one way or the other when you're rapid-firing. And, you know, empty the chamber. Fire all six rounds. You better your chances that way. We've got plenty of ammo and plenty of time."

Plenty of ammo is right, Sarah thought. *Plenty of time isn't.* She cracked open the cylinder to reload from a box on the shooting platform at her waist.

Sarah Locksley, born thirty-three years ago. Happy once. Not so much anymore. Dead in a river, killed by a psychopath who drove her to further despair by threatening to murder her, except she had nothing left to live for anyway because some goddamn out-of-control fuel truck driver ran through a stop sign.

She lifted the gun and aimed again.

That won't work. This is a memorial service. A little sadness and mainly nice, safe things said about someone whose life was cut short by tragedy.

That's me. I'm the someone. Or maybe, it's the ex-me.

The target loomed in front of her. She narrowed her eyes and hummed to herself to block out the noise of other weapons being fired.

Not a word about the truth of Sarah Locksley.

She smiled. A part of her wished she could go to the service. It would certainly help for her say goodbye to herself. *So long, Sarah. Hello, Cynthia Harrison. I'm pleased to make your acquaintance. And I'm delighted to take over your life.*

She could hear the gunshots echoing around her, and the gun jumped in her hand. *Cynthia Harrison,* she thought, *I wonder if you would be embarrassed or disappointed or angry to know that the very first thing I do with your name is kill a man. A very special man. A wolf who most assuredly deserves to die. After all, he's killed me once already.*

This time four of the six shots landed dead center, and the fifth tore a hole in the target's forehead.

Twenty minutes before the service was to begin, Red Three took the video camera she'd obtained at the mall and placed it in a spot where it was trained on the people who would come through the doors, stop and sign a "remembrance" book, then take their seats in the small room. It was set to record two hours' worth of video, which Karen had insisted to the funeral director be the length of the service.

She glanced toward the front of the room. Karen had put together a montage of photographs of Sarah and her dead family. There were bouquets of white lilies on either side of the pictures, which were mounted on a sheet of white poster board and placed on a tripod in front of the few chairs the funeral home had put out. There was a small podium with a microphone.

A part of Red Three wanted to stay. She imagined she could hide behind a curtain, remaining still, holding her breath. But she knew there was danger in staying behind, even if hidden. So instead she ducked out minutes before the first people pulled into the funeral home parking lot. She wore a dark hooded sweatshirt beneath her old parka, and she pulled this up over her head and walked away as quickly as she could from the funeral home toward a nearby bus stop.

For the first time in days, she knew she wasn't being followed. This didn't make sense to her, but Jordan wasn't about to reject the sensation, because it made her feel like she was doing something that might just help save her life.

When the bus wheezed up beside her and its doors opened with a familiar hydraulic *whoosh*, she climbed in. Jordan was aware that she was breaking any number of school rules by being off campus on a Saturday without permission. She did not care. She imagined that breaking a few onerous regulations was the very least of the trouble she was racing toward. *Breaking rules is bad*, she thought. *Killing is worse.*

This notion made her smile, and she had to fight to keep herself from bursting out in laughter.

Karen was in a side room, dressed in a trim black dress, looking as proper as a Puritan, poring over two sheets of paper on which she'd written a small speech, using details that Sarah had given her about her life.

The words on the page streamed together. She felt like a dyslexic, every letter jumbling and tumbling across the paper willy-nilly, threatening to short-circuit everything she planned to say. Just as she did before going on stage with a new comedy routine, she did some breathing exercises. Slow in. Slow out. Settle the racing heartbeat.

"I know you're here," she whispered. One of the funeral directors, across the room from her, looked up with a practiced, hypocritically wistful look, and Karen realized that he thought she was speaking to her dead friend, not a killer.

"People are starting to arrive," the funeral director said. He was significantly younger than the man she'd spoken to earlier in the week, but he already had down pat the solemn, sonorous tones of loss. She guessed he was a son or a nephew being shepherded into the family business, and this particular memorial service was definitely not a funeral home challenge. No need for the boss to be there. No casket. No body. Few flowers. Just some random sentiments.

If he's out there, it will be because he needs to know and he wants to see and he wants to hear. Karen could feel her pulse quickening at the thought that she was going to be standing up in front of the Wolf. "I'll go out now," she replied, weakly.

Earlier, she had placed a stiff-backed chair near the microphone. Smiling, nodding her head to people streaming in out of the parking lot, she went to it. She knew none of the faces that returned her smile. Each stride she took was walking deeper into a spotlight. As if speaking some oriental mantra, she kept telling herself that he wouldn't kill her right there. *Not now. Not now.* She had never heard of anyone murdering someone at a funeral home in front of assembled mourners. Bringing death to a place of death. This seemed so unreasonable that she tried to use its improbability as a reassurance.

Karen had never given a eulogy before, and certainly not for someone she barely knew and who actually wasn't dead. She thought the whole thing would be comic if it weren't the only thing she could think of doing that might keep her alive.

Don't speak ill of the dead, she thought. She wondered where that maxim had been coined.

Karen was pleased at the turnout. She had not known whether there would be five people or fifty. Zero had been a possibility, but the number was going to exceed her top guess. That was good. Perfect, even. *Large numbers will make him feel safe. He will think he can blend in. If no one had come, he probably would have shied away, not willing to risk standing out in an empty room.* She could feel electricity, not unlike what she felt going on stage.

Be good. Be persuasive. Make Sarah seem dead. She had given many performances, but none, she thought, had been nearly as important as this one.

Karen glanced over at a woman and a man. The woman was holding the hand of a small boy wearing a white shirt that was too tight and a red tie that had already come loose around his neck. The boy was leaning against an older sister, probably thirteen or fourteen, who was dabbing at her eyes with a handkerchief. The family paused in front of the photo display and spent a respectful few moments looking over the collection of pictures before taking seats. *A former elementary school student,* she realized, *and a younger brother who doesn't want to be here at all.*

Not a wolf.

The room began to fill up—a great variety of men and women of all ages, accompanied by a few children. The phony solemn music the funeral home piped in with hidden speakers flowed around her like smoke, almost as if the music could obscure her vision. She waited until the stream of people pausing to sign the remembrance book dwindled, and then she stood. Out of the corner of her eye she saw the young funeral director throw a small switch on the wall, and the music stopped in mid-note. She looked out over the gathered crowd briefly and launched into her speech.

"I'd like to thank you all for coming. This is a great turnout, and my dear friend Sarah would have been pleased to see so many people."

She wanted to make eye contact with every person in the room, on the off chance that she could recognize the Big Bad Wolf just by the glint in his eyes. But instead, she kept her head down, as if moved by the emotion of the fake service, hoping that Jordan's camera was doing the job for her. She read words that meant nothing, trying to sound deeply respectful when what she wanted was to scream.

It was all a gamble, she understood. *Maybe he's smart enough to stay away and this is all for nothing.*

But maybe he's not. Maybe he's drawn here, because the scent he's been pursuing is just too strong and he's not able to stop himself. That was what the three Reds were counting on.

She thought of the old saying: *Curiosity killed the cat.*

Maybe it can kill a wolf, too.

36

The funny thing, he thought, *is that with all the killing I've done, I just don't much like attending funerals. They make me really uncomfortable. They are too filled with excessive emotion and phony sentiments.*

He found himself whistling a series of disconnected notes, not a recognizable tune. *Real people like the Reds. Made-up characters in my books. Lots of different types of dying at my hands. But whether it's on a page in prose or laid out on a slab in a morgue waiting for the hearse and a trip to the crematorium or a berth six feet under, you are still stone cold. Whether you were killed by old age, illness, or sudden death, by a knife or a gun or even by an author's whim, in the end it's all the same.*

He snorted and thought he sounded like a preacher giving himself a sermon. "Ashes to ashes. Dust to dust," he said in a mock, deeply sonorous tone.

The Big Bad Wolf believed that he had perfectly blended his fictional worlds with reality. He was a killer in both. He considered himself equally a master of the real and the make-believe. To be so adept in both arenas fueled his excitement.

291

"Tick-tock, tick-tock. Clock is running, ladies," he said to himself. He laughed a little, and wondered which would be ultimately more tantalizing: killing or writing about it. They were both wildly attractive.

His only lingering concern was exactly how to express Red Two's death. This was the sort of challenging knot that all writers liked to undo, he thought. *James Ellroy.* L.A Confidential. *He likes to tightly wind things into complicated scenarios, and then dance his way out with compelling language. And violence. Lots of violence. Can't forget all that savagery he brings to the ending.* The Wolf knew he had to make her final moments on the edge of the bridge seem as alive as the ones he was about to deliver to Red One and Red Three. His problem was he hadn't been there. "Goddammit." He had to make sure that readers knew that when Red Two threw herself into the dark waters below, it was his push that sent her.

"You know enough. You have the details. It's just a matter of the right description," he said. It was always reassuring to speak to himself in the second person.

He made a mental list: *Panic: You know that. Doubt: You understand it. Fear: Well, who has a better handle on that than you? Bring them all together in Red Two's mind, and there you have it.*

He made a mental note to draw a bath when he returned home, immerse his head completely beneath the water, and try to duplicate the sensation of drowning. *It won't be the same. No black water and fierce currents pulling me under. But I'll get just enough of a little piece of comprehension to make it work on the page.*

Hold your breath. When you start to black out, you will know. That should do the trick.

Know about what you're writing. Hemingway knew war. Dickens knew the British class system. Faulkner knew the South. All good fiction writers have a little journalist inside them.

He had pulled his car into a small dirt parking area adjacent to a wildlife preserve not far from Red One's home. The preserve abutted the back end of her property. There was a hiking trail favored by local granola-and-boots types that led back into the forest and up a steep but manageable path to a hill that afforded fine views of the valley that he and all three Reds lived in. It was a popular spot. On a nice Sunday morning it was likely to be jammed with a dozen or more cars, and you could hear laughter penetrating the trees and scrub brush as people cheerfully made their way up and down the trail. But on weekdays, it was almost always empty, as few people wanted to take a hike, even a something-less-than-grueling one, after a long day at a boring job. This afternoon, there were only three cars in the lot, even though it was the weekend. The gray, overcast skies threatened rain soon, and the air was chilled deep enough that he could see his breath when he rolled down his window; higher elevations might see snow flurries. This concerned him. He did not want to leave tracks in frozen ground. Slick, damp mud would obscure his footprints. Mud that froze as the temperature plummeted would encase the patterns on his shoe soles almost as well as a plaster of Paris mold. He had read of more than one killer identified by a distinctive shoe print, and he was aware that even the most rural police force knew how to identify shoe prints and tire tracks.

He glanced around. He wanted to be certain that none of the few hikers saw him as he awkwardly changed from a cheap blue suit into jeans, fleece top, and waterproof shell, rapidly going from funeral attire to outdoors gear. He had to contort his body in the front seat of his car as he slid out of his pants, and he was reminded that he wasn't getting any younger. His knees creaked and his back tightened, but it couldn't be helped. He shucked off his wing-tip shoes and slid his feet into thick woolen socks and sturdy waterproof boots.

After changing, he double-checked his fake mustache and goatee in the rearview mirror, to make certain that it was still fixed to his face and hadn't become ridiculously skewed when he'd slid into his turtleneck sweater.

He had once read—back in the days before security cameras and video monitoring systems—of a bank robber who never wore a mask to obscure his identity, but who routinely used some Hollywood makeup to place a savage fake scar on his face, extending from above the eyebrow and across the cheek to below the chin. *Someone who truly understands the psychology of crime*, the Wolf thought. Every time the police had asked the bank tellers and other witnesses for a description of the robber, they had all uniformly responded: "You can't miss him because he's got this damn big scar," which they then described in great colorful detail. The fake scar was all they saw. Not his eyes or hair color, and not the shape of his cheekbones or the curve of his nose or the square of his chin. He had always liked that. *People only see the obvious. Not the subtle*, he told himself.

But *subtle* was the religion he worshiped.

Out of the trunk of his car, he took a common bright pink backpack purchased in a chain drugstore. Decorated with a prancing white unicorn, it was the sort favored by kindergarten girls. He also removed a knotty wooden hiking staff, around which he'd placed a rainbow-hued scarf that was a staple dress item for the local gay and lesbian community. He pulled a navy-blue knit cap emblazoned with the logo of the New England Patriots football team onto his head.

The Big Bad Wolf knew that all of these items taken together created an eccentric, incongruous package, one that, like the bank robber's scar, would make him invisible to anyone he might happen upon in the forest. *They will remember all the wrong things*, he told himself.

In the pink backpack he had placed six items: a sandwich, a small flashlight, a thermos with coffee, a pair of night-vision binoculars just in case he decided to stay until after the sun set, a folding spyglass, and a copy of *Audubon's Birds of North America*.

The book—which he'd never opened or bothered to read—was for anyone curious enough to stop him, such as a park ranger, although he doubted any would be up on the trails this afternoon. But it wasn't a bald eagle or a white-tufted owl he actually intended to spy upon.

He started whistling again. A carefree happy tune. He glanced at his wristwatch. *Timing is important*, he reminded himself. He waited until the sweep hand hit 12, and then the Wolf started rapidly up the path toward the preserve, looking for the small notch in a trailside tree that he'd made in the trunk to mark a route down through the woods that stretched behind Red One's home.

Trial run, he thought. Next time it wouldn't be a child's pink backpack and gay pride walking staff. The next time he would bring only his hunting knife.

He considered all that he had planned: *Tuesday. An ordinary, run-of-the-mill day. The dull middle of the workweek. Nothing ever really special about Tuesdays.*

Except, this Tuesday will be different.

He carefully counted the minutes it took him to wend his way through the thick tangle of woods. Later, he would count the hours until Tuesday evening.

Out the side door. Past the deli and the pizza shop. Duck through the walkway behind the parking lot. Keep your head down and walk fast.

Red Two hurried through the fading light of the late afternoon. It had started to drizzle again, and she hunched her shoulders forward and tucked her chin into her chest against the cold. She wore an old black baseball cap that was tattered and did little to conceal her mop of hair, but it was better than nothing. Some droplets formed on the bill.

The local Episcopal church had seemed like a good place for them to gather. It was four blocks from the women's center where Sarah was hiding, just off the bus line that served Jordan's school, and a quick walk across the town's main shopping area from the parking garage, where Karen could leave her car and make certain she wasn't followed by riding an elevator up and down a few times.

"The pastor has an office in the basement he says we can use," Red One had said on the phone. "I told him we were trying to help out a friend—that's you, Sarah—at Safe Space and needed a place to meet in private, and he was most understanding. He said he frequently sermonizes on family violence, so I made it seem like we were worried about an abusive husband."

She had not said, *"No Wolf will follow us into a church,"* which was what Sarah was thinking as she crossed a black macadam parking lot that glistened with rain. Some crazy thought about sacred or consecrated ground reverberated within her, but she told herself that was for vampires, not wolves.

Red One had told her not to use the main church entrance, so she made her way around to the rear. There was a small basement entry that had a sign next to the door that stated: NO ADMITTANCE DURING SUNDAY SERVICES. AA GROUP MEETS 7–9 PM MONDAY, WEDNESDAY, FRIDAY.

She stepped in a puddle, cursed, and hurried forward. She felt almost ghostlike, as if she were suddenly invisible. She wondered if this was because of the memorial service. *A lot of people think I'm dead. I can't let anyone who knew the old Sarah see the new Cynthia.*

She pulled the door open and entered the church's basement. A radiator was hissing and steam was clanking in some hidden pipes. Sarah pushed down a narrow corridor lit with uncovered bulbs that made the white-washed walls shine harshly. At the end, the corridor opened into a larger space that had a low soundproofed ceiling and a linoleum floor, a stage at one end, and several rows of gray steel folding chairs arranged in front of an empty podium. It was a dingy, cheerless space, and she guessed this was where the AA meetings took place.

Off in a corner, there was a door open to another room, and she heard voices. She moved that way, and saw Karen standing inside next to a sturdy oaken desk. On the walls were some pictures of a silver-haired man in robes performing ceremonies and a pair of divinity school diplomas, but there was no sign of the priest. Jordan was beside Karen, fiddling with a camera, some wires, and a laptop computer.

Jordan looked up, smiled, and jokingly said, "Hey, dead woman walking. How're you doing?"

"Not bad. Adjusting," Sarah said.

"Cool."

Karen came over and gave Sarah a hug, which surprised the younger woman. But she could feel a type of warmth flowing through the embrace: not exactly a friend's embrace, but a *we're-in-this-together* touch.

"How'd it go?" Sarah asked. She thought it was the most curious question, asking someone how her memorial service had been received.

Karen shrugged and smiled wryly. "It was good. A little weird—but actually good. You had many more friends than you said would come. People were genuinely sad . . ." She stopped before finishing the sentence, but Jordan jumped in.

". . . Because you killed yourself." The teenager grinned and laughed.

Sarah smiled weakly. She thought there was nothing in the least humorous in their situation, and what they'd done and what they planned on doing, and in saying farewell to her former life. But at the same time, Jordan's response was precisely right: It was all hilarious, an immense practical joke.

The three Reds were silent for a moment.

"Was he there?" Sarah asked.

"I don't know," Karen replied. "There were a lot of men, and families, but I couldn't be sure about any one specific man. He wouldn't wear a sign that said 'Hi, I'm the Wolf' or try to stand out in any way. I was trying to make eye contact, but it was hard—"

"He had to come," Jordan interrupted again, speaking with all the determination of an athlete and the self-confidence of a teenager who was absolutely 100-percent certain about something. The other two Reds were older and therefore more accustomed to doubts. "I mean, come on. How could he not show up at the service for what *he* created? He's been all over us in every fucking kind of way, so how could he stay away? It would be like winning a big lottery prize and not showing up to claim it."

Karen, of course, imagined a million reasons the Wolf would stay away. *Or one reason, anyway*, she thought but did not say out loud. *Because he's smart and he didn't need to be there. Because he's waiting for us outside. Or close by. Or around the goddamn corner, or at my house or in my office or somewhere I don't expect it and that's where I'm going to die.* She shook her head, not necessarily in reply to anything Jordan had said, but more in answer to her own ricocheting fears.

Karen had an odd thought, a memory culled suddenly from a college literature course, years before organic chemistry and statistics and physics and the interminable months of medical school training. It was a course on existential writing, and she hadn't thought about it in decades.

Mother died today. Or maybe yesterday; I can't be sure.

She wanted to scream.

Karen dies tomorrow. Or maybe the next day; I can't be sure.

Jordan looked up from punching buttons on the computer. "Hey, it's working. It's show time!" She laughed harshly. "All we need is some popcorn."

The three women leaned across the desk and watched as the computer screen filled with the images of people coming through the door to the memorial service. The canned solemn music played in the background. There was little other sound, as people were quiet and respectful as they shuffled unknowingly into the camera's vision and then out.

"Keep watching," Karen continued. "Sarah, you should identify every-one you can." She opened the remembrances book that the funeral home had provided, where folks had written short statements or merely signed their names.

Sarah stared at the first person to approach the book on the video. "Okay, that's my neighbor and his wife, and their two sons. The red, white, and blue superpatriot whose backyard you used the other night," she said to Karen.

Karen took a pencil and made a notation in the margin of the book.

"And those people are parents of one of my students. And that's their child. She was in my last classroom before I quit. She's grown in the last year." Sarah nearly sobbed. "She's becoming beautiful," she whispered.

Another notation went into the margin.

"Keep going," Karen said stiffly. Faces, sometimes names, often con-texts leapt out of the computer screen at the three Reds. Jordan used the computer mouse to slow the flow down, and once or twice to stop the picture as Sarah paused to place a person. The connections came to her hesitantly or instantly; it was a little like watching a strange sort of theater presentation, where there was no dialogue and no plot, but each separate image created a distinct and profound impression. Several times Sarah had to stop and walk around the room, as she delved deeply into memory to recall who someone was. The three Reds were alert to each man who entered the line, stopped by the book, seized the pen provided by the funeral home, and then passed out of the camera's eye.

"Come on, goddammit," Jordan whispered. "I know you're here." The flow of people dwindled and finally stopped. "Shit, shit, shit," Jordan cursed again. The image on the screen was the remembrances book idly waiting on the table. The music ceased, and they could hear the first words of Karen's eulogy. "Motherfucker," Jordan added.

"Let's watch it again," Karen said calmly. She had to fight to keep her voice from rising in panic.

"He didn't come," Sarah said. She felt herself plummeting. It was as if she'd lost a fingerhold on the side of a mountain and was suddenly tumbling through space.

Karen saw Jordan clench her fists and punch out in the air, trying to smash the face of the Wolf that was both with them and not with them. "Watch it again," Karen said, a little more softly, but with insistent fury. "We've missed something."

But she was filled with fear—because maybe they *hadn't* missed anything. She could feel anxiety threatening to crack every word she spoke, and her heartbeat increased. *This has to work*, she cried to herself. It wasn't as if she had any other ideas. She wanted to burst into tears, and it took an immense effort to will herself not to. "Start from the beginning. And Jordan, this time stop the image on *everyone*."

It was painstaking work. Slow and deliberate. With every person who wasn't the Wolf, the tension in the room grew. None of them knew exactly what they were looking for. They were being driven by the cockeyed idea that something would seem completely obvious—when each of the Reds secretly believed the opposite might be true.

Jordan wanted to grab something and smash it. Karen wanted to scream loudly and then continue screaming. Sarah, who felt like she was letting the other two Reds down, was near tears.

Jordan stopped the image on a family group that lingered at the remembrances book. "Okay," she said, frustration littering her voice, "now who the hell are they?"

"The man is an EMT who worked out of the fire station where my husband was shift commander. I think he's the one who was called to . . ." She stopped, unable to say the word *accident*. Sarah stood up and paced about the room a few haphazard feet, as if scared to view the pictures on the screen for a second time.

Karen understood instantly what had upset Sarah. She filled in, trying to coax Red Two back into the process. "Okay, so he worked with your husband, and the people with him are who?"

Sarah stopped her pacing and returned to the images. But she stayed a few feet back, as if the distance would somehow keep her safe from memories. "That must be his wife, the one with the toddler hanging on and the baby in her arms. They came to dinner once or twice. And I guess the woman right behind them is the mother-in-law. I remember that. They had a mother-in-law living with them. I think my husband said he was growing tired of hearing about all the complaints—"

"Okay. Moving on," Jordan said. "Unless you think an EMT is the Wolf."

Karen raised a hand. There was something that bothered her that she couldn't quite put a finger on. "No," she said carefully. "Just roll it back a little, and then forward real slowly."

She watched the family again. The husband was wearing a blue suit. It was a little too tight for him and he moved stiffly as he approached the signing table and book. He wore a tie that seemed to strangle him and a look that spoke of loss. The wife—Sarah's age, pretty, but with hair that seemed not quite combed and makeup that seemed haphazardly applied— wore a nice flowered dress and an overcoat with a baby bag slung over one shoulder, undoubtedly containing bottled milk, diapers, and rattles. She struggled to both hold a squirming child in her arms and control a toddler by the wrist so that he wouldn't sprint away from her. It was an all-too-common mother-child choreography, one of too many items, too many responsibilities for the narrow situation they were in—an adult moment not suited to small kids.

"That's not right," Karen said.

Sarah shook her head. "No, I know him. I mean, he's dedicated to his job. He saves lives. He's no killer."

"You can't know that for certain," Jordan said in frustration. "The Wolf could be anyone."

This wasn't what bothered Karen about the image. She leaned forward, staring intently. "Just inch it forward," she said.

Jordan manipulated the computer mouse.

The mother-in-law came onto the screen, but she was partially obscured by the wife, husband, and children as she bent to the book.

"That's not right," Karen repeated.

"What?" Sarah asked.

"The mother is struggling with the kids. Why wouldn't she hand one of them to her mother when she signs the book? But she doesn't. I mean, isn't that what the mother-in-law is there for? Another set of hands? And clearly, she's needed . . ." Karen stopped.

They all craned forward.

"I can't see her face clearly," Sarah said. "Damn it, turn this way!" she almost shouted at the figure on the computer screen.

"Did you ever meet the mother-in-law?" Karen suddenly asked.

"No."

"Then we don't know for sure that—"

She stopped. She twisted her body, as if moving herself would make the image of the woman clearer. Jordan advanced the picture just slightly, moving her face closer to the computer screen.

"Do you know who that is?" Karen asked abruptly.

"No," Sarah answered.

Karen took a deep breath. A gasp of sudden recognition.

"I do," she said.

There was silence in the room. She thought: *A woman who comes to a funeral who doesn't know the deceased.* The three Reds could all hear the heating system hissing in pipes concealed in the ceiling above them.

"So do I," Jordan said quietly. All her teenage bravado had fled her, and her face had paled.

37

She wrote down everything she could remember in a cheap notepad that she'd purchased at a local drugstore. She was excited, like a teenager waiting for a prom date. For the first time, she actually felt like she was a genuine part of the mysterious process. She described the other mourners in detail when she pictured them in her head: *This older man wore a gray suit that didn't fit him and a lime-green tie; this woman was at least seven months pregnant and really uncomfortable.* She quoted every word and phrase she could recall from the doctor's eulogy: "No one except Sarah knows why she made her final choice . . ." She identified the pieces of music that she recognized—Bach's "Jesu, Joy of Man's Desiring" and a sonata by Mendelssohn. She put down every banal snatch of conversation she had managed to overhear in the line of people filing into the small chapel-type room: "I hate funerals," and "This is so sad," and "Hush, kids, this is quiet time . . ."

At the very bottom of her report, Mrs. Big Bad Wolf added: *I'm certain that Doctor Jayson didn't recognize me. I averted my eyes and kept hidden behind other people. I sat in the very back, and ducked out as soon as she finished speaking. Then I waited across the street from the funeral home parking lot until everyone left, including the doctor. She didn't even look my way.*

She added one other note: *There was no sign of Jordan at any point. If she had come to the service, I would have spotted her immediately.*

Mrs. Big Bad Wolf had always believed that her nondescript, mousy features were a hindrance. She never stood out in a crowd, and all the years of her life she had been jealous of the popular girls—then women—who did. She was even a little irritated that her doctor hadn't seemed to notice her, even though she had taken steps to avoid being seen. But this sense of mild anger was replaced by the notion that her appearance—her very ordinariness and the way she blended seamlessly into any crowd—was suddenly an advantage. She did not know that her husband, had made nearly the same point early in his book.

I was a fly on the wall, she thought, *seeing everything and hearing everything and noticed by nobody.* She looked down at the pages filled with her report: clear, legible, concise handwriting, all in a secretary's precise style.

It was, she imagined, a totally different way of standing up and being counted. *You don't have to make a loud noise or be extra-special beautiful,* she told herself. *You don't have to be six feet tall, or have red hair like the women going into the book. When you have words at your disposal, it automatically makes you special.* It was wildly seductive for her, magical and utterly romantic. She looked at the notations stretched across the lined pages in front of her and hoped that her language was descriptive and accurate.

She suddenly realized that her husband had never asked her to write something for him before. This made it even more special. That she had been trusted with the task of attending the service was deeply satisfying.

"It's crucial for everything that's going into the new book," her husband had said as he watched her get ready, picking out a simple, nondescript gray jacket, dark slacks, and a pair of tinted glasses—not quite sunglasses, but just dark enough to obscure her eyes. "I can't be there, but I need to know everything that happens."

She had not asked why or questioned him when he'd told her that she had to avoid being recognized at all times. Instead, she had fixed her hair, combing it in a completely different style than usual. She had been surprised when she looked in the mirror at how the woman staring back at her wasn't her.

He had also coached her on what to say if someone did recognize her. "Just act surprised, and say that you knew Sarah's husband from some years ago, when he was a student. That will work. No one will ever ask a follow-up question."

Smiling, he had told her what school the dead husband had gone to and where he'd done his undergraduate work before joining the fire department. He also told her that Sarah's husband had been taking some night school graduate writing courses at the local community college. "Just say that's where you met him," he told her. "A shared interest sadly cut short by accident."

She had followed every instruction to the exact letter, and, she believed, done it better than he could ever have hoped for. She congratulated herself. *You should have been an actor. A performer. This may have been your first time on a stage, and you nailed it.*

For an instant, it felt to her like she was writing a chapter of her own that would go, word for word, directly into his book. This gave her a great thrill.

She could hardly sit still as she bent over her notes, rummaging through every memory of the service, adding every element that popped into her head, because she knew that even the smallest observation might be the one that made the entire description work, and that might make the scene work, and then the chapter, and ultimately the whole book.

Looking up, she suddenly saw headlights cutting through the night, turning into their driveway. She pushed herself to her feet, excited.

Mrs. Big Bad Wolf went to the front door to open it for her husband. It was as if her years reaching to the early edge of old age dropped away from her in that moment. She was no longer the quiet, sickly, worried woman who occupied the hidden, unimportant position at his side. She was as filled with intense passion as she'd ever been on any night since they'd first met. She was, she thought, Mata Hari. *A femme fatale.*

305

Now that they knew something, it only frightened them more, because it underscored how little they actually did know.

The three Reds argued shrilly.

"There's absolutely no reason for her to be there, which means there's only one reason," Jordan said forcefully. "She has something to do with this."

"We don't know that for certain," Karen responded fiercely. "Damn it, Jordan, we can't go jumping to every conclusion we *think* is obvious, because maybe it's wrong."

"That woman only connects two of us—not three," Sarah said, jumping into the midst of the fight. "Three. All of us. That's what we would need to understand who the Wolf is."

"The fact that you don't know who she is and we do, that's all we need," Jordan snorted.

"That doesn't make sense," Karen responded.

"So, let me ask you this: Does stalking and killing three strangers who just happen to all have red hair because you've got some kind of fairy fucking tale obsession make sense? Really, does it?"

"It must. Somehow. Some way. It does."

"Great. What you're saying is we're no closer to finding out anything and doing something about this fucking Wolf because we're not sure? That's just great. I mean, just fucking wonderful."

Jordan paced around the room, waving her hands in frustration. She knew one thing only: She wanted to do something. Anything. The idea of waiting to die was, she thought, killing her. The irony of this was lost on her. She knew she was being impulsive. She just no longer thought it was a mistake.

Sarah plopped herself back into a chair, trying to discern why a stranger had come to her funeral and why this would make her so upset. She told herself that there had to be funeral groupies who occupied their own desperate lives with attending every sort of service they found advertised, so they could shed false tears and think they were lucky because their own lives, as miserable as they might be, hadn't ended.

She stared at the computer screen, where the woman's partially obscured face was frozen. *Why couldn't she just be someone like that? Of course she could. But she might be someone else entirely.* Sarah looked over at Karen and Jordan. The two of them represented polar opposites. One was in a hurry to strike back. One was being overly cautious. It would have been nice, she thought, if she had fit in between, a force for reason. This wasn't the case. A part of her wanted to run, right at that moment, take advantage of her new Cynthia-life and leave the others behind to face the Wolf. She could be safe. He would be satisfied with the remaining Reds. She could be free. A wave of selfishness nearly overcame her.

She fought it off. "There's only one thing we can do," she said briskly, a schoolteacher imposing order on an unruly class. "We do some stalking of our own."

Jordan waited until she heard the sound of the closing door echo through her dormitory. She went to her window and watched until she saw the teacher who doubled as a dorm parent scuttle off into the evening darkness.

Right behind her was a gaggle of teenage girls, her dorm mates. They were all heading over to a dance at the school's art gallery. She could already hear the raucous chords of a local rock group covering the old Wilson Pickett song *In the Midnight Hour* wafting over the campus. She seized a small screwdriver, the type designed for fixing electronics, and her plastic-encased school ID card. She had already removed her shoes so she could move quietly down the hallway.

There was a notable advantage to living in a hundred-year-old Victorian that had been converted to single rooms for upper-class students. The door locks were notoriously ancient and flimsy, and a bit of common knowledge passed down from student occupant to student occupant was how to use the stiff plastic edge of the ID card to jimmy open any lock.

She hoped that the door to the dorm parent's one-bedroom apartment on the ground floor would have the same lax security.

It did.

She flicked the edge between doorjamb and lock, twisted her card with a practiced motion, and the door popped open. She was even lucky enough that the woman had left her desk light on, so that Jordan could move rapidly through the rooms without stumbling over the unfamiliar furniture arrangement.

What she was looking for would be either on the desk or near a bedside phone. It didn't take more than ninety seconds for Jordan to spot it.

Students were not supposed to have access to this blue-jacketed binder emblazoned with the school's name and logo beneath the words "Confidential Faculty/Staff Directory." If they—or their invariably upset parents —wanted to contact someone in the administration or on the faculty, the school's website listed e-mail addresses and official phone numbers. But the directory that Jordan had seized from beneath a stack of student papers had information not so readily available.

She flipped it open to the section entitled "Dean's Office."

There, next to "Administrative Secretary," was a name, along with office and home phone numbers and an address, and even more conveniently, in parentheses, a man's name. The secretary's husband.

Her hand quivered as she read the name. *Are you the Wolf?* For a moment, her head spun dizzily. Jordan breathed in deeply, settling her racing pulse and clenched stomach. Then she copied everything from the directory entry onto the back of her hand in black ink. She didn't trust herself not to lose a scrap of paper. She wanted this information tattooed to her skin.

She could feel a rush of fears and confidences all clashing together within her. She fought off every sensation, telling herself to remain calm, remain focused, to return the directory to the exact same position it had occupied when she found it. She reminded herself to make sure that she had disturbed nothing and left no trace of herself in the faculty member's apartment, not even the scent of her fear. The air in the apartment seemed harsh, like bitter smoke. She urged herself to use stealth, make sure that she exited the room with as much quiet and secrecy as she had used when she arrived.

Don't let anyone see you, Jordan, she admonished herself. *Be invisible*.

For an instant, she thought it was funny. She had broken in and acted like a burglar, violating a school rule that would get her dismissed instantly, but she had not stolen anything except a small piece of information that might be larger than anything she had ever before held in her hands. It was like stealing something that could be either priceless or worthless.

She moved across the room quietly and put her ear to the door. She could hear no one outside. She inhaled rapidly, like a diver readying herself to plunge beneath black waters, and slowly turned the handle to let herself out. She wished in that second that she'd brought her filleting knife with her. She decided that from that point on, she would keep it close at hand.

Now the band was covering the Rolling Stones' "She's So Cold," doing a passable imitation of Mick, Keith, and the lads, right down to the lead vocalist's plaintive pleas encapsulated in the lyrics. The local group was wedged into a corner of the art gallery's main room. Usually, the gallery sported student, faculty, and alumni works, but the open space was easily converted into a dance floor. Someone had replaced some of the overhead lights with a huge silver ball that reflected flashes of light onto the packed dancers.

The music reverberated off the walls; the students gyrated or collected in knots, closely pressed together, shouting above the band's sounds. It was hot and loud. There was a refreshment table to the side, where a pair of the younger faculty dispensed plastic cups filled with watered-down red punch. A couple of other teachers hung by the sides, eyeing the students, trying to make sure than none of them snuck off hand in hand for some illicit contact. This was an impossible task. Jordan knew that the heat in the room would translate into connecting. *Someone will lose his or her virginity tonight*, she told herself.

Three times, she had elbowed her way through the dense, twisting pack of dancing students, moving diagonally across the floor each time, pausing once or twice to twist her body in circles, so that she might be mistaken for one of the party-goers. Her eyes, however, were fixed on the exits and on the faculty trying to prevent the inevitable sneaking off to quiet, dark places.

Jordan had been to enough of these dances to know what would happen. The teachers would spot a couple trying to exit together. Or, they'd be smart enough to realize that the sophomore leaving from the right intended to meet the senior exiting on the left, and both would be halted.

She waited, biding her time. When she saw a couple trying to leave, she slid behind them. She knew what would happen.

"Where do you think you two are going?" came the demand from the teacher. He confronted the couple, who at least had the sense to stop holding hands, and who were replying sheepishly and nervously that they meant no harm and didn't mean anything and weren't doing anything and had no possible idea what the faculty member thought they might conceivably be up to.

And, in that moment of confrontation, Jordan slipped through the door.

She made her way rapidly down a corridor. With each step, the music faded a bit more. At the end of the hall, she stopped. To her right were stairs, to her left another hall that led to the bathrooms. There would be faculty watching each bathroom. It was too obvious a place for a quick grope between couples or a fast swallow of an ecstasy pill or snort of cocaine. The kids who wanted to use the dance to cover a marijuana smoke invariably were wise enough to head outside, so that the telltale scent of the drug couldn't be detected by the houndlike capabilities of the faculty noses.

The stairs to the right went down to a second flight, where there were drawing and sculpture studios. The studios would all be watched by a teacher making rounds every fifteen minutes or so, because they were a favorite making-out location. She intended to bypass these obvious spots, head out a ground-floor door, and, sticking to the shadows, make her way into the science and physics building next door. It was a little like being an escaping prisoner of war, dodging light towers and guards.

There was an advantage to being a four-year senior. By the time graduation would arrive, one knew all the little quirks and idiosyncrasies of the school—such as which doors weren't locked.

Ignoring the classrooms just inside the entrance, Jordan headed down another flight of stairs. The labs were below and their windows didn't look out on the main walkways and quadrangles of the school, but faced toward the playing fields. It was dark—the only light was reflected from the art building where the dance was being held, which was well illuminated. It was quiet; Jordan's sneakers slapping against the floor and her breathing were the only noises close by—everything else was rhythm and blues and rock and roll coming from the band a building away.

At the third lab door, Jordan stopped and turned the handle. The room was black and gray. She could make out the shadows of lab equipment spread out across wide tables, where students did experiments.

She whispered, "Karen? Sarah?"

From a corner shadow, they responded, "We're here."

38

The room itself seemed conspiratorial. Dark shadows seeping into corners, the wan light from the nearby art building, the odd shapes of scientific equipment spread throughout the long, wide space—everything made it seem like the sort of spot where bad ideas and wild schemes were hatched. It had been years since Karen had been in a school laboratory. Sarah's scientific sensibilities were defined by elementary classroom studies of ducks and frogs and barnyard animals. Jordan, however, loved the room, not because of the science that was contained there, but because it seemed to her to be the place where odd chemicals and strange substances could be combined into smelly failures or explosive successes, and that paralleled the position she imagined the three of them were in. She was encouraged as well by the idea that it was a place of well-defined formulas and eminent reason, so that the order and understanding that science tried to impose on the world might help them as they designed what their next steps were to be.

The three Reds sat cross-legged on the floor behind a long table. They had Karen's laptop between them, and they hunched forward as Jordan typed in various bits of information.

"Here," Jordan said. She pointed at the screen. "Gotta love Google Images."

The unprepossessing image of a man in his sixties stared back at them. He had a paunch around his middle and skin that sagged beneath his chin. He had shaggy gray-tinged hair around his ears, but a thinning top, and he wore old-fashioned horn-rimmed glasses perched on the end of his nose. The picture was taken a few years earlier at a local bookstore reading series. He was clearly a little shy of six feet tall, and not heavy-set, but not athletic-looking either. His ordinariness was his most dramatic feature.

"You think that's a killer?" Jordan asked.

"He doesn't look like what I imagined the Wolf would look like," Karen said.

"What do killers look like?" Jordan asked. "And what would a wolf look like?"

"Tall. Strong. Predatory. I don't see that," Karen said quietly. "You think that guy could chase you down?"

"He's a writer. Mysteries and thrillers," Sarah said.

"Does that mean anything?" Karen responded.

"Well, I guess it means he knows something about crimes," Sarah replied. "Wouldn't any crime writer who was good enough to get a book published know something about how to commit a felony?"

"Yeah, probably," Karen answered sharply. "But they'd also know how people get caught." She turned to Jordan. "Tell us about the wife," she asked.

"Bitch," Jordan snapped.

"That doesn't say much," Karen said.

"Yes it does," Sarah interjected.

"The woman sits up in the dean's office and never smiles," Jordan said. "Never says hello. Acts put out when you show up to get reamed by the dean for whatever you've done wrong, like you've somehow made her day worse."

"So, just because she's a little rude, you think . . ." Karen stopped. *Teenage think is simple think*, she reminded herself. *Except when it isn't*, *when they surprise you with some truly prescient idea or observation.* She looked through the dark at Jordan, trying to discern which of these moments this was. Jordan was the angriest of the three of them. Even in the room's shadows, she could see her face lit with barely contained fury. Karen imagined that it was the teenager's anger that made her risky. It also made her attractive. She wasn't beset by doubts—or, at the least, no doubts that Karen could see. She wondered whether she had once been like Jordan and suspected the answer to that question was yes, because the line between anger and determination was often thin. At least, she hoped she'd once been like Jordan. She suddenly felt old, then thought, *No, that's not what I'm feeling. What I'm feeling is defeated already by what we might have to do.*

"I still think she's a bitch," Jordan replied. The teenager hesitated, then gasped sharply, the sound echoing about the science lab.

"What is it?" Sarah asked.

Jordan's voice trembled. It was in sharp contrast to the blustery, fierce Jordan that the other Reds had grown accustomed to. "I just realized: The bitch comes to every basketball game."

"Well, what does—" Sarah started, only to have Jordan leap excitedly into a rush of words.

"Every game. I mean, she's always up there in the middle of the stands—I've seen her a million times, watching us play. Except I only *thought* it was us. Maybe it was *me*. And if she's there, I bet her husband is there, too, right next to her."

"Well, have you ever seen him?"

"Yeah. Sure. Probably. How would I know who he was?"

This made sense.

"And that's not all," Jordan said, her voice picking up momentum. "In the dean's office, she would have access to my school record. She would know just about every scheduled place I had to be. She'd know when I was likely to be in class, or eating lunch or going to basketball or heading to the library. She would know just about everything. Or, at least, could figure it out."

Sarah leaned back. Her mind churned. *You take one thing and add it to another thing, you combine one observation with something else you've noticed, and it all seems to mean something when maybe it doesn't.*

To Jordan, it suddenly seemed obvious: mean secretary. Husband. Games. Her every trip to the gym. All the failed appointments with psychologists to get her back on track. She thought, *It has to connect the dots. But not yet to the other two Reds.* Jordan abruptly punched computer keys, and pictures of the husband's four book jackets arrived on the screen.

The pictures were lurid, suggestive, and over-the-top images. A man wielding a bloody knife figured prominently in one. A large handgun resting on a table was in the center of another. A third sported a shadowy figure lurking in an alleyway. This jacket caused Karen to shudder.

"He hasn't published in years. Maybe he's retired," Karen said. Not one word that fell from her lips had any conviction behind it.

"Yeah. Or maybe something else," Jordan sneered. "Maybe he got tired of writing about killers and decided to try a real suit on for size."

The three Reds remained silent. They could hear distant music from the dance. The pulse of rock and roll contradicted the dark feelings they all felt.

"What do we do now?" Sarah whispered. "Maybe it's him. Maybe it isn't. I mean, what the hell can we do? What are our alternatives?"

Again silence enclosed the three women. It took Karen, the organized one of the three, a few minutes to reply. "One, we do nothing—"

"Great plan," Jordan interrupted. "And wait for him to kill us?"

"He hasn't yet. Maybe he won't. Maybe this is all just, I don't know . . ."—she waved her hand at the science lab equipment—"some weird experiment, the kind of bizarre thing a writer thinks up and—" She stopped. "We have no real evidence, other that the Wolf's word, that he intends to kill us."

"Bullshit! He's been stalking us and—" Sarah countered.

"What about your dead cats?" Jordan cut in.

"I don't know for sure they're dead. I only know—" Karen realized she was contradicting everything she truly believed.

"Bullshit!" Jordan interrupted, echoing Sarah. "You fucking well know."

Karen did, but she continued on, false reason and awkward compromise littering her voice. "Maybe that's all there is to it. Maybe he just wants to go on taunting us and teasing us and threatening us for years."

Jordan shook her head back and forth. "Any one of the shrinks my fucking parents have forced me to go to over the years would grin and say that's total denial, as if they were making some sort of really wonderful point that should straighten me out like instantly and turn me into a well-adjusted, happy, perfectly normal teenager, like there is such a thing anywhere in the world."

Both Karen and Sarah were glad of the dark, because they both smiled right past their fears. Karen thought this was exactly what she really liked about Jordan. *If she can live through all this*, Karen thought, *she will grow into someone special.*

The word *if* was nearly painful inside her, like a sudden clenched stomachache or a slap across the cheek.

"Okay, so *nothing* and *wait to see if he does kill us* is one choice," Sarah said. "And?"

"We can try confrontation," Karen said. "See if that scares him off."

"You mean," Jordan interjected, "like knock on his door and say, '*Hi. We're the three Reds. One of us has already faked her death, but we'd really like it if you'd stop saying you're going to kill us, pretty please.*' Now, that's a plan that we can all really get behind."

Sarah nodded. "Of course, we do that or something like that—let him know we know who he is—and it's just as possible that it would force him to make a move. He might accelerate all his plans. Think of all the movies you've seen, where the kidnappers tell the victim's family, 'Don't call the police,' and either they do or they don't, but neither answer is ever right because it sets everything in motion. It's like we've been kidnapped."

"One other thing," Jordan added. "If we just confront him, we lose all our advantages. He just denies he's the Wolf, slams the door in our faces, and we're back at square one. Maybe we're dead tomorrow or next week or next year. Maybe all he'll do is decide to invent a new plan and put that into action."

Karen put her head into her hands for an instant. She was trying to see clearly through a fog of possibilities. It was like sorting through symptoms belonging to a very sick patient. A misstep, a wrong diagnosis, and the patient might die.

"We don't know for sure that he is the Wolf," she said. "How can we act without being one hundred percent sure?" She was a little surprised at the hesitancy creeping into her words; she always tried to be aggressive, decisive. This was hard for her. She felt like she had just delivered a joke that fell flat, and she was being laughed *at*, not *with*.

Jordan shrugged. "So what? We're not a court of law. We're not going to the cops with some crazy-ass story about notes and a Wolf and sneaking around for all this time, just so a cop can think we're complete nuts." Jordan was speaking fast. Probably too fast, the other two Reds thought. "It's all about maintaining the edge. Keeping control. There's only one thing we can do."

Karen knew what Jordan was going to say, but she let the teenager say it anyway.

"We outwolf him."

"How do we do that?" Sarah asked. She already knew the answer to her question. It just scared her.

Karen, too, knew the answer. She leaned back and felt a ripple of muscle tension race through her entire body, as if she was quivering from head to toe. Her last remaining bit of reason forced some words out of her mouth. "We can't just go kill him, just like that. Wait outside his front door and when he comes out to get the newspaper, shoot him and then try to disappear? Do our own little urban drive-by? That's not who we are. And we'd all end up in prison, because that's not self-defense, it's murder, and the last time I checked, none of us are master criminals."

"How do we make it into self-defense?" Sarah asked. "Like a trap? Do we wait for him to try to kill us first? Except, maybe he's been doing that already."

"I don't know," Karen replied. "None of us has ever done anything like this before."

"Are you sure?" Sarah allowed frustration to creep into her voice. "We invented my death. We've all been manipulative, scheming, I don't know what, at some point in our lives. Everyone has. Everyone lies. Everyone cheats. You grow up and you learn how. We just have to create something that the Wolf would never expect. Why can't we do that?"

"What do you mean 'create something'—" Karen started, but was interrupted by Sarah.

"Something he would never expect."

"And what—"

"Don't you feel like everything he's done depends upon us acting like nice normal sensible friendly folks? We stop acting like all those things that make us who we are. Or, who we have been."

The three Reds were quiet for a few moments.

"I want to kill him," Jordan said slowly, breaking into a silence that seemed lethal. "I have since the very start. I want to be finished with the Wolf totally and completely. And I don't care about anything anymore except that we move, and move fast. And prison is better than a grave."

"You sure about that?" Karen asked.

Jordan didn't reply. *It's a good question*, she thought. This idea was immediately followed by the young person's automatic answer to all huge doubts: *Ahhh, fuck it.*

"But how?" Sarah asked sharply. "What do we do?"

She couldn't believe she was actually agreeing to a murder. She also couldn't believe she would not agree to murder, in this case. She wasn't even completely sure they were talking about murder, except that was what it sounded like. It was as if in the darkness of the science lab, any chance of rational thought was dissipating around them.

Karen was about to say something, but then stopped herself. *Are you a killer?* she suddenly demanded of herself. She did not know the right response, but she knew she was about to find out.

Jordan was nodding her head. She typed some numbers into the search engine on the computer.

A Google Earth image of a modest suburban home in an undistinguished neighborhood came up on the screen. Jordan hit *street view* and suddenly they were moving up and down the road where the writer and the secretary lived. It was not unlike Sarah's old neighborhood: trim, white-sided houses with well-kept yards. It was a typical New England neighborhood, not the sort that end up on postcards or in travel brochures featuring farms or stately old houses. These were simply rows of homes built thirty years earlier, with a postwar feel, well maintained by generations of blue-collar workers and their families, who took pride in ownership as part of the American dream of upward mobility. It was a place where folks generally went to the local high school to cheer for the football team on Friday nights and ate a post-church meat loaf dinner on Sundays. People would be rabid supporters of the Red Sox and Patriots, but unable to afford the exaggerated ticket prices except maybe once a year. Their kids grew up hoping for a good job with a union contract, so they could repeat the same arc as their parents, only just a little bit better, just as their parents had done a little bit better than their parents.

It was the sort of place that encapsulated all that was both right and wrong with America, because hidden behind all the mowed lawns and freshly painted aluminum siding were more than a few alcohol or drug problems, domestic violence, and the other sorts of afflictions that commonly run beneath the fake surface of normalcy. The three Reds all looked at the images of the house and the street—from above, from in front, from behind—and tried to imagine how something as evil as the Wolf could flower in that sort of spot. That a killer lived there seemed impossible. Red One thought, *These are the people who come to me for help when they are sick.* Red Two thought, *These people are just like me. I taught their children.* Red Three thought, *I have nothing in common with these people, and they would look at my private school, nice clothes, and money background and hate me instantly.*

Sarah spoke first. "I don't know if that's the Wolf's home," she said hesitantly, "but we have no other leads. No other ideas. No one else seems like a possibility. So I think that's where we should go."

"I agree," Karen said.

"You know," Jordan said softly, "Little Red Riding Hood doesn't exactly turn and run when the Wolf confronts her. She's observant. She voices her doubt. '*What big teeth you've got, grandmother.*' The others were silent. "We have to go ask this writer and his secretary wife some hard questions. We can't wait. We can't delay. Every minute we don't act, we give the Wolf time to close in on us. We have to change the game around completely, from this moment on. We take control. If we wait one more second, it could kill us. It's been like that from the very start, and we've probably pushed our luck to the damn edge. We have to be able to ask questions in such a way that he can't possibly lie to us. Then we'll know the truth. And we'll know what to do, because right at that minute it will be fucking obvious."

She paused, and whispered, "No lies, no lies, no more lies. No longer."

"How do we guarantee that?" Sarah asked. "How do you ask a question that someone can't answer with a lie?"

She knew the answer to her question.

So did Karen.

Jordan reached down and suddenly the others saw the knife in her hand. The thin, sharp blade caught a streak of diffuse light slipping through one of the laboratory's windows and glowed like silver mercury.

39

Red One thought it was like inventing an edgy stage routine for a difficult, unruly audience.

Red Two thought it was like a grade school child's papier-mâché project, pieced together with string and tape.

Red Three thought it was like studying for a hard examination in a course where she had skipped too many classes.

None of them actually called it what it was: *preparing to kill someone.*

Each of them created her own part of the whole. That had been Karen's rough idea, and she had insisted upon it—although precisely why, she could not have fully explained to the other two Reds. It just seemed to her that shared effort made sense, in a vaguely democratic way. None of the three Reds knew that the Big Bad Wolf would have found this aspect of their hurried and haphazard plan totally delicious and decidedly smart; he would have admired the inevitable confusion three people operating independently to create one profound killing would have created for any follow-up investigator.

The Wolf had honed his own design down to what he considered a satisfying simplicity. It was similar to the famous family fun board game that rested on some dusty shelf in virtually every play room or summer vacation cottage: Clue. Except, for him, it wouldn't be *Colonel Mustard in the pantry with a candlestick*. It would be *the Wolf with a hunting knife when they least expect it*. In actuality, the Wolf had entered into a Zen-like phase of murder: The actions were subordinate to the interpretation. He twitched with excitement in front of his computer screen: *They are already dead. It's the words that accompany the deed that are important. I have to bring people along with me on this journey. Arriving at the killings, it has to be utterly tempting for every reader; they can't feel revulsion, they need to feel their own lust. It needs to be like driving past an accident on the highway: You can't help but look even though you know indulging your morbid curiosity makes you somehow less of an honorable person.*

The three Reds and the Big Bad Wolf had reached the same decision: *Hurry up and kill.*

Everyone's future depended upon it.

Jordan left the library late in the afternoon, a copy of Truman Capote's *In Cold Blood* in her backpack. She was interested only in the opening chapters, which she had read through twice before skipping to deep in the middle to identify what had tripped up Perry Smith and Richard Hickock. She had also gone to the school's modest selection of films and found the original version of Sam Peckinpah's *Straw Dogs*—which she had never heard of—and the first installment of Wes Craven's *Scream* on a shelf. These were supposed to be signed out on a nearby sheet. She started to put her name down, and then realized it might be better to ignore this requirement.

Back in her room, she put the first movie into her computer's drive and took out a pad to jot down observations and notes. She had spent hours earlier in the day poring over Internet entries describing various crimes, but all with a pair of critical themes: *random killing* and *home invasion*.

Jordan reminded herself that by the end of the day, she would have to destroy everything she had written down.

As the idyllic English countryside in the movie came up on the screen in front of her, she also knew that she would have to wreck her computer. She paused the film, and wrote a quick e-mail to her estranged mother and father:

Mom and Dad . . . My damn computer keeps freezing up and it totally like lost an important paper I'd been working on so I have to redo the whole thing and it might be late which would affect my grade. I'm sending you this e-mail from a friend's laptop. I need to get a new computer asap because finals are coming up. I can get it at the mall today okay, but I'll use your credit card.

She knew that neither of her parents would refuse this request. They would likely be pleased that she had communicated something with them, if only the need for some money. She thought adding the bit about the lost paper was clever, because they would never deny her something that might be the difference between flunking and passing a course. And her request might provide them with something to argue about, Jordan believed, which would be an added advantage.

The computer she was staring at had a footprint inside its memory that was every bit as incriminating as a fingerprint left at a crime scene. Jordan smiled, and turned back to the movie. She was pleased that she was becoming a criminal.

All that hard work and studying is paying off, she thought.

Three pairs of men's running shoes. Three different sizes. Identical make and model. Three different sporting good stores to purchase each in cash. Her shopping list was extensive and the seemingly random manner in which she had to buy items added to the hassle. Ordinarily, Sarah would have complained about the added errands and the complicated, round-about way she had invented to accomplish them, but now erratic, nonsensical behavior was a strength and not a deficit. She imagined some detective arriving at the mall and staring incomprehensibly at the competing shoe stores, unable to understand why some killer went and bought the same item in three places instead of just buying all three pairs at once. This had been a suggestion Jordan made: *"Don't do things that make obvious sense."*

The Mad Hatter, Alice in Wonderland, the Red Queen shouting, "Off with their heads! And then we'll have a trial." Sarah looked around her at the most common staple in the American world—the shopping mall—and thought she was living an upside-down existence. *I'm a dead woman purchasing items to kill with.* It all seemed like some huge cosmic joke. She burst out in laughter—a few other shoppers turned and looked oddly at her—and then she went back to her duties.

Sarah worked her way through obtaining the items that she was assigned. She bought the first black hood at an outdoors chain that specialized in climbing gear and kayaks. At this place, she also acquired three matching sets of skin-tight black synthetic long underwear and three small, high-intensity flashlights. She went to the rival chain to buy two other hoods. She also bought a fish billy—an 18-inch-long polished wooden club with a leather strap that fit over the wrist that sportsmen used to subdue very large and feisty fish. She went to a store that featured leotards and dancing gear for three pairs of ballet slippers. In a hardware store she purchased a roll of gray duct tape, a set of screwdrivers, and a heavy rubber mallet.

Then, as if working without any rhyme or reason, she returned to the sporting goods store and added three black hooded sweatshirts to her list of purchases. At a nearby luggage specialty store, she bought the three cheapest small canvas duffel bags they had: one blue, one yellow, and one green.

When she walked out into the midst of the mall, surrounded by other shoppers carrying oversized paper sacks stuffed with cheap Chinese-made clothes and Korean electronic items, Sarah did a small dancer's pirouette. If people stared at her for an instant, that was fine with her. She felt free. Unlike the other two Reds, she knew she could flee at any moment.

She wanted to laugh out loud. In return for a new identity and a new future, she had only a single obligation: murder.

Sarah liked the symmetry of it all. Death gives life. She conceded that it might not be the wisest approach to starting anew, but she was locked into a world that had little past—her life as Sarah seemed to be fading more every minute—and connected only to two red-haired onetime strangers whom she now felt she knew better than any friend she'd ever had before, and to some man who wanted to be a wolf and a character in a fairy tale.

She reached down into one of her shopping bags and wrapped her hand around the fish billy. It had heft and a smooth, polished surface. It felt lethal to her touch. She smiled. She felt lethal, too.

If he sees me, we're screwed.

It was the only thought that penetrated Karen's fear. Once again, she was in a rental car. She wore sunglasses, despite the gray overcast of the afternoon. Her distinctive red hair was hidden beneath a ski cap. In her right hand she had the video camera, as she cautiously steered with her left. The window was down on the passenger side of the car, and she lifted the camera up and took video as she slowly drove down the blocks adjacent to the house where the Big Bad Wolf might or might not live. She knew it would be jumpy, dizzying, unprofessional footage—but just letting the other Reds see the neighborhood was likely to help them.

She pulled to the side of the road a half-block away from the house. Looking up and down the street, she made certain that no one was around. Surveillance was important, but secrecy and surprise were more so. She took some shots of the house from afar.

Karen could feel her heart pounding, and she admonished herself, *You can't be like this later*. Her hands shook, and she imagined that when she showed the other Reds the footage they would see how scared she had been, and that unsettled her, because she knew she had to be strong-willed.

It isn't reasonable, she thought. *I'm the one that's supposed to be in control.* She imagined that she was now only a doctor of doubt. Maybe a doctor of death.

Down the block, a teenage boy emerged from a nearby house and slid behind the wheel of a small dull-silver-colored pickup truck. The boy had absolutely nothing to do with anything, but she still ducked down, and as soon as he roared past her, she floored her own gas pedal and accelerated away from the neighborhood. It took miles for Karen to calm herself, and when her breathing returned to normal, she realized that she had driven into a totally unfamiliar part of the county.

It took her nearly an hour to find her way back to roads she recognized because she refused to stop and ask for directions, and another hour to return the rental, retrieve her own car, and make her way home in the dark.

She pulled up her driveway, descending into the woods that concealed her home from the road. More than ever before, she hated the isolation of her place. She stopped in front.

The automatic light system came on.

She was about to shut off the engine and head inside when she hesitated. She was nearly overcome by conflicted fears: The place that should have been her safe haven was also her biggest threat.

Karen suddenly slammed her car back into gear and did a tire-squealing U-turn. She drove as if she were being chased, even though she saw no one on any of the country roads that she took. It was suddenly as if the Big Bad Wolf had managed to kill everyone *except* her. She was alone in the world, last person standing, sole survivor, waiting for the inevitable. She screamed in her car as she accelerated down the highway, her voice rising through the small space, scaring her even more.

When she was able to get some slight control over her emotions, she drove up onto one of the main highways. Within a few seconds, she saw a sign: FOOD—GAS—LODGING.

The motel at the bottom of the exit ramp was part of a national chain. The parking lot wasn't crowded. There was only a single clerk at the desk. She seemed young, probably a recent college graduate in a management training program that required her to work late hours, and had an irrepressible, outgoing smile. The young woman checked Karen in, asking her whether she preferred a single king-sized bed or two double beds. Karen slid into nervous sarcasm. "I can only sleep in one bed at a time," she replied.

The young lady smiled and laughed. "Well, that's true. So a king-size?"

Karen handed over her credit card. This was dangerous. It made a record of her staying there. But there was little she could do about it.

"One night?" the young woman asked.

Karen shuddered. "No. Two. Business."

In the small, oppressively neat motel room, the first thing Karen did was to indulge in a blisteringly hot shower. She felt filthy, sweaty. She wondered whether fear could make someone feel dirty. She thought it far more likely that it stemmed merely from being in close proximity to the person they all imagined *might* be the Wolf.

Hair damp, a pair of towels wrapped around her, she went to the small desk in the room and pulled out her comedy computer. *No more jokes on this*, she thought. She started in with various real estate sites, like Trulia .com and Zillow.com, followed by sites maintained by big banks in the mortgage business. It did not take her long to find the house where the secretary and her husband the writer lived. There were only exterior pictures. She cursed this bad luck, then looked a little harder and discovered that a house across the street—and seemingly identical—had been on the market three years earlier. One of the sites helpfully provided pictures of the interior and a virtual tour of this home. *"Be the same,"* she whispered to herself. *"Please be the same."*

Like any prospective buyer, she followed the images on the screen. Front door. Turn right. Living room. Eat-in kitchen. Downstairs office space. Stairs up. Two small bedrooms "perfect for a growing family" and a master with its own bathroom. Finished basement.

She stared at the pictures. Suburban New England bliss. The great promise of the American middle class: home ownership.

Karen returned to the website showing the secretary and writer's house. She learned how much they paid in property taxes. She learned how much in the current market conditions their house was worth. Useless information.

She had a brief memory right at that moment, staring at pictures of the house she intended to visit. The lyrics to an old rock song that played on the oldies stations she listened to frequently jumped into her head, and she mumbled in time to internal music: "Monday, Monday. Can't trust that day."

Karen ignored this warning and sent a text message to the other two Reds: *Tomorrow. 2 and 2.*

She didn't think she had to add p.m. and a.m. They would know what she meant.

40

2 p.m.

He took her out to lunch—an unexpected pleasure.

Mrs. Big Bad Wolf left behind on her desk faculty assessments and student disciplinary reports that all needed to be properly assigned to permanent files. She put aside a long-winded analysis from a trustee committee investigating new revenue streams and a lengthy written request from the head of the English Department to expand course offerings away from traditional literature like Dickens and Faulkner and into classes on modern communications media, like Twitter and Facebook. She happily joined the Big Bad Wolf at a downtown Chinese restaurant, where they ate far-too-spicy foods and sipped weak green tea. She guessed that he had some motive for taking her out—as in any long-term marriage, spontaneous acts of affection were rare—but she didn't care. She reveled in steamed dumplings and miso sauce.

The waitress came and asked if they wanted dessert.

"I think a bowl of ice cream," the Big Bad Wolf said. He looked at his wife.

"No, no sweets. Got to watch my weight."

"Oh, come on," he said, a teasing tone in his voice. "Just this once?"

She smiled. He reached over and took her hand. *Like teenagers*, she thought.

"All right." She smiled at the waitress. "I'll have some ice cream, too."

"Two bowls of vanilla," the Wolf said. "We're just plain old folks."

This was a joke the waitress didn't get, and the two of them laughed together as she went off to fetch their order.

He didn't drop her hand, but leaned across the narrow table toward his wife. "The next day or so," he said, being as vague as he could, but speaking with a slight grin on his face, "I might have an unusual schedule. You know—rising early, staying out a little late, maybe missing some meals."

"Okay," she said, nodding.

"You're not to worry."

"I'm not worried. It's important?"

"Last bits of research."

She smiled. "Final chapters?"

He didn't reply, except to widen his smile, which she took as a *yes*. She didn't care. *Creativity isn't a nine-to-five job*. She looked across at him. Deep within her, many words reverberated, echoing doubts and fears. *Is he going to kill?* With surprisingly remarkable ease, she closed doors on all of them. She did not care in the slightest what he did or whom he might do it to. *It is only research, just as he says.* Whatever existed in the past, whatever might happen in the future, whoever he was once, whoever he might become, all was nothing compared to that moment right then, holding hands in a cheap Chinese restaurant. *There is nothing vanilla about love*, she thought.

The Wolf dropped his wife off at the school, giving her a playful wave as she disappeared into the administration building. Within seconds, however, his focus was elsewhere.

He had a few items left to acquire. None of them were particularly difficult to find: an insulated camouflage hunting suit available at the same sporting goods stores that Red Two had frequented the day before, and an inexpensive blue blazer and gray slacks from the local Salvation Army used clothing store. For Red One, he had to blend seamlessly into the forest beyond her house. For Red Three, he had to look like a faculty member, or a visiting parent, which required a jacket and tie—just on the limited chance that someone might see him on the campus. Of course, he wouldn't stand out: A fake beard. Glasses. Hair slicked back. The chances of someone recognizing him were near zero, and who would lend any credence to some prep school kid's identification of someone they only saw at a distance for a few seconds? And beyond that, it would be hours before Red Three's body was discovered. He thought this was what was most exceptional about the twin murders he'd planned. In each, he would be nearly invisible.

The Wolf went over his mental list:

Clothes. *Check*.

Transportation. *Stolen plates would help*.

Weapon. *He had honed his knife to razor sharpness*.

All that remained was descending into the total concentration necessary as he closed in on the remaining Reds. As he drove away from the school, savoring what the following day held, he imagined it was like getting a phone call from an old and distant, but dear and important, friend. He summoned up memories from fifteen years earlier, the same way a distinctive voice coming over the years was still intimate and totally familiar.

The priest was using his downstairs office to work on a sermon for the next Sunday, so the three Reds met amidst the wooden pews in front of a huge wooden sculpture of the crucified Jesus wearing His crown of thorns, head bent as death neared.

They sat uncomfortably as Karen played her street video for them. They shifted against the hard wooden surface, trying to memorize details, landmarks. It was difficult for each of them to concentrate. They knew they had to be instant experts at killing, and yet, right when their attention should have been laserlike, each of the three Reds found her mind wandering in unhelpful directions, as if the realization of what they intended to do forced them to mentally go someplace else. Karen started to apologize for the quality of the video, but stopped herself because she didn't trust her voice. It all seemed incredibly haphazard and shamefully unplanned for someone who prided herself on cautious organization. Karen felt it was her unhinged wild comedy-club persona that had taken over designing a murder, instead of her disciplined-doctor side. She didn't know how to make the right part of her take the lead. Instead, she punched the computer keyboard, and a couple of clicks brought up the real estate information she'd acquired the night before.

When the images ended, all three Reds leaned back, silent.

Sarah reached down to the polished floor at their feet and pulled up the three duffels. She handed each of them a bag she'd packed with her purchases. She kept the yellow one for herself.

In a situation that demanded dozens of questions, they remained quiet for several minutes. A passerby might have believed they were praying together.

Jordan looked up once from the screen and fixed on the religious images that surrounded them. The sculpture was a deep brown wood, inlaid with streaks of gold paint where there should have been red-colored blood. The church ceiling reflected blues, greens, and yellows from large stained glass windows. She thought it was an unusual place to be planning a killing, but then she involuntarily shrugged, and realized that *any* place a spoiled teenage private school student was planning a murder would probably be pretty unusual. She glanced over at Karen. *She's a doctor. She's seen death*, Jordan thought. *She has to know what she's doing.* Then she turned to Sarah and much the same thought penetrated her imagination. *She had death come knocking on her door completely unfairly. It had to make her so angry that now she's ready to kill.*

Jordan believed she was the only one of the three Reds not to have an intimacy with dying. She did not expect that virginity to last the night.

2 a.m.

The motel had a side exit that operated with the electronic room key. Karen used this to avoid the young woman at the front desk. She peered into the darkness, trying to measure the distances between parking lot lights. She wanted to grip shadows the way a climber holds a safety rope. She threw herself behind the wheel of her car, tossing her blue duffel bag on the seat beside her. She fumbled with the keys before starting the ignition.

She was shaking, and took several deep breaths to try to calm herself down. *You read books. You watch television. You go to the movies. Think of all the times you've seen good guys and bad guys act out some murderous plot or scheme in some fictional situation. Just do what they do. Only this is real.*

This, she knew, was ludicrous self-advice.

Maybe you've seen a million fictional murders, she told herself. *But all those put together don't tell you what to do.*

Putting the car in gear, her eyes constantly switching between all the mirrors, she drove fast. She had one critical stop to make before she picked up the others: her medical office.

Jordan hadn't slept.

Around one in the morning, after having lain immobile on her back staring at the ceiling of her dorm room, she had risen and dressed. The black long underwear went on beneath jeans. She slipped into the black sweatshirt. She put her cell phone and her knife into the green duffel bag, and fitted the black balaclava over her head. She took the new running shoes that Sarah had purchased and put them on top, where she could reach them as soon as she got outside. She slid her feet into ballet slippers.

She stood up and turned slowly around. The clothing she wore didn't even rustle.

Jordan looked around her. The only light in the room was from an outdoor streetlamp just beyond her window that pushed a yellow glow into a few corners. It was like packing for a vacation—she was worried that some key item would be left behind. Only on this occasion it wasn't a bathing suit or a passport that she was afraid she would forget.

The mere act of dressing for murder made her hands twitch. Her breathing was shallow. Her throat was parched and it felt like her right eyelid had developed a tic.

She wondered where all her bluster, confidence, and bravado had fled to. Now, just when he might have a name, and an address, and suddenly become something other than a vaporous threat, her confidence was evaporating. She felt like a small child, afraid of the dark. She wanted to whimper.

An immense part of her protested that it would be smarter to strip off the killing clothes and hide under the covers of her bed and just wait patiently for the Wolf to come for her. She fought this desire off, reminding herself that the other two Reds were counting on her.

Imagining that she was entering into the last night of her life as she once knew it, Jordan went to her door. It was the most crippling sensation: It was as if over the time she had been stalked by the Wolf she had grown accustomed to a certain kind of fear, but this night promised to replace it with a totally different kind, when she'd just gotten used to the first kind. She wanted to scream. Instead, she listened carefully to make certain that none of the other girls in the dorm were up, either studying or taking a late night trip to the bathroom.

At some point or another, every student in the school had snuck out of a dormitory after hours, defying hard and fast rules, risking expulsion. *Nobody*, she thought, *ever did this for the reason I have.* No late night assignation with a boy. No late night drug or alcohol run. No just-less-than sadistic late night prank being played on first-year students. This was something different.

She put her hand on the door handle, and as she opened the door she felt as if it would be a new Jordan who would take the first step out into this utterly new world, leaving old Jordan behind forever.

She eased out of her room. The slippers concealed her footsteps but she walked gingerly, afraid that the old wooden boards in the floor might creak and groan in a telltale way. Each step, the person she once was steadily disappeared behind her. It was like leaving a shadow behind.

When she managed to work her way slowly through the front door, the cold air greeted her. She shivered as she pulled off the ballet shoes and tied on her new running shoes. Even though she could feel sweat beneath her arms, the bitter cold felt close to overwhelming as she made her way to the rendezvous with the other Reds. Jordan was afraid she would freeze in position, and so she raced through the night.

Sarah's exit from the women's shelter was equally stealthy. Her problem was making it past the night security guard—a volunteer from one of the local colleges who came on at nine and stayed, bleary-eyed, until the morning shift: a retired police patrolman, who arrived with fresh coffee and donuts. The night volunteers were taught to always err on the side of caution. Any disturbance, anything out of the ordinary, could result in a call to the shelter's gun-toting boss, or 911.

So Sarah waited for nearly an hour, poised on the second-floor landing just out of sight, knowing that eventually the young woman would get up to stretch, or go to the bathroom, or head into the side office to pour herself a cup of coffee, or maybe just drop her head down on the books and take a nap.

Her husband's gun was in her duffel bag, along with a change of clothes. But at this moment, she was dressed exactly as Jordan was, down to the sound-muffling ballet slippers. Karen would be wearing the same outfit.

Sarah didn't even glance at her wristwatch. She wanted to say some sort of prayer designed to make someone go to the toilet. Her entire body was rigid with anticipation.

She licked her lips, which were suddenly dry and cracked. She felt embarrassed, dumb. All her thoughts had been bent toward what they would do when the three of them arrived at the house where they believed the Big Bad Wolf lived. Suddenly she almost burst out laughing, but stifled the sensation. It wasn't anything amusing as much as it was the accumulation of fears.

We've got it all fucking backward, she thought. *It's the wolf that goes to the three little pigs and blows their houses down, except for the smart one, who built his house out of brick and stone.*

Wrong fairy tale.

It had not occurred to her that her first problem might be insurmountable: simply getting out of a place designed to keep people protected without being seen. She suddenly felt like she was in the oddest kind of jail.

She heard a shuffling from below. She leaned forward, listening. This was followed by the sound of a book being slammed shut. She heard, "Goddamn, this stuff is impossible. I hate organic chemistry, I hate organic chemistry, I hate organic chemistry," repeated in a frustrated, angry tone.

After a second or two, the phrase "I hate organic chemistry" turned into a haphazard, invented song, one second being sung high-pitched, next in a basso profundo. She heard footsteps crossing the foyer. Then she heard the bathroom door open and close, and she launched herself down the stairs, tiptoeing to stay quiet, hurrying to get outside. It was crucial that the world thought the woman now named Cynthia Harrison was asleep in her bed.

41

The three Reds waited in the rental car a hundred yards away from the house. They should have been going over the last details of their plan, such as it was, but mainly they were quiet with their own thoughts. It was shortly before three in the morning. Karen had simply pulled to the side of the road and parked beneath a large oak tree. Jordan was in the backseat, Sarah the passenger. Karen placed the car keys on the floor and made certain that the others knew where they were. Then she distributed three sets of surgical gloves, which they all shakily pulled on. All three sets of eyes swept up and down the block. Other than an occasional outdoor light left on by a forgetful home owner, the street was dark and asleep.

Language was at a bare minimum. None of the three Reds trusted their voices not to quaver, so they choked out words laconically. It was as if the closer they got to murder, the less there was to say.

"Two doors," Karen said. "Sarah and me, in back, breaking in. Jordan, if the Wolf tries to get out the front, you've got to stop him. When we've made it inside, we'll let you in."

They all nodded.

None of them spoke the question—"If it is the Wolf"—although each of them had the same thought.

Nor did Jordan ask: "*What do you mean 'stop him?'*" or "*How exactly do I stop him?*" or finally, "*What happens if I can't stop him and he gets away?*" Uncertainty had bred with finality; all three Reds had entered into some odd sort of state that traveled well beyond reason. It was a fairy tale of their own making.

"Upstairs and to the right. Has to be the master bedroom. That's where we're going. Move fast. They will be asleep, so we will have the element of surprise, but breaking in will probably wake them."

"Suppose . . ." Sarah started to ask, then stopped. She suddenly realized there were hundreds of *supposes* and that trying to anticipate all of them was impossible.

Jordan's voice was stifled, weak.

"In *In Cold Blood*, once inside they separate the Clutter family. Are we going to . . ."

She, too, halted in mid-sentence.

None of the three said the words *home invasion*, although that was exactly what they were engaged in. This was the sort of crime that assaults some deep-seated American notion, that one should always be perfectly safe inside one's home. Bank robberies, drive-by shootings, illicit drug turf wars, even estranged couples divorcing with gunfire— all made a kind of contextual, rational sense. A home invasion did not. It was usually driven by bizarre fantasies of rape or hidden riches that rarely materialized. It was the type of crime that Jordan had studied over the past days. Usually, though, in this type of crime, Jordan had learned, it was the psychopathic bad guys assaulting the safety of some complete innocents. This night was the reverse—it was the innocents attacking the home of a murderous Wolf. But while this seemed the case inside the car, she guessed that somewhere out in the cold all the roles would switch around 180 degrees.

"Anyone want to say anything?" Karen asked.

"Answers," Sarah coughed in response. "Let's go get some answers."

The three Reds slipped from the car like spills of black ink creasing the nighttime. They tugged hoods down over their heads, adjusted their face masks, and moved swiftly toward the house. A dog barked from inside a neighbor's place. All three Reds had the same frightening thought: *Suppose he has a dog—a pit bull or a Doberman willing to defend their master.* None voiced this concern. It seemed to Karen that every stride they took forward underscored how little they knew about committing a crime, especially one as profound as they were engaged in.

Each Red wanted to grab the others, stop in mid-attack, and say, "What the hell are we doing?" None actually said this; it was as if the three of them were tumbling headlong down a steep hill, and there was nothing to grab that might arrest their momentum.

Red One felt sick to her stomach.

Red Two was dizzy with doubt.

Red Three felt suddenly weak.

Each Red was nearly crippled with tension as they moved silently through the night. The cold air did little to dissipate the heat of anxiety. It seemed to them that all that had happened to them made each of them somehow smaller.

At the front of the house, Karen quickly gestured toward bushes adjacent to the main door. Jordan ducked in, concealing herself as best she could. The two other Reds slid seamlessly around the edge of the home, heading toward the back.

Suddenly being alone in the night nearly crushed Jordan. She listened for some sound, afraid that her own breathing was so loud it would wake the occupants, wake the neighbors, wake the police and fire departments. Any second she expected to be surrounded by sirens, flashing lights, and voices ordering her to stand with her hands up. Police or Wolf. She was trapped between the two.

She slowly worked the zipper on her duffel bag as quietly as she could. She removed her knife and gripped it tightly.

She no longer believed she had the strength to wield it. The ferocity that had come so easy and natural a few days earlier now felt impossibly difficult to achieve. It was as if the athlete Jordan, the faster-than-the-others Jordan, the Jordan stronger than anyone else on the team, the smarter, prettier, and roundly taunted and teased Jordan, all disappeared in that moment of waiting, replaced by some stranger Jordan couldn't recognize and certainly didn't trust. If she had known any prayers, she might have tried them. Instead, she hunkered down by the front steps, her black outfit fitting as perfectly as a jigsaw puzzle piece into the night, her muscles twitching and quivering, hoping that this new and unrecognizable Jordan would be able to summon the necessary fury when she needed it.

Break the window. Reach inside. Throw the dead-bolt lock. Attack.

Karen's plan had little subtlety. In the movies, it always appears so simple: Actors are calm, intelligent, unhurried, and they make clever choices and behave with easy determination. *Life isn't so simple*, she thought. *Everything conspires to trip you up. Especially the person you are. And this is not who we are. I'm a doctor, for Christ's sake. I'm not a break-in artist. And I'm not a killer.* She held the rubber mallet in her hand, getting ready to smash her way into the house, and had just begun a fierce backswing when Sarah abruptly grabbed her arm. Karen heard the younger woman's sharp snatch of breath from the cold night. She turned toward her, wondering what had made her act so precipitously.

Sarah said nothing, but pointed to their right. On the window in what they guessed was the kitchen was a sticker. It was a shield emblazoned with the words: PROTECTED BY ALPHA SECURITY.

Karen's head spun dizzily. A simple irony wasn't lost on her: This was the same company that she had hired to install the system on her own house, after the Big Bad Wolf's first letter. It had never occurred to her that a killer might hire the same home security company.

She hesitated. Then she whispered: "Okay, here's what happens. We break in. It triggers a silent alarm at the company headquarters. They call the home owner, who has to respond with a predetermined signal that indicates they're either okay, it's all a mistake, or that there's trouble, which makes the company call the cops, who are here in a couple of minutes."

Sarah nodded. The two Reds were stymied for an instant. "What should we do?" Sarah asked.

"I don't know," Karen responded. She was suddenly becoming aware that every second they remained outside, every moment they left Jordan hanging at the front, their risks grew exponentially. It was like watching diseased cells on a laboratory slide join together, becoming larger, more complex with each passing instant.

"Make a decision," Sarah said. "Either forward or back."

A slow, burning anger took root inside Karen. *If we run, we might be running into death. Maybe not tonight. Maybe tomorrow. Or the next day. Or next week. Or next month. We will never know when.* She sucked in cold night air. "Got your gun?" she asked.

"Yes."

"Okay. You go for the upstairs bedroom on the right as soon as we break in. I'll be behind you. I'll let Jordan in. And Sarah . . ."

"If it is the bedroom. We don't know for certain."

Karen wanted to say "*We don't know anything for damn certain,*" but instead she merely added, "Don't hesitate."

Sarah nodded. *Easy to say. Hard to do.*

Left unsaid was what she was supposed to not hesitate and do. *Kill them both? Just start shooting? What if he's not the Wolf?*

Karen knew that if she waited one more second, panic would replace determination. She grabbed the mallet and swung it hard.

At the front, Jordan heard the tinkle of glass breaking. If seconds earlier she'd thought her breathing was thunderously loud, this noise seemed to her to be violently explosive. She shrunk back, clinging to shadow edges with a drowning person's embrace.

A stray shard frayed the cloth of Karen's sweatshirt. For an instant she believed she had sliced her arm open, and she choked out some guttural sound from deep inside her chest. She imagined dark arterial blood would pulse through the fabric, and she expected a sheet of pain to strike her. This did not happen, which surprised her. Her skin was not even scratched. She reached inside the broken window and threw the dead-bolt lock. Within a second, she had thrust the door open.

Sarah pushed past her. She raced forward, her flashlight in one hand and her gun in the other. The small beam of light swept back and forth crazily as she sprinted into the house. *Up and to the right. Up and to the right.* She grabbed at the banister and leapt up the stairway.

Karen ran to the front door and fumbled with the locks. It took her a second, and then she threw it open. "Jordan, now!" she whispered as fervently as she could.

Jordan was crouched by the side, hidden in the darkness. The night seemed like tendrils wrapping her so tightly she was immobilized. She could feel herself giving commands to muscles that wouldn't answer. Then, as if she were floating above herself, looking down like some spectral figure, she saw the stranger Jordan rising, nearly tripping on the front steps, half-tumbling into the house, and grabbing at Karen to keep from falling.

Karen pushed the youngest of the three Reds to her feet, closed the front door behind them, and then jumped to the stairs and raced to catch up to Red Two.

It was not a lot of noise they were making.

But it was enough.

Ripped by the sounds of the break-in from the vaporous territory between dream and reality, the Big Bad Wolf felt a blistering bolt of fear slice through his core. He sat upright in the bed, his breath suddenly coming in shallow gasps, and swung a fist through the black air, punching at unknown and unseen terror, choking words off in some sort of animal cry, unsure whether he was striking out at a nightmare or at something real but ghostlike. At his side his wife coughed out a scream of her own that became more gurgle than shout. Mrs. Big Bad Wolf felt her throat close, as if someone were choking her.

The bedroom door burst wide, and a figure—in the dark they could not tell if it was human; it was just a shape that matched the night—thrust toward them. Wild blades of light sliced across the bedroom, as Sarah waved her flashlight back and forth.

She raised her gun, trying to remember everything she had been taught by the director of the women's shelter.

Use two hands.

Flick off the safety.

Hold your breath.

Take careful aim.

Make every shot count.

She fumbled and dropped the flashlight to the floor as she tried to handle the gun as she had been shown, and the couple on the bed in front of her disappeared into crazy shadows. She thought she was screaming "*Kill him! Kill him!*" but again she couldn't hear the words, or even feel her lips moving with sound. In that second of hesitation, a shock of orange and red exploded in her eyes as the man she wanted to shoot clubbed her across the face with a wild roundhouse punch. The Wolf, all battle instinct, had thrown himself at Sarah, knocking her sideways. Mrs. Big Bad Wolf had jerked forward, flailing crazily at the dark, viciously grabbing at any shape she could find.

Sarah staggered, and as she did, a second blow landed on her chest, knocking the wind from her lungs. She bounced off a bureau and was suddenly thrown sideways and fell across the bed. She felt a hand grabbing at her gun. She knew only that she had to fight back, but exactly how to do this slipped through her consciousness. The only thought she had was *Don't let go! Don't let go!* She was twisted about, spinning like a top, and she felt her feet slipping as she fell from the edge of the bed and slammed against the floor, a sudden immense weight pressing down on her and sharp nails clawing at her face as if trying to rip her mask free.

Behind her, two other black shapes barreled into the room. Karen had the billy club in her hand and was swinging it wildly, ineffectively.

It smashed into a bedside lamp, shattering china. A second uncontrolled swing crashed into knickknacks on a drawer top, sending debris flying.

The darkness cheated them all.

The Big Bad Wolf and Mrs. Big Bad Wolf fought desperately. The two of them kicked, bit, punched, used teeth, fists, feet. Bedclothes landed in piles. The wooden frame of their bed groaned beneath their frenzy. It was Mrs. Big Bad Wolf who'd grabbed the gun in Sarah's hands, holding it by the barrel, wrestling it back and forth, trying frantically to pull it free. She barely understood what *it* was—she knew only that *it* was something that could kill them and that she had to seize it, and not let go. Animal-like, aware only that they had plunged from sleep into a fight for their lives, they fought ferociously. Guttural grunts and sounds of battle filled the room.

The Wolf leapt through the black at Karen. He smashed a blow against her ear. Her head spun. Another blow slammed into Karen's midsection and the doctor felt a rib crack and sheets of agony pummel her body. Gasping, she expected a third, something that would knock her unconscious, and she swung the billy club crazily, feeling it crunch against skin and bone. She heard a high-pitched cry of pain.

A second sudden howl pierced the room. Jordan had slashed at the Big Bad Wolf with her filleting knife, catching his arm just as he pulled it back to slam into Karen. With a roar, the Wolf grasped Karen and swung her savagely into Jordan, knocking the youngest Red to the wall, slamming her head into a framed picture that shattered with an explosion.

The Wolf battled, knowing now that there was a club, a knife, and a gun, which his wife seemed to have a grip on. The only light in the room came from the abandoned flashlight that had rolled uselessly into a corner, so the fight had little organization and no rationale; it was simply bleeding, gouging, kicking, and trying to survive in darkness and shadow.

He still did not know whom he was fighting. If he'd had an instant to reflect, he would have perceived three forms, all female, and perhaps this would have made the mathematics of the struggle clear. But the blows raining down, the pain from his sliced forearm, and the shock of going from sleep to a deadly attack all conspired to push clarity aside. All he could think of was getting to his hunting knife on the desk in his downstairs office, or seizing the gun he knew was somewhere in the room, and evening the odds.

He pushed Karen aside, tossing her against the same wall that Jordan lay slumped against. He threw himself on the two figures—his wife and a shadow—locked together in their struggle for the pistol. He smashed into the two of them not knowing which body was which, pummeling everything he could feel. In the confusion, the Wolf heard the distinct clatter of the weapon coming free and falling to the wood floor. He groped around for it, but could not find it.

And then, suddenly, a hand grasped his forehead and his head was jerked back savagely. He felt a blade at his throat.

Words seemed to come from oblivion. "I will kill you if you move again."

Jordan was behind him, almost straddling his form, one hand holding his head, the other gripping the knife, like a farmer ready to slaughter some animal for dinner.

His first instinct was to burst forward. The pressure of the knife dissuaded him.

And then the telephone rang.

42

"What Big Teeth You Have, Grandmother . . ."

At first the telephone's insistence seemed utterly bizarre, some infusion of mundane normalcy into a situation that had none. It stifled the fight, froze everyone in position like in a children's game.

It was Karen who immediately understood the ringing's importance. It had to be answered without delay. It never occurred to her to answer it herself.

She frantically seized the flashlight from the corner where it had fallen, and shined it into the eyes of the Big Bad Wolf. "Answer it!" she shouted. This was impossible—he was pinned beside the bed, kneeling on the floor, between Jordan and her filleting knife. The phone was on a bedside table across the far side of the room. Each ring screamed louder. Karen focused her light on Mrs. Big Bad Wolf, who was entwined with Sarah. "Answer it!" she cried again. She raised her billy club as if ready to crush the woman's skull—which, even in the near-panic that Karen felt surging though her, she knew would defeat the purpose of the threat. "It's the alarm company. Answer the fucking phone!"

Sarah, suddenly grasping the urgency of the situation, pushed Mrs. Big Bad Wolf up and toward the phone. The gun, lying nearby beneath a bureau, half-hidden by sheets and blankets tossed aside in the frenzy of the bedroom battle, suddenly seemed less important, but Sarah grabbed at it, reclaiming it for her own. She, too, pointed her weapon at Mrs. Big Bad Wolf.

Mrs. Big Bad Wolf hesitated. Her eyes widened as they fixed on the knife blade at her husband's throat, ignoring the gun barrel staring at her. He managed a small nod, and she scrambled across the bed and grasped the receiver. "Hello?" she said shakily.

"This is Alpha Security. We have a silent alarm at your location. Are you the home owner?"

Mrs. Big Bad Wolf stammered, trying to catch her breath and reply simultaneously. "Yes, yes. The alarm, uh, what . . ."

"Your alarm system is showing an intrusion."

She held the phone near her ear, but her eyes were on her husband. "An intrusion?"

"Yes. A break-in."

"We were asleep," she said. Her mind was working as fast as it could. "You just woke us up. The phone ringing scared the bejesus out of both of us. We have a new puppy," she lied. "Maybe he set it off. Can you give me a minute to check?"

"You need to give me your security code," the voice on the other end said briskly.

"Okay, let me just check," she repeated. She used an old person's whiny, shaky voice. "Won't take more than a second or two. I have to go downstairs. I know I wrote down that code in the drawer there . . ." Again she looked toward her husband.

But it was Karen who whispered a direction. "If you don't give the right code, and do it right now, he will call the cops. That's fine," she said, a smug grin flitting across her face, "We can all just wait here quietly for the cops to show. Then we will happily tell them everything. Think about it: Is that what you want?" This was directed to the Big Bad Wolf.

A part of Karen that seemed cruel found the situation suddenly deli-cious. *So, Mr. Wolf, Mr. Killer, Mr. Whoever the Fuck You Are, you want to explain to some surprised cop just what's going on here tonight?*

She smiled sickly as she spoke in a low, fierce tone. It was as if her words carried extra weight spoken in the dark shadows thrown by the flashlight. She felt on the verge of total savagery. Karen the comic, Karen the doctor—both had been replaced. She did not know that the other Reds were feeling similar conversions. She whispered, "The cops will want to know exactly why three women who are strangers to each other chose this night to join up and break into this house. Not some other fancy house, where there's money or jewels or expensive art, because we're sure as hell not here to rob anything. This specific house. A pretty fucking ordinary place, right? And they will hear a story from the three of us that they will have a lot of trouble believing. But it will only make them more curious. And then they will have questions for you. Those will be hard questions. Do you want to answer their questions? Is that what you feel like doing tonight?"

His eyes widened.

"So, if you are *not* the Wolf," Karen said slowly, "by all means give the emergency response. Bring the cops here as soon as you can and they can lead us all away in cuffs. But if you are . . ." She reached up and pulled off her black hood, spilling her red hair out. The other two Reds did the same.

At the phone, Mrs. Big Bad Wolf gasped.

The Wolf hesitated. He could still feel the blade tickling his throat. He could see the fear in his wife's eyes. He was trying to sort through his options, and saw only one available. *Delay.* And this did not include a con-versation with the police. The local cops were ineffectual and incompe-tent, but not totally. "Give the code," he muttered angrily. "Tell 'em we're okay. It was the dog we don't have, just like you said."

Mrs. Big Bad Wolf removed her hand from the telephone receiver. "We're all okay. Just fine. It was a mistake. The dog set it off," she care-fully repeated. "Our all-clear code is *Inspector Javert.* That's J-A-V-E—"

"Thank you," said the voice. "That's a cool code. Very literary. I saw *Les Misérables* on Broadway. I'll reset your system from here."

Mrs. Big Bad Wolf replaced the receiver on its hook.

"Now we should just kill them both," Jordan said. The words coming from her lips surprised her. The weak, scared-outside-in-the-shadows Jordan had been shunted aside and replaced by the fierce, uncompromising, murderous Jordan. It had happened in the matter of seconds. Perhaps, she imagined, it was shaken loose inside her by the physical contact; being slammed against a wall can open up unseen resources that are rarely called upon. Regardless, she felt a cold, homicidal urge come over her, and she moved the knife blade back and forth just slightly, tearing the surface of the Wolf's skin, so that a thin line of blood started to trickle down to his chest and stain the top of his pajamas. She bent forward, leaning her head down, so that her lips were next to his ear. "You thought it would be the other way around, didn't you? You thought *you* would be holding the knife to *my* throat, huh? And then what were you going to do?"

He didn't answer. He wore a snarl on his face and he could barely contain his own rage. He wanted to wrap his hands around her neck. *Any* neck. But he was locked in position.

Sarah struggled to her knees. She had her gun in both hands, holding it straight out. She was right in front of the Wolf with the barrel of the weapon pointed at him from perhaps six inches away, aimed right between his eyes. She thought, *Pull the trigger and you end everything. Start over again right now and the new you will be safe forever.* The Wolf was bracketed by the two Reds. The gun and the knife were like deadly parentheses.

"I thought you were dead," the Wolf said bitterly.

"I went to your service," Mrs. Big Bad Wolf said piteously from across the room, where she suddenly slumped onto the bed, tucking her knees up under her arms like an unhappy child. She spoke in a whiny tone, as if this trick was a cheat and unfair.

"I am dead," Sarah answered brutally without taking her sight off the Wolf. She squinted down the barrel. "Jordan's right," she said coldly. "Let's kill them both right now."

The Big Bad Wolf felt his muscles constrict. He breathed in sharply. He fantasized himself bursting forward, miraculously slamming Jordan's knife aside, wrestling Sarah's pistol away from her with a single immense and magical tug. He would kill them all. Right then and there. Right on the floor of his bedroom, in front of his wife. He would save her. They would kill together. He could hear the sharp reports from the gun. He could see the bleeding forms of the three Reds in front of him. He would win. It was always supposed to be that way.

And then, suddenly, he could not move.

Inwardly he shouted commands: *"Move legs! Hands! Arms! Now!"* Outwardly he remained frozen. And he thought, *Am I going to die now?*

Getting older was inevitable. Being forgotten was something he understood. Getting caught was always a possibility.

But being murdered had never occurred to him.

"No, please," Mrs. Big Bad Wolf moaned. A small stream of blood was dripping down from the edge of her mouth where Sarah had landed a lucky punch. Her hair was frizzed out in a tangle of knots. She had paled and the doctor in Karen thought she had seen the woman age years in the space of seconds. She suddenly wondered about the woman's heart. *It could give out any second. We'll have caused a heart attack. Is that homicide? Or is it justice?*

Mrs. Big Bad Wolf turned to Karen. "Please Doctor, please . . ." She swung around toward Jordan, "Jordan, you're a good girl, you can't—"

"No I'm not," Jordan furiously interrupted her. "Maybe I was once, but I'm not anymore. And I can." It was obvious what *can* implied at that precise moment. Jordan gripped her knife more tightly.

"Wait," Karen said. The other two Reds looked at her. "We don't know enough yet."

Red Two and Red Three stared at her quizzically.

"Before we kill them, I need to know everything," she said. She felt an ice within her. It was as if for the first time since she'd received the Wolf's letter, her life was coming into focus. Clarity had finally bubbled up close to the surface, where she might just be able to seize it. She bent down, lowering her face close to the Big Bad Wolf's, so that her breath washed over him.

"My oh my, what big eyes you've got, Grandmother." She smiled with a harshness that she did not know she possessed.

"You remember that, don't you? And where it comes from? A fairy tale. Can you believe it? A goddamn fairy tale that none of us have read since we were kids. Anyway, the proper response is: '*All the better to see you with, my dear.*'"

She was nearly whispering. "Can you say that?"

The Wolf did not reply.

"I think you can," Karen said.

Duct tape is remarkable stuff, Karen thought as she taped Mrs. Big Bad Wolf's hands and feet together. *Better than a rope and knots. Sticky and convenient. I bet real criminals happily use it all the time.*

The two wolves were side by side on the living room couch, immobilized by the wrappings of gray tape. They looked a little like awkward teenagers on a first date—not quite touching, slightly ridiculous. Mrs. Big Bad Wolf was having trouble controlling her emotions. They seemed to career around within her willy-nilly. Her husband, on the other hand, had descended into a sullen anger. He wasn't saying much, but his eyes tracked each of the Reds.

"All right," Karen said, stepping back and admiring her handiwork.

Red Two and Red Three were a few paces behind her. Each still wielded her weapon. "What now?" Jordan asked.

None of the three Reds was aware of the tidal change that had taken place in the small house. The Big Bad Wolf was completely alert to the difference. It was well within his area of expertise.

He laughed, just slightly. "You've made a mistake," he said. He held up his taped wrists. "Big goddamn mistake."

"What mistake?" Jordan blurted out.

The Wolf smiled.

"You know nothing about killing, do you?"

The three Reds did not answer this. He didn't expect them to. "In a fight, in self-defense," the Wolf lectured softly, keeping his voice low and even, which only seemed to underscore his knowledge, "you can do almost anything. Remarkable things. It just depends on how desperate you are. Stab someone with a knife. Pull the trigger on your big hand-cannon. Beat in somebody's brains. It's a very simple thing to defend yourself in battle. Anyone can find the strength to win and do whatever it takes in all that heat and blood and struggling."

He leaned back a little in his seat. "But now we're not fighting. The battle is over. You've won. But you haven't, really, because now you will have to kill. In cold blood. It's a bit of a cliché, isn't it? But you can all feel it, can't you? Any of you think you have that particular kind of strength? A fight is one thing. Murder is something very different."

The three Reds were quiet.

The Wolf didn't seem frightened or even all that put out by the situation. "A mother, she could heartlessly kill to defend her children. A man might without thinking if he was defending his home and family. A soldier will to protect his comrades—doesn't even need a command. But that's not what we have here tonight, is it? Which one of you thinks she can be a killer? Who is going to be first?" He started to laugh.

Karen was taken aback, almost as if the psychology of the moment had slapped her across the face. Jordan realized she was suddenly hot. *But we won!*

At that moment, Sarah pushed past the other two Reds with a slippery burst of energy. "You think we can't kill you?" she shouted. She stepped quickly across the room and thrust the gun barrel up against the Big Bad Wolf's forehead. His wife whimpered, but he merely grinned.

"Prove me wrong," he challenged. He kept his gaze directly in Red Two's eyes, belying the gamble he was taking.

Sarah thumbed back the hammer. Her finger tightened on the trigger. She let loose with a long, angry groan.

And then she stepped back.

"Not so easy, is it?" the Big Bad Wolf said.

She immediately thrust the pistol back against his forehead. "I can do it," she said fiercely.

"If you could, you already would have," he calmly replied.

Red Two and the Wolf quivered slightly. Karen and Jordan were sure she was going to pull the trigger. And they were both sure she would not.

Karen spoke first. "Sarah, step back."

A second passed, then another, and finally Sarah lowered the hammer on her pistol and moved away from the Wolf.

"You see, you think you've accomplished something here tonight," he said, almost gloating. "But you haven't. You know nothing about killing and I know everything. You know nothing about me, and I know everything about you. And that will mean you will always lose and I will always win." He smiled again. "You want to know something that's obvious to anyone who really knows murder?"

The three Reds didn't respond, but the Big Bad Wolf continued anyway. "There's no strong woodsman coming through the door with his trusty axe. There's no loving grandmother safe and hidden in the closet ready to emerge and embrace Little Red Riding Hood. There's only one real ending to the story, and it's the only ending that was ever possible. The first ending."

They were all silent.

"You could never save yourselves. Not once I started." He grinned. "You are all smart," he continued. His voice was almost friendly. It had a kind of familiarity that suggested the banter between old friends meeting in an unexpected manner. "That's why I picked you in the first place. And you are all clever enough to see there is absolutely no way out for you tonight. You should never have come here. You should have let me do whatever I was going to do. Or maybe you should have killed us both upstairs. Maybe you could have done that. And maybe even, like Red Two says, you can kill me now. Maybe, just maybe, you are that angry and scared. But are you also capable of killing her?" He nodded his head toward his wife. "Because she's completely innocent," he lied easily. "She hasn't done anything."

The Wolf shrugged his shoulders. "Now, that takes a special kind of evil. Killing someone just because they are in the right place at the wrong time. Or maybe the wrong place at the right time. That's hard, even for an experienced professional. You think you have that strength? Can you be that evil?"

He smiled again. "One, two, three," he said. "Three little psychopaths. Or, perhaps not."

Karen's head spun. It was as if someone had loosed some scent in the room that was causing her to be unable to think clearly. She imagined that everything the Wolf was saying was true. They would never be free. *Kill the man, and I'm no different from him. Maybe. Let the man live, and always wonder if he's stalking me again. Maybe. Kill the woman, and live forever with guilt. Maybe.* She felt nauseous.

At her side, Sarah's hand shook. The gun suddenly felt incredibly heavy, and she was unsure whether she had the strength to continue to hold it. She wasn't even certain she had the physical ability to pull the trigger. It was as if all the energy had been drained from her muscles. Beside her, Jordan slumped back against the wall with a groan.

And directly into that moment of weakness for all three Reds, Mrs. Big Bad Wolf blurted out, "It's just a book, you see. It's only the book he's writing. No one has to die tonight."

The silence in the room crowded them for what might have been only seconds, but which seemed far longer.

"Find the words," Karen whispered to Jordan. The youngest nodded and left the room.

All writers need stories, Karen thought. *They steal from their own lives and from the lives of people around them. They steal from their families and their friends. They steal from history and from current events. They rob news articles, what they see on the street, overheard conversations, and sometimes they even steal from each other.*

Then she heard Jordan shout, a half-scream, half-cry, the sound that someone who has cut herself accidentally might make in surprise and shock. Karen's eyes went instantly to the Big Bad Wolf, who snarled, some of his offhand, unafraid appearance abruptly slipping away. She realized, *He knows.*

"You go," Sarah said to Karen. She quickly waved the gun in the direction of Jordan's explosion. Sarah had slumped down on the floor across from the two Wolves, her back up against the wall, her weapon balanced on knees drawn up to her chest, trained on the two captives.

Karen heard Jordan yell out, "In here!" and she followed the sound of the voice, which seemed to shake with some new tension. As she entered the room just down the hallway from the kitchen, she heard Jordan sob. *That's not right*, she thought. *Red Three is strong. She's been tough from the start.*

What she saw first when she entered the Wolf's office were tears streaming down Jordan's face. The teenager wasn't able to speak. She just gestured at the wall.

It had not taken Jordan more than seconds to find the locked office door. *Locked door. This is obvious: Go inside.* Nor had finding a key been hard—there was one on the Wolf's chain, hung right by the front door.

It was only when she stepped inside and saw what he'd accumulated there that she had really started to lose control.

Pictures. Schedules. Outlines. A wicked hunting knife.

It amounted to a detailed study of each of their lives and the means to end them.

Karen followed Jordan's eyes and saw a long-distance shot of her sneaking a smoke. She saw Jordan on the basketball court. She saw Sarah outside the liquor store. A collection of all the familiar places, image upon image, gathered together into a montage of deadly obsession. Close-ups. Long lens shots. Action images next to pictures that seemed more like still lifes. Lists of favorite places and daily breakdowns, maps and bird's-eye views of their homes, offices, school—the intimacy of their day-to-day lives. But what she saw that went beyond the shock of seeing their personal histories detailed was the energy she knew must have gone into creating everything on the walls. It was as if all three Reds were standing naked in the Wolf's office. The violation was profound. It was as if they had never had a private moment. The Wolf had been close by their side every second—they just hadn't known it.

It was the investment of time and dedication to death that finally overwhelmed her. Karen felt her knees weaken, and she dropped down.

From the other room, Sarah called out, "What is it?"

Karen replied weakly, "It's us."

Jordan was overcome with rage. She grabbed Karen by the shoulders and jerked her up, shaking her. "We've got to kill him!" she said hoarsely. "Look at this! What choice do we have?"

Karen did not respond. All she could think was: *If we kill him, how do we get away with it? And if we do get away with it, what will that do to us? He's the killer. Not us.*

Her shoulders slumped. Jordan released her and with an angry, anguished cry approached the wall and started ripping down every picture. She tore into every representation of their lives. She clawed at each element of the mural in front of her. Paper flew around her in shreds. She was sobbing something guttural.

Karen reached out to stop her, but hesitated. *Destroy it all*, she thought. She joined in, grabbing at a picture and tearing it into tiny pieces, flinging it across the room, both of them feeling that by wrecking everything the Wolf had built to kill them, they could somehow free themselves.

As Jordan beat senselessly on the display, showering pieces of the design of their deaths throughout the room, Karen turned and saw the computer and the pages of manuscript on the writing desk beneath a leather-bound scrapbook. She reached for her billy club and was about to smash the screen, when Jordan said, "Wait."

She paused in mid-blow.

"If all this is up here," she said, pointing at the debris from the wall, "do you suppose even more is in there?" Jordan nodded at the computer at the same time as she reached out for the Wolf's personal scrapbook, opening it to pages of reviews and accounts of murder.

Karen nodded.

"What else is there?" Jordan asked.

And in that moment of hesitation, surrounded by all the signatures of obsession, Karen saw an answer.

43

Karen spread three items out on the floor directly in front of the Big Bad Wolf. If he'd been able to stretch his foot out, he could have touched them with his toe.

His computer.

His manuscript.

His scrapbook.

She said nothing. A fourth item—his hunting knife—was in her hand. She waved it in the air idly, as if trying to cut atmosphere. She just wanted the Wolf to stare at these things for a few minutes, digesting what she might be able to do with them.

He shifted in his seat.

Karen wondered for a moment: *Has anyone ever spent this sort of evening with a serial killer and lived?* She suspected the answer was *no*.

She gave the Wolf a wry, small smile that she hoped would unsettle him further. Inwardly, she was warning herself: *Push. But don't push too hard. Act, but don't overact. Medical school didn't teach me anything about the stage.*

I had to learn that for myself. She wondered whether any comedian had ever faced as hostile an audience as she had this night.

She left Red Two and Red Three across from the Wolves, not saying anything to them while she went first to the kitchen, then to a bathroom. It did not take her long to find what she needed: Plastic baggies. Scissors. A bread knife with a serrated edge. Cotton swabs. A black marking pen.

When she returned to the living room, it looked to the others as if she'd been on a very odd shopping trip. She was grinning, even though her ribs throbbed where she'd been struck. This was all performance on her part, but she also knew how to not let an unruly crowd upset her routine. *Keep telling jokes. Don't let up. Don't let the heckler or the disruptive asshole take over the show. You're in charge.*

She began singing disjointed snatches of a hit 1960s song. No matter how clumsily she did it, she knew that the Wolf would probably recognize her version of the tune Sam the Sham and the Pharaohs once made famous: *Little Red Riding Hood.* She hoped it would irritate him.

She waited for a moment, picked up the scrapbook—idly flipping through a couple of sheets, using the hunting knife to turn them—and looked up: "So, how many people have you killed?"

The Big Bad Wolf didn't immediately answer. His eyes narrowed and his smile widened. He had a sudden surge of confidence. His hands and feet might be restrained, but Red One was engaging in conversation. This was seductive. "None. One. A hundred. Do you mean on the page or in my head or in real life? How many do you think?" he replied.

Karen looked at the Wolf. She tried to pick out some feature in his face, some indication in the way he sat on the couch, some body smell, or posture, or tone of voice—anything that would give away what he was. It was like staring into a shapeless gray-blue sea in the last minutes of daylight. The ripples of waves on the surface hid all the currents that could join together with winds and tides when darkness fell to suddenly become dangerous. That was where his power lay, she understood: in the unprepossessing appearance that obscured his true nature.

Beside him, Mrs. Big Bad Wolf's entire body shook with rage. She scowled and nearly shouted her answer to the same question: "What makes you think he's killed *anyone*!" she burst out. "I checked! I even spoke with the cops. There's no proof of anything! He's just a writer. I told you, he has to research!"

Karen nodded, ignoring what Mrs. Big Bad Wolf said. "You always get away with it, don't you?"

The Wolf shrugged. Not a *yes*. Not a *no*.

She turned to Mrs. Big Bad Wolf. "And you . . ." she began, but then she swallowed her question. She could see every answer she needed in Mrs. Big Bad Wolf's face. *Your life is changing tonight, too, isn't it?*

Karen shuddered. She took a deep breath and turned back to the Wolf.

"What do you really like to use?" she asked. "Guns? Knives?" She waved the hunting knife in the air again. "Your hands? Something else? How many different ways are there to kill someone?"

"There are advantages to every weapon, and disadvantages, too," he responded smugly. "Every thriller writer knows that." He glanced over at the manuscript on the floor in front of him. "It's in the book," he added sharply.

Karen the doctor and Karen the comic had learned one lesson from both her lives that she was applying at this moment. "Can you kill someone with uncertainty?" she asked.

She continued, coldly, fingering the blade, but speaking about something different: "Is doubt a weapon?"

Again silence crept into the room. Karen used it just as she would have a moment on the stage. *Make him think. Make him wonder. Make him unsure.*

All these words were as effective as razors.

"Have you ever imagined what it is like to be a victim?" Karen asked.

All three Reds saw the Big Bad Wolf's face freeze. *Doubt can do that*, Karen thought, as if making a diagnosis. His wife, on the other hand, merely looked confused, as if she didn't understand the question.

Karen stepped forward. She put the Wolf's knife on the floor and picked up the scissors. The first thing she did was cut a lock of his hair. This went into a baggy. Then she swiped a cotton swab in the blood congealing on his throat where Jordan had nicked his skin. This, too, went into a baggy. She used the black marking pen to identify each, carefully writing the time and date on the outside. Then she held up her surgical-gloved hand and snapped the sterile surface as if it were a rubber band. She whispered to the Big Bad Wolf, "I suspect your fingerprints are all over that computer. Shouldn't be too hard for an expert to obtain them. But ours are not." She snapped the glove in his face a second time. She took out another cotton swab. "Open wide," she said, just as if she were in her office.

The Wolf clenched his teeth together. Karen looked at him. "Come on now," she said, in a pleasant voice that hid all her fury. It was the tone she would have used with a scared pediatric patient, reluctant to do as asked.

He opened his mouth. She swabbed the inside. "A few extra cells," she said. She dropped this swab into another plastic bag. Then she moved over to Mrs. Big Bad Wolf. "Same drill," she said.

Mrs. Big Bad Wolf looked genuinely astonished as a lock of her hair disappeared into a bag with her name on it, followed by a blood sample and a swipe from the inside of her mouth.

Karen took her collection over and placed it all in Sarah's duffel, alongside the hunting knife. "We'll be keeping that," she said smugly. Then she took one of the cell phones and quickly snapped several pictures of both the Wolves. She took close-up shots, being careful to get images from full front and profile. "Smile," she said. Neither Wolf did.

When she was finished, she turned to the Big Bad Wolf. "Tell your wife what we've done," she said.

"Blood. Hair. DNA. It's the medical version of who we are," he said. *The softer his voice, the greater his fury*, Karen thought. She ignored this.

"Maybe not medical," Karen said, shaking her head. "Do you think *forensic* might be a better word?" Then she added, "I wonder if there's anyone out there who might be interested in those samples. You think there's a cold case cop somewhere who might find them . . . I don't know . . . *intriguing*?"

She smiled. "Here's the situation. All this material is going into a safe place. Maybe a safety deposit box. Maybe a lawyer's office safe. Maybe we'll just dig a big hole somewhere and bury it. Maybe we'll send it all wrapped up with a nice red bow to one of those police agencies. Of course, we could do that today. Or tomorrow. Or maybe next year. It's up to us, and we'll figure it out. But you can bet it will be someplace you could never find. Your computer, the scrapbook, your manuscript . . . we're taking everything tonight. Three people will have access to that stash: Red One, Red Two, and Red Three. Maybe . . . we'll let Sarah—because she's the one you will never be able to trace—pick out a nice hiding place somewhere far away. Or maybe it won't be her, it'll be me that hides it. Or Jordan. She's real good at keeping secrets. Anyway, you will know, from this second on, should anything, anything at all, ever threaten any of us Little Red Riding Hoods again, the remaining Reds will know what to do with this stuff. Have you got that?"

The Big Bad Wolf nodded. His face had darkened. All three Reds imagined that every muscle was straining to rip free of his duct tape bonds. His anger would be murderous. But as they watched, they saw throbbing veins on his neck relax and a frightened resignation slip unbidden into his eyes. It was as if he saw a different kind of restraint, far tighter than duct tape, binding him.

He had become them. They had become him.

Karen's smile had disappeared. For an instant, she thought, *How many people have you killed?* And she understood with a doctor's understanding of death that there was nothing she could do about the people who had already died. But she could immunize everyone else from that moment on. So, she used the flat tone of voice that she would employ if she were delivering harsh news of a virulent and inexorably fatal illness to someone she truly hated.

"You gave us nothing but uncertainty, and then you were going to kill us. Now we're giving you the same. You will never be able to hear a knock on the door without thinking it's the police. You will never look up and see a cop car behind you and not think that this time it's all over, or walk down a street and not imagine that some detective is following you. When you wake in the morning, you will know it might be your last day of freedom.

When you go to bed at night, you will not know if the next day your little fucking pathetic life is going to end. And it's not just the cops. No, I imagine there just might be some family members of victims out there who would be interested in these connections. Or maybe some defense attorneys who can use this stuff to set a client free. And I wonder just how some poor fucker who has spent fifteen years on death row is going to feel about you. I don't think he will be generous."

She gestured toward the items. "Think of all this as a disease. A terminal one." She hesitated, then added, "Don't try to run. If you disappear, we will know it—and all this will be . . . *properly distributed*. And don't think that you can say goodbye to us and find some other poor woman to kill, and get your kicks that way. Someone new dies, some new *Red* wherever she might be, and this lands in the right hands. It's just all over for you. Totally. Whoever you were right up to this minute, now you are finished. From now on, you're just an ordinary guy with absolutely nothing special about you. No killing. No writing. No nothing at all. In fact, if I were you I wouldn't even go outdoors."

She paused for an instant, before continuing: "You see, from now on, we're watching you."

Karen took a deep breath. She was unsure how much of what she said was a bluff and how much wasn't. But neither did the Wolf. She stared at him and thought she detected a twitch in his lip. She thought that to fall so fast from Wolf grandiosity to less than zero might be fatal. She hoped so. *Humiliation*, she thought, *is a dangerous weapon*. "I'll ask you again: Can you kill someone with uncertainty?"

There was silence in the room.

Karen turned to the other Reds. "Ladies," she said. "Time to leave." She took the serrated bread knife she'd lifted in the kitchen and placed it on top of the television set. "Here," she said. "I sure hope it doesn't take you too long to make your way to this, get it into your hands, and figure out how to cut yourselves free."

She couldn't resist a final sardonic joke. "It's almost morning. Hey, don't be late for work."

They picked up everything. As they started to exit, Jordan also couldn't help herself. She whispered to the other two Reds, "You know something? I've learned that I absolutely hate fucking fairy tales." She cackled with an unrestrained enthusiasm. Then she turned to the Big Bad Wolf as they were heading out the door, waved the manuscript pages tauntingly at him, and said, "I guess there's gonna be a different last chapter than the one you expected, huh?"

The cold air outside hit all of them at once. At first they remained silent as they carried the items robbed from the Big Bad Wolf toward their car.

Sarah spoke before the others. "Are we really safe now?" she asked quietly.

"Yes," Jordan said.

"No," Karen replied.

"Maybe," Sarah answered her own question. "So what do we do now?"

"Everything," Jordan said.

"Nothing," Karen muttered.

Sarah paused again. They had reached the car, and Karen opened the trunk for the stolen materials.

"Something," Sarah said.

8 a.m.

Jordan made a point of jamming every inch of her breakfast tray, with bowls of cereal and milk, a plate of toast and eggs, fruit, coffee, and orange juice. She waited at the end of the line for a hulking linebacker on the school team to move in front of her as he headed toward the breakfast bar, and then she swung the tray into his path. It fell to the floor with a clatter of breaking dishes, an instant disgusting mess. There were close to seventy-five students and faculty in the dining hall that morning. The students—as was typical when a tray was dropped—broke into applause. The faculty—equally typically—immediately moved to get a janitor to clean up the debris and to silence the cheering students. All Jordan could think of was that everyone would remember her that morning, and the idea that she had spent the better part of the night facing down a killer would seem crazily irrational, like some completely made-up teenage fantasy that no one in their right mind would ever believe. She knelt down and began to wipe away at the mess on the floor. *Goodbye, Red Three*, she thought.

Sarah slid into the group of women getting a gaggle of children ready for the school bus outside of the women's shelter. Even with all the stress of threats from estranged men, the kids still had to go to school. It was always a time of tension, with the scary idea that one of the men might arrive on the scene suddenly mingled with utter *don't be late for school* normalcy. It was a bit of a melee, and the other women staying at the shelter appreciated the extra set of hands and eyes as they tried to maintain some sense of order in lives that had been completely disrupted by domestic violence. None noticed that Sarah had joined the pack not from inside the shelter, but from outside. They knew only that the single woman named Cynthia was being really helpful, double-checking with children that they had their lunches packed and their homework done, teasing and laughing with the kids in a friendly fashion, while simultaneously keeping a wary eye out for any of the threats the women knew might show up at any moment. They did not realize that for the first time in days, Sarah, who became Red Two and was now Cynthia, was imagining that she just might actually be free.

Karen greeted her first patient of the day with a cheeriness that might have seemed inappropriate for dealing with someone suffering from a painful case of shingles. She kept up a warm banter as she did a physical examination and then prescribed medications. She was careful to make certain that all her notes were time-stamped on the electronic medical records sheet for that patient. When the appointment was over, she walked the patient out to the main waiting room so that all the other people scheduled for that morning could see her on this incredibly typical, nothing-in-the-slightest-out-of-the-ordinary day. But before she went to see her second patient of the morning, Karen turned to her receptionist.

"Oh," she said idly to the woman behind a small partition, as if this were the most unremarkable thing in the world. The doctor with the secret love of comedy handed the receptionist Mrs. Big Bad Wolf's chart. "I'd like you to call this patient this afternoon and schedule an appointment for sometime in the next few weeks. I'm just really concerned about her heart."

EPILOGUE:
The First Chapter

He took the gun and cracked open the cylinder. It was a snub-nosed .38-caliber Smith & Wesson type favored by fictional police detectives in the noir books popular in the '40s and '50s because it fit snugly into a shoulder holster that could easily be concealed beneath a suit coat. *A zoot suit*, the Big Bad Wolf thought. Detectives who wore snappy fedoras on their heads and said things like "Forget it, Jake. It's Chinatown." The Wolf knew that it was an inaccurate weapon, although singularly deadly at very short range. It was no longer in common use. In this modern era real cops preferred heavier semiautomatic arsenals that carried more bullets and delivered more impact. He had purchased this weapon from a private gun dealer in nearby Vermont and had paid a premium price for it because of its slightly antique and romantic qualities. The dealer had asked few questions when he'd seen cash.

The Wolf removed five of the six bullets from the cylinder and placed them upright in a row in front of him. He had performed this procedure every morning for more than a month. They were directly adjacent to a new passport and a fake social security card. *Run and become someone new. Die.* Two choices. Neither good.

He closed up the weapon with a satisfying *click!*

Holding the weapon out in front of him, he paused.

Hemingway. Mishima. Kosinski. Brautigan. Thompson. Plath. Sexton. He pictured them and many others.

An abrupt shaft of tension creased through his chest. He could hear a distant siren somewhere in his neighborhood. Police, fire, or ambulance—he could not tell the difference. He hardly breathed as he listened. The siren grew louder, closer; then, to his immense relief, it began to fade away, and finally disappeared.

The Wolf walked across the bedroom and stared into a large mirror. He lifted the gun and placed the barrel by the side of his forehead, thumbed back the hammer, and teased the trigger with his index finger. He wondered just how many pounds of pressure it would take to fire. One pound? Two? Three? A real tug or only a slight caress? He held that position for a good thirty seconds. Then he shifted the gun, so that the barrel was now in his mouth. He could taste the harsh metal resting on his tongue. Another thirty seconds passed. Then he moved the gun a final time in a ritual as familiar to him now as brushing his teeth or combing his hair, so that the barrel was pointed up, prodding the flesh beneath his chin. Again, he remained frozen until he was no longer aware whether it had been seconds, minutes, or even hours. *One more murder,* he thought. When he slowly lowered the gun, he could see a reddish indentation where the barrel cylinder had been pressed against his skin.

He thought he could no longer recognize himself.

Gray, thinning hair. Crow's-feet lines around his eyes. Teeth yellowing. Eye sockets receding. Vision out of focus. Veins protruding. Chest sunken.

It was as if he—just like the distant siren—was fading away. He knew that soon enough he would look in the mirror and see a dead man. And when that minute inevitably arrived, he would finally pull the trigger.

Mrs. Big Bad Wolf stared out her office window at the graduation ceremonies beginning on the quadrangle in front of the administration building. She could not bring herself to go down to join them. She lifted the window sash, and could hear the soaring music of a bagpipe band that marched the graduating seniors into their seats with pomp and flourish. Through a tangle of green-leafed trees that swayed in the sunlit breeze of the fine early June morning, Mrs. Big Bad Wolf searched the collection of proud parents, friends, and family who were there to honor the graduates. From her vantage point, it was impossible to make out faces or identify forms. Twice she imagined she saw two red-haired women in the audience sitting together, and then, when she looked through the branches another time, she was completely unsure. The only Red she absolutely knew was there would happily prance across the stage to receive her diploma within a few minutes. *The nice thing about graduation is that it is all about the future*, Mrs. Big Bad Wolf thought. *Limitless, unrestrained future.* She left the window and returned to her desk. She had spent many lonely days and nights since she'd managed to slice the duct tape from her wrists and ankles in time to get to her job, just as the doctor had told her to.

She had never spoken to her husband about that night.

She did not have to.

"How things change," she whispered. Mrs. Big Bad Wolf centered herself in front of her computer. She was filled with fear, doubt, and a near-certainty that what she was about to do was somehow terribly wrong and terribly right all at the same moment. She could feel a little nervous sweat gathering beneath her arms as she adjusted the keyboard so that her hands rested comfortably above the letters. She glanced around quickly to make sure that no one was watching her. She clicked a few keys.

A new, blank document flashed onto the screen in front of her. She paused again and told herself that there would never be a better moment. She wrote:

Chapter One: The Three Reds

She indented a few lines, and then she typed:

I did not know on my wedding night that the man who crept beside me into bed was a vicious killer.

Mrs. Big Bad Wolf looked at the sentence. It wasn't bad, she insisted to herself. It *might* just work. She did not know much about nonfiction or memoir, but this didn't seem to her to be a poor start.

She asked herself whether somewhere within her there was another sentence to follow, and where she might find the language to construct it. And in that most rare of moments, spectacular arrays of words suddenly burst from her imagination. Words rollicked and rumbled, shined and shouted, they bounced around within her, suddenly unchained, adventurous and yearning to be free, exploding in the heavens like fireworks, gathering together into a great pyrotechnic display of phrases. Mrs. Big Bad Wolf felt a wild hot rush of excitement and hunched over, eagerly bending to the task at hand.